"All alone, my

Northrup strode back to her, his gait loose-limbed and sure. A predator's stride. One might try to run, but it would be useless.

Daisy drew her shoulders back and faced him head-on. He noted the gesture, for a contented smile oiled over his features. She ignored it, and the little flutters that were running riot in her belly. "Thank you for letting me stay."

He sat next to her on the settee, and the fresh, wild scent of him hit her anew. "I've never been one to deny a beautiful woman." He looked her over slowly, as if contemplating how to start a particularly fine meal. "Especially when she is so eager for a moment alone with me."

"Hmm. A penny compliment. I'm all astir."

Sharp canines flashed in the firelight. "Immune, are you?"

"Only when flattery is given by rote."

"Then I shall have to try harder."

"Or give up."

Northrup dimpled, his teeth clicking as his smile grew wolfish. "I never give up."

He said it lightly, yet a flash of something dangerous, almost feral, lit his eyes, and Daisy wondered at the notion of truly being the object of this man's obsession. A chill chased over her skin. Rather like being hunted, she thought...

Praise for FIRELIGHT

"A compelling Victorian paranormal with heart and soul... The compulsively readable tale will leave this new author's fans eager for her next book."

—*Publishers Weekly* (starred review)

"*Beauty and the Beast* meets *Phantom of the Opera* in this gripping, intoxicating story... An exceptional debut and the first of what promises to be a compelling series."

—*Library Journal* (starred review)

"4½ stars! Top pick! Seal of Excellence! Like moths to a flame, readers will be drawn to the flickering *Firelight* and get entangled in the first of the Darkest London series... Callihan crafts a taut tale filled with sexual tension. This is one of the finest debuts of the season."

—*RT Book Reviews*

"*Firelight* draws readers in... Murder, a secret society and overwhelming desire keep Archer and Miranda on their toes—and keep readers turning pages." —BookPage

"A perfect 10! *Firelight* is a debut novel that will knock your socks off. Readers are not going to be able to casually read this novel. It's a page turner... The growing passion between Archer and Miranda steams up the pages... Excellent secondary characters and an amazing premise... I can't wait for the next book."

—RomRevToday.com

"All this reviewer can say is *wow*! The sexual tension and story suspense is so thick it becomes tangible like the very fog of Victorian London."

—TheRomanceReadersConnection.com

"This is one powerful story…Never read anything quite like it. Could not imagine the ending either. Read it—if you dare."
—RomanceReviewsMag.com

"Evocative and deeply romantic…a beautiful debut."
—Nalini Singh, *New York Times* bestselling author, on *Firelight*

"A sizzling paranormal with dark history and explosive magic! Callihan is an impressive new talent."
—Larissa Ione, *New York Times* bestselling author of *Immortal Rider*

"A dark, delicious tale of secrets, murder, and love, beautifully shrouded in the shadows of Victorian London."
—Hannah Howell, *New York Times* bestselling author of *If He's Dangerous*

"Inventive and adventurous with complex, witty characters and snappy writing. Callihan will make you believe in the power of destiny and true love."
—Shana Abé, *New York Times* bestselling author of *The Time Weaver*

"A sexy, resplendent debut with a deliciously tortured hero, an inventive supernatural mystery, and slow-building heat that simmers on each page. I can't wait to see what Kristen Callihan comes up with next!"
—Meljean Brook, *New York Times* bestselling author of *The Iron Duke*

"A dazzling debut, sexy and thrilling. Callihan now has a place on my to-buy list."
—Anya Bast, *New York Times* bestselling author of *Dark Enchantment*

"Utterly phenomenal! Sword fights, magic, a heroine with secret strengths, a hero with hidden vulnerability, and best of all, a true love that's hot enough to burn the pages."

—Courtney Milan, *New York Times* bestselling author of *Unraveled*

"A compelling and emotional page turner that will have readers burning the midnight oil."

—Anna Campbell, award-winning author of *Midnight's Wild Passion*

Moonglow

Also by Kristen Callihan

Firelight

Ember (short story)

Moonglow

Kristen Callihan

FOREVER

NEW YORK BOSTON

Forever
Hachette Book Group
237 Park Avenue
New York, NY 10017

www.HachetteBookGroup.com

Printed in the United States of America
OPM
First Edition: July 2012
10 9 8 7 6 5 4 3 2

Forever is an imprint of Grand Central Publishing.

This one is for my sisters,

Karina and Liz.

They were there at the beginning and will be here until the end.

A greater gift, I cannot comprehend.

Acknowledgments

Again, I must thank my wonderful agent, Kristin Nelson, who always looks out for me. I am so grateful.

Thank you to the talented team at Grand Central/Forever, Lauren Plude, Jennifer Reese, Christine Foltzer, Amy Pierpont, and a host of others who help me in so many ways.

Thank you to my first readers and brainstorming partners extraordinaire, Karina Callihan Escobar and Rachel Walsh. Thank you to beta readers, Jill Archer, Claire Greer, Jennifer Hendren, and Susan Montgomery.

Thank you to Jill Shalvis for keeping me sane during the second-book-revision syndrome. And to Emily Greenwood and Jill Archer for much of the same.

The family: Thank you to my sisters/slave laborers Liz Callihan, for maintaining my website, and Karina Callihan Escobar, for doing all of my graphic design work. And to my brother, Michael Callihan, for putting up with talk of syphilis and my mad plotting that one summer day. And to my mom, Hilde, for listening to general whining—I know you're used to it!

And, of course, to my wonderful husband, Juan, and my children, Maya and Alex, for always being there for me and always understanding when I had to work late. I love you so much!

And last, but certainly not least, I want to thank my editor, Alex Logan. You are my captain and my wing-man. Every writer should be so lucky as to have an editor like you.

MOONGLOW

Prologue

Art thou pale for weariness
Of climbing heaven and gazing on the earth,
Wandering companionless
Among the stars that have a different birth...
—Shelley

London, April 1, 1883

Lord above, was there a better sight than a woman flush with passion, her skin dewy and pink, her breasts bouncing from the force of his thrusts? The woman beneath Ian moaned and arched up to meet him, her red-gold hair catching the afternoon light as it spilled over white linen. What could be better than tupping a woman? A *paid* woman. Did she truly want to be here? Want him? He frowned as his concentration slipped a notch, and with it, the thick knot of pleasure in his balls eased.

Bugger. Stay on point, lad! His locked arms wobbled once. Once. Enough to put him off rhythm. Enough that the smell of penny perfume and stale sheets drifted up to him. Then came the foul scent of oft-used woman and boredom. His pleasure ebbed like seawater off sand. *Shit!*

The whore stilled, her fine red brows pinching in confusion.

Head in it! Head in it! Alas, neither head was listening. More like retreating. Horror washed cold and sure over his skin as little Ian died a quick, limp death.

"My lord?" The whore was lifting her head now, her green eyes bewildered. So close to the original, she looked. But not enough. It wasn't enough anymore. "Something amiss?"

For a moment, Ian couldn't answer. Really, what did one say? He'd didn't have the experience to know. Her confusion faded, replaced by something worse: gentle pity.

"Aw, now, love. 'Tis all right." She patted his arm as he remained frozen in shock, save his cock. The lazy bastard slid out of her, shrinking back like a frightened turtle. She had the good grace not to visibly take note, but held his gaze. "Happens to everyone."

Not to me! He wrenched away and rolled onto his back to face the gilded ceiling. Perhaps the mattress would open up and swallow him whole. "I've been tired, ah…?" Did she have a name? Had he asked? His skin grew clammy, crawling along his frame. Ian wanted nothing more than to close his eyes and sleep for a few decades. Oblivion was getting harder to find.

The woman leaned on one elbow to regard him. In the cool light, the lines around her eyes and mouth deepened, betraying a hard life burned far too quickly. "Yes, tired is all." Another pat, like pacifying a lame dog, and then she sat up. The bed creaked as she put her legs over the side of the bed and tossed the thick mantle of her hair over a bony shoulder. "We needn't speak of it again."

He flew upright and rounded on her. "No. We needn't."

Her brows lifted, a tremor of fear making her perfume sharper. Ian relaxed his expression and forced himself to breathe. He'd growled. Damn it all. Control. But the wolf within him was getting harder to hide away lately. He tried for a pleasant expression as he reached for his coat. "I didn't please you, lass, and I'm sorry for it."

A sound of shocked amusement left her lips and the corners of her mouth twitched. "To speak plainly, sir, it isn't your job to please me, now is it?"

Ian laughed shortly. "Ah, now, Jeanine, your honesty is a humbling thing."

Jeanine. That was her name, though more likely Jenny. Despite certain techniques, she was about as French as a pint of blue ruin. He pulled out far more notes than planned and handed them to her. "Consider that my apology."

Her fingers curled around the money as she eyed him. She was a shrewd one. He didn't like them stupid. Made things harder in the end. They got ideas of becoming mistresses. Fortunately, with a reputation as a profligate, no one much cared what Ian did as long as it was outrageous. Good entertainment always calmed the savage beast that was London society.

Jeanine-Jenny's mouth curled into a friendly smile. " 'Tis a fine apology, me lad."

Now that they were done, she'd let her Irish show.

Jeanine-Jenny slid from the bed and gathered her things, giving him a flash of firmly rounded arse. Not even a stir of appreciation. Trying not to think of little Ian, the bastard turncoat, he rested his hands upon his knees while she dressed in thick silence. His contentment almost returned as she reached for the door. But her green eyes flashed at him from over her shoulder at the last moment. Every muscle in his body tensed as he read that look.

"I'll be as quiet as the grave," she assured.

The door shut with the muted thud of a lid being placed upon a coffin.

Chapter One

London, April 18, 1883

Three hundred sixty-six days, ten hours, fifteen minutes, and...Daisy glanced down at the heart-shaped gold watch pinned to the dip in her bodice, a strategic placement designed to draw the eye. Strategic placement, perhaps, but it made it a bugger to read the time. The tiny face flicked in and out of shadow as the carriage lantern swayed gently overhead.

Seconds needn't be counted anymore regardless. She was free. Daisy looked out into the boiling gray fog that shrouded the streets of London. Moreover, three hundred sixty-six days, ten hours, fifteen minutes, and however many seconds was quite sufficient a time to stay in mourning over a man one hated. Even if that man had been one's husband. Especially if, she corrected, smoothing out a wrinkle in her azure silk skirt. Azure. Lovely word. It rolled over the tongue, promising adventure and foreign climes. She loved azure. Loved color. Though, for a time, she had loved black too. Black had been her banner of freedom. A marker announcing the shift from the bondage of marriage to the emancipation of widowhood.

Daisy was finished with black now. One ought to curse the queen for her dogged devotion to mourning, thus causing countless widows to guiltily follow suit. Only it was quite romantic, and Daisy could not fault a romantic heart. As for herself, she'd done her year of mourning, enough to satisfy wagging tongues. Now it was her time.

Barnaby, her driver, called out to the horses. The carriage made a sharp turn down a narrow lane that would take her to her future. Amusement, laughter, life. A place where women did not wear black, unless one wished to be thought of as mysterious. No one had ever thought of her as mysterious. Infamous, perhaps.

Suddenly, her insides clenched with such force that she trembled. Loneliness and fear urged her to shout at Barnaby to turn round. Her bed was safe and warm. What if she was all talk? What if the infamously fun-loving Daisy Margaret Ellis—she refused to call herself Craigmore—was nothing more than a coward?

"Why don't we get a bit of fresh air?" The man nuzzling Daisy's neck let out a small laugh at his jest. "Fresh" air being a myth in London. Daisy refrained from rolling her eyes. After all, his lips felt wonderful as they made a soft, slow circuit over her skin. It had been over six years since she'd been touched in passion. He nipped the tender juncture at the base of her neck, and she shivered, her nipples tightening in anticipation. Wine coursed through her veins, heating her blood and painting her world in soft, nebulous colors.

Around them, couples had paired off, finding their own dark corners in the overcrowded town home to do what they might. Men with the single-minded purpose to win congregated around gaming tables, barely noticing the women who adorned their shoulders. A few danced to the endless tunes played by the orchestra Alexis had hired for the night. As for Alex, Daisy hadn't yet spotted her.

Being newly widowed herself, Alex had chosen to live among the demimonde. The *ton*, Alex declared, was too tiresome. Daisy agreed. The *ton* had all but turned their backs on Daisy when Craigmore died and left her nothing by way of monetary support. Surely the bloody man had assumed she'd end up in the streets as a destitute wretch. Little had he known about her own resources.

Daisy eyed the man before her, a well-formed youth with a slightly coltish way about him. "Fresh air would be lovely."

A languid heaviness stole over her as she leaned into him. He smelled of cheroots, fine wool, and young male. His hard body against hers was a wonder. What did it matter that she'd forgotten his name?

His arm locked around her shoulders as he led her through a maze of corridors. Gaslight flickered low. Blue smoke and hot flesh turned the air hazy.

Daisy stumbled, and his grip tightened. "Careful. Don't want you on your back. Yet."

A true wit, this one. She cleared the thought away. She didn't need to think, only to feel.

With a laugh, they burst through the back door. Daisy caught a breath of dank, coal-tinged air and saw the flash of wet pavers glistening in the moonlight, and then her companion shoved her against the wall. Thick ivy rustled against her ear as he leaned in and took, his mouth brutal.

Daisy opened to it, ignoring the pain, looking for the pleasure. So elusive, pleasure. So easy to remember one's self and lose the feeling. His tongue thrust past her lips, cool and thick. Ought a tongue feel cold?

Clouds scuttled overhead, and the bright disk of the moon shone down, setting the dismal little alleyway to glow like blue daylight. Daisy blinked up at the moon as her lover's hands drifted lower, catching up her skirts, his breath hot and damp above her breast. Daisy strained against his questing hand as it groped her. This is what she'd been waiting for. Six years of living in hell, she'd waited to be wanted, to be looked upon as a desirable woman and not a thing of disgust.

Temptress of man, harbinger of lust. You are a worthless vessel whose only use is to receive man's sin.

Anger coiled with her revulsion. *Forget Craigmore, he is dead. His words cannot touch you. Follow the pleasure.* But it skittered away as the wind shifted, brushing ice cold against her bare arms. Ah, but this alley smelled. Queer, like sticky sweet rot, and copper mixed with dirt. The stench sent a finger of ice over her spine. She murmured a protest. They were too exposed here, and she no longer wanted this.

"Easy, pet." Hard fingers raked her thighs.

"I want to go inside."

"Relax," he said.

She pushed at him. "Inside."

"I'm trying," he said with a laugh.

She turned her head to get away from him and caught the sight just to the left of his shoulder. A spill of gray satin skirts, the ruffled edges kicking up in the wind, a pale length of arm extended outward as if begging for help, the sparkle of diamonds on a white throat, large, glassy eyes staring. And blood, so much blood. Black and shining in the moonlight. Daisy's mind pulled the shapes, rearranging them to form a story. Alex. Alex's torso torn open. And something bent over Alex, its face buried in the gore, nosing about as if sniffing the body. A scream locked in Daisy's throat, so hard and cold that she could not get it out. Terror uncoiled, giving her the strength to push her lover away.

"What the devil?" he said.

A whimper broke from her lips as she tripped over her skirts and her companion turned. As if called, the thing lifted its head. A drop of crimson blood dripped from its jaw, and Daisy screamed. It snarled, rising on hind legs that were long as any man's. Her would-be lover scrambled back, bellowing in fear as the monster charged.

Daisy's head smashed against brick. Something hot and wet splashed over her cheek and neck. A body fell upon her, jerking and thrashing, grinding her into the hard ground, and then the screams, screams upon screams, pure unadulterated terror. It washed over her, taking her wits, sucking her down into the cool embrace of darkness.

Not far away…

Six whores and six failures were enough to make even the most optimistic of men throw in the sponge, as the Americans would say. There was fortitude, and there was humiliation. Ian knew he crossed that line around whore number three. So then, no more tupping. *Fornicating* as his father would have called it.

"Bloody, buggering, fucking, hell!" Ian's curse was lost to the night, dissipating like heated steam in the cool, clean air of Hampstead Heath.

Sweating and swearing, he ran faster, his feet pounding

into the soft earth. Defeat never sat well with him. Worse, there was nothing left to him other than this. Running, pushing his body to the limits of endurance. Biting back another foul oath, he ran harder, his blood pumping through his veins like molten glass, as his legs screamed for mercy. Only here did he feel alive.

The great black dome of the night sky soared overhead. Beyond lay London, a jagged landscape of church spires and haphazard buildings bathed in the silver light of the moon. A shiver of feeling danced over him. The moon. That glorious seductress. Her power pulsed through him like so much wine. She fueled him, and in return, the beast stirred.

For decades, Ian had ignored this part of himself. He'd kept his beast so tightly leashed it had become nothing more than a faint echo in his mind. And he had suffered for it. Grown weak and apathetic. Now its howl rattled about in his skull, growing louder and stronger.

Part of him reveled in the beast. Why not? He'd lost all other sources of pleasure. Why not let the beast at last have its fun? Why not let it out to play? Even as the thought rolled over him, an innate sense of self-preservation protested. He had not struggled through one hundred and thirty years of life to let a little thing like temptation suck him into total annihilation.

Swearing again, Ian turned toward London, away from the wild things that called to the beast, the small scurrying rabbits and the fearful does that, even now, Ian could scent. A bitter laugh escaped as his feet ate up the ground, leading him into London with uncanny speed. Perhaps one day he'd be back to take down a deer with freed claws. Would he soon find himself muzzle deep in hot, wet blood, eating warm flesh with mindless pleasure?

Earth gave way to stone, clean air turning thick and fetid as he pushed into the city. Around him, the buildings were a blur, the odd pedestrian little more than a streak of color and the stir of air as Ian ran past. He was that fast. Faster than he would be all month now that the full and glorious moon fed him.

A dray loomed before him, plodding along with its load of coal. He leaped, arcing over it, to land on quick feet and run onward. It was more populated here, throngs of idle humans mixing with street traffic. He wove around them without care, his feet splashing through some unholy muck and kicking up the scent of rot.

His shoulder brushed past a coffee monger pushing his cart along. What would he see? A man in leather moccasins brought back from the American West? The loose gray trousers and cotton shirt of a laborer? Items Ian Ranulf, newly titled Marquis of Northrup, would not be caught dead wearing. Surely not that trussed-up dandy. Lord Northrup would never be confused with this wild man running amok.

All at once, the strength left him, and he slowed. His breath puffed even and steady. The beat of his heart was as strong as ever in his chest. Unstoppable. Unending. The thought nearly brought him to his knees. Around him, the chatter of men and women enjoying the clear night scraped against his nerves.

Slowing to a stroll, Ian wandered down a twisted street where the press of bodies thinned out to lighter foot traffic. To his left, yellow light poured in wide blocks from the windows of an older town home, still beautiful but shabby in this unfashionable neighborhood. The strains of a reel and feminine laughter rose above the din of London nightlife.

Ian moved away from it, into the shadowy mouth of an alley, when through the thick mash of human sweat, rotting water, and sewage came the distinctive tang of blood. Human blood. Just below that, a finer note, that of wolf.

It was that scent, the wild, rangy stamp of wolf that had his hackles rising and a growl rumbling deep within his throat. Seventy years of doggedly keeping away from his kind was almost lost as he instinctively turned toward the scent, ready to tear into whoever dared to encroach upon his territory. He came to an abrupt halt. It wasn't his territory. Not anymore.

Fight or flight, it warred within him until his chest felt ready to rip in two. A trickle of sweat rolled down his neck. He nearly moved away when a sharp feminine scream rent the air, followed by a snarl of rage. A man bellowed in pure terror. The snarls grew and then came the distinctive sound of tearing flesh, a man gurgling as though drowning. Blood, the perfume of it washed over Ian, making his knees buckle.

"Bugger!" He ran toward the scent without another thought.

Men were already spilling into the alley as Ian charged headlong into the fray. Someone shouted in shock. A woman fainted. A ripple of terror went through the throng of onlookers, heightening the sharp smell of fear. Men both retreated in horror and shoved forward in fascination. Women were quickly ushered away.

Ian shouldered a rotund man aside. The scent of wolf overpowered his senses. Wolf and blood. *Jesus.*

When yet another gentleman stepped in his way, Ian found his voice and said words he hadn't uttered in years. "Move aside! I'm a doctor." Though from the overwhelming amount of blood he smelled, he rather thought his rusty services would not be needed.

The crowd parted, and Ian took in the scene. Bile surged up his throat. Blood was everywhere, coating the walls of the town house, pooling upon the ground, and running along the cracks between the cobbles. A man—what was left of him—lay in a tangled heap against the wall, his face an unrecognizable hash of claw marks, his torso eviscerated. Just beyond, a woman suffered the same fate, though her face was unmarred. She'd died first. He'd bet his best walking stick on it. Already the stench of decay crept over her, and the body was stiff and white in the moon's glow.

Ian crouched low and inhaled. Scents assaulted him. He let them come and sorted through the mix. Beneath the rot, terror, and blood was the rangy scent of wolf imbued with something off, bittersweet yet sulfuric. Sickness. What sort, he couldn't tell, but it was well-developed. An odd fact indeed, given that werewolves weren't susceptible to disease.

"He's past help," said the man beside him. Ian held up a staying hand and inhaled deeper.

Beyond the filth came a fainter scent—rose, jasmine, vanilla, and sunshine. Those notes held him for one tense moment, pulling the muscles in his solar plexus tight and filling them with warmth. It was a fresh, ephemeral scent that made the beast inside him sit up and take notice.

A small groan broke the spell. Someone shouted in alarm. The dead man moved, rolling a bit, and the crowd jumped back as if one. Ian's pulse kicked before he noticed the soft drape of blue silk beneath the man's twisted legs.

"Bloody hell." He wrenched the body aside. It pitched

over with a thud to reveal the crumpled form of a woman covered in blood and, oddly, vines, thick and deep green as they flowed down from the town house wall to envelop her.

"Step back," he said sharply as one wayward man tromped forward.

"Lud! Is she alive?"

Ian made quick work of the vines, extending only the very tips of his claws to rake through them, but his hands were gentle as he touched the woman's wrist to check her pulse. Slow, steady, and strong. It was from her that the scent of flowers and vanilla arose. Her features were lost under a macabre mask of crimson blood. Ian cursed beneath his breath and ran his hands over her form in search of injuries. Despite the blood, she appeared untouched. It was the man's blood, not hers. She'd seen the attack, however. Of that, he was certain. She'd been the one to scream. Then the man.

He glanced about the alley and imagined the events unfolding. This couple had seen the first victim. They shouted, and then they were attacked. Ian brought his attention back to the woman.

She was a handful, lush curves, neat waist. He gathered her up in his arms, ignoring the protests of those around. Her head lolled against his shoulder, releasing another faint puff of sweet scent. A curling lock of hair, red with blood, fell over his chest as he hefted her higher and stood.

"She needs medical attention." He moved to go when a gentleman stepped in his way.

"Here now." The gentleman's waxed mustache twitched. "You don't look like any doctor I've ever seen."

The crowd of men stirred, apparently taking in Ian's odd attire for the first time.

Ian tightened his grip on the female, and she gave a little moan of distress. The sound went straight to his core. Women were to be protected and cherished. Always. He stared down the gathering crowd. "Nor a marquis, I gather. However, I am both." He took a step, shouldering aside the man with ease. "I am Northrup. And it would do you well to get out of my way."

Another murmur rippled among the men, but they eased away; not many wanted to risk tangling with Lord Ian Ranulf, Marquis of Northrup. Those who weren't as convinced, he pushed past. He'd fight them all if he had to. This woman wasn't getting out of his sight. Not until he'd questioned her. And he certainly wasn't letting her tell the whole of London that she'd just survived an attack by a werewolf.

Chapter Two

"There now, that's a good lass. Wake up, dear."

Daisy was warm. Warm and heavy of limb. It felt wonderful. The thought formed, and then confusion chased it away. Beyond her dark cocoon came the comforting sound of tinkling water, like that of a bath being drawn. Where was she? Who was that crooning? And what had happened...Her eyes flew open on a gasp. The flickering light of gas lamps wavered above her. She caught a glimpse of mahogany paneling before a woman's face came into view, wrinkled and kind, a gray halo of hair about her head.

"Easy, lass." The woman clasped Daisy's shoulder.

Daisy blinked down at her shoulder and realized that she was naked. Swaddled in eider down, but naked. "Where..." She swallowed. "What..." Her throat closed.

The elder woman gave her a little pat and then turned to adjust the taps on the enormous copper tub sitting in the center of the room. A man's bathing room, with velvet brocades and a silver shaving kit gleaming on a nearby table. A masculine fragrance of wool, linen, and vetiver lingered in the warm air.

"You've had a terrible fright, I suspect." The woman closed the taps and dipped a hand in the water to test it. Neither plump nor thin, the woman's frame was sturdy. "Just right."

The woman looked Daisy over. "You're in the Marquis of Northrup's home. His Lordship found ye and brought ye here." She moved to Daisy's side and gave her a kindly smile. "I was of a mind to wake ye before I got you in the bath. Bit of a nasty shock to be awakened by a bath, eh?" The woman's eyes went soft. "Ye need cleaning up, lass."

Daisy followed the direction of the woman's gaze and saw her hair cascading around her naked shoulders in a red tangle of dried blood. So red it reminded her of her sister Poppy's hair, and then she remembered. "Oh, God..." Her breath came in dry pants, the urge to gag, to scream making her shake. "That thing... my... friend..."

Her pants became rasps, and the woman wrapped a strong arm about her. "Hush, child, hush. You're safe." Work-worn palms soothed her arms. "Ease yerself before you become ill."

Like a child, Daisy let herself be led to the bath. The water was blessedly hot, smelling of lavender and chamomile, and Daisy let out a sigh. The woman smiled in satisfaction before reaching for a pitcher and a bar of soap. "Let's get ye clean, then." Her movements were brisk, and Daisy relaxed under the efficiency until the woman hit a spot at the back of her neck. She hissed at the sting and reached up to feel a row of punctures in her skin. A violent shudder wracked her body.

"It bit me," she whispered. She did not want to

remember what *it* was. Her insides lurched and swayed, and she swallowed convulsively.

"Let me have a look." Gentle fingers probed the wounds. "'Tis not very deep," the woman said soothingly as she washed it clean. "'Twill heal in a tic, to be sure." Even so, the woman got up and came back with a jar of ointment. Her fingers were strong and sure as she smeared the pungent stuff on Daisy's neck.

The sting receded, and Daisy relaxed a bit more. "What is that?" she asked.

"An old recipe. Helps speed the healing." She sat back down behind Daisy and took up washing her hair. "I'm Mrs. Tuttle," the woman said. "You may call me Tuttle if ye like." She let out a short laugh. "I havena been called anything else in an age."

Daisy stared at the small coal fire glowing at the other end of the room. "I'm Daisy."

The sound of her own name felt wrong. She felt wrong. Numb.

"Would you send word to my sister?" The sudden need to see one of her sisters was almost painful. Poppy, however, would ask too many questions and make her feel like a goose for recklessly attending a party with the fast crowd. No, she needed Miranda, who would offer comfort without judgment. Her voice cracked when she spoke again. "She is Lady Archer."

"Of course, dear. I'll send a messenger out directly."

Strong fingers massaged Daisy's scalp, and creamy cascades of foam slid over her breasts and arms, the foam pink with old blood. In the dim of the elegant dressing room, she could almost believe the blood to be a trick of light. Only it wasn't. Bile rose in her throat. She drew her knees up and closed her eyes to the sight.

"Tuttle? The..." She licked her dry lips. "The man?"

Tuttle's movement stilled for only a moment. "Passed on." She crossed herself and then picked up the pitcher.

Warm water eased over Daisy's head as she squeezed her eyes shut. "I don't even remember his name." Her mouth trembled. She'd only been looking for a bit of amusement, harmless pleasure. She felt sick to her soul.

Tuttle made a soft sound. "'Tis a terrible business, ma'am. Bless the Lord that yer unharmed."

Daisy curled into herself as another round of water flowed over her, taking the gore away. "And Alex." She swallowed down bile. "Alex was my friend."

Tuttle washed her with neat economy and then gently helped her to her feet to wrap a thick towel about her. The quiet movements were oddly comforting, and when Daisy was settled again on the green-velvet settee, she felt a bit more clearheaded. Unfortunately, it also led her to realize that she'd let Tuttle see her unclothed. Unease tightened the muscles on her back. She glanced at Tuttle. The light was dim here, and Tuttle hadn't remarked on anything. So perhaps she hadn't seen.

Daisy adjusted the towel higher up her back as Tuttle handed her a glass of brandy. "The master sent this for you. It ought to be whiskey, but he thought that might be too strong for ye."

Daisy took a sip of brandy as Tuttle bustled about. Liquid fire melted the ice in her belly, and her thoughts turned to her kind host. She couldn't recall meeting Lord Northrup. Then again, it had been a year since she'd been out in society, and she hadn't run in such lofty circles. Names, titles, and faces filtered through her mind, and she finally remember that the Marquis of Northrup was an old title belonging to some lord in Scotland for at least sixty years now. The man must be ancient.

Tuttle came near, holding up a rather flashy dressing gown of celadon green satin. The color would suit her sisters but most likely make Daisy look peaked. However, as it was that or go around swathed in a towel, Daisy slipped it on. Unfortunately, the garment, which smelled of cheap violet water perfume, puddled on the floor, the arms of it flopping far past Daisy's hands. Made for a woman of Miranda's stature too, Daisy thought grimly as Tuttle helped her hook up the front. The hooks strained over her breasts, and Daisy grimaced at the ill fit. Lord Northrup, the randy old goat, apparently favored tall redheads who wore harlot's perfume.

Ian fiddled about with the decanters on his drinks table. He'd already poured himself a measure of scotch and had no real purpose for pulling out the random crystal stopper only to put it back in. With a sound of disgust, he pushed away from the sideboard.

The woman was above, getting bathed by Tuttle. If he closed his eyes, he could hear the gentle tinkle of water and smell the fragrance of his bath soap enveloping her.

He blew out a breath and plopped down in his chair by the fire. Grabbing his glass from the side table, he took a hearty swallow before scowling down into the amber liquid.

The woman. He had exactly one glimpse of her pale throat before Tuttle had shooed him away.

"I'm a physician," he'd protested, when an implacable Tuttle had batted him back from undressing his patient.

"Oh, are ye?" Tuttle's expression had been dubious. "I thought ye'd given that all up."

Fine, he hadn't practiced since 1865 but the knowledge was still there. "Cheeky woman, do not split hairs now. I've seen countless nude females in that capacity, and it doesn't affect me in the least."

"Aye," Tuttle had snapped back. "An' when ye can look at her with the detached politeness of a healer and not leer like some randy lad, I'll let you examine her. Until then, out you go."

This is what he got for treating his staff like pack instead of servants, and while he craved the close familiarity of others, now wasn't one of those times. "Blast it, woman, I need to ascertain whether she is injured."

"Ascertain, eh?" She shoved him toward the door. "Is that what you're callin' it now?"

With only a harried assurance from Tuttle that she'd check the lass for damage, he'd been banished from his own room as though he were some deviant incapable of basic professionalism.

A grumble sounded in his breast. Very well, he could admit that part of him had been looking at the woman with the interest of a man, and damned if he knew why. The poor thing had been covered in blood, and in all likelihood, was traumatized. That his breath had begun to quicken as his hands undid her top buttons suddenly made him feel small and wrong, a right cad.

"Bloody hell," he muttered and took another long drink. The liquor sent a pleasant path of warmth down his throat and into his twitching gut. But it did not calm him. The silence in the library irritated the hell out of him. It struck him that silence was fast becoming his constant companion. Certainly he heard many things, talked to people on a daily basis, but on the inside he was alone.

Ian sank farther into his chair, and the twitchy, itchy

weight of his situation intensified. As he looked at the door, his ears pricked up at the sound of the woman's tread coming down the main stair, and his heart kicked within his chest. A pleasant jump along with a tightening of his gut. Although he hadn't felt the sensation in months, years really, Ian realized the feeling for what it was: anticipation.

A sense of the surreal settled over Daisy as Tuttle led her through Northrup's elegant town house. She ought not be walking. She ought to be dead. That she lived, breathed, felt the slip and slide of silk over her legs with every step was at once so normal yet so abnormal that she almost laughed. Her friend was dead. And her own would-be lover? She was prepared to shag him, for really she couldn't call it making love, and now the man—whose name she still could not remember—was gone, slaughtered.

Temptress of man. Harbinger of a man's lust and destruction.

God help her, her late husband's words rang too close to the truth. Were it not for her going into the alleyway with that poor man, he might still be alive.

Her heartbeat sped up as Tuttle opened the door to a cozy library and ushered Daisy forward. What had her rescuer seen? Her steps faltered because suddenly she resolutely did not want to know.

As soon as she stepped into the room, he rose up from the leather wing chair by the fire in one fluid move. His eyes narrowed, taking her in just as she studied him.

Her breath gave a little catch as she moved closer. Most certainly, this was not the elderly Lord Northrup, but perhaps his heir. Good God, but this man was beautiful. Distractingly so. His was a masculine beauty that artists often replicated. Lean of face, saved from femininity by the sharp V of his jaw and the strength of his chin, with high cheekbones so defined they might have been cut from marble. Only his mouth was soft. Soft and mobile, the corners twitched as if wanting to smile.

However, there was nothing soft about his eyes. Deep set under dark brows that were currently slashed in a scowl, they pierced into her, their light color indistinguishable until she came close. A chuff of air escaped her. "Azure."

One brow lifted a notch. "Pardon?" His voice was at once lilting and light, yet rough. Silk over gravel.

Daisy stopped and let her gaze travel from the tips of his polished shoes, over his lean form dressed to perfection, and up to those azure eyes that now danced with amusement. She would have remembered this man had she seen him before. "You are too pretty to be a noble."

A bark of a laughter shot out, and Daisy felt a quirk of irritation. Damn her loose tongue.

Lord Northrup stepped closer, bringing with him the heady scent of vetiver and clean male. "I don't think I've ever been called pretty before, lass."

Very correctly, he caught up her hand and bent over it, his lips brushing her knuckles. His dark hair was the one wrong note in his otherwise flawless attire. It flowed in shining waves to the top of his shoulders. Barbaric. "If you're not careful," he said, "I'll soon be blushing."

Neither of them wore gloves, and his skin was dry and very warm. A stir of feeling wisped through her insides, and she fought the urge to back away. "I doubt that. I am certain you are quite used to such accolades." She gave a careless shrug as she retracted her hand. "In truth, I should take care not to stand too close or risk being eclipsed by your splendor."

He flashed a quick, practiced smile. "Oh, I don't know." He reached out and tugged a curl dangling by her cheek, the action making her insides jump. "You exude quite a shine yourself."

No, she would not blush. Daisy never blushed. Not over a man's attention. Yet her cheeks felt suspiciously warm as she turned away from him and wandered around the room. "Nonsense."

He strolled near. "Ah, but sometimes speaking of nonsense is the best cure." The gentleness in his tone made her heart skip a beat. He knew what she was about. He knew she strove to ignore the panic welling up like acid in her belly.

"Pay no mind to me, sir. There are times when my mouth and brain forget to hold a conversation."

His mouth quirked, true amusement making him appear almost boyish. "Happens often, does it?"

Cheeky sot. Daisy gave him a repressive look from over her shoulder, and he chuckled, clearly unperturbed by her annoyance.

"I see you are quite well, physically, at least. But let us sit." Catching hold of her hand once more and ignoring her murmur of protest, he tugged her gently toward the settee by the fire. He folded his long length next to hers. "I'm intrigued. If not by beauty, how then does one spot the garden-variety nobleman?"

He was too close, his gaze too warm for her comfort. Sliding her clenched fists under the borrowed dressing gown, she shrugged.

"Easily," she said. "One need only look for the promise of beauty not quite fulfilled, a nose too large, eyes a bit too close together, or ears ready to set sail."

Northrup's head snapped back, his eyes widening. "You, madam, are a snob."

She bit back a laugh. "Oh, to be sure. As I am certain you men are not cataloging a woman's every feature from the moment she steps in the room."

He grinned with the ease of a man who did so often. "As you did with me, you mean?"

Her lips tightened. "Pray, do not hold your tongue on my account."

"Said one spade to the other." He was smiling again, leaning in as if he might gobble her up. Damn the man, he had an infectious smile. She resisted the urge to return it.

Among the *ton*, Lord Northrup's type of charm was as prevalent as weeds in a meadow. Light, amusing, and devoid of any true meaning. She used to long for such interactions. But after tonight's horror, even that small amusement had lost its flavor. Yet she appreciated his efforts to distract her. Despite the bath and the bracing effect of the brandy, residual shivers of panic clung to her. She wanted to rub her arms until the feeling was gone.

Northrup rested an elbow on the seat back, and the light reflected in his long hair, turning it auburn. Wine and chocolate. Delicious. The look in his eyes said he had at least some sense of her line of thoughts.

"You wear your hair longer than fashion," Daisy blurted out. "Why?" The question was in poor taste, but the cornered often react in haste. At least that was the reasoning she used on herself as she felt her cheeks prickle with embarrassment.

Obviously as surprised at her bluntness as she was, he took a moment to address her. "I'm in mourning for my father." The corners of his lush mouth turned down as he glowered at some unseen thing before his expression cleared. "It is the Ranulf custom for a man to let one's hair grow for three years after the death of a close family member."

"Oh, I had no idea." Her discomfort grew.

"How could you?" he answered with unexpected kindness.

Daisy found herself reacting to it. Her hand settled on his forearm for a brief moment. "I am sorry for your loss."

He looked at the spot she had touched. "Thank you. Your concern is unnecessary, but kind." He went back to studying her, and a look of bemusement wrinkled his brow. "You remind me of someone. Though I cannot place it."

The feeling was mutual. He seemed at once utterly familiar yet completely foreign to her.

His look of concentration grew. "But I have never seen you before tonight. I would have remembered." His tone was soft now, a confession that moved beyond small talk.

She had to smile at that bit of odd logic. "Certainly." She meant to say it lightly yet her voice caught and faded as she met his gaze. Everything within her stilled and warmed. As if similarly affected, his smile slipped and his expression grew unguarded. Daisy's breath hitched, for she saw in the depths of his eyes something that looked like longing.

It mirrored feelings she'd rather not think on, and so she sought to turn the conversation back to the benign. "Were you living in Scotland before the previous Lord Northrup's passing?"

His straight brows drew together. "How did you know that my grandfather passed on?"

It was Daisy's turn to frown. "Your title... Was Lord Northrup not your father?"

The current Lord Northrup's look of confusion faded. "Ah," he said with a little smile, and then sat a bit straighter. "My father was Lord Alasdair Rossberry. It is a bit of a muddle, I grant you, but he and my grandfather both passed"—a strange look flashed in his eyes before he continued—"around the same time. Thus I inherited two titles."

The tips of his ears reddened as he grimaced. "I beg your pardon for not making a proper introduction. Ian Alasdair Ranulf, previously known as Viscount Mc-kinnon, at your service...Hell, I haven't even asked your name." One side of his mouth kicked up. "I'm usually much better at this sort of thing, only I confess—"

"I distracted you," she finished wryly, but her heart had started to pound. Mckinnon, the name was familiar. Why? Alarm bells clanged within her tender skull.

"You're very good it," he admitted in a low voice.

"Only when I'm trying." Daisy licked her dry lips and inclined her head. "Daisy Ellis Craigmore."

Whatever she expected of him, it wasn't the sudden shock in his eyes or the way he straightened and stepped away from her. "You are Miranda's sister."

Apparently shock was catching. All the warmth within her left as though she were caught in a draft, and then she knew. "You!"

Northrup's slanting brows furrowed, but his tone was light when he spoke. "Me? Whatever do you mean?"

Daisy's elbow slipped a bit as she scrambled to sit up straight. "You're the beastly man who tried to poison Miranda's mind against Archer." Miranda had told Daisy all about it months ago, how Mckinnon had tried his best to convince Miranda to carry on an affair with him. And now Daisy was sitting in the parlor with the vile man.

He scowled. Whether it was toward the veracity of her statement or the fact that he'd been caught out, Daisy couldn't be sure. The only certainty was the feral gleam in Northrup's eyes and the way it made Daisy feel unaccountably nervous. However, having lived with much worse, intimidation did not easily cow her. She returned his look pound for pound, and his irritation seemed to grow.

"'Beastly' is it?" he all but growled. "I'll kindly ask you to remember who took you in and saw you set to rights."

A qualm of guilt lit through her, and he must have seen it for he stepped closer to loom over her in righteous indignation. "And I don't recall you thinking me so beastly a moment ago."

No, she'd rather liked him, damn the man. It made her cheeks burn to realize he had noticed this as well. In the heavy silence, she heard the clatter of a carriage pulling up beyond the front windows. A coach door opened and shut. Northrup's nostrils flared as if catching a scent, and a strange look passed over his features. "Well, won't this be cozy?" he said, as he straightened his coat. "I believe the lady in question has come to call."

Chapter Three

She was here. Miranda. He hadn't seen her in months. And then it had been only a glimpse at some ball. He had wanted to speak to Miranda one more time. To apologize. Not for warning her about Archer—the bastard had no right to marry a woman without telling her the truth of what he was—but for putting the wariness in her eyes whenever she looked his way. Despite what others thought, Ian did not hold with frightening women. He had played out his dance with Miranda poorly.

He heard Miranda's voice in the hall, sharp with worry as she asked his butler Diggs where to find Daisy. How she knew to come here Ian did not know, but her presence plucked at the nerves on the back of his neck. Ian closed his eyes for a moment and pictured Miranda, golden-red hair, her long, willowy form, and alabaster skin.

At one time, he'd fancied himself in love with her. And now? Seeing her was the last thing he wanted. He was thoroughly tired of redheaded women.

Beside him, her sister gathered herself together. She

looked nothing like Miranda. Curling hair of morning sunlight mixed with polished gold. Enormous doe eyes, not the color of celadon but of summer skies. Daisy. A preposterous name. Frivolous. And yet he could not think of her as Mrs. Craigmore. The name did not fit.

Ian's gaze slid lower. The unfortunate dressing gown she wore, a sad little orphan of some long-ago mistress's wardrobe, did not fit but most certainly highlighted her undulating curves and that plump arse that practically begged a man to take hold of it. She surely was built for frivolity.

Ian resolutely tore his eyes from her lush form as the door opened and Miranda appeared, so beautiful it made a man's chest hurt to look upon her. She spared him but a glance before rushing to her sister's side.

"Daisy!"

"Panda. Oh, God." Daisy pulled her close and shuddered so hard that Ian feared the woman might faint.

Miranda hugged her sister tight. "I was so worried. When you sent word that you'd been hurt..." She said nothing further but held on as if she might never let go.

They stayed like that, their bright heads close, glowing like sunrise and sunset, their slim arms locked in an embrace. Too pretty a picture for him. Damn, but he did not want this woman to be Miranda's sister.

"Where is Archer?" Ian asked. The man usually hung about her skirts like an overgrown shadow.

Miranda lifted her head. Her words came out halting and reserved. "Home. Given the way you two are apt to get at each other's throats, I thought it best that I come alone."

He couldn't help but laugh a little. "I am surprised he let you go."

She gave him an admonishing look that was much like

the one her sister had given him earlier. "It is you whom Archer does not trust, not me."

Touché. He inclined his head in deference.

Miranda turned back to Daisy. "Are you harmed?"

Daisy shook her head, which made the wild tumble of her curls tremble. "I am well. Only frightened."

A pair of green eyes turned to Ian, and he found himself bristling. "Because I get such joy in frightening innocent women."

Miranda blanched. "Of course not. I am simply curious as to how my sister came to be in your care."

"Then let us sit," he said.

The sisters immediately curled up together on the settee, Miranda clasping Daisy's hand in a show of comfort. Oddly, this made Ian want to smile. The temptation faded when Miranda pinned him with her green gaze. "Well then, how did you come across my sister?"

He hesitated. Hell, it was one thing to coax a story out of a frightened young lady. It was another to give up *his* secrets. Archer knew them. At least some. What was not clear was how much Archer had told Miranda. Right now, she was looking at him with a mixture of weariness and impatience. As to Daisy, he rather thought that if he revealed himself at this moment, she'd up and flee the room. He would not resent her one bit if she did.

Ian ran a hand through his hair. "I was in the area. I heard a scream and caught the scent of blood and ran to help. I found Mrs. Craigmore—"

"Daisy," interrupted the very woman. She glanced around, taking in their shocked looks. "Don't go reading anything into it. Given the choice between having to hear that name in reference to me and shocking society, I'll take the latter every time, thank you."

Ian admired her nerve. "For the sake of fairness, you must call me Ian."

Miranda's eyes narrowed a fraction. Good. He ignored her, or did his best to appear that he was. "At any rate, I found Daisy, saw that she was overcome, and took her to safety. End of the story."

It was clear that Miranda didn't believe that was all to the story, but she held her tongue, and Ian took advantage of the moment to turn to Daisy. "I am more interested in knowing what you saw, Daisy."

Daisy took a deep breath and her breasts strained against the tight confines of the hideous green dressing gown. Ian found he couldn't stand the sight of the gown. It shamed him that she should wear a whore's clothes.

"I fear you will not believe me," she whispered.

"Be assured, madam," Ian said, "I will."

Her bright blue eyes surveyed him as if checking for any sign of insincerity. "You seem so certain"—a bitter laugh escaped her—"when I wouldn't believe myself."

Ian leaned against the settee back. "What you saw appeared as something out of a fantasy, yes?"

"More likely a nightmare," Daisy said with a burst of breath. But she would not continue. Her golden brows drew together as she glared down at her tight fists.

Ian looked at Miranda. Initially, he had wished she hadn't come. But now he wondered if her presence might help. "I do wonder," he said to Miranda, "how close a family you are."

Fortunately, she read the question lurking there. Miranda touched Daisy's hand. "Daisy, Lord Northrup knows about me."

Daisy's eyes flew to Ian in horror. Indeed, what Miranda could do was equally fantastic, and Ian suspected her family had kept her sister's secret for a lifetime. After all, what would society say if they knew the lovely Lady Archer was a fire starter?

"And about Archer as well," Miranda added.

"Which is why," Ian said, "you can tell us what you saw without fear of judgment."

Daisy cleared her throat, and as she recounted her tale, rage and the urge to do violence tumbled about in Ian's chest. Hells bells, he knew too well the terror of confronting a fully turned werewolf. That this woman had faced one made the hairs rise upon the back of his neck and gave him an unsettling sense of helplessness. Yet he remained outwardly calm.

"I did not get a long look at it," Daisy said, finishing her tale. Her eyes squeezed shut. "But that muzzle, the fangs, and the claws. It was a wolf. And yet it moved in an almost human way..." With a grimace, she shook her head and went quiet.

Ian sighed and told her the truth. "A werewolf is what you saw."

It was almost comical the way her mouth opened and shut as if trying to form words and failing. All the color leached out of her soft cheeks. Her mouth kept working as she looked from Miranda to Ian and back around again. A little laugh escaped, but it died when she swallowed with visible effort. "A werewolf." Her tone was scathing. She laughed again. "Right, then. A werewolf. Some fantasy beast of lore."

"You think those claws and fangs nothing more than an elaborate costume, do you?"

"No! Although I...I suppose it is what I had hoped."

"Unfortunately," Ian said, "hope and reality are often at odds."

The words settled like a shroud over the room. He regarded them for a moment. "I must ask a favor of you, Daisy."

Gold curls coiled atop of her shoulder as she tilted her head. "What, pray tell, do you want?"

Ian crossed his arms in front of his chest. "I want you to refrain from telling anyone else what you saw." He gave Daisy a small smile. "Given your reluctance tonight, I gather that you aren't likely to say a word, but I need to be sure."

"Consider yourself assured," Daisy said with a touch of asperity. "I have no desire to be pronounced a raving lunatic."

Her candor made him want to chuckle, and he wondered if this woman would ever hold back her opinion. "That is most sensible of you, madam. I have no doubt you would find the accommodations in Bedlam beneath your standards."

Despite the insults she'd hurled his way earlier, Daisy slanted an amused look from beneath the bronze fan of her lashes, which set off an answering stir within Ian's gut. Beside her, however, Miranda's eyes narrowed in suspicion, and Ian fancied he could see the cogs turning in her brain.

"I well understand why Daisy would be reluctant to speak," she said, "but it seems to me that your concern goes a touch beyond casual."

Beneath the fold of his arms, his hands curled to fists, but he answered her easily. "Were the good people of London to hear that a werewolf is roaming the city, there would be panic. I don't believe any of us want that outcome."

"Understandable," Daisy agreed, but she was frowning. "Only, well...ought they not be warned? What if it..." Her pretty lips parted on a strangled breath and she went pale. "What if it bites someone, and...well, turns them into one too?"

Myths indeed. His mouth twitched but he kept a straight face. "You cannot be infected by a bite, luv. A man is either born with the capability to become a werewolf or he is not."

"Are you sure?"

"Absolutely." He could see the questions forming on the sisters' faces; they gathered and brewed like clouds over a darkening sea. Ian stood, needing to quell the storm before it broke. "Look," he said. "Go home, get some rest. All will be well. I swear to it."

Daisy did not look so sure. Miranda, however, nodded as if his word, while not good enough for her, would have to do for now. Ian rather thought she would like to get as far away from him as possible. He did not like the Ian Ranulf that Miranda saw, but he had been that man for so long that he almost forgot who he had been before. The suffocating feeling was back, threatening to swallow him down. Because he did not know how to climb out of the abyss and walk with the light steps of his old, true self.

Miranda's skirts rustled as she stood. "Well, then, thank you, Northrup, for looking after my sister. It was good of you." Steeling herself, she offered him a hand in friendship.

Between her haughty look and Daisy's earlier disdain, the devil in Ian could not resist coming out to play. *They thought him a cad, did they? Then he would be one for them.* He clasped Miranda's hand and pulled her close. "Will you not call me Ian?" he murmured, bending over her hand to lightly kiss it. "After all we've been through? Together?"

He could hear her back teeth meet. He ignored it and leaned in until her scent surrounded him. A familiar, pleasant scent but surprisingly not enough to excite him anymore. "You know, the hero usually receives a boon in such circumstances. A kiss perhaps?"

Her mouth slanted. "Are you quite through?"

Ian gave her an innocent grin and let Miranda believe that he still wanted her. He didn't, but bloody hell, her suspicions irritated. "Well, you know where to find me, sweet, should you feel the need to visit. Or perhaps I shall call on you."

Daisy too had risen. The sight of her sent a qualm of disappointment through his gut. *Beastly man was he? She had no idea.* He turned his smile on her, refusing to look apologetic. He bent over her hand and murmured pretty words of some sort or other. It didn't matter what he said; he just wanted them gone.

Miranda headed toward the door, her slim back straight and proud. Ian moved to follow when, through the buzzing within his ears, he realized that Daisy had not stirred.

He stopped, and seeing the action, Miranda did too. Daisy clasped her hands tightly before her. "I would like a private word with Lord Northrup." Her blue eyes sought his. "If I may?"

Miranda scowled. "Daisy, it really isn't necessary."

Her sister's expression was implacable. "I believe it is." A soft blush colored her cheeks. "It may take more than a moment. If you do not want to wait, I will understand."

Surprise had Ian rooted to the spot, but hearing those words spurred him out of his frozen state and he found the ability to speak. "She may take my coach home." He made a small bow. "It is at your disposal, as am I."

Daisy gave the smallest of smiles. "Good." She turned

back to her sister. “See? It is all arranged. Now stop mothering me. That is Poppy’s manner of deportment. I am fine, really.”

Annoyance colored Miranda’s high cheeks and pinched at her mouth. “Of course I shall wait for you.” She gave Ian a glare that promised swift death should he try anything untoward, which made him want to laugh. He managed to appear benign as he escorted Miranda from the room, while inside his heart pounded.

What did Daisy want? And why had she stayed? He had a fairly good idea. A smile spread over his lips, one that he feared looked rather wolfish. As it should be, for the wolf had a delectable morsel of prey waiting in his den. It was time to play.

The door clicked quietly shut as Northrup returned to the library. In Daisy’s mind, it might was well have been the slamming of a cage door. She pressed her damp palms against her thighs and tried to steady her erratic breathing.

Northrup set his hunter’s gaze upon her, and her heartbeat tripped with a pained thud. She knew why he believed she had stayed behind, and damn if some small part of her didn’t agree with him.

“All alone, my dear. As requested.” He strode back to her, his gait loose-limbed and sure. A predator’s stride. One might try to run, but it would be useless.

She drew her shoulders back and faced him head-on. He noted the gesture, for a contented smile oiled over his features. She ignored it, and the little flutters that were running riot in her belly. “Thank you for letting me stay.”

He sat next to her on the settee, and the fresh, wild scent of him hit her anew. “I’ve never been one to deny a beautiful woman.” He looked her over slowly, as if contemplating how to start a particularly fine meal. "Especially when she is so eager for a moment alone with me."

He was so sure she would melt. And for some reason, that spark of confidence in his eyes made her want to take him down a peg. She ought to flirt. Flirting was a well-loved cloak that fit her perfectly. Only now, the very idea of flirting made her ill. Still, she would do it, if it laid a trap for him.

"Hmm. A penny compliment. I'm all astir."

Sharp canines flashed in the firelight. "Immune, are you?"

"Only when flattery is given by rote."

"Then I shall have to try harder."

"Or give up."

Northrup dimpled, his teeth clicking as his smile grew wolfish. "I never give up."

He said it lightly, yet a flash of something dangerous, almost feral, lit his eyes, and Daisy wondered at the notion of truly being the object of this man's obsession. A chill chased over her skin. Rather like being hunted, she thought.

She shrugged, lest he see her disquiet. "There is a fine line between persistence and being a pest, my lord."

He chuckled, the wild light in his eyes shifting to genuine amusement. "Now why do I suspect you've crossed that line more than a few times, my dear?"

Daisy didn't know whether to laugh or be shocked. "Perhaps you'll find tonight to be one of those times."

"Will I now? Then it is my turn to be stirred."

He was making it too easy. A bubble of disappointment rose within, for she thought he'd be harder to lure, but then his blue eyes ran over her as heavy as a caress, and she became aware of the globes of her breasts straining against the deep V of the ill-fitting dressing gown.

"That gown is a tragedy on you," he murmured in a low growl that rasped against her skin.

"So sorry," she managed to say past the flush that left her oddly breathless. "You'll have to take your objections up with the man who provided it for me."

He grunted in amusement, his gaze not shifting from her body. "He is a fool. He is of a mind to take it off, lest it offend him further."

Heat blossomed over her skin and settled between her legs. Such a shock, she almost choked on it. Her breasts rose and fell over the edge of her bodice in cadence with her breathing, and his eyes followed the movement.

"Oh, you are good," she whispered as all that heat turned to delicate throbbing. Here was the excitement she'd craved earlier. Only now that she'd found it, she felt disoriented, as if she were a rider about to be unseated. Were he not possessing a tendre for her sister, she might have considered giving in to his charm. "I suppose this is you trying?"

One corner of his mouth kicked up. "Is it working?"

Yes. "If you need to ask, it probably isn't."

A snort escaped him. "Probably?" His eyes lifted to meet hers, and she almost crossed her legs against the unwelcome onslaught of feeling. Good God, he was potent. She'd underestimated him entirely. In heavy silence, they stared at each other.

His nostrils flared as if scenting her, and he suddenly grinned outright, a wolfish grin that set off tremors of alarm in her belly. "Liar," he said. "I can almost taste your wanting, it's so thick in the air."

And then she knew; he'd been toying with her as well. Her pulse jumped, but she merely returned his look with one of bland disinterest, refusing to lose this game. "You, sir, are a bore."

Something near a growl rumbled deep in Northrup's chest. "If this is you bored, I cannot wait to see you excited."

Slowly, oh so slowly, the blunt tip of his finger lifted to trail under her sleeve and along the bare crook of her arm with infinite care. Goose bumps rose in its wake, a pleasurable chill that had her yearning to lean into the warmth of his lean, strong body. Why did it have to be this man who made her breath quicken?

She smacked the finger away and stared into his too-blue eyes. "Do not mistake me for some witless hen who follows whatever cock is thrown into the roost."

His chiseled features froze for a moment and then a smile slowly spread over his mouth, lighting him up from within. Dimples pulled at his cheeks, and Daisy caught her breath. *No, she would not be moved.*

"Cock?" he intoned, a hairbreadth from laughing. Blue eyes twinkled. "My dear, I'm the wolf." He leaned in, bringing all his tempting warmth and masculine strength closer. His voice rumbled over her skin. "I eat the hen," he murmured, "before I carry off what's left of her."

She laughed. She hadn't meant to, but she could not stop it from rolling out, full and thoroughly unladylike. Lord Northrup scowled down at her, his expression so put out that she laughed again.

Daisy fought for a breath. "I'm sorry. It's only... You are so... practiced."

"Practiced," Northrup repeated faintly, his fine features twisting into a male glower. He wiped a tired hand over his face. "Well," he muttered as he slumped back against the settee, "if that doesn't drive the final nail in the proverbial coffin."

Her laughter died as abruptly as it had started, and she

turned away from him. Daisy blinked up at the ceiling and suddenly a tear leaked from her eye. She whisked it away but he had seen. Something shifted in his eyes. "Ah, now, lass," he whispered.

"You must think me a lunatic," she said.

His voice stayed soft and soothing. "You have no idea what I'm thinking."

She continued to gaze up at the coffered ceiling. "I always do that. Laugh when I ought to cry, cry when I ought to laugh." She shook her head and a curl fell over her eye. She was too weary to bat it away. "My father died last year. When I heard the news, I just laughed and laughed." A sigh left her. "I loved him, despite his faults, but I..." Daisy turned and gave Northrup a watery smile. "It wasn't until a week later that I cried. Ridiculous, isn't it?"

How she wished she could truly cry now, the messy bawling sort of cry. She felt it bottled up within her throat, but it wouldn't break free. The dead deserved tears. She was making hash of everything this night.

Northrup settled down in a comfortable sprawl of long limbs and then looked up at the ceiling as she had done. "Oh, I don't know. My father was murdered. When I heard the news, I did not cry, didn't say a word actually."

Northrup's words tugged at her memory. Archer had known his father. The mad woman who chased after Archer had killed old Lord Rossberry, Daisy realized with a jolt. She cleared her throat and tried to sound calm. "What did you do?"

Northrup turned his head to peer at her. "I shagged a dozen whores."

"All at once?" she muttered, which made him laugh. Flushing, Daisy looked away, but she could feel his knowing smile. Unfortunately, his nearness and the heat of his body made him impossible to ignore, or to stop from picturing him engaging in the act. She flushed again.

"No, luv." His eyes crinkled at the corners as he watched her, but his voice was soft and serious when he spoke. "And it wouldn't have mattered. Distraction works for only so long, you know."

The room blurred before her as the tears finally came. Slowly, as if he feared startling her, Northrup reached out and took her hand. It was a shockingly intimate thing to do, and yet she felt comforted. His palm did not possess the smooth, cool skin of a gentleman but was rough and very warm. All that warmth seeped through her arm and up into her chest, and she found herself lacing her fingers with his. With his free hand, he passed her his kerchief and sat silently while she wiped her tears.

After a moment, he expelled a tired sigh. "You wanted time alone with me, lass. Now, why is that?"

Daisy turned and the springs of the couch groaned in the quiet. Northrup's mouth parted on a breath, but his eyes held a hint of wariness. And rightfully so. She smiled a little sadly, suddenly wishing she hadn't started down this road. She hadn't expected to like him. "I want you to leave my sister alone. She isn't for you."

Her words hit him with visible effrontery. A laugh burst from his lips even as they twisted in a snarl of irritation. He let her hand go, but did not retreat into denial as a gentleman might. Instead he lifted a brow in challenge. "And if I do not?"

Northrup closed the small distance between them until she could see the ice-blue striations in his irises. "What shall you do then? Hmm?" His lips almost touched hers as he spoke. "Stomp one of those dainty feet in protest?

Take me over your knee and rap me with one of your little evening fans?"

Daisy shook her head, and the tip of her nose brushed his. Northrup made an odd sound but did not pull back. She hadn't expected him to. "As much as it would surely disappoint you, no. I don't have to do any of those things. My sister is safe from you. She loves Archer and always will."

His eyes narrowed to slits. "Then why warn me off?"

"As I said before, there is a fine line between persistence and being a pest. You, sir, have crossed it, and it paints you a fool."

Dull crimson washed over his high cheeks as a growl rumbled low in his throat. Time to go. Daisy calmly gathered up her skirts and brushed against him as she rose. "You did me a kindness this evening, despite your unfortunate behavior toward my sister." Northrup outright snorted at this, and she let her voice rise a touch. "The least I can do is return the favor and set you to rights before you make an even greater ass of yourself."

It was rather gratifying the way his mouth hung slightly open, his body seemingly frozen upon the settee. "Good night, Lord Northrup. I thank you for your assistance."

Her hand closed over the door latch when suddenly he was there, his big hand coming down on hers and holding it. "D'ye think ye can dress me down and simply leave, lass?" His Scots burr thickened with his agitation, rolling so deep and luscious that she shivered. Northrup crowded in, pressing against her hip, and she felt the hard length of him in crude detail. "I'm thinking you'd prefer I'd play with someone else."

She eyed him over her shoulder. "Me, you mean?" she asked coolly, as if her heart was not bounding like a frightened rabbit within the cage of her ribs.

His square jaw bunched as he gave a sharp nod. Speechless for once. What a thought.

"You're welcome to try, my lord." She shoved him with her shoulders, catching him off balance, and he faltered back a pace. Daisy opened the door but stopped to look at him.

Northrup's broad chest heaved with the rapid breath of a man in a temper, his vivid eyes flashing while his fists clenched at his sides. It ought to have frightened her, but it served only to send an unwelcome bolt of heat straight to her sex.

"However, I doubt that you could handle me. Somehow I think you prefer your women either unavailable or subservient. I am neither."

Chapter Four

Bout time you got here." Henry Poole shifted on his small feet, looking left and right down the street as though expecting to be set upon by thieves before glaring up at Ian. In the distance, the soft chimes of church bells sounded. "Adele will be wondering where I've gone any moment now. We have breakfast together. Usually."

"I am precisely on time, old boy," Ian said as he strolled toward Poole. Despite the casual stride, edginess plucked at Ian's spine. In all these years, he had never made peace with death. And avoided it whenever he could.

He eyed the small, rectangular outbuilding that made up Poole's surgery. Not even the broad, well-trafficked streets of central London could blot out the subtle, sticky sweet smell of decay wafting from the building's high crescent windows. He shifted his weight away from the building.

"And the hour was picked by you," Ian reminded.

"Hmm..." Poole extracted his pocket watch to frown down at it in accusation.

Short, round, and turned out like an Antarctic penguin in his immaculate morning suit, Henry J. Poole was not the image one would picture for London's foremost forensic surgeon. And though his round eyes and snub nose appeared childlike, the man had a sharp mind and a near vicious tenacity when it came to the study of human anatomy.

"Been avoiding Inspector Lane for hours," Poole said, "on account of your little request. That man wants to view the bodies something fierce. Have you any idea the lies I've had to tell?"

"I'm certain they were quite inventive, Poole."

"Bah. I don't need the hassle. Ought to be concentrating on my practice, getting fifty quid to diagnose Lord Something-or-other's dizzy spells." He glared at Ian as if to make sure Ian was following his rant. "I don't need to be helping the police. Or you either. I've got better things to do."

"By all means," Ian said, "let me incommode you no longer. I am certain Lord Something-or-other would be happy to pay for your services."

Poole harrumphed. As well he should. The police needn't use his services. There were other surgeons who were more than happy to oblige. But like most geniuses, Poole was fiercely competitive and thus protective of his unofficial role as the CID's pathologist, lest some crack charlatan fill the position. It was a little-known specialty and did not receive the recognition it should. Something that irked Poole to no end.

"Let's get on with it then," Poole muttered.

"Not quite yet," said a deep voice from behind them.

Ian silently cursed as Benjamin Archer strode forward, his gray eyes flashing equal parts amusement and censure. The nosy blighter.

"Planning a bit of fun without me, Northrup?" A smug smile stretched his face.

"As fun and you are generally at odds," Ian said, "then yes, yes, we were." He turned to glare at Poole who had made himself appear as small and unnoticeable as possible. "Ratting me out to Archer, are you?"

At this, Poole drew himself up. "So happens I owe him a favor or two as well."

Ian snorted as Archer drew abreast of him. "Which includes," said Archer, "letting me know the moment you contacted him to view the victims of this attack."

Ian's teeth ground together. Damn but this was work to be done by delegates of the *lycan* clan. And yet, after sending his man Talent to scout, Ian discovered that not a single clan representative had come out of the woodwork. Why? Ian feared he knew the answer, and he did not like it in the least. So now he was here. Where he least wanted to be.

Poole tucked away his watch. "Let's get on with it, then."

At the sound of someone clearing his throat, all three men whirled about, and Poole yelped. Inspector First Class Winston Lane of the Criminal Investigations Department leaned against the corner of the building, pipe in hand.

Wreaths of gray smoke encircled his head, obscuring his features but not the sharp gleam of his eyes. "Seems my invitation to the party was lost in the mail."

Poole's muttered string of obscenities filled the ensuing silence. Ian agreed with all of them. Having Archer along was an annoyance, but at least the man knew with what they were dealing. Inspector Winston Lane did not. Humans were never to learn of the other world. The results would be calamitous. Starting with mass panic. It had been Ian's hope to obscure certain evidence before the CID got to it. He shot Archer a glance, and the man blinked once. *Understood.* At least in this, they were partners.

Lane took a deep draw on his pipe, and the tip burned red hot in the blue light of the morning. He let the smoke out slowly. "Hello, brother," he said to Archer. Aside from being an annoyance in this matter, Lane was also husband to Miranda and Daisy's eldest sister, Poppy. Whether that would turn out to be a further nuisance or a boon remained to be seen. "I ought to have expected you here as you do turn up in the oddest of places." Lane did not wait for a reply from Archer but turned his keen gaze on Ian. "Lord Northrup, I understand you took my sister Daisy to shelter after the attack. I thank you for that."

Ian inclined his head. Lane was an odd piece, carrying himself with a pride that went far past his station, yet conveying the manners of a man long used to bureaucracy. Had Lane been of higher birth, he would undoubtedly be running for parliament. Regardless of his station, one look from him had Poole squirming.

"I'm certain Lords Northrup and Archer will have a reasonable explanation for their presence here," Lane went on softly. "As for your colorful evasion of me, Poole, we shall discuss it later."

Poole grunted and avoided Lane's gaze. Lane waited for one of the men to confess his sins as it were. Archer merely stared at the man. A good tactic for Archer, as his stare was quite effective. Ian, however, hated keeping quiet. "I do hope you like waiting, Inspector, as you will be doing a fair bit of it."

Lane smiled blandly. "Patience is a virtue most valuable to an inspector." Lane knocked his pipe against the sole of his boot, sending red embers tumbling and the release of fragrant tobacco into the air. "Now that we're all here, let us proceed."

"Are we certain?" Ian asked. "No others are forthcoming? No wives? The bootblack boy? Perhaps the muffin man I passed on the way?"

The only answer was Poole's rather shocking hand gesture, to which Ian would rather not acquiesce.

Poole pulled out a set of large iron keys. The door swung easily and in stepped Poole, his once nervous visage turning instantly to one of cool professionalism.

Ian followed at a pace behind, hating the damp coldness upon his neck. The narrow corridor, painted institutional green and lit by two stingy lamps, made a sharp turn and the cloying smell took on a decidedly sulphuric taint.

"Cost me twenty quid to delay matters." Poole's sandy-colored head bobbed along in the greenish gloom. "The Fenn family wanted the burial today. Today. Had to tell the coroner I'd sent the body on to the wrong address to give us more time. Rubbish, and the coroner well knows it. I've never misplaced a body in all my life." He shot a glance at Lane. "And you can well blame these two." He jerked a thumb toward Archer and Ian. "Tell me, what's a man to do when a marquis and baron are breathing down his neck?"

"Inform the lead inspector?" Lane offered.

Ian let Poole rant. He knew the man helped him not out of desire for money but from the fact that Ian had stepped between him and the wicked edge of a thief's knife on one dark night. Loyalty ran deep within Henry Poole. What Archer had on Poole, Ian didn't know. Nor did he care.

The little surgeon stopped by a massive iron door, and Ian's insides turned.

"You've read the report?" Poole asked him.

Ian forced himself to nod. Behind him, Lane made a sound of disgust. "You sent him an official report?"

Poole pretended not to hear as he led them into the room and closed the door with a ringing clang. "I don't know what more I can tell you. But it's best to take a look."

Compared to the corridor, the examining room was as light as midday and washed clean, the blood having long since flowed down the drain in the tiled floor. The space was Poole's pride and joy. The men accepted the heavy leather aprons Poole offered and followed him to the row of bodies that lay upon the steel tables lining the room's center. Bathed in the sunlight slanting down from the overhead windows and the power of four large gas lanterns, the scene appeared oddly peaceful—were it not for the stench.

When Poole was busy laying out the tools of his trade, and Lane watching the process, Archer stepped close to Ian, his strong features still and guarded. The shock of seeing Archer as he was now had yet to wear off. For seventy years, the devil had worn black masks and gloves to hide himself from the world. Transformed by an evil demon, Archer had slowly been turning into a monster of ice and stone, and would have become a demon himself had Miranda not saved him.

Ian swallowed down a bite of regret that he had stepped in between them. The truth was, the greater part of him was relieved to see Archer whole and human again. Even if he'd never admit it to a living soul.

"Ian." Archer gave only the slightest of nods, his eyes icy. He leaned in, lowering his voice to a murmur. "Miranda says you were the one who found Daisy." His eyes narrowed. "A werewolf, was it? It was very...convenient that you were at the scene."

And there it was, the cold accusation in those gray eyes. Ian had been waiting for it but still his claws itched to break free. "Yes, you would know all about being at crime scenes at the wrong time. Or mistaken identities."

Archer flinched. As he should, the blighter. Archer himself had been suspected of murder based on mistaken identity. "Fine then, do you know who did it?"

Ian's annoyed whisper was but a breath. "If I did, I wouldn't be here, now would I?"

A small twitch moved the corner of Archer's mouth. "Fair enough." He moved away to join Poole by the examining table.

Poole put on his spectacles and leaned over what had once been Mr. Mark Ashford. "You can see what's been done to the poor bastard," he said, oblivious to Ian's disquiet. And why shouldn't he be? He'd given Ian several lessons in anatomy, Archer as well. Trained them both to conduct their own dissections at a time when performing one could get them all tossed into Newgate. Thankfully, the law had finally seen the benefits an autopsy provided the medical profession.

Ian had long since worked past every normal man's fear of blood. The human body, from skin to flesh, sinew, and bone, was a miracle. Every organ, the blood that pumped through its veins, a wonder. The perfect order of it, the way all parts worked in harmony to keep it alive, boggled his mind. Ian had often found himself overwhelmed by the beauty of it all. But the wolf in him hated death. Its natural instinct was to let the dead alone and concentrate on the living. Which was why Ian had given up practicing medicine; one could stave off death for only so long.

The body before them had been all but destroyed. Only the limbs lay relatively intact. Beside Ian, Winston Lane shifted his feet. The man's skin had taken on a greenish hue, and he'd pulled out a handkerchief to press to his mouth. Archer stood silent and still as a statue, betraying nothing of what was going on in that head of his. A neat trick, that.

"Not much left by way of evidence," Poole went on. "But look here."

Ian let his eyes move past the raw, open ruin of the chest. It was a body. Nothing more. Shapes and colors and smell.

Poole pointed to the edges of the flesh. "See there. The incisions along the *pectoralis major.* They are still relatively intact for proper study."

Clean cuts, four in an evenly placed row, the flesh, muscle, and sinew severed in one neat swipe. Claw marks. He didn't need to look at Archer to know the man had picked up on the fact. Ian bent closer, pretending to inspect the wounds, and let Archer do the talking.

"Made from a knife?" Archer murmured aloud, tilting his head.

"I agree," said Poole as Ian took the moment to inhale deeply. "Look there. Ripped into the abdominal cavity like it was soft butter."

God, the stench of death. His insides rebelled, his morning's meal threatening to surge up. He forced himself to get past the ugliness of it to the very essence of the body and caught a distinct note on the body's skin. A slight presence of perfume. The same Ian had smelled in the alley. He lingered on it for a moment, relishing the sweetness, the way it made his wolf relax, then moved on. There. There it was, the scent of sickness and wolf.

Poole bent close as well, startling Ian. "Note the depth on the slash at the trachea. Nicked the spine at the fifth vertebra. The victim bled out within moments due to massive hemorrhaging."

Archer and Lane nodded, Lane still looking rather peaked. Ian did not blame him in the least. "Still new to this bit of business, Lane?" Ian asked him.

The man glanced up. "I've been to my fair share." Lane's mouth twitched. "Admittedly, every time feels like the first."

Poole laughed. "Can't say that about everything, now can you?"

"Quite right, Poole," Lane murmured dryly.

Ian straightened. "The other body, if you please, Poole."

Poole glowered, clearly wanting to give a full lecture, but he shrugged. "Suppose it makes no difference, as they died the same way." His snub nose wrinkled. "At least these two bodies here did."

Lane jerked his head round to Poole. "And the other victim?"

"A bit . . . more. She'd been violated, I'm afraid."

The men bent their heads for a moment, and then Ian moved to the second body, the widow Alexis Trent. *Just get through it. Do not think.* "Let us see this one first."

Poole pulled back the sheet, and one of the men cursed. Poor woman was as ruined as the man, but her once lovely face stared up at them as if silently begging for justice. "Not much difference, as I said. Slashed with the same marks." He tossed away the sheet. "The odd bit of it is, were it not for the precision and size of the incisions, I'd be pressed to think this was the work of an animal. But there you'd be looking at lacerations rather than incisions."

Lane perked up. “An animal, you say? Would be a rather large one to do such damage.”

“That was why I said ‘if,’ ” Poole retorted without much heat. “We don’t have anything larger than a dog roaming our city streets, and this isn’t the work of a mere dog.”

Archer remained impassive, but Ian knew he’d gone on full alert. “I should think the populace of London would notice a large predator walking its streets,” Archer added and then leaned in to study the wounds. “And Poole is correct. Wounds from animals are usually more ragged lacerations than clean incisions.”

Ian had to give the man credit; he was excellent at diversion. When Winston blinked in confusion, Ian said, “Lacerations have jagged edges, such as might occur when an animal tears into a body. Incisions are clean, deep wounds as occur from the slash of a knife or sword.” Or the razor-sharp claws of a *were* or lycan. Now as to a *were*’s teeth, they certainly would cause lacerations. Ian wondered at the lack of bite marks. There were none he could see on the organs or interior cavity either. Had the thing not wanted to eat its prey? Odd. If it hadn’t been eating, what was it doing?

The only possibility that came to him was that the *were* was scenting the body. But why? What about Mrs. Trent would attract the beast so intently?

Archer tilted his head as if contemplating. “Mmm… Curved blade. Something extremely sharp.” He accepted the pair of forceps Poole handed him and delicately peeled the skin back from the flesh along the upper edge of a cut, which also quite effectively disturbed a set of the incisions, ruining the shape of them. Poole was too intent upon Archer’s lecture to notice. “Sliced down to the bone in some places. A single-edged knife. And large.”

Poole nodded. "Exactly."

"Well, that narrows it down a bit," Archer said wryly.

Poole's grim smile widened in response. "Yes, quite. Knives in London being as common as a crab in a whore's...ahem...But why always four even cuts, each obtaining the same depth, as though the bastard used four knives at once?"

Rather pasty and swallowing quite frequently, Lane clearly forced himself to study the marks. "Perhaps a torture device of some sort?"

Ian leaned in, pretending to decipher the nature of wounds so obviously left by a full-fledged werewolf. "I agree. Well done, Lane." Bracing himself for the hit, he breathed in. Wolf. Sickness. Something inside of him stilled.

Again came the scent of spring, sweetness, and decadence. Delicious. It was Daisy's perfume, he realized with a hitch in his chest. That maddening woman who'd called him out and left him to hang in his humiliation. Damn if her sass didn't stir him. He'd thought of little else since, and though it rubbed him raw, he itched for another encounter. At the very least, a chance to best the clever little cock tease.

Alexis Trent had worn the same perfume. Odd. She was a friend to Daisy. Perhaps they had shared?

He stood back. "The other body, Poole. The poor lass." The police had found her tossed like rubbish in some dark bowery corner not three days before the attack in the alleyway. According to Poole's report, they'd only made the connection between the three bodies due to the violent abuse done to each of them.

Gods, this poor girl had died days ago. *Days*, and his kind had done nothing to stop the mad werewolf or protect the people of London, as was their duty. Anger boiled within his veins. The Ranulf, the bloody king of Clan Ranulf, was supposed to act, not sit with his head stuck up his arse. Even Ian, who'd willingly turned his back on the clan, knew as much. The stink of it was Ian could not even approach them to ask why. He was in exile.

"One Miss Mary Fenn of Camden Town," Poole said, bringing Ian's attention back to the fore. "Found her reticule with the body, if you can believe. Seems even the lowest of scavenging thieves hadn't the stomach to approach her." Poole shook his head sorrowfully, but then hesitated. "See here, she isn't..." He glanced at Lane, and the man bristled. "Well, inspector, you usually just read the reports. These men are used to such sights, being surgeons in their own right. This poor girl's been dead much longer. Given the recent heat and the work of rats, there isn't much left of her. The rate of decay is quite advanced."

"Then how do you know she'd been violated?" Lane countered, his skin pebbling with sweat.

"Found her with her skirts tossed up." Poole flushed crimson. "Legs spread apart."

Lane nodded. "Of course. It was in the report, was it not?" He touched the side of his head as though pained by his lapse in memory. Ian knew it was the morgue, the specter of rot and death at work on him.

Lane suddenly looked tired. "Same marks? From what you can tell?"

"Yes, sir. We needn't view her."

Oh, but it was most certainly needed. Ian had to compare her scent. He glanced at Archer. The man's eyes narrowed a touch. Ian pressed his lips together. He didn't know how to insist without it looking odd. And there was the grim fact that the more subtle scents would be overwhelmed in a highly decayed body. Ian would have to all but stick his nose into it, a notion to which his wolf, and his stomach, thoroughly rebelled. Unfortunately, Archer's expression made it clear that he hadn't any brilliant ideas either.

Irritation swelled and then a thought hit Ian. "Have you her clothing, Poole?"

Poole's eyes widened but he went to a storage locker. "Certainly."

Under the watchful eyes of Lane, Ian accepted the ragged bundle of clothes. Archer stepped back toward the body of Alexis Trent. "If you would, Poole, I've a question about the damage done to the greater omentum."

At Lane's look of confusion, Ian smiled. "Fancy physician speak for that fatty looking mass in front of her intestines. You know, the lumpy yellow-gray bit hanging before them." His grin widened as Lane went decidedly green. "If you are feeling faint, you can stay with me. I wouldn't blame you in the least."

The man glared at him, but strode off on wobbling limbs to stand by Archer's side as the men waxed lyrical on many methods of evisceration. Ian shook his head, his smile remaining. Predictable as the sunrise, calling a man's courage into question to get him to react.

But his smile faded as he studied the gown he set on a working table before him. It was in tatters but oncc quite respectable. A machine-made, plain cambric dress with wide skirts and a bodice slightly out of date. The clothes of the middle to lower class. And most thoroughly soaked in the same perfume as worn by the other victim—and the luscious Daisy Craigmore. He needn't even inhale. It was there, just beneath the muck and dried blood crusting the fabric. Dread sucked at him. The *were* wasn't attacking at random. It was attracted to the perfume. Daisy's perfume.

Chapter Five

Ian tracked her easily through the crowded streets. Though her mourning gown blended well within the sea of working-class worsted, the widow Daisy Craigmore stood out. Her pace was steady and serene as a lady's ought to be and yet that stride of hers was pure eroticism, hypnotic in its bump and sway. The elaborate gathering of fabric over her bustle only served to highlight the motion, enough to glue more than one man's gaze to her rear as she walked. And though his hackles rose with each covetous glance, she paid the men no notice. Beneath the black taffeta, her shoulders were set and tight, and he wondered if she thought of that night when death brushed its hand too close to her cheek.

That Daisy had chosen to walk after the funeral of Alex Trent wasn't so strange. He understood the need to clear one's head. Only he'd expected her to find a pretty park in which to take her promenade. Instead, she moved farther away from the safety of Mayfair. The neighborhood they entered was working class, but not so poor as to be dangerous. Simply a place decent men lived, worked, and played. Ian stuck out like a brass tack in old leather.

Not breaking stride, he took off his ruby stickpin and stuffed it into his pocket, along with his gold watch. He didn't fear theft. Pity the man who tried it. But he'd rather not shout out his presence; the cut of his suit and the cost of the cloth already did that enough.

At the corner, a paperboy stood, his little voice a mighty shout as he waved the latest edition over his head. "Mad killer stalks the fair people of London! Victims' livers eaten for his supper!"

Daisy's pace faltered, a small bobble of her feet that had Ian wanting to stride ahead and take hold of her arm for support. He needn't see her face to know she was as white as milk.

"When will he strike again?" cried the paperboy. "Who among us is safe? Read all about it!"

Daisy moved past the boy without a glance. With the ease of a frequent patron, she walked up to a tavern, the Plough and Harrow, and entered. He gave her a moment before following.

The taproom was dim and smelled of ale, men, and roasted meat. Filled with the midday-meal crowd, shouts of laughter and genial conversation rumbled in the air. It was a comforting sound that invited a man to join in.

Ian slid the brim of his hat down low and followed her movements with a sideways glance as he tucked himself into a shadowed corner of the bar. She'd gone directly to a giant old gent dressed in homespun and sporting a stained apron. The man's bushy brows rose in happy surprise as he caught her in a fond embrace.

"Meggy-girl! Now there's a sight for sore old eyes." He

kissed her proffered cheek lightly. "What ye been up to, darling lass?"

Her laughter brightened up the room. "Oh, a bit of this and a bit of that, Clemens." She drew away and tucked her hand into the crook of the old man's arm. "Have you a seat in which an old friend might rest her weary bones?"

"Tosh, ye have to ask?"

Clemens led Daisy to a table by the window in the back, where a man sat nursing a pint. " 'Tis the best seat in the house for my Meg."

Without ado, Clemens grabbed the idling man by his scruff and tossed him aside. "Out with ye, Tibbs. Go prop up the bar if ye've a mind to stay. Miss Meggy needs the seat."

Tibbs grumbled something incoherent as he stumbled to the bar.

Miss Meggy's protests of Tibbs's ill treatment were ignored.

"He'll be there day an' night if I let him," Clemens said as he swept away all proof of the unfortunate Tibbs before holding out her seat as proper as any Belgravia footman might.

"Will it be your favorite for luncheon then, lass?"

Daisy took off her mourning bonnet, revealing hair of gleaming gold and silver moonbeams parted demurely down the center and gathered in the back in a riot of curls. "Yes, Clemens, thank you."

Ian waited until Clemens departed to pounce. His tread was undetectable in the din of the room, his movements easy and at one with those around him. In short, nothing about him drawing near should have alerted her, yet the moment he pulled away from the bar, her head lifted and her summer-sky eyes pinned him.

He let his stride slow to a leisurely stroll, watching her watch him approach, and damn if heat didn't flash down his groin, his balls drawing up tight with anticipation and the pleasure of having her eyes upon him.

"Daisy." He stopped in front of her and, doffing his hat, gave her a bow. "This is a pleasant surprise."

She sat back against her chair, letting one arm drape over the back of it. The pose was indolent, relaxed, and not at all ladylike. Thank the devil for frock coats or she'd see how it affected him. "Yes, quite, Lord Northrup. One would never presume to find you in such a plebeian establishment."

He didn't wait for her to bid him to sit, for he gathered he'd be waiting a long time. "It seems I like slumming as much as you." He had to stretch his legs out under the table or risk knocking his knees against the tabletop. "Well, perhaps not as much. You appear to be quite the regular."

Daisy's soft mouth pursed. "Not that it's any business of yours, but I'll tell you for fear of suffering constant prodding."

"The prodding is my favorite part."

"This was my father's local pub," she said in an overloud voice, all her creamy skin turning rosy. "When he could afford it. I frequent it as well when I can. It's clean, and Clemens keeps the riffraff away... ah, Clemens!" She looked up with a smile as the scowling Clemens stomped over with a tray in hand.

Clemens set down a tankard of peaty ale with a thud. His small eyes narrowed on Ian. "This nabob botherin' you, lass?" A meaty fist curled near the vicinity of Ian's head. "Shall I toss him for ye?"

Ian lifted one brow a touch. "Am I, Meggy?" he asked

Daisy as he stared down the barman. Ian wouldn't hurt the man, as he admired those willing to protect women from unknown threats. But there was no reason to let anyone else realize that.

Daisy gave a small sigh. "No need, Clemens." She inclined her head toward Ian. "Mr. Smith won't be staying long."

"If you're sure, lass. You can't be too careful these days, what with a killer on the loose." The man didn't notice Daisy blanch.

"It is good of you to worry, Clemens. But I am all right."

"So long as you are certain." Though his eyes were hard on Ian, he gently placed a plate of Welsh rabbit before Daisy. "If ye be needing anything. I'm just there." He kept his eyes on Ian as he jerked his head toward the bar. "Right. There."

"And not a step farther," Ian added genially.

With another glare, Clemens thundered off, making a point not to wait for Ian's order. Just as well since he didn't fancy drinking anything offered by good old Clemens as it'd likely be spit in, or worse.

"Mr. Smith?" Ian asked when Daisy ignored him and set about eating her meal. He did not miss the way her hands shook just a fraction, but she seemed determined to let her worries go. "Why not simply call me Northrup?"

"Perhaps it is best to keep your anonymity," she said.

He leaned on one elbow and watched as she daintily cut her cheese on toast into neat little pieces. "Perhaps I don't want my anonymity."

"Mmm." She took a bite, savoring it for a brief moment. "Who says I was referring to *your* sensibilities? Perhaps I'd rather not be associated with you."

He found himself grinning. "Perhaps, perhaps, perhaps. You make my head spin, Meggy-girl, with your round-robin talk." She scowled, and he swallowed down a laugh. "It is Meggy? Or Daisy? I wouldn't want to be confused."

"It is my name. Daisy Margaret Ellis." She took another bite, eating her food with a strange combination of pleasure and economy. "Father called me Meggy before he settled on Daisy. Clemens took to it rather too fondly, I'm afraid. Frankly, I find both names deplorable. Why not Margaret or Meg?" She waved her fork in emphasis before catching his eye and seeing his broad grin. Instantly, she resumed her disinterested air. "You are a pest, you know that? Go away, will you? I'm not in the mood to play."

The pain and sorrow creasing her eyes made him ache in sympathy. He knew that feeling of loss too well. Which was precisely why he would stay. "Ah now, I can't be too terrible. After all, you are letting me share your table."

"Better to do that than make a scene." She patted her rosebud mouth with her table linen, and Ian shifted in his seat. A woman should not be allowed to possess such a mouth. "Besides," she said, seemingly oblivious to his interest, "I wanted to know why you were following me."

"Cannot this be a happy coincidence?" he asked lightly. He liked toying with her. When he batted, she always batted back.

"You've been following me since the church."

"Oh?" He made a track through the condensation beading the pewter mug between them.

"Yes, 'oh.'" Her knife sliced the bread cleanly. "I caught your scent not two feet out of the graveyard. Perhaps before." Her shoulders lifted in a surprisingly Gaelic shrug. "I was distracted until then."

"Ha! I bid you to prove it." Though he made a show of smiling, it unnerved him just a bit to think he'd been caught out so soon.

The corners of her eyes tilted upward when she smiled in return. Much like a cat's, he thought with a sudden qualm.

"Your valet uses champagne in his boot polish mix—very ingenious of him as your boots are like mirrors. He draws your bath with oil of rose hip and sweet orange, which makes me believe you suffer from dry skin. You wear Le Homme Number 12 from Smithe's, an expensive cologne featuring essences of vetiver, amber, and sandalwood. And though its popularity among nobs might lead me to confuse you with another, one cannot overlook your natural scent, which is a subtle mix of meadow grass, fresh rain, white wine, and well... you."

Ian stared at her with his mouth surely agape. She did not flinch, though a fetching pink flush colored her cheeks. He snapped his mouth shut. "Fuck me," he breathed with genuine surprise. So rare that anything truly shocked him these days.

Her flush grew. "Thank you, but no."

Ian shook his head to clear it. He felt dizzy, as though he'd been running and had come to a sudden stop. Jesus, but this woman kept him on his toes. "I'd say you were bamming me if it weren't all true."

The table creaked as she leaned in on her elbows, coming close enough that his insides heated again. He resisted the urge to pull away, if only to clear his reeling head. Her voice came at him in a satisfied purr. "And you had black tea and toast with bitter marmalade for breakfast."

Heads turned at his shout of laughter. He ignored them in favor of the golden-haired olfactory genius sitting before him. Her sense of scent was as good as his, if not better, as he studiously ignored his for fear of being overwhelmed.

Daisy dropped her gaze and went back to eating with methodical determination.

"I'm a nose," she said between bites.

"I should say so."

She glanced up. "It's an undignified talent for a lady to possess, I'm told." Her shoulders lifted. "However, quite useful in detecting strange men intent on following my person."

"I'd say it was bloody brilliant," he countered. "Strange men or no."

Her lids lowered as she took a sip of her ale. "Why is it that you are following me?"

Wariness fairly hummed about her, as if she were bracing herself for his retaliation, believing that he would want revenge for the way she'd put him in his place.

Admittedly, the idea had occupied his thoughts, but sitting with her now, retaliation was the furthest thing from his mind; he was enjoying himself too much. The experience was so novel to him now that he wanted to bask in it, the same way his wolf liked to lie out in the moonlight and soak up its strength.

His reply was forestalled as a short, portly fellow stomped up onto one of the center tables and made himself heard. "All right, gents. Now then, it be well known I'm a man of my word."

A collective groan went through the room, and the man waved another hand. "Aye, I know. But"—he slapped his hands together—"a bet's a bet. I lost, and it's me turn to settle accounts."

"What's the damage this time then, Gus?" shouted a man to Ian's right.

"An ode. By yours truly. Public's choice."

Instantly, the men and women in the tavern began calling suggestions. "Do Gladstone!"

"The Queen!"

Funny how Ian could feel Daisy's cunning smile. Foreboding had his shoulders tightening as he turned. Her grin was that of a child at Christmas. "Marquis of Northrup," she shouted.

Gus, who had been considering offers with a very serious air, jumped at the opening. "There," he cried. "Now that's a superior toff what's worth me song."

Ian resisted the urge to slide down in his chair. If only they knew that said toff was sitting among them.

Daisy laughed, her eyes resolutely not on him, which only made her notice of his every move all the more obvious.

Gus cleared his throat as the crowd went silent in expectation. His voice came out surprisingly clear and fine. "O woe is to be that lofty he. Our fine dandy, the Infamous Lord Northrup. How it pains the dears, this gentle' man hears, that he can't get it up for a tup!" Triumphant, Gus held out his empty mug as he sang on: "O have ye sers a dram to spare, so's he can find his courage in a cup!"

The tavern shook with the roar of laughter. Ian refused to flush. Blast if that damn ode wouldn't be sung on every street corner by nightfall. Courage in a cup indeed.

Daisy's eyes sparkled with mirth as she caught his gaze, and the crowd went back to shouting out requests. The corners of her mouth dimpled as she held back a smile and the urge to laugh suddenly bubbled up within him. Either that or punch someone.

"Well," she said, "at least I know my sister is no danger from, shall we say, an untoward advance due to your virile nature."

Ian ground his teeth hard enough to feel his jaw creak. Aye, he'd known it was coming. It still didn't cosh the desire to wipe the grin off her mouth, preferably with the use of his. Perhaps his tongue down her throat would clear up any questions of virility or lack thereof. Because with her, he was getting the sneaking suspicion that it would not be a problem. But he found himself looking away, not liking what he saw in her eyes, the judgment and the pity. "Your sister was safe from me long ago. I've no interest in chasing after what doesn't want to be mine."

"Hmm." Slowly, methodically, her nails rapped over the wooden table, playing a rhythm that made his eye twitch. "And yet you seem to favor redheaded women when trolling for whores."

Mary Mother of... Slowly, methodically, he counted to ten. God save man from curious women. "Been checking up on me?"

Her look was the sort one gave to an ignorant child. "That would imply effort, when one need merely mention your name to learn of it. No wonder Archer wants your head." A golden curl bounced at her temple as she shook her head.

His fingers twitched. Damn what Archer thought. Damn her too. He wanted to growl, howl his irritation, bare his teeth, and set her in her place. He scowled at the barman watching them instead. The man flinched and quickly turned back to wiping the glass in his hand with a rag. "You assume that your sister is the only ginger-haired woman in the world."

He forced himself to meet Daisy's eyes. "That a man cannot have lived as long as I have without the possibility that there might be another woman in his life possessing similar coloring?" *Don't speak of it.* His heart was going too fast. The pain was rising.

Daisy paled. "Who was she?"

Ian studied his fingers, unsurprised to find the nails had grown long, lengthening into the beginnings of claws. He relaxed on a breath, and they retracted with a pinch of pain.

"Doesn't matter," he said finally. "Whores are at the root of my current predicament."

Predicament. He almost laughed. A fine word for losing heart. He couldn't look at Daisy and say the words, yet he'd started his mouth running so he had to finish.

"I can't...Christ. It ought to be more than a financial transaction." And damn Archer for putting that thought into his head those many months ago. But there it was. He couldn't pay a woman to swive him anymore. Not when he remembered what he used to have. Companionship as well as passion. The stink of it was, he didn't want to finesse a woman into his bed either. When had sexual relations become so complicated?

Laughter, the clink of a glass, and the murmur of conversation swelled around them. Daisy moved, a subtle gesture that brought her an inch closer to him. Her eyes, when he made himself look, did not hold pity but the dark pain of personal understanding. "I find it hard," she said in a voice so low a normal man might have missed it, "to imagine any available woman you set your sights on not offering herself to you freely."

A smile tugged at his lips. "Is that an offer then, Daisy-Meg?"

"I prefer to leave you with bated breath rather than answer," she said tartly before her expression turned sorrowful. "You were at the funeral. Why?"

He sat a bit straighter. "To pay my respects."

"You know something." Her slim throat worked on a hard swallow. "About that night."

"Aye." He dragged a hand through his hair. "I went to the autopsy."

"Isn't that the sort of business best left to the police?"

"Police." He snorted. "They couldn't find their cocks to take a piss."

Ian felt a moment's qualm when she colored, but her lips twitched. What was it about her that made him forget even basic manners?

"Careful now," she said as if reading his very thoughts. "My brother-in-law is police, and I shall have to be insulted in his stead."

"Winston Lane," Ian confirmed with a nod. "He's seems capable enough. But there's no getting around the fact that he cannot help with this particular issue."

Again came the subtle paling of her cheeks. She was trying mightily to take the notion of werewolves in stride, but it wasn't quite working. Could he blame her? Hadn't he blanched when he'd learned that his kind wasn't the only thing to go bump in the night?

"Does Winston know about... werewolves?" she asked.

"No. He thinks the killer is using a knife. Archer and I were not inclined to dissuade him of the notion."

"Archer was there?" A little furrow had worked its way between her golden brows. She waved her question away. "Of course he was. What good is one meddling noble when you can have two? Never mind. Tell me what you found."

As practical as a Scot, she was. "There was another victim," he said. "Murdered before your attack. A woman. Young lady, actually."

"Poor dear." Daisy's hand trembled as she took a deep drink of her ale. "The same... did she..."

He nodded dully. He'd be damned if he'd tell Daisy about that poor girl being violated. Swallowing down his rage, he told the bare facts of her death.

"God." Daisy shuddered. "He's got to be stopped."

"He will be." Ian reached out, laying his fingers lightly on her wrist. At any other time, he might be smug about the way her pulse leaped. Now he sought only to keep her there should she bolt. "There is a link between the women." His grip tightened a fraction. "Daisy, did you let your friend Mrs. Trent borrow your perfume? Or you hers?"

Her eyes darted over his face. "My..." Her breath hitched. "Why do you ask?"

"All three of you wore the same perfume." He closed his eyes. "Tea rose, ambergris and jasmine, a hint of sandalwood mixed with neroli." He looked to find her mouth softly open. "A lovely floral perfume. Although your natural scent is sunshine on summer grass, vanilla, and spice, and you, as it were. Which I confess, I much prefer."

Unfortunately, his light jest did not take the pain from her eyes. "Alex admired my perfume," Daisy said hoarsely. "Her party. She wanted... to be a smashing success. So I let her..." Tears welled up in her eyes.

Gently, he wiped one away with his thumb. "It is not your fault."

"No?" She took a shaky breath and looked away.

"No. Never think it, do you hear?"

Staring off into the crowd, she nodded and then began to tap a steady rhythm with her fingers. "My perfume is an original blend, Northrup. I created the formula myself. Why was this girl wearing it?"

"Perhaps it is a coincidence. Perhaps the girl blended

something similar on her own." He didn't believe the words any more than she, apparently.

Her nose wrinkled. "That would be very great odds indeed," she said with a sniff, and then turned to him. "Do you need my help then? Is that why you've come?"

Something quite like tenderness turned over in his chest, and he fought valiantly not to smile. Though she argued with him at every turn, she clearly understood partnership and how to strategize before going into battle. She was like a wolf that way. Like pack. The realization did strange things to his insides. "No, not that."

When she scowled, he leaned toward her. "I am here because you are in danger." His thumb ran over the delicate skin of her fingers. He didn't know why holding her hand should feel any better than holding another woman's hand, but it did. "For whatever reason, this wolf is attracted to that scent, and believe me, if a wolf latches on to a particular smell, he won't easily let it go."

Her eyes went wide and glimmering as she searched his face, but her voice stayed calm. "If my perfume is what attracts this beast, surely if I cease to wear it, the beast won't bother."

"You understand scents," he said. "You have to know it doesn't work that way. I could smell that perfume on you the other night, even after your bath. You might cease to use it, have your maids clean your clothing, or order new garments. But it will take time for the scent to fully leave your person, at least to the level at which a *were* would no longer detect it. Time in which this beast might come for you."

He had said as much to Archer and Miranda after the autopsy. They hadn't been pleased.

Neither was Daisy. She drew herself up and away from him. "Then I'll go to Miranda and Archer."

He caught her hand again. "You'll be staying with me," he all but growled.

"You? Don't be absurd."

Miranda had said the same thing. Rather, she'd said, "Over my dead body." Which was, unfortunately, a possibility given the speed and strength of a mad werewolf. The only way he'd been able to convince Miranda of his plan was to point out that the *were* was likely carrying a contagious disease, something Miranda, for all her firepower, had no defense against. After that, Archer had been adamantly in favor of Ian taking care of Daisy's safety. Smart man.

Daisy, however, did not appear as convinced. "Why on earth do you think you can protect me?"

And here was the moment he had dreaded. For she was going to run. And he would chase her.

Ian tightened his grip on her hand, securing her to him. "Because, luv, he is the darkest version of my future."

Chapter Six

His words hung between them as Daisy's gaze darted over his face, trying to understand. "Your future?"

The last human he'd willingly revealed his true self to had been Archer. Of course, Archer hadn't been precisely normal himself, which made it easier. But if Ian was to properly guard Daisy, she needed to know the truth. Even so, the words were hard to utter.

"The same sort of beast resides inside me." On a silent sigh, he let his inner wolf show through his eyes, knowing she would see the inhumanness and the way they now appeared utterly lupine.

He was prepared when she reared back. "Calm down," he said as she yanked at her hand. Her chair screeched as he hauled her close.

A few men glanced their way, and Ian gave them a sharp look of warning before leaning into Daisy. "Hold, lass," he whispered.

Her breath blew hot and scented with fear against his face. "You...you're a werewolf," she hissed. Daisy's pulse beat a wild tattoo against his fingertips. He fought the urge to stroke it.

"No," he said in a low tone. "But I could become one."

"Am I to understand the difference?"

"There is a great difference. And I'll tell you if you can calm yourself."

The tang of human sweat and beer was thick in the air. He could hear her heart pounding within her breast. But she stopped struggling. For that he was grateful. When her pulse slowed, he looked her over. "Are you calm then?"

She glared but nodded shortly.

"You won't run?"

Daisy made a noise. "Just get on with it, Northrup."

Lovely woman. He moved closer so that only she could hear him. "What you have to understand is that a lycan—"

"Lycan? What is that?"

"If you'd let me get a word in—"

"It is a pertinent question."

One. Two. Three. He opened his eyes and focused on the little furrow between her brows.

"Lycan is the name we use. It hails from the Greek lycos, which means 'wolf,' and the myth of Lycaon, the Arcadian king who served Zeus the flesh of man disguised as a roast. An angered Zeus turned him into a wolf as retribution."

"How very gruesome," Daisy murmured with a moue of disgust.

He couldn't contain the smile that tugged at his lips. "Quite."

"But why not simply call yourselves werewolves?" she asked, folding her arms on the table to provide a lovely bed for her breasts.

No. Do not look.

"Because there is a difference. A lycan," he said, raising his voice, for the blasted woman had opened her mouth again—as curious as a pup, this one—"has control. He turns at will."

"So stories of the full moon and all of that..."

He laughed shortly. "Doesn't turn us. Mother Moon does, however, intensify our strength. The brighter she glows in the night, the stronger we are. And we are weakest on the new moon, when the sky is utterly devoid of her silver rays."

"Why? What is it about the moon's rays that give you strength?"

"I don't know."

She frowned the way a child might, as though put out for not getting the answer she wanted, and a strange, aching sensation spread within his chest.

Damn if she didn't remind Ian of himself. Before he had lost heart. When he had tackled life with lusty abandon, and frank curiosity. But there was a look that clouded her eyes, as if something was killing her natural vivaciousness, like a frost creeping along tender spring grass. As if she too were slowly giving up the struggle. He found himself wanting to banish that look, perhaps save in her what he couldn't save in himself.

He almost laughed. Ian was no one's savior, and no one wanted him to be. He shook himself out of such fanciful thoughts and gave her his best schoolmaster expression.

"Look, we don't know how we started, why we live this endless life, or from where we came. It's all speculation. But the closest our elders can figure, it has to do with reincarnation. Once we were wolves. Over several lifetimes, our spirits evolved and we became men, but the wolf spirit lived on as well. Think of it as a soul divided."

"Two souls in one body?"

"Precisely. So wolf and man are at odds." He spread his hands out in supplication. "Man wants to be in control and so does the wolf. A lycan is a being in which the man's soul is in control but the wolf's soul alters his makeup to create an immortal capable of using the strengths of both. Man may call upon the wolf, shift into a hybrid of wolf and man, gaining extra strength and speed, but man is always in control."

She sat back with a little huff. "Seems hardly fair to the wolf trapped inside of you. Surely, he wants his time in the sun?"

His beast whined, agreeing, and Ian pushed against it. Discomfort and irritation coiled within. "Had the wolf his way, the wolf would remain so, the man's body shifting fully to wolf and his soul fading into the background, never to return."

"How can you be sure?"

"Because," he hissed, "it has always been so. Have you any idea how many of my brethren I've seen lost to the wolf? None came back."

"Perhaps it is because the wolf has had to fight for his right to be free. Perhaps if it were given a turn..." His wolf paced within him, making his bones ache, surely lighting his eyes if Daisy's paling expression were any indication. She closed her mouth abruptly.

He took a sip of her ale and felt the fangs that had threatened to grow recede. "D'ye think any man wants to risk his soul to test the generosity of his wolf by fully shifting?"

"No." She trailed her nail along a groove in the wood. "I suppose not."

"I give him what I can," Ian said. "I let him run far and

long each night." His conscience and his wolf chided that this was not precisely true but was a recent occurrence. Ian swallowed down his guilt. "It is essential that I keep control."

She didn't seem frightened anymore but curious. "And if you fully lose control, that is the werewolf of which you speak?"

"Yes. The wolf is in control but he is not a normal wolf. He is bigger, much bigger, his head at the height of my shoulder."

Daisy's blue eyes went as round as saucers. "Yes, exactly."

"And he is damaged. Rage and unpredictability rule him. A *were* often kills because it feels compelled." At this, Ian lowered his head. "It isn't the wolf but the man, yearning to return, that prompts this, I'm afraid to say. Murder is man's specialty. Wolves do not kill for sport. Only for food or dominance within the pack. A werewolf is an unstable beast, and it is a lycan's responsibility to put him down, which is not easy as a werewolf has the full strength of the wolf while the lycan must retain some of his human frailties."

"And this werewolf that attacked Alex"—Daisy's voice pulled to a thin whisper, her milky skin going the color of whey—"you called him mad, but aren't they all?"

"Not in this way." He felt the weight of his words as he spoke them. "His scent is heavy with sickness. I fear that it makes him even more unstable."

"I smelled the sickness in him as well. A rotten scent."

She never failed in surprising him.

"Aye," he said.

Daisy nibbled on her bottom lip. "There is one thing I do not understand. We both smelled illness on the werewolf. How can that be if you are all immortal? One would think sickness doesn't affect you."

Ian reached for her mug and took another drink. "Lycan do not become immortal until we reach physical maturation. Until then, we are as mortal as you. We can get sick..." The mug in his hand rattled as he set it down. "We can die. If one was to contract a degenerative disease beforehand"—Ian shrugged—"our makeup is such that the change into becoming full lycan would not destroy the disease, only slow its tide. The disease would be working on this *were's* body, slowly breaking him down. Unfortunately, that doesn't lessen the *were's* strength, but simply makes the beast's behavior more erratic."

She moved to take a hasty sip of ale but set the cup back down when she found it empty. Her hands wrapped around the pewter mug as if to keep them still. "So where do we go from here?"

"As I said before, you will stay with me so that I may protect you."

Daisy sat back abruptly. "No."

"What do you mean, no?" he said. "Have you not heard a word I've been saying?"

"I heard every word, Northrup."

His mouth was hanging open for he could not fathom her resistance. "Surely you can understand that you need protection."

"Of course, I understand. Only I don't see why *you* have to be the one to protect me."

There were a few tempting oaths he'd like to shout, but he bit them back and went to the heart of the matter. "Are you afraid of me? Is that your worry?"

Daisy was silent for a moment, nibbling at the corner of her lip as she considered, but when she spoke, she looked directly at him. "Well, you would know I was lying if I denied feeling fear when you told me."

He gave a short nod and she continued. "But looking at you, and sitting with you now, I don't feel afraid." She shook her head slightly, and a small, self-deprecating laugh escaped her. "I suppose I must be daft"—her blue gaze grew sharp"—for annoyance is the most prevalent emotion I feel when I am around you."

"Annoyance I can live with," he said, hoping that he wasn't grinning like a fool. "Come along then, we'll go and collect your things."

This time it was Daisy who caught ahold of his sleeve. "That was a lovely attempt, Northrup, but I'll not be managed by you."

He sat back with a grunt and ran a hand through his hair. "What is your objection then? What fool notion is it, for I'm sorely tempted to throw you over my shoulder and haul you off without further discussion."

"You wouldn't dare."

He simply raised a brow, and she crossed her arms in front of her chest as if the action could somehow stop him. "Are you worried about your reputation?" he asked.

"Posh," she said with a snort. "My reputation had been reduced to tatters long before you came sniffing around. Craigmore made certain of that." Despite her bravado, her golden brows knitted as if the memory pained her.

Craigmore sounded like an ass.

"Well," Ian said in satisfaction. "Then we needn't resort to complicated subterfuge. Society will simply presume you are my mistress for the season."

Her nose wrinkled as if she'd scented something foul. "Such is man's logic. Has it not occurred to you that I'd rather not be thought of as your mistress?"

"You could do a lot worse!" Hell, the bloody woman could twist a conversation. Unable to help himself, he caught her hand again, not precisely caring what she thought of his need to touch her. "I would say we are fairly comfortable in the other's presence. At least enough to spend a couple of weeks together." She looked so aghast that he smiled grimly. "Maybe less if we're lucky."

"Well, that *is* comforting." She rolled her eyes and pulled at her hand.

"It should be," he said, not letting go. "Perhaps I need to make a few things clear. I am a lycan. Which means I have a superior sense of smell, hearing, and sight." He inclined his head toward the bar. "Thus, I can hear your man Clemens over there berating his serving wench for not watering down the gin."

Daisy's gaze shot past his shoulder, no doubt seeing Clemens leaning over some woman named Alice as he grumbled on about lost revenue. Daisy's lips compressed in stubborn refusal.

"I heal quickly and have the strength and agility equivalent to five men." Ten when he was in top form, though he was getting closer to that once more. Every day that he let his wolf have more freedom, his strength grew.

At this, however, Daisy did scoff. With his free hand, he clasped the pewter mug between them and crumpled it. The ball of metal wobbled about as he let it go. Ian but took a small bit of pleasure in seeing the way her eyes went wide and her pretty mouth fell open.

"It is my duty to protect those under threat of my own kind. You, my dear, are under threat. It is that simple."

She made what sounded suspiciously like a snort. "I shall hire guards until you hunt the beast down." Her expression went wry. "I assume with all your boasting, you can do that, yes?" Her gaze strayed to her wrist where he held her tight. She tugged again, harder. "Now, let me go, Northrup."

The devil. "No."

She glared daggers at him. "This is your revenge isn't it? Systematic torture disguised as good intentions."

"Torture is it?" He made a sound of annoyance. "To see you carry on... Do you think it is my driving ambition to play nanny to an unwilling woman? To one who thinks so poorly of me?"

She had the grace to blush and lower her lids, but she did not protest his claim.

"Let me get this clear. You'd rather cling to that stubborn resistance and get your fool head murdered than listen to reason and stay with me. Is that it? Well, hell, why don't I wring your neck now and save us all a great deal of time and trouble?"

"Why you... you... ass!"

It was too easy to deflect her kick under the table. He grinned wide. "Temper, temper. You wouldn't want to hurt your protector."

Daisy Craigmore, while having a most angelic countenance, could glare bloody murder quite well. "I don't like you."

He pulled her close, forcing her to lean into him. "Like has nothing to do with it. I'm watching over you until this thing is done, Daisy-Meg. You'll not fight me on this, or you'll see how great a pest I can be."

Chapter Seven

Winston Lane was accustomed to being lied to. Even the innocent tended to shrink away from his direct gaze, as if they felt the need to protect secrets he truly had no care to uncover. Lies, evasion, distrust, such was the environment in which a police inspector dwelled. Lies he understood and recognized immediately.

The Lords Northrup and Archer were lying to him. They knew things about this case that he did not. He could feel it in his bones. And the female victims were the key. Lord Northrup had been particularly keen to study the females. Most especially Miss Mary Fenn's clothing. Northrup had smelled them; Winston was sure of it. He'd seen the man's nostrils flare, as an animal scents for danger. Most curious. Why had he done so? What had he discovered?

With a suppressed sigh, Winston eyed the hostile woman before him, a birdlike creature who likely held onto every farthing that passed her way. "Mrs. Marple, would you say Mary Fenn was a proficient worker?"

According to Mary Fenn's mother, the proprietress of Marple's Millinery worked her daughter to exhaustion. Not a surprise, really. However, it was an easy enough question to establish if Mrs. Marple was going to lie.

"Fair enough." She scratched at her sleeve. "Showed up on time, did her work, though her bonnets tended to be overdone on the flowers." She gestured to the rows of bonnets lying in a profusion of color on the shelves behind her. "Costly, silk flowers. Better to fill in with wax fruit and the like."

Beside him, his partner Sheridan made a sound of basic male annoyance, the rudiments of female fashion being beyond his ken or interest. Winston cut him a glance before forging on. "And you found her character beyond reproach?"

Mrs. Marple's eyes darted between Sheridan and himself, figuring out the angles, wondering what he wanted of her. A dicey thing, questioning the witness. Phrase it the wrong way and you led them to answer with information that sought to please, which wasn't necessarily the truth. Put the thing too bluntly and they might turn on you and close up like a lockbox. Step, turn, guide, release, one danced through an interrogation.

"Wouldn't hire a girl with poor character, now would I?"

"Certainly not."

"However," interjected Sheridan, "if you had without knowing, what is a gentlewoman to do?"

Mrs. Marple bristled at that. "Why, turn her out, of course!"

"Even if it meant losing a highly proficient employee?" Winston asked, pushing just a bit.

"See here." She took a step closer, her bony hand raised in ire. "Having a suitor doesn't make a girl untoward."

"Miss Fenn had a suitor?" Winston already knew this from interviewing the mother. A Mr. Thomas James, mild-mannered accounting clerk.

Mrs. Marple blinked. "Only saw him the once. He came by to say a word of hello last week during luncheon. Mary said they were engaged to be married. I heard he dealt in perfumes. Created them, I believe. Mary was quite proud of the scent he'd last given her."

Sheridan stood straighter as did he. Mr. Thomas had not been a perfumer. "Could you describe the man you saw?"

Again her eyes darted between them. "Why?"

Winston's gaze didn't waver. "The description, if you please, Mrs. Marple."

"He didn't come in the shop. I only saw the back of him from afar as she met him on the corner." Mrs. Marple pointed to the shadowy corner that turned into an alley.

Winston could not quite keep the surprise out of his expression, and the woman flushed. "What harm was it to let them meet alone? She was a good Christian, Mary was." The woman went back to scratching her arm. "Why, to accept the suit of a cripple, she'd nearly been a saint."

Crippled? Mr. Thomas was certainly not crippled. Winston gave a nod of encouragement as if it were all old news to him. He prayed Sheridan would do the same. Thankfully, the lad was learning. "Heard it was true love," Sheridan chimed in.

"What else could it be?" Mrs. Marple's worn face eased, a dreamy expression coming into her eyes that made Sheridan cringe. "To overlook such a twisted and hunched figure, it had to be true love."

"Indeed," Winston said. Frustration pulled this way

and that within his belly. The damage done to the victims was the work of a man with incredible strength. He couldn't imagine a cripple capable of doing the deed.

He gave the woman a tight smile and thanked her for her time. He and Sheridan were halfway out the door when her voice stopped them.

"You might try talking to Miss Lucy Montgomery," she said. "She was Mary's closest friend. Thick as thieves, they were. She works as a maid in some great lord's household. Ranulf House if I remember correctly."

A lead was a lead. Winston touched the brim of his hat. "Thank you, madam."

Her face was tight. "Just find the mad man who did this. No girl deserves to die that way."

Winston thought of his sister-in-law Daisy. Resolve tightened in his chest. Nothing would stop him from finding the fiend.

Despite Northrup's rather dire claim that he would harass her into compliance, Daisy saw neither hide nor hair of him the following morning. True, there had been a moment last night in which she thought she saw his shadow lurking under the street lamp by her townhome, but the figure was gone as soon as she leaned closer to her window, and she couldn't be sure it was him. She supposed she ought to have been alarmed at that sight, but it had brought a reluctant smile to her lips. Now, however, she felt mildly irritated that he was absent, and *that* irritated her as well. The blasted man. Had he played up the danger in an attempt to frighten her? Revenge, perhaps, for being treated as a fool by her the other night? Surely if it were truly dangerous, he'd be dogging her every step?

Whatever the case, she wasn't one to sit around and

wait for this beast to be caught. She ordered the coach brought round.

Number 98 James Street housed Florin, one the most famous perfumers in the world. For a time, Daisy's father had provided Florin with the exotic oils and essences used to create their heavenly concoctions. This trade brought about her love of perfume. However, it was her special talent that made her intimately acquainted with the shop.

A crisply dressed shop clerk hurried out to greet her, offering a hand down from her coach. After gently ushering her inside, he assumed his post by the glass-paneled doors, poised and on the alert for the next shopper.

As it was nearly time for tea, the store was empty of shoppers, for which Daisy was thankful as this visit did not promise to be pleasant. Behind the glossy mahogany counter, Mr. Abernathy held court, standing rod straight in his starched suit. The man's watery blue eyes widened upon seeing her, but he kept his expression composed, his mouth turned up with just a hint of a pleasing smile beneath his trimmed, white mustache.

"Madam," he said in proper tones. "How may I be of service?"

"While I appreciate your efforts in subtlety, Mr. Abernathy, I have no desire to remain anonymous for the moment." She set her reticule upon the glass-topped counter. "Let us get to the matter directly. I am quite cross with you and I suspect you know why."

He blinked back at her in the picture of perfect innocence. But she did not miss the way the pulse leaped at his throat. Nor the small twitch of his mustache. "Mrs. Smith, I could never imagine doing you a wrong that would warrant your censure. Please be assured that there must be some mistake."

Her smile was thin. A warning. "Mr. Abernathy, we've done good business together. Beneficial on both sides, I should think."

And the man knew it. Daisy, in her role as the enigmatic Mrs. Smith, had provided the shop with numerous perfume formulas, all of which had become highly successful, including the much anticipated scent currently in development for the Queen. In return, Daisy received a generous portion of the shop's profits and would never have to go hungry—despite Craigmore's efforts to see her in the gutter. Yes, it was a beneficial relationship, but one in which certain players held more power.

Her finger tapped firmly upon the glass. "I would not like to see our relationship end due to pettiness. There are several establishments more than happy to purchase my formulas."

Abernathy jerked his head as though slapped. "Here now, madam! You wouldn't dare."

"Wouldn't I?"

A deep red flush crept up from his high, white collar. "Have you no sense of loyalty?"

"Have *I*?" She leaned into his space, fighting the urge to poke his starched chest. "It is not I who sold secret formulas to an outside partner. A matter about which I am certain the members of the board would love to learn."

His large Adam's apple bobbed. "Now, Mrs. Smith, you cannot possibly believe that I would—"

"I can, and I do." She gave him her best Poppy glare, as effective on liars as it was on sisters. "You are the only one who handles the production of my personal perfume. It is not to be created for mass distribution, and you know it."

"I cannot presume to understand—"

"Then I will put it to you plainly and use small words

so there is no misunderstanding." Her hand curled around his lapel, and the fabric crackled beneath her fist. "Another woman was wearing my perfume. You will tell me to whom you sold my formula, and in return, you may keep your position and my services. Or we will proceed by another route. Believe me when I say that such a course will not be to your advantage, Mr. Abernathy."

Sweat pebbled down his brow as he gave her a stiff nod of agreement. Daisy smiled sweetly.

"The name, if you will, Mr. Abernathy."

"Oi! You'll wrinkle the silk."

Ian spared a glance at his valet who was busy brushing his waistcoat as if Ian had lit it on fire instead of merely buttoning it in haste. The young man was worse than a nanny. "Talent, you do realize that I have dozens more?"

Talent scowled. "Oh, right, which makes caring for one's things such a tiresome exercise." Carefully, he pulled out Ian's evening coat and helped Ian into it. "Hell, you've got forty cravats, as befitting a spoilt marquis, why not burn the one you're wearing now? Save me the trouble of cleaning and ironing."

Ian closed his eyes and wondered for what must be the hundredth time why he'd agreed to let Talent be his valet. And then remembered that the blasted lad hadn't taken no for an answer. Bruised and battered within an inch of his life, the youth had been found literally on Ian's doorstep ten years ago. And while Ian would have gladly employed young Jack Talent for other tasks, for the lad had the makings of an excellent spy, Talent hadn't wanted what was offered. No, the man simply wanted a home, a place with the others.

It was the one reason Ian could not reject. Damn if the

little bastard didn't know it, Ian thought irritably as he adjusted the cravat Talent had just tied, earning another growl of disgust. It was a petty little victory in the war that was the state of Ian's wardrobe. The laughable part was that society often touted Ian as a natty dresser, when really it was Talent's insane and exacting standards that had Ian dressed to the nines and a leader of fashion.

"I think you're cracked to go to Lena," Talent said when Ian strode to his cabinet and pulled out a glossy wooden stake. "She's just as likely to have your bollocks for dinner as help you."

Ian thumbed the point of the stake. Not quite sharp enough. He pulled out the sanding block. "You think I'm incapable of defending myself?" The idea was laughable.

For once, Talent looked aghast. "Course not. Only, well, she's ungodly." With a shiver, Talent crossed himself. Talent's piousness, as it were, had the tendency to rise up when he wanted to dole out a lecture and to go completely missing when it proved inconvenient to his own needs.

Ian laughed then. "You, my young friend, are the proverbial pot calling the kettle black." Ignoring Talent's scowl, he blew over the tip of the stake and wood dust swirled golden in the air. "We creatures are all ungodly in the eyes of humans, and they would likely have your bollocks on a spit if they knew what you were."

"They'd have to catch me first," Talent muttered as Ian slid the stake into his boot. "Just watch your back, all right?"

It unsettled Ian that someone still cared enough to warn him away from danger. It was that small thing that had Ian giving his staff leave to treat him with undue familiarity; they were all he had. Ian moved to step away from Talent and his concern, but not before giving the man a hard look. "Watch after her."

Ian had stalked Daisy for much of the day, following her to such innocuous haunts as Florin and her milliner's. Not that she'd noticed; he'd learned his lesson and stayed far downwind this time. Ian had caught her looking over her shoulder more than once. A smile tugged at his lips. Anxious for his company perhaps?

He came home to change only when his groom, Seamus, had arrived to take over the watch. Seamus was a strong, capable lycan. But Ian preferred Talent's subtlety for the job.

"Do not let her out of your sight for anything. She can protest all she likes, but the lass is coming home with me tonight." He would see this thing done with Lena and then he was collecting the stubborn Mrs. Craigmore.

"She'll never even see me," Talent promised.

Ian believed it. Talent's skills were such that he could be practically under one's nose and the poor sot wouldn't be the wiser.

"So you're set on bringing the girl here?" With a precise flick, Talent laid out Ian's top hat and gloves. He knew better than to try to put them on him. Ian took to being dressed only so far. "Never seen you ask a girl to stay, I'll give you that. Usually it's a contest to see whether the door hits their sweet backsides before they get clear of it on their way out."

"Lady," Ian corrected with a twinge of irritation as he donned his gloves. The smooth leather scraped raw over his twitching skin. Damn, he was thinking about her again. Was she taking her tea? Changing into her dressing gown? He cleared his throat. "One cannot call a woman such as she a girl." Not with that figure. "And she's not coming here to stay. This is solely a matter of protection."

Talent muttered something best left ignored as he followed Ian out of the dressing room and into his bedchamber.

"Now," Ian said, "what of the *were*?" He needed to be well-informed when he faced Lena.

"Word on the streets is of no good. Not one lycan that anyone knows of has turned." Talent shrugged as he poured Ian a glass of port. "Could be a country lycan gone bad, but with the Ranulfs controlling the borders, I cannot see that happening."

Ian took the proffered glass and drained it in one gulp. "Aye, the Ranulfs would know if a werewolf came into London. Hell, the sorry bastard would be taken out before he made it to Hampstead."

Certain as the sun rising in the east, a wolf clan always protected its territory. And London was the territory of the Ranulfs. No beast dwelled within the city proper without the Ranulfs knowing about it. Which made Ian's teeth grind. Being an ousted member of Clan Ranulf, he was well acquainted with their vigilance in regards to territory. Damn it, and now his hands were tied. On a silent curse, he turned away, handing Talent his empty glass.

As if reading his thoughts, Talent's expression turned shrewd. "You're going to ask Lena to approach The Ranulf about it, aren't you?"

The Ranulf. Ian almost laughed. Even after all these years, he'd be damned if he called Conall The Ranulf. The very notion turned his wame. "Something of the sort." He drew a hand through his hair and then put on his hat. "It isn't as if I can approach them."

He knew he sounded bitter. It had been Ian's decision

to leave the clan. He didn't regret it, and yet the very notion of still being exiled twisted his guts. He hadn't realized how very lonely it would feel. Allowed to live on the fringes due to his royal blood, but unable to return to his clan. But he had willingly thrown his birthright away with both hands, and it had been for the best.

Chapter Eight

Daisy counted herself an overzealous fool once more as her coach rolled up before her quarry. The only information she had to go on were past conversations in which Miranda talked about her days in the streets, days in which their father had forced her to steal for him. Dirty blighter. Had Daisy known of his machinations, she would have put a stop to it, even if it had meant taking a parasol to her father's rather thick skull.

Her driver jumped down and murmured a few words to the man lounging against a lamppost. The man nodded, money discreetly changed hands, and Daisy's stomach rolled in sudden anxiety. Outside her window, an enormous crow circled once, then twice, cawing as if in agitation, and her pulse sped up. She was not generally superstitious but the overgrown bird's presence simply cried out "ill omen."

Her coach door opened. His smell hit her first, ripe onions and old sweat, poorly masked by a copious amount of surprisingly fine cologne. The coach rocked as he hefted himself inside, clearly not a man accustomed to entering conveyances. Daisy shrank away from the stench until her shoulders hit the bolsters.

Shrewd eyes, shadowed by a bright orange bowler trimmed in royal purple, studied her as a toothy grin erupted over his narrow face. "Well, 'ello, 'ello." His long length oiled in next to her. Too close. " 'Tis me lucky day, I see. Usually don't provide services meself. But for you, I shall hav' to reconsider." He rubbed his hands in clear anticipation, leering at her breasts as he did. "Ah but yer a fine full bushel. Wot will it be? A bit o' tip the velvet muff? Bump the goat?"

Daisy could only blink in shock. This was the infamous Billy Finger, Miranda's former partner in crime? And here Daisy thought she was the sister with the lewd knowledge.

"Mayhaps somthin' darker, eh? Cat 'o nines tickle your fancy? Course, I wouldn't object were you so inclined toward working the gutter lane over the old lobcock here." With that he grabbed his crotch like an offering.

Her voice finally broke free. "Oh, do shut up!"

Billy frowned, but then shrugged, his bony shoulders moving under a canary-yellow frock coat. "Right then. A silent meetin' o' flesh, as it were. I understand perfectly, me lady. Dirty puzzle, you are. Let's get you unrigged."

He reached for her, and she slapped his hands. "What? No! Contain yourself, you idiot. I'm not here for an assignation."

A scowl twisted his face as he scratched the greasy hair peeking out beneath his hideous example of haberdashery. "An' what's a gent to expect, invitin' him into yer coach? I've got no time for chin music with a mad hattress."

"I'm here for assistance," she said with precise deliberation.

The scowl grew. "If yer wantin' me for your cove, you've got the wrong man. I'm no Nancy what will give up me round mouth for a poke!" He moved to go.

Daisy's lips twitched, stuck between a laugh and a scream of frustration. "You are Billy Finger, are you not?"

Billy froze. Slowly he turned and looked her over with a calculating eye. "Haven't heard that name in an age."

Daisy forced her hand out and gave what she hoped was an amiable smile. "Call me Daisy. I'm Pan's sister."

His chuckle was slow, his brown eyes alight with mischief and fondness. Billy Finger, now called Burnt Bill on account of his scarred arms, a souvenir from tangling with Miranda, was known to hold great affection for her sister. By the looks of his smile, Miranda had not exaggerated. "Ah, Pan. I should have known. Is she getting along all right, then?"

"Perfectly well, and said to tell you hello." A small lie, as Miranda had no idea what Daisy was planning, but Daisy wasn't sorry for the way Billy beamed. "I do apologize for the confusion Mr... erm... Finger. I ought to have said at once, only your—ah, enthusiasm surprised me."

"Enthusiasm, eh?" His thin brows waggled. "Can't think of any man what would blame me."

He leaned forward, setting off another wave of the scent she'd forevermore think of as "criminal male."

"Now then, sweet sister of the lovely Pan, what mischief did you have in mind?"

Ian leaped from his coach in front of the ramshackle building that served as home for the club so charmingly named Hell. Well, that wasn't precisely true. It was both

Heaven and Hell. Heaven serving the upper floors of the house, and Hell being the domain of the lower.

Leaning drunkenly over the garbage-strewn West Street in one of London's foulest neighborhoods, the dilapidated building gave no hint of the decadence hiding within. Indeed, a few young fellows out for a lark dithered on the curb, unsure if they'd found the right place.

Ian had no such hesitation. It wasn't his first visit here, nor likely his last. A year ago, he'd stumbled out of these hallowed walls from a night of gambling to find Lady Miranda Archer in the act of setting the whole street afire with naught but the power of her mind. A shock, to say the least.

Tonight, however, had the singular distinction of being his first visit in which he wasn't interested in procuring a willing partner or losing himself in drink and vice. The idea made his step light as he descended the dank stairwell to Hell.

He stopped before a gate of ornate wrought-iron, and the stake in his boot pressed upon his calf. It was a small comfort knowing that its strong point was capable of piercing flesh as hard as plaster.

Ian tugged the bellpull dangling before Hell's gate. A moment later, the door opened. The form of a ridiculously tall man loomed in the shadowed hall, his black eyes shining in the flickering light of the candelabrum he held.

"Evening, Edmund." It was all Ian need say.

The black eyes didn't blink. Well, they never did. But Edmund stepped back to let Ian in.

In contrast to the outside, the inside was pure luxury. Crimson silk-lined walls were lit by crystal gas-fueled sconces. A rug lay underfoot, thick and deep red. Given the amount of foot traffic Hell received, the rug was likely changed out repeatedly. To lay such a rug here was a direct flaunt of the enormous wealth of the club. Ian's feet trod over it soundlessly.

Male laughter and feminine squeals filled the air, mingling with the sweet smoke of cigars and heady incense imported from India. They walked past parlors as elegant as those in Mayfair, fitted with gilded chairs sturdy enough to hold two and deep satin-covered couches that could hold three or four. And everywhere, everywhere, naked flesh undulated.

They passed a long dining room with walls lacquered in blood red. Upon a matching dining table lay a lass, her legs spread, her sweet breasts pointing up to the ceiling. Jaded or not, Ian was a man, and the sight was hard to ignore. She'd been covered in fruit, some pushed into interesting places. She writhed as men feasted upon her.

Edmund led him along a familiar route, down another set of stairs that descended farther into the earth. Lamplight hit the fall of Edmund's long hair, casting it bone white against his black frockcoat. Like a lass's hair, Ian thought, resisting the urge to rake his own hair back. He still wasn't accustomed to wearing it longer and decided that he'd draw the line at hair that fell to his middle back. But Edmund's kind liked to flaunt their differences.

Down below, the sex games continued, but the fiends participating here feasted on flesh in an altogether different manner. Here, fangs punctured smooth skin and blood ran freely. But as all participants were willing, Ian wouldn't judge.

Lena was waiting for him when he entered. Diminutive and wraithlike, she sat curled up in a large black-leather wing chair by a crackling fire. Firelight caressed the curve of her paper-white cheek as she smiled, a catlike curl of red lips. As always, Ian was struck by the sight of her. The strange way she arranged her raven hair, the top parted and twisted into small rolls at the back of her head, the rest left to fall down her back. It called to mind drawings from the Far East. An image heightened by the lacquered sticks spearing her coiffure and the silver silk dressing gown that hugged her body. She was like a doll. A beautiful, deadly doll.

He heightened his senses as he came near, and the coppery scent of her enveloped him.

"Lena." He bowed. "It has been too long."

"Ian Ranulf." The rich depth in her voice belied her size. "Still as handsome as the devil." Obsidian eyes traveled over his form in a leisurely perusal. "Perhaps more so with that hair."

He saw the interest in her and knew what it was to bed her: cold, exciting, too dangerous—hence the excitement. In the darker hours of his life, Ian had been fairly addicted to that sort of bed sport. Now, however, he gave her a benign smile. "And you, Lena, are incomparable as always."

She laughed at that, showing a bit of sharp teeth. "Flatterer. Sit." A white hand indicated the seat next to hers. She leaned in when he did, setting the carnelian beads in her hair sticks to clattering. "Come, let us drink, then we shall talk."

Deftly, she poured a good measure of vodka into two cups—one silver, the other bone—and handed him the bone cup. A friendly gesture, as lycans, while tolerating silverware well enough, did not like to drink from silver cups.

She waited until he had a mouthful of cold, clean vodka to attack. "The rumors are true then."

Ian took his time swallowing. There were rumors, and there were rumors. He no longer cared about the one but the other… "Given their very nature, I wouldn't put much stock in rumors, Lena."

Unfortunately, her mouth curled again. "Not those stories, darling. I could never believe that of you." As she had had him in his prime, he could see why. He remained silent. "I have every confidence you will soon have need of my girls again." A cold hand patted his. "It's just a lull, I am sure."

Little witch. He looked at her askance as she took another long drink of vodka. Aside from blood, vodka was the one substance that Lena's kind could imbibe. Thus she drank a lot of it. The silver cup clinked as she set it down. "I refer to the human you brought home the other night, and you well know it. Ah, a scowl is it? Already, you are taken with her. It is written all over your handsome face."

And there it was. He set his cup down. "I've vowed to protect her. I take my vows seriously."

One ink-black brow lifted. "Oh? And what of your familial vow?"

He forced himself not to move, but deep inside his wolf growled in agreement. "I do not recall taking any vows that I have broken."

"No, you turn from them before making the expected commitment."

His fingers clutched the thick leather armrests. "What I do or do not do for my family is not why I am here."

Lena shifted in her seat, curling her slim legs under her rump. "Forgive me, dearest, but that is precisely why you are here." Her cold, black eyes pinned him. "You seek this mad wolf, and yet you do not go to The Ranulf. You come to me. And we both know why."

Ian forced his fingers to unclench. "I'd rather keep my head if that's all right with you." Should he approach the Ranulf court without express invitation, his would be rolling on the floor.

Lena hummed. "It is a lovely head. And a pity that you chose exile rather than to lead."

Ian sat forward and let his eyes linger on her. Lena loved to be admired, and he was not above using her vanity. "But then I wouldn't get to see you." He lowered his voice to a rumble. "I'd much rather you provide me with what I need."

Aside from running the popular club, Lena was a ranking captain in The Society for the Suppression of Supernaturals, commonly referred to as the SOS. It was her duty to keep informed of all supernatural beings and their activities. More so, she was responsible for keeping their deeds from the human world. The SOS was the last defense, and he needed them.

Lena ran her tongue along the tip of her tiny fang. "I am listening."

"I suspect the SOS has an idea as to who and where the werewolf is," he said. "I am asking for Mother's help."

There it was. A plea. Mother, the enigmatic head of the SOS, had never been seen. No one but Lena knew who or what she was. And no one was granted Mother's, and hence the SOS's, permission without first going through Lena. A little fact that gave Lena a rather extraordinary sense of superiority.

One she reveled in now by smirking at him. "And here I thought the putting down of turned lycans was The Ranulf's duty. The question of the night is, why does Ian Ranulf come here, searching for the outlaw, and yet The Ranulf sits on his throne and does nothing?"

A series of small pops sounded, and Ian realized his claws had sunk into the leather. Lena's eyes gleamed with victory. "I suspect you know the answer as well as I do."

Ian's wame pitched. He swallowed hard, the vodka running like vitriol through his veins. Damn it, but she was right. Conall had not hunted the *were* down. Which was not only against the clan's honor but a direct violation of their arrangement with the SOS.

She tilted her head toward the door, and her beads clacked again. "You act the ostrich, sticking your head in the sand while the world about you falls apart. Do you know how many lycans have come to me in the past months seeking asylum?"

His jaw tightened. "I suspect you will tell me."

"Do not be churlish, Ian Ranulf. They come and tell me tales. Of Conall using corrupt humans to fund his empire."

Despite his irritation, Ian's eyes shot to hers.

She poured herself another drink and downed it in one graceful swallow. "They come because The Ranulf believes they exist to serve him."

"They do." But he knew what she'd meant, and it made his insides twist. No lycan would leave the court of a proper alpha. Bloody hell. He could not go back to that life. He wanted to forget. Ah, but the wee bitch knew it, and still she wouldn't let him breathe.

"I am not a nanny," she said. "I send them to America and Canada when I can, but this business tires me."

"Send them to me," he said. "I will situate them."

"Very well, they are your problem now. And you are being duplicitous," she added. "What is worse, you have ignored your wolf, ignored who you *are*, for so long your power has atrophied. No wonder you cannot bed a woman."

Ian shot forward, slamming his forearms on his thighs. "Enough. Will you help me or no?"

She didn't flinch. "No."

"Right." He stood to go but her sharp voice stopped him.

"You are alpha, and you know it. It is time you took what is yours."

Ian stared down at her. "Conall is the alpha. I will not challenge him, if that is what you are after."

She stood as well, a rustling of silk and limbs. Her chin barely reached his collarbone, but she held power enough to match him, perhaps break him should they face off on the night of a waxing moon. Hell, she was right, he had ignored his wolf for too long, and it had made him weak.

"You cannot even call him The Ranulf," she snapped. "He wants to expose our world to the humans, and yet you run from the truth with your tail between your legs."

Ian turned away. God, he hated politics. He didn't want to be a lycan, nor a wolf. He only wanted to be a man and live a normal life. "Conall—The Ranulf—knows his duty. He might be lax, but he'd never expose us."

Lena's eyes were black steel. "Bullshite, as your kind would say. If you really believed that, you would not be here with your hat in hand. Because The Ranulf would have already eradicated the threat."

"Then help me find the *were*," he said. "Tell me what you know, Lena."

"I have given you my answer. I will not pester Mother with a problem that you can easily solve."

For a moment, he couldn't see. The red haze had him. With effort, he gulped down a lungful of air. "Do not make war with me, Lena." His mouth felt thick with extended fangs. "For the memory of what we once had together, do not."

Sadness flitted over her face but it was shut down by a wall of cold determination. "Then do what is right, Ian Ranulf. Take control of your clan."

With a vicious curse, he swept the drinks table aside, sending cups scattering and vodka splashing into the fire. It flared high as he shouted. "Bloody hell, woman! Do you no' understand? I cannot go back to that life. I lost everything that was dear to me when I was that man. I'll no' do it again."

Lena took a step closer, crowding him with the scent of copper and the cold of her body. "If you lost everything, then there is nothing left to lose, no?"

He scowled, but Lena laughed, a deep throaty sound that made his fists clench.

"If we don't act, more will die. We do not harm the innocent, Lena."

"You do not harm them. I am not so particular."

A growl rumbled in his throat, his claws burning to break free. "Find someone else to play the pawn. The only thing that you'll accomplish by coming after me is getting bitten."

She glared back, ice in her gaze and teeth glinting in the firelight. "I like the bite, Ian, you know that."

Their stalemate was broken with the entrance of Edmund, looking harried and followed by an overlarge black crow. The crow circled once, cawing frantically, before settling on Ian's shoulder.

His blood ran cold at the sound and what it meant. Damn it all to bloody hell. He was already running from the room as Lena's laugh cut through his wild thoughts. "I see your human needs you already. Pray, Ian, do not forget her while you think on what I've said."

Chapter Nine

And here Daisy thought Billy stank. The streets were worse. Daisy burrowed deeper into the scarf around her neck and inhaled. Alas, even her perfume could not completely dampen the stench. Rotting water, rotting food, rotting bodies. It was a potpourri of rot, as if the city were slowly dying from the inside out. Perhaps it was. Old Nichol, Billy called this place. The people here appeared forlorn, the light in their eyes dimmed by a hard life, worn out by hunger and pain.

They walked slowly, yet with purpose. Billy had warned her not to meet anyone's eye but to move as though she owned the world. She could do that. But inside, her heart pounded. Her escort kept one ropey arm slung about her shoulders, his large hand dangling irritatingly close to her breast. They were to look like a couple off in search of fun. Every so often, he'd lean in and whisper something naughty in her ear, and she'd laugh accordingly.

Thankfully, the warmer weather had burned off much of the fog, leaving only a muddy layer to hover a foot or so off the ground. People walked as if without feet, phantoms that seemed to float along the ether. The street was narrow here, sad little houses sagging against crumbling buildings that had once been grand homes. And leaning against them, the men and women who lived in this hovel.

Beneath lowered lids, Daisy watched these people as she passed, saw the gap-toothed smiles of strutting men who wanted to be cock of the walk and the hunched, thin shoulders of women scuttling by. A few brazen women loitered about on corners, their bosoms all but hanging out like Monday washing.

Not, Daisy rectified, that she was in a position to throw stones. Daisy glanced down at her own rather abundant display of flesh spilling from the top of her low-cut bodice. She'd dressed the part, donning an old evening gown of brilliant green satin. While perfectly respectable in a ballroom, out here, with her hair loosely knotted and naught but a thin scarf for covering, she might as well be another moll hanging on the arm of her man.

"I'm goin' in first," Billy said at her ear. "He's not particularly keen on visitors, right? So's let me do the talkin'." The arm about her gave an unnecessary squeeze. "You just stand back lookin' lovely an' agreeable."

She gave his ribs a jab with her elbow, and he grunted. "You get me in, and I'll talk," she countered. If this so-called perfumer was purchasing stolen formulas, she doubted he'd be inclined to confess. He might, however, hold a passion for perfume and find himself unable to refrain from discussing the art of developing a scent. She was banking on that small hope. "Just remember who is paying whom."

Billy looked at her sidelong. "I'd rather you'd pay for a bit of hide the pickle," he muttered.

Daisy snorted lightly. "I bet you do. Just keep that pickle of yours in its jar and your mind alert."

Billy muttered a bit more about iron-hearted *buors*—which she presumed meant women—and pains in his arse, but he led her down a dark alleyway where the general smell grew to a nearly overwhelming stench, so rank that even he couldn't help but comment upon it.

"Sweet aunt fanny," he said, pulling out a ratty, scarlet satin neckcloth from his pocket to press against his nose. "Smells fouler than a dock whore's twat down here."

She bit her lip. No, she would *not* laugh. Not when her eyes were watering and her stomach was in danger of voiding. Despite herself, she leaned closer to Billy. The offensive smell touched something inside of her that called forth a desperate need to flee.

Billy's grip tightened as well. "Something's off, chips. Let's come back in the daytime at least."

Fat, gray clouds scuttled over the bright moon, whose rays cast the alleyway in a palette of blues and blacks. Nothing stirred here. It was as if the fetid air had chased all life away.

"Nonsense," she said past the lump of fear in her throat. "We've come this far."

Above them, a timber creaked, and her heart jumped. But there was nothing to see, just the settling of an old building.

Billy heaved a sigh and then made a gagging sound as if the action had let in an unwanted mouthful of the stench. "Gor, that's ripe." He pointed to the end of the alleyway where a dilapidated building listed sadly to one side. "His spot is there."

She was strangely hesitant to take another step. "Doesn't look like the home of a successful perfumer."

"Mayhaps he has posh digs elsewheres," Billy drawled. "But that's where he works his capers so's that's where I'm taking you." His brown eyes softened with surprising gentleness as he glanced down at her. "Come on then, luv, Old Burnt Bill will protect you against what beasties might hide in the night." He pulled a wicked-looking hunting knife out from behind his back, where it had been hidden beneath his coat, and held it up as if to reassure her.

They'd taken two steps when something large and hulking dropped in front of them in a blur of movement. Daisy screamed as it slammed Billy into the side of the alleyway and forced Billy's wrist high above his head in one deft move. The hunting knife fell to the ground with a clatter.

"That's some pigsticker," came the silk and sand voice of Ian Ranulf, Marquis of Northrup. Moonlight hit the hard curves of his face, highlighting the cruel smile that curled his mouth. "Save it will do you no good if you're dead."

Daisy snapped out of her shock and strode forward. "Let him go, Northrup!" Heedless, she slapped Northrup's shoulder with her reticule. "Get off him, you big beast."

Northrup released his prize. Billy slumped down the wall as Northrup turned to glare at her. "Ye gods, woman, what do you have in that wee bag of yours? Rocks?" He rubbed his shoulder irritably.

"A handgun," she retorted, fumbling to get said gun free.

Billy, who was rising on unsteady feet, spat on the ground before glaring at her as well. "Well, that's a fine place to keep your iron. Might have been a bit more helpful in yer hand, eh?"

Northrup grunted. His gaze alighted on the swells of her bosom, and his nostrils flared. A wicked light came into his eyes. "Oh, I don't know. She'd probably shoot off her own...*foot* at that."

Daisy refused to dignify their remarks. Instead, she shoved the gun back into her reticule; it was useless now at any rate. "What the bloody hell are you doing jumping off rooftops anyway? Trying to scare the life out of people?"

Northrup's brows slanted. "I had to jump off the roof to get down here, aye?"

"Is there something untoward about walking along the street as normal people do?" She hit his shoulder with her bag again. The brute had scared her witless, and no doubt had taken pleasure in doing so.

"Ow! And no, I cannot," he said. "Not when I am in a hurry to chase down one fool woman." He snorted in disgust. "I'm of a mind to take ye over me knee for sheer stupidity, never mind insulting me to the core. Ye gods, I should have known you'd get up to something, as single-minded as you are. But I never fathomed this depth of idiocy."

Daisy muttered the vilest oath she could think of and he rolled his eyes. "I'll consider that one day. Until then, why don't you tell me whom it is you're after."

"The perfumer," she said. "Apparently, my legitimate perfumer sold the formula to my perfume to a man who then concocts a cheaper version and sells to other stores or private buyers."

Northrup turned to scowl at the perfumer's hovel. "Of course. I hadn't thought to go right to the source," he mused and then glared at her. "Might have saved me an evening's worth of trouble had you mentioned that little tidbit."

Daisy swallowed the niggling feeling of guilt down.

"Lookit," said a voice. "Seems to me you two are cozy like. Why don't I leave you alone?"

Billy, she thought dimly. She'd almost forgotten him. She glanced his way to find him edging back from them. "Oh no, you don't." Daisy pushed away from Northrup and stalked Billy. "I paid good money, you." She pointed a finger at Billy. "That includes not fobbing me off on the first man who gets in your way."

In truth, the idea of being alone with Northrup unsettled her in more ways than one. She ought to have included him in her plans. She ought to have trusted him, for she could see that he cared about her welfare despite his rather snide comments. The idea of facing him with that knowledge made her insides writhe with shame.

Northrup caught her arm and wrenched her back. "Fob you off?" His dark brows lifted in outrage. "Have ye gone daft?" He glowered at Billy, and the poor man twitched. "She stays with me. Go on before I lose my temper with ye."

"I'm not staying with you if it means being sent home, Northrup!" Daisy wriggled to get free, but Northrup only tucked her more securely at his side.

"Call me Ian," he snapped. "And ye surely are goin' home."

"Don't go playing the Scottish lord with me." She kicked at his foot, only to miss. "I decide where I go and with whom, not you."

Northrup's nose bunted against hers. "What in the devil's name are ye talkin' about, ye dafty wee besom?"

"You know very well." Daisy ignored the way her breath hitched when he got too near. "You get riled up and off you go, throwing that Highland accent about as if to intimidate." She dropped her voice in an imitation of his. "Ye will do as I say or I will take ye overrr me knee an' stroop yer backside!' "

Utter silence fell between them, punctuated by Billy's mutterings about insane women. Northrup's eyes narrowed, his lips a thin line that twitched at the corners. Then like a thunderclap, his laughter broke free, rolling over her rich and full. The corners of his eyes creased as he bowed and let his brogue roll to full effect. "Aye weel, lassy, ye canna blame a man fer wantin' ta get his 'ands on such a fine, plump arse such as yers, now can ye?"

She flushed hot. "Ass," she hissed, which only set him off again.

The crook backed away farther, lifting his hands in the air as if to placate Northrup. "Sorry, luv," Northrup growled at the endearment, and Billy's steps quickened, "but might makes right, and all that." With an apologetic wink, he turned and fled.

"It's 'right makes might,' you little rat," she yelled after him before turning on Northrup. "Look at what you've done. You've scared him off."

Northrup crossed his arms over his chest. "This concerns me how?" The feral look returned to his eyes and sent a chill over her skin. "Does it bother you to lose him? Seemed quite cozy walking at his side. Where did you find him, anyway? Passed out in a gutter?"

She could only laugh in shock. "Are you jealous of Billy Finger?"

His square chin jerked as if hit but he stalked closer. "Answer the question, Daisy."

"Which one of the four?"

Northrup's eyes glowed in the moonlight. "Where did you find him?"

"Lord, but you have more curiosity than ten cats—"

"Wolves generally do," he intoned blandly.

Her heart skipped a light beat but she did not let her haughty expression alter. "He is Miranda's friend."

As expected, her sister's name took the wind out of his sails. He turned to look thoughtfully down the empty alleyway. "I thought he appeared familiar."

"And just how do you know him?" Daisy countered.

Northrup hesitated for only a moment. "I saw him once, with Miranda in Bethnal Green. She set the street on fire," he said. "I don't suppose you possess the same sort of talent? It could come in handy."

She'd been expecting it, yet his query punched into her with painful force. "No." She looked away, blinking hard. "Yet another disappointment, I gather."

Northrup had been in the process of glowering at the distant house, but his head whipped around. "What?" When she said nothing, he stomped to her side and grabbed her hand, forcing her to face him. His expression was fierce, but when he spoke, the words came out surprisingly gentle. "The only thing I find disappointing about you is that you pop up where I least want you to be."

Emotion lodged in her throat, and she had to fight hard to clear it. "Where is it that you want me to be?"

The soft line of his mouth compressed, and for a moment, she thought he wouldn't speak. But his tension eased and the pad of his thumb glided over her gloveless fingers. Fast women did not wear gloves. "Not anywhere near here." He tugged at her hand, pulling her closer. "Let me see you home, Daisy-girl."

"Look here, Northrup, either we argue for an undue length of time in this foul air and then go into the shack, or we agree now and go into the shack."

Northrup's lips twitched as if he were debating whether to laugh or shout, but suddenly, he heaved a sigh and ran a hand through his hair. "Fine. But I'm going in and you are waiting out here." He lifted a finger and gave her a look worthy of a governess. "No objections, or I will throw you over me shoulder and march you home, whether ye will it or no."

"Your Scottish is showing again." She grinned at his scowl. "All right, all right. You win. Now may we please get on with it?"

His world was pain and darkness. Brilliant flashes of his life shot through his mind. Memories he did not understand. Instinct made him yearn for fresh air and fields of grass and flowers in which he could run free. And the hunt. The taste of blood and meat. How he wanted that most of all. His stomach rumbled, hunger and thirst, an ache that made him howl.

The lycan had captured him. Bastard. His tormentor. The one that kept him in a constant state of agitation.

Pain wracked his body with the force to break bones, making him cower in the dank corner of his cell. Water dripped. Made him thirst. The clatter of horse hooves from beyond made him wince. He sensed the moon's power. He'd felt her rays warm him the other night. And then they found him again. Imprisoned him again. His teeth gnashed.

Like a balm, the memory came, of bright blue eyes and a smiling mouth. Hair golden as the sun on wheat. He didn't understand color. Didn't see it now. Only in memory. He whined, confusion hurting. Deep inside him came a cry. A man's cry. The man wanted the female. The man ached for her. Her scent was a constant tease and torment.

His woman. The only one who ever cared for him. A flash of memory burned again. His woman lying dead upon a pallet, her body ravaged like his human body had been. Sores and pain. She could not be dead. He scented her still. How could that be?

Rage and confusion blurred until he surged up, smashing his skull against the bars, his teeth snapping at the metal.

Out. He wanted out. The man inside him wanted out, too.

"To her," the man pleaded. *"Find her and the pain will end."*

The wolf had to believe it so. He and the man had been one for so long. What was his memory was the man's. They only needed to be let out. The wolf banged against the cage again, and again. And each time, the metal bars bent a bit more.

Northrup got his Scottish under control, but not his muttering. Complaints drifted through the quiet as he led her back down the foul alley to the abandoned dwelling of the perfumer. Daisy's eyes watered as the stench hit her. She allowed one pull of the air into her nostrils so that she might detect anything of use. Beneath the horrible fug of death and decay came a strong, almost painful mix of numerous base notes and florals. Yes, perfume had been made here.

Distaste flattened Northrup's mouth as he turned to regard her. "Stay here. Take your little gun out and shoot whatever comes close. No hesitation." He spoke in halting tones as if trying not to breathe or smell if he didn't have to. "I shall not be far."

He moved to enter the hovel but she stopped him with a hand to his arm. "Take this." She offered the flimsy protection of her scented scarf.

A small smile lifted one side of his mouth. "Kind of you, lass. But I'm afraid I'll be needing my nose." His skin shone slightly gray in the moonlight. Daisy's stomach turned in sympathy. She could not imagine willingly inhaling the source of the smell. The wry yet resigned look in his eyes told her they understood each other perfectly on that notion. He said no more, and Daisy was left alone in the thick darkness.

Nothing stirred except the faint sounds of Northrup moving through the shack. The mouth of the narrow alley was an impenetrable wall of inky black. Simply looking at it made her heart pound. Something small and rodentlike skittered past. She shivered and focused on the gaping front door of the perfumer's home and willed Northrup to hurry. Waiting in the shadows while surrounded by the air of death, one minute felt like an hour.

Daisy huddled farther down into her scarf when a thought occurred. Northrup was only there to scent out the wolf. But more needed to be done. She hesitated. Despite what she'd said to him, she did not want to go into the shack. But she knew she must. Bracing herself, she clamped the scarf more firmly to her nose and strode forward.

Moonlight pouring in from a hole in the roof illuminated the wreckage in the front room, highlighting the glinting edges of broken bottles and the dull shapes of furniture strewn about.

Daisy's breath came in short bursts as she crept forward, her booted feet crunching on bits of glass. Northrup was nowhere to be seen, and her voice was trapped in her throat, hindering her from calling out. The dark corners of the room seemed a living thing, intent on following her, pressing in on all sides as if to swallow her up. Deep within, she knew Northrup was close, but it did not stop her body from trembling or her mind from urging her to run away.

The smell was a tangible thing, coating her skin, clinging to her hair. She swallowed against the bitter taste of it, and her stomach rebelled. A creak to her left had her whipping about, her heart in her throat. The sight that greeted her was too much.

Lips curled back in a ghoulish grin, the dead woman seemed to mock Daisy. A fat fly buzzed about dull yellow curls before landing on a grizzled cheek. A cry, almost animalistic, broke from Daisy's lips, just as a pair of warm hands closed over her arms. She screamed again, and he pulled her close.

"It's me," Northrup said, hugging her tight. "It's me."

Daisy sank into his strength and shuddered. "Was it... did the werewolf do this?"

"Not to her, but there is a man beyond the bed. The perfumer, most likely. The *were* certainly had at him. No"—he tugged her back when she glanced at the dark shape against the corner—"don't look." He cupped the back of her head for a moment. "Are you well enough to move?"

She nodded and then, steeling herself, she pushed away from him and began to search the room in quick, halting steps.

Northrup was at her side in an instant. "What are you doing?"

Casting aside an overturned chair, she opened her mouth only as much as necessary. "Record book."

They made quick work of searching, Daisy keeping as far away from the bodies as she could. Her hands drifted over the disarray of bottled oils and essences. A fortune in the perfume market, and most likely stolen. When she turned around, she found Northrup standing stone still at the foot of the dead woman's bed. His head was bent as he stared down at an object in his hand. But it was his expression that worried Daisy, for he looked as if he'd seen a ghost. Given where they were at present, the idea lifted the hairs along her arms.

"What is it?" she whispered, drawing near.

At the sound of her voice, Northrup twitched and broke from his apparent stupor. "Nothing." He pocketed the object, something small and gold, and his troubled gaze met hers. "Nothing we need discuss in here."

Northrup touched her elbow. "I have it." Indeed, he held a small ledger in his free hand.

She did not resist when he led her directly out. He moved with quick, jerking steps. No words were spoken as they walked out of the alley and down another street. When they'd gone several blocks and the air was fresher, he let go of her, and they stopped.

Shaking, she reached into her reticule and pulled out a small flask. "God, that was a vile business," she muttered before taking a deep drink.

Northrup eyed the flask with humor as she handed it to him, but he pulled a long swallow as well. His eyes widened as he did, undoubtedly shocked at the burn of good scotch whiskey going down his throat instead of the expected ladylike lemonade or watered wine.

Daisy lifted a shoulder. "A bit of liquid courage never hurts when one seeks to employ a known thief and raid the home of a possible murderer."

Northrup's eyes danced but his expression remained somber. "Indeed not." His silk-and-gravel voice was raw. "Perhaps you'd favor a touch more just now?"

"Perhaps a touch," she agreed and took a sip. The peaty-sweet spirit burned away the foul taste death had left and eased the tightness in her limbs. Even so, she feared nothing would ever erase the memory of what she'd seen.

Daisy wrapped her arms about herself and shivered. Northrup noticed the action and slid out of his coat and wrapped it about her shoulders. Grateful, she sank into its heavy warmth. "What was it that you found back there?"

His expression was at once thoughtful yet disturbed as he slowly pulled out a moonstone stickpin. The little carved unicorn seemed to glow with an inner light as he passed it to her. It was a lovely piece, and she said as much.

"Where did you find it?" Daisy asked as she handed it back.

Oddly, he didn't look at it but quickly pocketed the pin. "On the woman's bodice."

"It is familiar to you though, isn't it?" She could see that much.

His nod was perfunctory. "I had one much like this, long ago." His dark brows drew tight.

"Is it yours?" The very idea unsettled Daisy. Why would Northrup's stickpin be with a dead woman?

"No." He sounded very sure and yet the look of confusion remained. "Mine was lost to time." His expression closed down, resolute and final. "But it is…curious. I need to think on it." He seemed to shake himself into alertness. "As to the ledger, let's have a look then."

He balanced the book on his hand and opened it.

"Look for entries made after March fourteenth," she said, happy to have a problem she could help solve. "That was when Mr. Abernathy, the manager at Florin, sold my formula to him."

A half smile pulled at Northrup's mouth as he thumbed

through the pages. "And here I thought you were merely purchasing cosmetics at Florin."

Daisy started. "You were following me?"

"Of course." He flashed her an evil grin. "It was quite gratifying to see you searching for me."

She pursed her lips. "Pest." His grin widened, and Daisy eyed him with suspicion. "Have you been following me all along this night?"

"No. Talent, my valet, has been keeping watch since teatime."

She ought to have known. "Another lycan, is he?"

Northrup shook his head as he searched the book. "No. Before you go off asking, I'm not at liberty to say what he is, only that he'll keep you safe when I cannot." His eyes flashed as he glanced at her. "And you'll never see him following, so don't bother looking for him."

Daisy muttered under her breath and leaned over his arm to read along as the blunt tip of his finger traced down the entries.

"A few sales for men's cologne, one for some liniment," he said. "Then... Here. Marked two days before the first murder occurred."

Daisy moved closer, and Northrup's warm breath stirred the curls that tickled her temple. She fought to ignore the way the sensation made her want to lift her head and nuzzle into him. "M. Randal, Number 2 Glower Street. One bottle Daisy." Her blood heated. "The blasted man even called the perfume by my name."

Northrup couldn't quite hide the laughter in his voice. "It is rather catchy. Is that what you called the scent?"

"I called it mine," she snapped, knowing she sounded defensive. "But yes, I put my name on the top of the formula." A stupid bit of whimsy that irritated her now. She pushed the feeling away. "But Daisy was never meant for public sale. It was my personal scent."

The corners of his vivid eyes crinkled. "A nose," he said softly. "You mentioned before that you had a perfume supplier, but I wasn't minding. You create perfumes then?"

Daisy kept her gaze upon the ledger, wanting to have done with the conversation, but his attention did not deviate and she was forced to answer. "For Florin."

Northrup's eyes widened, but she ignored him. "I knew Craigmore intended to leave me with nothing. It was either plan or starve. I was not about to let that man have the last word."

His raspy voice was a current of warm air against her cheek. "Well done, lass."

Her cheeks were overwarm as she tapped a nail upon the ledger entry. "M. Randal. Do you suppose that is a man or a woman?"

Northrup stirred. "I cannot see a lady coming to a place like this for perfume. A gentleman either. But it is more likely than a woman doing so."

"Agreed," said Daisy. "Well, if it was a man who purchased it—"

"Then perhaps it was a gift." Northrup turned his head to look down at her, his warm eyes and firm mouth scattering her thoughts.

"Seems logical." She cleared her throat and stepped away from Northrup and his unnerving presence.

"Northrup, you said the werewolf killed the man. But what of the woman? How did she die, do you suppose?" A flash of bones, blood, and flesh filled her mind's eye, and she swallowed.

"There were no slashes or bites. I think—" Northrup

paused, biting his lips closed for a moment as if he were fighting against the memory of the corpse, and then he took a breath. "She expired from disease. There were tumors, her skin covered in papules. All the signs of tertiary syphilis." His expression went grim. "She carried the same scent of sickness as the *were* does."

"A lover's disease." It hurt Daisy's heart to think of what had become of the poor woman. And the man. Was he her lover? What of the werewolf? "Whoever bought this perfume must be warned."

He snapped the book shut and offered up his arm. "Glower Street isn't far off. Shall we?"

Chapter Ten

It was Friday evening; thus finding a hack proved difficult. Daisy had long since sent her own carriage home, and Northrup appeared to have tracked her down on foot. Thus, they were forced to walk to Mr. Randal's residence.

Daisy glanced at the man at her side. His casual bowler tilted at a rakish angle and his stride confident yet carefree as though he owned the very earth beneath his feet, Northrup caught the eye of every female, and some males, as they passed. A charming fiend.

Night painted the landscape in colors of blue and charcoal. A chill touched the air, making their breath visible. His warmth beside her was a welcome thing. Daisy wrapped her fingers more securely around his forearm.

"What is that clinking sound?" Northrup shot a suspicious glance in the direction of her skirts.

"Some essential oils I took from the perfumer's shack." She pulled out the bottle of verbena for him to see.

His nostrils flared slightly as though already scenting

it. “Why on earth would you take something out of that hellhole?”

Daisy laughed. “And let them go to waste when they are perfectly usable? You must be mad.”

“I should think you have wealth enough to buy your own oils should you so wish,” he said, looking bemused.

“Posh. Waste not, want not. Besides, Poppy loves verbena. I’m going to make a perfume for her with it.” She uncorked the verbena to take a whiff. The sharp lemony scent would chase away the lingering taint of death that clung to her.

Northrup reacted instantly, flinging himself away from her and covering his nose with his arm. “Ye gods, woman, put that away. Are you trying to kill me?” A violent eruption of sneezes shook his frame.

Quelling a smile, Daisy closed up the offending bottle. “Don’t like verbena, do you?”

He gave her a repressive glare between bouts of sneezing. His hand shook as he pulled a linen kerchief free. “Not many lycan do. It burns something fierce.”

“I shall keep that in mind, in the event you decide to get out of line.”

Northrup rolled his eyes. “And you call *me* a pest.”

They walked on in silence, but she felt the weight of Northrup’s stare. “What is it?” she finally said. His attention made her insides twitch, damn his eyes.

His buttered-toast voice rolled over her. “You are fearless, you know.”

She would not allow her cheeks to heat. Her cheeks ignored her. “I am not.” She studied the sway of her skirts as she strode forward. “I was terrified back there.”

“But you forged on, did what had to be done.” He stopped beneath a lonely lamppost, and his auburn locks, tangling about his collar, glowed under the wavering lamplight. Daisy admired them, and the clean lines of his countenance.

Northrup's head tilted as he continued to look her over as if just truly noticing she was there. "For all your frippery, you're a brave lass."

Daisy didn't know whether to be insulted or not. "Careful now, Northrup, or I'll start to believe you like me."

His teeth flashed in the glow. "I think I like you too well at that, Daisy-girl."

His words gave sway to a spot deep inside of her. She prattled on as if she hadn't heard, lest he realize he affected her. "You talk of frippery when it is all too apparent that you rather like playing the fop as well. Do not try to deny it."

"I wasn't going to." Self-deprecation colored his chuckle. "Birds of a feather, are we?"

Her lips quirked, and she glanced away, the fluttery feeling inside her stomach making her long to run away so that it would stop. She was astounded that Northrup had let her come along with him. She couldn't account for it; Craigmore was of the decided opinion that women stayed within the home. Of course, she knew on an intellectual level that all men, thankfully, were not like Craigmore. But it did not stop her from expecting them to be.

"Northrup?"

"Mmm?"

"I apologize. For not telling you about the perfumer before I went to find him. I am not..." She took a deep, coal-tinged breath. "I am not accustomed to having a man finding me worthy of being a partner."

His gaze made her heart pound and her fingers shake. She hated feeling so exposed but found she hated his hurt and disappointment more.

"I would say that it was your previous partner who was unworthy."

Really, he took her breath away at times. When he looked at her as if she mattered. Her, not Daisy the ornament, or Daisy the tease, but her. Swallowing past the tightness in her throat, she said what he deserved to hear. "And for the other bit."

His voice gentled, and she heard the humor hiding there. "What bit?"

He was watching her, a smile playing about his mouth, forgiveness already softening his eyes.

"For making you think I do not trust you to keep me safe. I do. Trust you, that is."

His smile grew. "It relieves me to hear it, Daisy-Meg."

There was an invitation in his voice, a lure for her to step close and forget herself.

He caught her expression and his smile grew fiendish.

"Don't go getting calf-eyed on me," he warned with amusement. "Or I'll start to believe that you like me, too."

"And we couldn't have that," Daisy said, feeling almost dizzy.

Northrup's eyes were indigo in the dim. He looked at her as though he knew her every thought. "After all," he said in a thick voice, "what would happen, Daisy-Meg, if you liked me?"

She couldn't think past the heat filling her. Desperately, Daisy nibbled on the inside of her bottom lip. Control, she needed to gain control. This was why she stayed away from men, because her lusts, once set free, were too great to contain. A small voice prodded that she hadn't been this overcome by her unlucky suitor in the alleyway the other night. Nor by the countless other men who flirted with her over the years. No, only by *him*. This man whom she liked all too well.

His voice was a husky whisper and a taunt that plucked at her nerves. "What might you let me do?"

No, not with him. Not now. Carnal knowledge of the casual sort was one thing. This—*he* was something else. Flushed, Daisy turned and began briskly walking, taking a turn onto the main avenue. It was busier here, with people darting to and fro, sellers hawking evening fare for harried clerks on their way home.

Northrup's long legs kept pace with hers with vexing ease, his deep voice a buzz about her ears. "So you would run from me now?" He chuckled, but the light in his eyes had dimmed. "Don't you know we wolves like the chase? It only makes us want to—"

He said no more but froze. Daisy turned back in confusion. His expression altered to one of such pain that her breath left her.

Chapter Eleven

Memory was a cruel thing. It could attack without warning. All it needed was for the scene to be laid, a seemingly random sequence of events, a certain combination of scents, the quality of light hitting the street just so. A sound, a touch, if set just right, could suddenly fell a man and bring him to his knees.

As it were, such events conspired against Ian as they turned a corner. Hitting the precise note in the landscape of his mind, the sensation opened hidden corridors he'd rather keep closed. The scent snared him first, the slight breeze touched with the warmth of fried haddock mixed with the buttery sweet note of toffee that the vendors hawked along the square. Then the light of the lanterns, misty blue-green in the fog, and a woman's laugh, holding the same overloud trill. It was all the same, as it had been decades ago.

"Da, why d'ye suppose that fellow's teeth all fell out?" That small hand, how it fit so well into his own larger one. *"Well now, Maccon, I suppose he ate only toffees and not his parritch. Let it be a warning to you, lad."*

Ian's step faltered. *Don't. Don't. Don't.* He wouldn't picture him. But it came, the sight of those eyes, deep brown and shining, like sunlight in a tidal pool, and his little nose wrinkling with disgust.

"Go on with you, Da! You're just trying to get me to eat parritch."

"There's a smart lad. But how else are you going to grow big and strong like me, I ask you?"

A black hole opened in his chest, and by gods, it hurt. It hurt so that he could not move. Street traffic buffeted him as he stumbled to a stop and tried to breathe through the pain. A scream of frustration built behind his clenched teeth, for nothing on earth could bring back what was lost. Someone banged his shoulder, the bloke muttering in irritation. Then a different touch, soft and smooth over his fingertips, brought him back.

"Northrup?"

Out of the black misery, her face came into view, her blue eyes narrowed, that pouting mouth a flat line of concern. "Is something amiss? You look ill."

He could only blink down at her as his throat closed. Loneliness, need, and despair made him quake. A flash of something darkened her eyes as she looked him over, understanding, pain that was her own, and then it was gone. If she treated him with pity, he'd howl and leave her standing alone on the street, but her pert chin merely lifted. "If you've plans to swoon simply so you can look up my skirts, I'll kick your head and leave you where you lie."

She grabbed his empty hand, filling it with her warmth. "Come along and cease your dramatics." She proceeded to tug him down the street with cool efficiency, her hand staying in his, holding it firmly. Warmth spread along their connection, up his arm and into the gaping maw of his chest. His feet worked to keep up, despite his longer stride and the mincing steps forced on her by her skirt.

"I don't know whether to be insulted or amused at such a blatant attempt." The sound of her snappish voice was a balm. She glanced over her shoulder at him with an assessing eye. Whatever she saw in him did not meet full approval for she tugged harder, her look turning saucy. "I expected more creativity from you, Northrup. This is your idea of a chase? It's pathetic, really."

The painful lump of emotion in his throat softened and turned tender. Lightness bubbled up from within as her barbs continued. "You can do better, I'm sure. In the future—"

He stopped short, using their momentum to whip her about. His free arm snaked around her neat waist to hold her against him. And his mouth came down upon hers.

He meant it to be a peck, a lighthearted thank-you for seeing his pain and offering diversion instead of pity. That was what he had intended. But the moment his lips touched hers, his body decided on a different course. On a breath, he tilted his head into the kiss and fitted her closer.

Sweet mother, her mouth was as hot and delectable as he dreamed. He kissed her as if he'd done it a thousand times before, opening her mouth, shaping her lips with his as if he owned them. Shock made her rigid for just a moment, and then all that tightness turned to soft warmth and pressed into him, forcing a pained groan from his mouth. Her free hand fisted his lapel, and then she was kissing him back.

Jesus, she knew what she was about. Heat shivered over his skin as her tongue tangled with his. Coming up on her toes, she angled her head and suckled his lower lip with a little greedy noise. His fingertips sank into the soft curve of her cheek as he held her still and gave her what she wanted.

They stood locked together on the street, attacking each other. He could think of no other word for the fierce biting, needy kisses, and the blinding speed of it. Their lips parted on a gasp as if they'd been struck by an electrical current.

With his arm still wrapped about her waist, he panted lightly as he stared down at her, taking in the lovely flush of her cheeks and her plump pink lips, wet now from his kiss. She blinked up at him, speechless apparently. So was he. She'd twisted him around her finger without effort, and all he wanted now was for her to twist harder. Christ, he was in a bad way. He did like her. Too much. And she was human. Destined to die someday. He couldn't go through it again. It would kill him.

His hands shook, *shook*, damn it. But he played the part she expected of him and slipped one hand beneath her bustled train to give her rump a squeeze, getting a satisfying squeak out of her in the process. "In the future," he said, straining to appear calm and unaffected, "I shall be more direct in my quest to get up your skirts, Daisy-Meg."

Chapter Twelve

As it turned out, M. Randal was the Honorable Mr. Jonathan Randal, fourth son of the Earl of Kentwick, who, unfortunately, had not been at home. After a bit of Northrup's not inconsiderable persuasion, they finally spoke with Mr. Randal's valet, who had informed them that the perfume had been given as gift.

"For Miss Annika Einarsson, Mr. Randal's fiancée," Randal's valet had told them. The man stood rod straight in Mr. Randal's proper, if unadorned, front parlor. "I purchased it myself. Sent out, of course, by Mr. Randal."

"And you decided to purchase perfume from a back-alley perfumer rather than a reputable supplier?" Daisy asked, unable to hold back her curiosity.

The valet sniffed but his expression remained implacable. "He may be the son of an earl, but he's the fourth son. Mr. Randal barely has blunt enough to rub two shillings together." The valet smoothed his immaculate lapels. "His father pays my salary. His mother provided the betrothal ring. Miss Einarsson is the money in this match. Can a man blame Mr. Randal for wanting to give her something on his own?"

Daisy had thought it rather lovely, actually. Northrup, on the other hand, had been impatient to track Annika down. The valet directed them to Holly Lodge in Highgate, where the couple were presently attending their engagement party.

After a quick return to Northrup's home to ready a small and light cabriolet, they set out for Highgate. Now, on the coach seat next her, he sat in that proper yet languid way of his as he drove the cab, apparently unaffected by the heated kisses they'd shared earlier. On a public street no less. His mouth had tasted of caramels. Rich, decadent, and so delicious it made her teeth ache. Daisy always had a weakness for caramels and could most likely thank them for maintaining the fullness of her curves. In her indulgence, she'd slip one soft, sticky candy into her mouth and let it melt, savoring the flavor on her tongue, the way it tasted sweet yet salty at the sides of her mouth. A shiver lit over her skin. She wanted to dip her tongue in Northrup's salty-sweet mouth and let his flavor wash over her again.

Northrup's collar was slightly askew, the only sign of their exchange, and her gaze moved over the exposed bit of flesh just below the sharp curve of his jaw. A tender area, that bit of throat on a man. Did his skin taste of caramels as well? She swallowed hard, for she could imagine it did, of caramel and salt. God, she wanted to suck that spot. Heated desire tightened her skin, making her breasts heavy and her thighs ache.

She took a steadying breath and thought of benign things such as new hats, fine kid gloves, and, no, not caramels, but perhaps that new striped parasol she coveted.

Unfortunately, her gaze returned to him like a magnet drawn to its opposite.

His dark hair flowed from beneath his top hat in glossy, uncivilized waves that brushed the tops of his shoulders and glinted auburn in the coach's lamplight. He had said he grew it long out of mourning.

"Was it your father you thought of before, on the street?" Her voice sounded thick and unsteady, as much a surprise to her as the question that had popped out of her mouth.

Northrup's shoulders twitched just enough for her to know he'd been surprised as well, as if he'd forgotten about her presence, she thought irritably. He took a moment to address her. "No. Not just then." His voice was thicker as well. The corners of his lush mouth turned down as he glowered at some unseen thing.

He sat straighter as he turned up the long drive to Holly Lodge, a grand estate owned by the esteemed Baroness Burdett-Coutts. "My father was a bastard most of the time. But I do miss him." The corners of his eyes crinkled faintly. "Some of the time."

She thought of her own father. Northrup might just as well have been describing her feelings. "And your mother?" she asked. "Did you lose her as well?" She ought not to have asked. It felt cruel, especially when seeing his wistful expression, but she'd been thinking of her own familial losses.

"She's been gone for ninety years," he said quietly.

If he noticed her squeak of shock, he didn't show it. Sweet God, how must it feel to live so long? Daisy suddenly felt her own mortality as if it had reached out and tapped her shoulder. With cold horror, she realized that one far-off day, she might run into this man and find him unchanged, while she would be old and gray.

"She was human, you see." Northrup shifted in his seat, yet his hands remained easy on the reins. "Call it nature's way of culling an aberration, or sheer dumb luck, but a female lycan is a rare thing. Maybe one is born every hundred years. In truth, it is very rare for us to impregnate a woman at all." The corners of his wide mouth curled, but his eyes held a painful hint of hopelessness as his gaze turned inward. "So rare that a man might outlive many human wives without—"

He sucked in a sharp breath, and his face went ashen. Daisy's hand moved to take his but Northrup's arm lifted to drive the horse around a sharp bend. His expression was easy now, back to the same teasing manner of his usual employ. "Let us simply say that you won't find many bastard lycans." The coach stopped at the grand entrance to Holly Lodge, and Northrup inclined his head. "We are here."

The air was cold and wet, beading in the wolf's fur. Fog clouded his sight, confusing him. He relied on scent to take him to her. The woman. Sweet, thick, sticky. Pollen in flowers, the smell of human female mixed with spring. He moved quickly, weaving past piles of rubbish that clogged his nose and threatened to overwhelm the scent of her.

But the woman was dead. Wasn't she? *No. No. No.* Panic set in and made the wolf cower. He growled. No, it was she. Her scent. He could taste it on his tongue. He wanted to taste her in his mouth.

Beyond the press of fog, the moon was full and strong, sending power through his flesh, making his bones hum. Closer. She was closer now. His fur stood on end. She was with a man. He could scent him. Man mixed with wolf. Lycan. The human voice inside him screamed in rage, and he howled in response. The lycan could not have her.

Chapter Thirteen

Though they hadn't an invitation, no one tried to stop Daisy and Northrup from entering the Baroness's garden party. Indeed, many gave Northrup a diffident smile or nod of the head. Daisy ought not be surprised; he was a marquis after all. Only the man she'd come to know was not some lofty peer, sneering down his nose at her, but irreverent and playful. He was simply Northrup.

They reached the terrace that led to the wide lawn and Daisy halted. Hundreds of white paper lanterns hung from the trees to twinkle with a soft, ephemeral glow. Ladies in satin gowns darted to and fro like colorful butterflies as they mingled, their laughter light and correct, never full and bawdy.

Daisy tensed. Why hadn't she thought this task through? To face these people once again, in front of Northrup no less, was too much. Northrup headed down the steps, but seeing that she didn't follow, he stopped short. He studied her in silence, his expression showing nothing of what he might be thinking, which Daisy appreciated as she rather thought it might be pity; she knew her face mirrored her trepidation. Irritation washed through her. Barbed words might cut her, but she'd bleed on the inside. Never again would they see the damage they wrought upon her.

Daisy took a step and came alongside of Northrup. His warm breath touched her as he leaned in. "Good. Do not fear their censure." A soft touch skimmed the edge of her upper arm. "I have seen generations grow from babes and then be put into the grave. And their words all lost to time."

He was trying to comfort her, she knew, and yet when she glanced at his clean profile, so youthful and strong, she felt an ache for him. How could she fret over trivial things when he would be forever unchanging and alone as time ebbed and flowed past him? Daisy rested her hand on his forearm and gave it a small squeeze.

He placed his hand over hers and guided her through the throngs of people milling about the wide lawn. "If I remember correctly," he murmured at her ear, causing unwanted little shivers to dance down her spine, "Randal is a lad of about twenty and two, curly-haired and distressingly cherubic in appearance."

Daisy's lips twitched, and she wondered how any person could maintain an ill humor when in Northrup's presence. "Distressingly? Really, Northrup, I cannot see what could be distressing about a cherub."

His brows drew in a scowl. "They're baby angels, for God's sake."

As if this explained all. It mattered not. Jesting with Northrup made her feel right. The sensation was like that first true breath she took after removing her corset for the night, yet she felt a qualm of unease. Men were sources of amusement or pain, not comfort.

"The weather is turning," Northrup said as they glanced about the crowds. Indeed, a thick fog was rolling in, as if cast out of London to haunt the bucolic peace of Highgate. With the fog came a chill that cut to the bone and made one's insides quiver. "Perhaps they've gone inside the tent."

Once inside the massive garden tent, they separated. Daisy searched the packed crowd for a cherubic-faced youth and his young fiancée, Annika. It was warmer here, the glittering light of two massive crystal chandeliers and the press of bodies heating the air.

Daisy had gone but a few steps when a nasal voice stopped her.

"Why, Jeffery, I do believe it is Mrs. Craigmore."

"I believe you are correct, dearest. Though I would not have expected to find her here."

"Here," the tone of his voice implied, indicating a place of quality.

Grinding her teeth, Daisy turned to face the proper Mr. and Mrs. Bean, once good friends to Craigmore. The older couple lifted their thin brows in unison as if daring her to speak.

"Jane and Jeffery," she said with a false smile. "How good to see you."

As expected, Mrs. Bean's thin mouth wrinkled at Daisy's irreverent familiarity, and she sniffed as if smelling something foul. "I am surprised that you ventured out so soon." Her eyes went to Daisy's deep-green dress, or rather, to the low cut of the bodice and the abundant display of Daisy's breasts. "Lovely gown, my dear."

A hit. Very palpable. Yet predictable. Daisy's bosom would never be demure. Nor would she try to hide it. To wear an ill-cut gown would be a sin. She smiled again, taking a breath deep enough to make their eyes widen. But her smile felt pained, and her skin as brittle as ice crusted over deep snow. She didn't belong here. She didn't belong anywhere or with anyone. For a moment, the pain of such loneliness made her want to sob. It took effort to parry. "Thank you," she said airily. "One tries to keep up with fashion, not be a slave to it."

She paused as she took in Mrs. Bean's monstrously ugly evening bonnet. "What a wonderful bonnet. That quail looks as though it shall take flight at any moment." And perhaps be shot down by hunters.

Mrs. Bean's eyes narrowed. "It is a dove."

"Oh?" Daisy peered closer. "Yes, it is. My mistake. I'm rather dismal at categorizing fowl. Even when it is right before me."

Unfortunately, Mrs. Bean was quite comfortable with social blood sport and refused to back down. "I see you arrived with Lord Northrup. Quite a big fish to catch." The long nostrils on her aquiline nose flared as she let her eyes travel once more over Daisy, inspecting and dismissing in one swoop. "Though I fear the bait might be lacking."

Northrup's scent touched Daisy a moment before his warm hand landed on the center of her back. "Ah, now, Mrs. Bean," he said over Daisy's shoulder, "surely you can do better than that." He smiled with teeth. "For example, there are times when a simple 'bugger off' works quite well."

Daisy's shocked gasp was lost among the Beans'. Northrup didn't wait for a reply but spun Daisy away from the couple. "That was fun," he said.

Daisy gaped up at him. "You really don't care, do you?"

"About those fools? No."

She laughed despite herself. "Good lord, but their faces." She pressed a knuckle against her mouth to contain her mirth. "I've never seen such outraged shock."

The corners of his eyes crinkled, but his grin faded into something softer. "You look beautiful when you laugh, Daisy. I should like to see you do so more often." Before she could answer, he leaned in close and his tone became serious. "We have a problem."

Quickly, he ushered her over to a young man who stood alone at the edge of the tent. Northrup's assessment of a cherubic appearance had been correct. The man's eyes widened when they approached him. "I cannot find Annika anywhere," the youth said without preamble.

"Mr. Randal, I presume?" Daisy asked.

He gave her a quick nod. "Madam." Randal turned back to Northrup. "Explain this to me again, sir. You believe that the London killer we've all been reading about is going after ladies who are wearing Annika's perfume? How do you know this?" The tips of the lad's ears turned deep red. Likely he did not want to discuss where he had purchased the perfume.

"He has already attacked Mrs. Craigmore." Northrup inclined his head toward Daisy. "And two others who have worn the scent. It is imperative that we get her to safety."

The young man's frown deepened as he scanned the crowd. "She can't have gone far. I saw her only moments before you found me."

The cold air seemed to pluck at Daisy's spine as she too looked about. "What color is she wearing?"

Randal straightened. "Pink. Pale pink." His gaze darted between Daisy and Northrup. "Surely there is no harm in Annika wearing the perfume here? Where there are so many people about?"

A soft breeze swam over the lawn to play with Randal's dark curls. For a moment, he appeared just a boy. Daisy's unease increased.

"You have no notion as to what this killer will do," Northrup said. He glanced at Daisy. "Perhaps check the house?"

The crystal chandelier inside the tent tinkled faintly as the breeze shifted toward them and Daisy caught the pungent smell of wolf. She turned to Northrup but his expression had gone blank. His nostrils flared, and the look in his light eyes grew deadly. Without a word, he sprinted toward the shadowed part of the lawn where no one had bothered to tread.

"What the deuce," exclaimed Randal as Northrup's lean form disappeared into the dark, and a stifled scream cut the night.

Daisy did not think but simply ran straight toward the sound. She reached the hedge line and halted as she saw the pale length of a pink satin skirt. She blinked at it before a rough shove sent her tumbling as Randal barreled past.

"Annika!" the young man screamed, his face white in the moonlight. He stumbled past the garden border to where she lay and gathered up her limp form. "Annika!"

Behind them, the garden full of people hushed upon hearing the commotion. Daisy's heart felt hard and cold within her chest, but her gaze moved from the couple to the greenery where a few branches swayed with undue force, as if something had just slipped past them. Northrup was nowhere to be seen.

Chapter Fourteen

Northrup was gone. But the girl needed help. Daisy stepped closer and licked her dry lips. "Is she…?"

The girl moaned and her fiancé touched her face with a trembling hand. "Anni," he whispered. "Dearest, what happened?"

Annika burrowed her face deep into Randal's coat and trembled. Her words came out muffled and halting. "Thing. Grabbed me. He was on me…" She shuddered violently and shook her head as if she could speak no more.

A sigh of relief left Daisy upon seeing the girl unharmed, and she sank back as a mass of humanity surged forward to see the spectacle. Someone elbowed her roughly, and another pushed her to the side. Angry voices tangled one over the other, rising high in an effort to be heard. Daisy drifted back from the gathering crowd and the heartbreaking sound of Annika sobbing. Daisy clenched her cold arms and wished for Northrup to be here. Only he was chasing after a werewolf. God help him.

Questions rang out in the night air.

"What happened?"

"Did anyone see?"

"The poor girl. I hear someone molested her..."

Jonathan Randal's cut through the babble. "...Lord Northrup..." Daisy edged farther away, walking backward as more people pushed forward. "...said a killer was after Annika..."

"Northrup?" a man said sharply. "Wasn't he there when the first attack occurred?"

The crowd grumbled in mass, heads swiveling around to look for Northrup.

Fingers of dread crawled down Daisy's spine. They'd blame Northrup. And her. She quickened her pace, keeping her eyes on the crowd as a man with an awful walrus mustache surveyed the grounds.

"Don't see him..." His voice drifted and swelled as more people began to protest and Annika started to sob once more.

"...was with a woman. Blonde, I think..."

"It was Mrs. Craigmore. Horrid woman." That from Mrs. Bean.

Daisy turned and slipped into the shadows that flanked the house. Keeping her head down, she ignored the way her blood pumped and she walked with steady purpose around the side of Holly Lodge and to the gravel drive where the carriages were kept. They'd find her. Any minute, they'd come for her. And what could she say? *No, sirs, it wasn't Northrup who attacked those people, but a werewolf.* She almost laughed.

She did not give the young groom time to question her, but simply took the reins of Northrup's cabriolet and gave a prayer of thanks that driving a coach was one mannish skill her father taught her how to do well. Cool air slapped at her heated cheeks as the horse pulled away. Her insides were so tight she feared she might be ill. She didn't even know where to go. The idea of leaving Northrup behind went against every instinct she had, and yet she was alone and vulnerable. She needed to find help.

Moonlight shrouded the country lane in misty blues and wavered in watery patches where it peeked through the towering trees. The skin along her neck prickled and dampened with perspiration. As the cab rounded a bend, she saw the large branch lying across the road. Daisy cursed loudly and pulled up on the reins.

God. God. God. It was a chant that went in time with Daisy's pounding heart as she jumped down and, with coach lamp in hand, went to see if she could move the tree branch. Her rapid steps crunched along the gravel, the wind moaning just enough to unnerve. Where was Northrup? Had he caught the werewolf? Was he hurt? She took a deep breath and then tried to move the blasted branch. It did not budge. Tears of frustration prickled against her lids, and she blinked rapidly.

Behind her, the horse nickered and tossed its head. She eased over to the animal, but the poor thing was overwrought and pranced, rocking the carriage back and forth as it shied away from Daisy.

"Easy now," she murmured to little effect. If anything, the horse's agitation grew. Its harness clamored as the horse reared back and then stamped the ground. Daisy stepped back, not wanting a personal meeting with those slashing hooves.

"Can't we come to some sort of agreement?" she whispered to the horse when a long, vibrating howl rent the night air. Until that moment, Daisy hadn't understood the term "bloodcurdling." She did now and shivered so hard that her teeth rattled. The horse was similarly affected and made a squealing sound, and then bolted. Daisy dove to the side just as the horse and carriage thundered past. Damn if it didn't bounce right over the tree limb.

Wide-eyed, Daisy watched as the blasted animal and her last hope of salvation faded into the night. Fog swirled about her like a phantom as the trees overhead rustled and sighed.

"Bloody, buggering..." Her words faded as another howl rang out. Daisy's stomach turned over, and she swallowed convulsively.

She needed shelter. A place to hide. She grabbed the coach lantern, her hand cold yet slick with sweat, and began to run. Before her loomed the high, gothic edifice of Highgate Cemetery's west gate. Daisy's fingers almost lost their purchase on the lantern, and she held it tighter. Forlorn and shadowed in the gloom of night, the gate might as well have been the doorway to hell. And she was going into it.

Ian flew past the shrubs and into the woods. Leaves and branches slapped at his face and obscured his vision. The *were's* scent, tinged with sickness, hung heavy in the air. And when Ian wove past a copse of trees, he saw the beast, its back humped and its fur molted and indigo in the moonlight. Rage fueled Ian's speed and made his blood boil. His wolf snapped against his bones, wanting out. *Mine. My territory. My prize.*

Bloody hell, but the beast was fast. It was nearly out of sight now, using its four legs and greater agility to leap over downed tree trunks and large bushes. A thick trunk lay in the *were's* path, and the thing simply smashed it to splinters with a swipe of its claws.

Hell, Ian ought to be running the other way. One lycan against a werewolf was suicide. The intelligent part of his mind was shouting at him to stop and get help like a sensible chap. The other part thought of what it had done to those poor women, and Ian saw red.

The bastard howled long and wild and then picked up speed, doubling back. It was circling around. Toward Daisy. Ian growled. He would tear its throat out. His boots dashed over hard-packed earth, and his senses heightened as they hadn't in years. This was a chase, not a mundane run. To chase, to hunt, this his wolf understood, craved. His body swelled in size, the wolf pushing to the fore, giving him a burst of strength. It was both a thrill and a warning. Control. Keep control. Get the *were*. Save the women.

Ice filled his veins because he feared he hadn't a chance.

Chapter Fifteen

The lantern in Daisy's hand gave off a sickly yellow glow, not showing the way so much as highlighting her vulnerability. She longed to toss it away, yet feared losing her last link with civilization. The air here was ice cold and damp, as if a breath from the beyond. Trees tilted drunkenly, their gnarled branches leaden with tendrils of ivy that seemed to reach out with long fingers in the faint breeze. Nearly lost amid the ferns and overgrowth were the carved shapes of cherubs and angels resting atop headstones. Little white faces watched her hurry past.

There was a presence here, as sure and definite as a cruel hand pressing down upon Daisy's neck. She could not falter. Even now, she could hear howls and snarls growing louder. Her sides pinched and her thighs burned as she ran into the mouth of a twisting path. She could *feel* that thing coming for her, as if it knew precisely where she was. Her stride faltered.

God in heaven. It was her scent. Her blasted scent

leading the wolf right to her. Daisy looked around wildly. Her mind racing.

She plunked down the lantern and grabbed handfuls of dirt, soft and loamy. The earth smeared with ease over her cheeks and along her arms. The fragrance of it musty yet oddly appealing to her in a way she didn't understand. Please let it be enough.

Northrup. Find me. Be safe.

A loud crash broke the silence. Something slamming into the west gate. Daisy's heart clenched in fear. The beast still scented her. Daisy slammed her hand against her thigh and felt the hard lump within her dress pocket.

Daisy turned out the lantern and then promptly smashed it against a tree. The acrid stink of lamp oil burned her nostrils. Would it be enough to overwhelm the wolf's more sensitive senses? Her hand shook as she wrenched the bottle of verbena essence out of her pocket and ripped off the stopper. The sharp scent filled the air as she splashed it about, before tossing the bottle far. She'd mourn the loss of it if she lived.

She moved to go but stopped. The leaves around her had rustled, a soft sigh that...spoke to her. Everything within her went tight and quiet. Through the thuds of her heart, she heard it again.

Turn to us. We will protect you.

Her gaze darted to and fro, taking in the crumbling headstones and rich greenery. No one was there. She willed her feet to move. She needed to move! Yet she found herself sinking to the earth. *Stop! Rise!* Gritting her teeth, she tried to rise. Instead, her hands sank into the loam. Disgusting. Yet...

A surge of power went through her, tightening her nipples, making her breath quicken. Whispers filled her ears, not human but a chorus, as if the plants around her had a voice.

Yes. Listen. See.

Before her eyes, thick vines, ferns, and clusters of honeysuckle began to rise and cover the path. Her breath caught and held, the air about her growing heady with lush fragrance. The forest was swallowing her up! Ye gods, she was being haunted. Her vision swam, but when she tried to let go of the earth, it wouldn't let her. Not until a veritable wall of flora had grown. Then suddenly she was free and tumbling back on her bottom.

In a daze, she gazed up at the plush growth. A haunted place, to be sure. Another howl, followed by a high yelp, prompted her to move. Jumping to her feet, she lifted her skirts and ran.

Her lungs were nearly bursting as she flew down a set of stairs and rushed headlong through a gate flanked by two sets of Egyptian columns. High walls formed a curving passage with tombs on both sides, doorways to the wealthy's eternal rest. Behind her came the sound of fighting, snarls, snapping teeth, and a man's scream of pain. Northrup? Daisy almost turned back. Sobbing, she pushed on until she spied a door that did not possess a lock.

Cold wood bruised her shoulder as she slammed into the door. It swung open with a gasp of moldering air. Inside, the darkness was complete. The thick smell of mold, bones, and decay was oppressive. She fell and landed with a thud that rattled her teeth. Beneath her, the floor felt gritty and uneven. Something sharp poked at her thigh. Daisy tried not to think of bones, or of haunted cemeteries that made the trees grow with unnatural speed. Later. Later she would be frightened. Her boots pressed hard against the door as if that could keep it closed. What folly.

* * *

Daisy's scent was a trail in the air. Like a wavering silk scarf beckoning toward Highgate Cemetery. Ian prayed that she'd stayed in the relative safety of Holly Lodge, but he knew his nose wasn't wrong. She was out in the open. Vulnerable.

The *were* slammed into the high iron gates, his movements clumsy in his need to reach his prey. Ian tackled the beast. They tumbled into the cemetery in a whirlwind of claws and teeth.

Rage. Pain. Ian felt himself slip under. Claws lengthened. His jaw snapped and popped as it grew. *Red.* He saw it. Felt it as he sliced at the furry body beneath him. The beast got its hind legs under Ian. In an instant, Ian was hurled back, crashing through the trunk of a tree with bone-shattering force before landing with a spray of earth.

Blood poured from his broken nose. He couldn't smell a thing, only taste the rich, sharp flavor of his own blood. Maddened, he sprang up, catching the *were* by its tail before it could escape. With a roar, he swung it round and into a Grecian tomb. Mortar and old bone exploded outward. The *were* yelped high and pained as it landed in a tumble.

Ian heaved a breath but then the beast rose on its back paws. And looked directly at him. The hairs along Ian's arms lifted and a queer slide of foreboding went through him. Oddly, his inner wolf howled for him to stop and not fight this beast. But it was too late to run. The yellow stare was utterly insane and filled with only one objective: death.

"Bloody hell," Ian whispered before the *were* charged.

Chapter Sixteen

Kill the lycan. It roared through the wolf's head as he charged. His teeth sank deep into the lycan's shoulder and the lycan screamed. The sound speared the wolf's brain, scattering shards of pain. He looked down at his prey, and his blood stilled. That face. Panic surged, choking and hot. He knew this face, this lycan man. No, no, no! His lungs seized. Memories threatened to drown him.

He lashed out, his claws hitting the lycan's face to obliterate it, make him die. Blood splattered. But the lycan did not die as humans did. Instead, he snarled, his own wolf coming to the fore, his human body growing, twisting, and bending, bones popping, changing, fur growing thick upon smooth skin.

The wolf remembered how it felt to turn from man to beast. Agony and dread. The thought confused him and made him slow when he should be quick.

The lycan used the advantage and sank his claws deep into the wolf's belly and wrenched it open. Pain and more pain. The wolf howled and scrambled back. He did not want any more pain. He wanted her. He needed her. But her scent was gone, replaced by the burning stench of human lamp oil and verbena.

The lycan rose over him, now more wolf than man, jaw elongating into a snout, his hands deformed by six-inch claws. Lycan bastard. *He* did this. He took the wolf's woman. And he would die. The wolf lunged, his teeth bared to rip out the lycan's exposed throat, when something stabbed his side. Darts. He knew them and feared them. Howling, the wolf fell hard upon the ground.

Strength gone and gasping for air, the wolf saw the lycan's body jerk as he too felt the force of the poisoned darts. The lycan tumbled to his knees and then landed dead away on the cold earth.

Sight fading, and his body going numb, the wolf heard the man walk out of the wood, his voice familiar and maddening. His captor. "Ah, laddie, why must you insist on defying me?" A pair of boots stopped before the lycan lying on the ground. "Well, well, what do we have here? Ian Ranulf comes to the rescue." *Ranulf.* He knew that name. The answer came to him just before the hard kick of his captor's boot knocked the wolf senseless.

Minutes passed. Or had it been hours? Daisy's rattled mind couldn't distinguish the difference. Her body tingled from the strain of keeping still. The sound of her own disjointed breathing filled her ears. Ink-black colored her field of vision. Maddening, when she wanted more than anything to see, and to know what was happening.

Nothing stirred. Bloody hell, a quick death would be better than this. Sharp prickles broke out over her limbs as she rose. Heart pounding like an anvil in her breast, she eased the door open and cringed as it creaked in the silence. Moonlight poured down through the trees, dappling the ground in celadon and silver.

The pins-and-needles sensation returned as she carefully looked outside. Dizziness threatened, and she realized she'd stopped breathing. Daisy sucked in a deep, much needed breath. All was quiet.

Just beyond the archway to the tombs was a familiar figure bathed in the ghostly rays of the full moon. He knelt on hands and knees, his broad shoulders shaking as though he'd taken a mortal chill. The expanse of his rib cage rose and fell in rapid succession. His shirt and trousers were shredded and blotchy with stains that she feared were blood. She approached him cautiously, for there was something about his state that had the hairs on the nape of her neck lifting.

"Northrup?" she whispered.

He did not answer but continued to pant with unnatural speed. When her skirts brushed against the tips of his boots, he made a sound that was unnervingly like a growl. He whipped around to look at her, and ice crawled down her spine. His irises, shining an unholy blue, filled his eyes until there was not a hint of white. The look of it was so animalistic that she felt a prey's urge to flee.

His lips curled back in a snarl. "Get. Away."

Drying blood crusted his upper lip as though his nose had bled. Crimson rivulets of blood ran from the edges of his mouth, and she realized with a horrified gasp that he was biting his lips.

"Dear God, Northrup—"

"Now!" His shout echoed against the walls, and she jumped.

But he was hurt. She could not simply walk away. "Let me—"

He was on her in a heartbeat, knocking into her and pressing her against the cold ground with his hard body. She cried out, and he swallowed the sound with his mouth. Daisy tasted his blood, hot and metallic, felt the slickness of it on her lips. It was Northrup, and not. And she felt the strange push-pull of wanting and revulsion.

His movements were rough, uncoordinated, and uncontrolled. He growled again and thrust himself against her in a clumsy move. Hard hands groped her. Fear and humiliation rushed like the tide through her veins. Held down. Forced. Shamed. Her hand wrenched free, and she struck him. Hard. Once. Twice. The slaps cracked through the air, knocking his head aside from the force, and left her hand aching.

On a shout, he rolled away from her, and she scrambled back, her feet tangling in her skirts as she fought for purchase.

Northrup lay in a heap, his shoulders shaking slightly. Daisy could only stare. Her lips throbbed. The feel of his touch did not abate but burned with a low flare that made her stomach pitch.

Slowly, he raised his head. His eyes, when they met hers, were desolate and utterly human once more. His gaze landed on her mouth, and he squeezed his eyes shut. "Oh, God, Daisy. I did not mean..." He broke off, breathing hard.

Daisy wiped her mouth with the back of her hand and cringed when it came away bloody. Not her blood, but his. She did not know what to say. He had warned her. She hadn't heeded. He was not Craigmore. Not that brand of evil. She knew this. Yet her heart was still going like a snare drum within her breast.

"Did I hurt you?" It was a stark question that echoed against the tombs.

"No." She curled her legs close to her chest. "No, I'm all right."

"I did." He swallowed with visible effort. "I hurt you."

She couldn't look at him. "Let it go, Northrup." Her voice wavered. "Please."

He nodded sharply and then stood with the slowness of an old man. There was only a slight tremor in his hand as he extended it to her, asking for her permission in assisting her to rise.

Daisy stared at his hand, broad of palm and long fingered. No claws now. She knew that hand to be warm and strong. Not Craigmore.

Even so, her head shook. "No."

When he frowned, she made herself speak again. "I just..." She shook her head again.

Northrup's expression went blank, and his fingers curled into a fist before his hand dropped away.

Daisy eased to her feet alone.

Chapter Seventeen

Alone in a room that was not her own, and tucked into a bed that was not her own, Daisy stared up at the half-tester curtains that hovered overhead. Her head ached. Indeed, the whole of her body ached. Which, she reflected wryly, was not a surprise given how she'd spent the evening. Northrup sat on the other side of her door. He'd crept up silently, but Daisy was well-versed in listening for footsteps outside her door. Craigmore never sought her out for sexual attentions, but there were far worse attentions he often wanted to inflict upon her. She had quickly learned to lock her doors and keep her senses sharp.

The thick down counterpane rustled as she turned onto her side. She stared at the door, which was little more than a hazy gray rectangle in the predawn hours. A terrible awkwardness now lay between her and Northrup.

"This is your home," she had said earlier when she realized that the hack Northrup had hired was turning into an unfamiliar drive. The townhome before her was far grander than her own, with high wrought-iron gates that all but cried out *Keep out*.

Sitting in the seat across from her, he had flicked a glance her way, the first in the long and tense drive back from Highgate. "Yes." His voice was devoid of its usual teasing lilt.

"You intend for me to stay here?" Though she had fussed about the arrangement earlier, after tonight, the thought of going home alone made her stomach clench. Only pride kept her from crawling into Northrup's lap and putting her head beneath his ruined coat. He might have acted like a beast in the graveyard but he was the beast she knew.

Mistaking her query, he'd looked away as if pained, and the light of the coach lamp set off his features in a sharp study of golds and brown. "I can't let you go," he whispered before clearing his throat and speaking with more strength. "Not yet."

In his hand, he twirled one of the long, wicked-looking darts that he had pulled out of his chest before they'd left the cemetery.

"What is that thing?" Daisy asked.

"Lycans use them to hunt down werewolves. The tips are poisoned with a drug that will weaken us." The twirling dart stilled between his fingers. "Use enough of them and we'll be knocked into oblivion, only to awaken confused and disoriented."

Daisy had sucked in a sharp breath. Confused and disoriented. *I am not myself.* Cold shame filled her, for Northrup had warned her to keep back. And she had ignored it to both of their detriment.

"Lycans did this to you? There are more of you around here then?" He gave her a speaking look, which made her feel foolish. "Precisely who are these lycans?"

Northrup hadn't met her eyes, but studied the dart. "They are the Clan Ranulf. My people." The scowl on his face grew fierce then. "Before I chose exile."

The thought of him in exile made her sad. She ought to not care, but Northrup was such a social being. To be cut off from his people must have hurt him, at least on some level. "Why did you leave?" she asked softly.

The glossy locks of his hair hid his expression, but his voice was low and clear. "Because I no longer wanted to be like them."

And what could she say to that? An uncomfortable silence filled the coach before she broke it. "Does this mean that your clan captured the werewolf? Is it over?"

Northrup had laughed then, short and humorless. "If it were over, they would not have shot me as well." He sighed and his blue eyes became as opaque as sea glass. "Instinct tells me that we are in more danger than ever."

"Why?" It was more of a plaintive cry than question.

Northrup's scowl returned but this time there was a bite to it, as if he'd gladly tear into a Ranulf clan member should one appear. "Because they now know I'm involved."

She'd been too tired and battered to say anything further then. Northrup had handed her off to the care of Tuttle as he stalked off with his valet, a young man whom he'd introduced as Jack Talent. Mr. Talent was a suspicious sort, who looked at her askance, as if waiting for her to do something foolish. She refused to be cowed by him, or hurt by Northrup's curt good-night.

Now, warm and clean after a hot bath, she lay cocooned in a bed he provided, as he stood guard outside her door. A sense of desolation filled her. The memory of his hands so rough and wild upon her made her stomach turn. Had that been Northrup, or the beast within him? Did it matter? Stretching her hand out toward the door, she drifted off to sleep, heartsick yet knowing that he would watch over her.

Chapter Eighteen

Spring had well and truly arrived in London. A soft breeze touched with warmth danced over the new green grass carpeting Hyde Park. Winston closed his eyes to the sensation and felt the sun upon his face. Rare indeed for him to feel the sun. The places his work usually took him were cramped, ugly tenements that light and fresh air forsook.

It was early yet, vendors having just arrived to claim the choice spots near well-trodden paths. Along the streets, drays rumbled past as milkmen and grocers made their deliveries for the day. Maids beat rugs in the small alleys between the grand houses, and here and there, boys swept up horse droppings and rubbish. The pampered gentry, however, were still tucked in their silk-lined beds, no doubt sleeping off their excessive, late-night revelry.

For all the glamour and comfort their world promised, Winston had never wanted to be part of it. A man was not his own keeper when he must kowtow to the mores of a society poised on the edge of their seats to see him fall. One mistake, and you were nothing. A sham. As if a man's worth could be quantified by etiquette. Hard work, the use of one's mind, that is what made a man's life worth measure. Such things gratified him more than the lure of being waited on hand and foot. He knew this with the certainty of a man who had lived on both sides of the velvet curtain.

He tipped his hat to a pretty young girl who loitered near a coffee stall. The smell of chicory and baking bread sent his stomach rumbling. Winston eyed the vendor making a show of cleaning a row of porcelain mugs.

"Top you off, sir?" The vendor lifted a basket top enticingly, releasing a cloud of steamy, scented air. "I've currant rolls fresh from the oven. 'Tis me wife's special recipe."

"Keep them warm for me," Winston said. For as much as he wanted one, work came first.

He turned the corner, and the grand mansion he wanted came into view. A colonnade in the classic Greek style fronted the mansion. Massive pillars of polished black marble ran along its length. At both ends, triumphal arches held up pediments of limestone carved with the crest of Ranulf and surrounded by a frieze of fearsome wolves.

It rankled Winston that he knew virtually nothing of this Lord Ranulf, who was listed as the Duke of Ranulf in Debrett's Peerage book, and apparently owned a great deal of Scotland. In all his years, Winston had never come across the man. When he'd asked his superiors for permission to speak to Ranulf, they'd been adamantly against the idea, almost fearfully. Ranulf, they warned, was an intensely private man and a favorite of the queen. He also happened to share a name with Ian Ranulf, Marquis of Northrup. Which might be a coincidence, given that every Scot whom Winston met seemed to be related to one another in some fashion. But Winston did not like coincidences and intended to call upon Northrup as soon as he could.

Winston's steps slowed as he spied a man walking down the front walk of Ranulf House.

The cut and cloth of his suit claimed the visitor as a gentleman. Indeed, the man walked with a bearing that spoke of pride and utter confidence. However, it was unfashionably early to pay a call, which had Winston on alert. As did the way the man watched the world about him, fierce eyes scanning the street for possible trouble as he walked.

They drew abreast of each other, and the man's cold eyes met Winston's. For all the fine attire and regal posture, this man did not look like an English aristocrat. For one thing, he was too dark, with nearly black eyes, thick black hair that curled at the temples, and olive-toned skin. The man's features were too boldly carved to be British. Deep-set eyes over a strong brow, a nose that would look too big were it not for his square jaw. An Italian, if Winston had to guess.

Winston took it all in a glance, as he was trained to do, and then lowered his eyes. The sunlight touched upon the man's wine silk waistcoat and his watch fob glinted bright, catching Winston's eye. It was a pretty piece of work, intricately wrought silver shaped into an angel perhaps. The man moved away before Winston could be sure, having only discerned the shape of outstretched wings and a woman's figure.

Something chilled Winston's gut. Defying basic manners, Winston turned to watch the man depart. An unexpected jolt hit him as he met those dark eyes once more. Caught out, he could only stare back as the man touched the brim of his hat before turning to stroll away.

The feeling of being judged, cataloged, and dismissed by the man, while ironic enough to warrant a smile, left Winston distinctly edgy instead. Shaking the feeling off, he made his way to the servants' entrance of Ranulf House and found a maid in the midst of descending the back stairs, probably hurrying to fetch coal from the chute.

"Good morning, miss," he said, making himself appear as harmless as he could under her wary gaze, "I am Inspector Lane of the Criminal Investigation Department."

Beneath the heavy fringe of her dark hair, her eyes went wide. He stepped in closer. "I need to ask a few questions to a parlor maid employed here. A Miss Lucy Montgomery."

"I'm sorry, sir." The young woman made a furtive curtsy. "But as I said before, Lucy don't work here anymore."

Winston paused in the process of pulling out his notebook. "What had she done to warrant dismissal?"

"Oh, no, sir, nothing like that. She's been let go on account of illness. I hear tell she's living with her brother now." The young lady frowned. "An' she wasn't a parlor maid. Not when she left, anyhow. She was personal nurse to one of Lord Ranulf's guests."

The telltale tinge of pink on the maid's cheeks and the way she avoided Winston's eyes set the cogs in his mind turning. So Miss Montgomery's rise from lowly maid to nurse had the servants talking.

"And do you know whom this guest might be?"

"Oh, no," she said. "We don't ask such questions."

So they were afraid of this Ranulf as well.

"At the risk of being indelicate, Miss...?"

"Lauren." She gave a quick curtsy.

"Miss Lauren, do you happen to know the nature of this illness?"

The maid's cheeks burned bright, and she glanced over her shoulder. But the yard was quiet and still.

"I shall be the soul of discretion," he promised.

"Well"—she nibbled her bottom lip—"Mrs. Armitage, the housekeeper, says it's consumption, but Hanna, the one maid let into his rooms, says he suffers from the French Pox. An' something terribly at that." A little shudder wracked her frame. "Him being twisted and crippled beyond recognition."

Syphilis. A lover's disease. Winston would bet his next week's pay that Miss Lucy Montgomery now suffered from the same illness.

The girl leaned closer. "In truth, sir, the staff has taken to wonderin' if he's even alive any longer."

"Why do you say that?"

"A few nights ago, just before Lord Ranulf returned from Scotland, a large state coach pulls up and they made to bundle the guest into it. So he could rusticate, says Mrs. Armitage and Mr. Timms, the butler. Only the fellow got into a rare state of rage. He tore out of the coach and ran off into the night. No one saw him return."

Winston handed the maid his card. "Give this to Mr. Timms. I shall talk to him and Mrs. Armitage now, if they have a moment." And if they didn't, he'd talk to them anyway.

The maid eyed the card as if it were poisoned. She licked her dry lips quickly. "Sir..." A noise from within the house made her jump and her breath shorten. When she spoke again, it was a rush of words. "They won't answer you. Not truthfully. It isn't allowed."

"Even to the CID?"

A sheen of perspiration was apparent on her brow. "Most especially to them." She glanced over her shoulder and tensed. "I've got to go now."

He wanted to push but knew it would be futile. But there was more than one way to skin a cat, as his superiors liked to say. He started to put his notebook back in his pocket but stilled, a cold realization washing over him as his mind played back what the maid had told him. "I'm sorry, but you say you've repeated this all before?"

"Aye." She nodded vigorously, her mobcap in danger of falling down. "To the gentleman who was just here." Her brown eyes narrowed. "Come to think on it, he said he was a Yard man as well." She shook her head as if pitying. "You fellows really ought to get your chores straight now, hadn't you?"

Chapter Nineteen

When the light of the sun crested over the sharp edges of London's horizon, Ian went down to breakfast. The slight quickening of Daisy's breathing told him she would soon wake, and he didn't want her to find him sitting outside of her door, guarding as he had done for the remainder of the night. Already, she was withdrawing from him. He did not blame her, but given the fact that a werewolf had nearly killed them both, he had to find a way to keep her with him. Blasted, hardheaded woman would probably fight him at every step.

Try as he might, he could not block out the memories of Daisy's eyes when he had come to his senses last night. On a groan, Ian sank his head into his hands and shuddered. Christ, he had lost control. He could not blame the drug entirely. He'd scented her fear. Mixed with the luscious perfume of her flesh, it had been irresistible.

"Jesus." He swallowed several times, fearing he would be ill. His hands were steady as he looked at them, but inside he shook. He'd seen his hands changing during his fight with the *were*. Too far. Nails had turned to claws, long and deadly, bones had distorted, fur taking over skin.

Control. It was a lycan's curse. All that inner power, and yet the constant struggle to keep the wolf in check. He had failed last night, too driven by rage over the werewolf and too desperate to touch what he should not.

Daisy. She'd looked at him as if he were a monster. And she would be right. In his youth, he had reveled in his wolf, drawing it out until they were nearly one. A deadly dance to be sure. Such power and wildness. Ian blinked down at his hands. The longer he remained in Daisy's presence, the more he felt.

Inside, his wolf whined, a placating sound, as if to remind Ian of what they once were and how good it felt to have that strength pushed to the limit. A helpless laugh left him. Aye, but he loved the beast, and that was the stink of it. Love and hate. Two sides of the same coin.

He caught her fragrance, warm, clean, and lush, just before he heard the slight swish of her skirts on the stairs. A ghost of a smile haunted his lips. She would never be able to catch him unaware. He had her scent now, as surely as if he owned it. The smile faltered when she entered the room, because while he might have her scent, he would never have *her*. Manners and honor demanded that he rise and greet her, and yet he could barely make his limbs obey. He did not want to see the disgust and fear in her eyes again.

"Good morning." His words sounded thick, as though filtered through water, and he fought for a lighter tone. "Would you care for breakfast?"

She hovered in the doorway, her eyes so weary that his heart grew leaden. He spoke to fill the awkward pause. "I have sent a man out to get your clothing." She was wearing the same gown she'd worn last night. Though tattered and dirty, it clung to her abundance in a loving embrace and shimmered as she moved.

She cleared her throat, a delicate yet awkward sound. "You needn't have bothered. It is easy enough for me to return home to change."

Ian knew he scowled. Bloody woman. Did she not realize there was no going back? Not anymore. Oddly, his frown seemed to buoy her. She took a good look at him and then strode forward as though determined to make the most of a bad situation.

Silence became a thick shroud as they sat opposite of each other and picked at their breakfast. Daisy helped herself to a piece of buttered toast. Neat, white teeth bit into it with a crisp sound.

God, it almost felt domestic, sharing a meal with her as if she were a proper wife. Save there was nothing proper about the way he felt watching that little pink tongue of hers sneak out to lick up an errant, buttery crumb resting on the corner of her mouth. He shifted in his chair, and she caught him looking. Frowning, she lowered the toast and stared at it as if she didn't quite recognize it.

Her voice was rough with regret when she started to speak. "Northrup—"

"I don't know how to apologize," he said. "Not in any way that can make things right. I can say that I wasn't myself, but it wouldn't be entirely true. That was me last night. A great part of me, at any rate." Shame rolled within him. "I try to control it, but the beast is always there, wanting out."

Daisy looked away, her fine brows knitting. Sunlight, pouring in from the tall windows, gilded her in tones of silver and gold, and he fought the urge to reach out and draw his fingertip down the small slope of her nose.

"At the very least, you know who you are." Her gaze returned to him. "There are days when I look in the mirror and don't even recognize myself. I've become merely shapes and colors. In truth, I hardly know who I am anymore, or if I was ever anyone at all."

I know who you are, he wanted to shout. *You are brave, funny. Fresh air in this smothered town. And utterly blind if you cannot see what I am.* Ian owed it to her to make it clear. "Then I envy you," he said. "For I've had lifetimes to learn each line and plane of my face, and I can't stand the sight of it."

Her lovely eyes creased at the corners as though his words hurt her. He could not account for it, nor the rawness in her voice when she asked, "Why?"

Ian wanted to look away, but he would not. Not with her. "I look like my father, before he was burned. I look like every lycan male in the Ranulf line. Every time I see this countenance, I remember what I really am. A monster." He made himself smile, laugh at himself as he always did. "A monster hiding behind a pretty face."

She did not smile with him. "You are not a monster."

"How can you say that?" His voice had gone raw, weak. "After what I've done?"

"And what have you done? Saved me? At great personal risk." Daisy spoke on. "You warned me to stay away. I did not listen."

When he began to protest, she shook her head slightly and the golden curls at her temples trembled. "I know who the true monsters are. They are ordinary men who do terrible things."

"What do you know of monsters, Daisy-Meg?" Who was it that terrorized her?

She looked at him with eyes wide and pained, and the

very air seemed to still about him. "Enough to know that you are not one of them."

The temptation to tell her everything was so strong that, for a moment, he could not breathe. Nobody knew him, not wholly, but in pieces that he rationed out like a miser. He reached for her, ready to let it all out, the pain and the loss, but she jerked as if she feared he might attack. It was a small movement, and one she might not even know she'd made. But he was too attuned to her to miss it.

The gesture hurt. More than he'd imagined it would. *You ruin everything, Ian. You and your beast.* Ian stood with an easy grace he did not feel. "Well, then," he said as best as he could manage. "I'll leave you to your breakfast." He strode out of the room without looking back.

Daisy stared at the empty doorway through which Northrup had just made his hasty exit. She had hurt him. She didn't know how or why, but she felt that tangible emotion roll off him as he quit the room. And it did not sit well with her.

"Blast," she muttered, and then went to find him.

He was in his library, sitting on the bench before the empty fireplace. He visibly tensed when she entered.

"Do you need something?" His voice was light, unaffected, but he didn't look at her. As good a sign as any of his distress, for Northrup always looked a person in the eye.

"Yes." She came farther into the room. "I want to know why you left me just now."

He made a sound of amusement. "Left you? How dramatic. I was simply finished with breakfast." Still he would not turn.

Slowly she walked toward him, noting the way his body seemed to twitch with every step she made. "Do you know," she said, "that I can tell when a person is lying?" She stopped. "It's quite a useful trick. Drove my sisters mad."

He frowned down at some invisible spot on the carpet. "Daisy... It was a long night. Now go on with you. I fear I am not of a mood to parry."

She ought to know better than ignore his request. Last night was proof of that. But this Northrup was not on the verge of violence. No, this was something darker. Closer to despair. She knew that emotion well. So she did not move away. "Tell me what I can do to help you."

Northrup's expression told no tales as he continued to sit in stubborn silence, with only the small rise and fall of his shoulders giving testament to his being made of flesh and blood, not stone. Daisy's heart constricted. Despite the insouciant facade he often presented to her, Northrup had a great capacity for caring. Likely, he'd laugh it off, should she remark upon it, but he could no longer fool her.

Clear morning light highlighted the tired lines around his eyes. The network of muscles along his back and shoulders were so tense that she could see them bulging beneath the excellent cut of his gray day coat. She moved closer, as cautious as one approaching a stray dog. The skin over his knuckles tightened, but he did not retreat from her.

His hands were finely made, elegant yet slightly rough, and so much larger than her own. She'd been held in comfort by those hands. And she'd been held down by them. The memory of his actions still brought forth a visceral clench of fear to her chest, strong enough that she'd flinched at his attempt to touch her a moment ago. Yet she had not lied to him; she knew the difference between men who hurt because they could and those who had made a mistake. She had made mistakes in her life. Not since she had lived with her sisters had anyone forgiven her for a blunder. She'd forgiven Northrup, but she had yet to show him. Daisy glanced down at the set expression on Northrup's face, and she knew she must bridge the gap between them now or it would grow wider.

The line of his jaw bunched as if to tell her he would simply wait her out until she moved off, and she almost smiled at his stubbornness. Her skirt billowed in a cloud of forest green as she knelt next to him.

When she raised her arms, he inhaled sharply and shied away. "What are you doing?"

"Taking off your cravat and collar."

From under the fan of his lashes, a painful mix of curiosity and uncertainty warred within the blue depths of his eyes. "Why?"

"You shall see."

He hesitated for a pulse beat and then lifted his chin to allow her access. Had she fully thought her actions through, she would have asked him to do the deed, for Daisy realized that she must kneel between his bent knees to reach him. Surrounded by the warmth of his body, her hands trembled as they went to his cravat. Touching him was unavoidable, and her knuckles grazed the sandy skin of his neck where his morning beard grew. For a moment, it seemed unbearably intimate, helping him as a wife might. Though he would not meet her eyes, his awareness of her betrayed him in the stiffness of his body and his light exhale with each tug of the cravat.

He was too close, his warm breath touching her cheeks. Were she to tilt her head just so, her mouth would be on his. And it would be good, so very good. She could taste him again, slowly, the way she yearned to, with deep explorations until they both became breathless. Heat radiated over her breasts and up her neck, and the tremor in her hands increased. She felt him swallow, edge just a bit closer. She merely had to look up, and it would happen. All of her concentration went to the tie in her hands. Her finger slipped and then the knot finally came undone. The silk hissed as she slid it free, and the tension radiating from him seemed to grow.

Setting the cravat and collar aside, she stood. "And your coat."

His head bent as he slipped it off and set it aside. Daisy moved on unsteady limbs to stand behind him, then cleared her throat. "When I was a girl, there were days when my father used to come home so weary." Though she spoke in a hushed whisper, the sound of her voice slashed through the dense silence. "Some nights, he would ask me to rub his shoulders." Swallowing hard, she set her hands lightly upon the warmth of Northrup's shoulders and felt them twitch. "Permit me?"

Rigidity gathered along his muscles, turning what once felt as sinewy as corded hemp rope into tight steel bands. He inhaled and held his breath for a moment and violent tremors rippled under her palms. Then he nodded, as though having lost the ability to speak. Anxiety gathered within her breast as she began to rub the unyielding muscles. Her thumbs dug into the small hollows on either side of his spine where large knots held reign. Northrup made a noise deep in his throat. She bit her lip as her fingers worked upward, slipping over the satin of his waistcoat. With a brush of her hands, his thick hair slid forward and exposed his neck. The thick column of muscles there tensed then softened under the hard push of her fingers.

Silently she worked, easing the pained stiffness from

his shoulders. Gradually, Northrup relaxed with small sighs of relief, mingled with little grunts of pain—and each of them eliciting a different sort of sweet pain within Daisy. It had been a bad idea to touch him. Her gown was too tight now, heavy and smothering against the heat radiating from her body. The desire to simply melt into him made her head light and her arms shake. Her pace faltered and then stopped, and her hands settled upon the hard caps of his shoulders as she struggled to gain purchase over her uneven breathing. She could no more move than he could speak.

A near-imperceptible shift skittered over him like a warning, or perhaps a promise. Gently, he took hold of her hand and brought it before him. The shuddering sound of her breath filled her ears as he slowly turned her palm upward and cradled it. Every nerve in her hand focused on the tip of his finger as he traced the various scrapes and cuts she'd gained during her struggles in the cemetery, a delicate and curious touch, like a scholar intent upon translating an ancient tome.

She nearly flinched when his silk-sand voice broke the silence. "Hear me, Daisy-girl. By my vow, on the grave of my father, Alasdair George Ranulf, and on the blood of Clan Ranulf that flows in my veins, I will never hurt you again." The warm puff of his breath heated her palm as he lifted her hand to his mouth. "I will keep you safe till this business be done. Or die trying. This I pledge to you."

He pressed a kiss into her palm's center, and her heart skipped a beat. Northrup groaned softly, his teeth scraping over the sensitive skin before his tongue slid out to lick her. With a gasp, she wilted against him, her breasts pressing against the hard line of his back. Soft lips skimmed along the length of her finger and her breath grew rapid, anticipation hammering against her throat. He paused at the tip for one agonizing moment and then drew her finger into his warm, wet mouth and sucked it.

"Oh, Christ..." Her free hand clutched his arm, the tense heat at her center tightening to near pain. His tongue enveloped her, pulling and sucking. And she uttered a muted cry. She could not think clearly, nor find the will to move away. Her head fell to the solid strength of his shoulder. On a smooth glide, Northrup released her finger and pressed her knuckles to his lips.

For a moment, they simply breathed, then Northrup's raw voice broke over her. "I cannot think."

She closed her eyes and concentrated on the cool feel of his shirt against her hot cheek. "Why?"

"My mind is filled."

Her free hand, heavy with languor, drifted along his arm and he trembled softly.

"With what?" she whispered.

"You. All the time. You." He sighed. "Daisy has taken up residence here." Yet it was to his heart he pressed her hand, to feel its pounding. "How to keep you safe. How to keep you out. How to keep... you."

His grip tightened a fraction. "It is madness. I want..." His breath hitched when she turned and pressed her lips against the back of his neck.

"What do you want?"

Before he could say a word, the hairs on the back of his neck bristled, and he eased away to rise. His voice was the beast's as he looked down at Daisy.

"Whatever may happen, do not run from them."

Chapter Twenty

There were four of them. Tall, well-dressed, and rather attractive men who entered the large front hall to face Northrup. The physical gracefulness in which they moved, and the slightly wild gleam in their eyes, mirrored Northrup's mannerisms in such a way that Daisy knew they must be like him. Lycan. She had no doubt that they'd sensed the very moment she'd snuck into the corridor to watch them. Daisy cursed herself for not staying in the library.

Northrup appeared calm, yet she did not miss the way his eyes took in their every move.

A ginger-haired man spoke up first. "We've come to take you to The Ranulf. Presently."

"A formal invitation," Northrup said. "I am all aflutter. Let us proceed." He moved to take his coat from his butler, who like all good servants appeared as if out of the ether with Northrup's hat and coat in hand.

The ginger man stepped into Northrup's space. "We'll be taking the lass as well." A pair of amber eyes focused on Daisy with stunning accuracy, and she sucked in a sharp breath. Damn.

The very air about Northrup seemed to shift and boil as his body tensed. Though he spoke calmly enough, no one in the room could have missed the steel behind his words. "She's not important."

"That is for The Ranulf to decide."

"The Ranulf does not rule my home."

The three other lycan men shifted their stance as Ginger slowly unfurled a predator's smile. "Thought you might say that." He scratched the back of his neck as he eyed Northrup. "Give you ten seconds to change your mind, you being MacRanulf an' such."

Northrup's teeth bared, gleaming white and alarmingly sharp. "Don't need it."

The fight happened with such speed that they were a blur of white shirts and the length of trouser-clad legs. Northrup used the momentum to his advantage and rolled one man over with a snarl that sent chills skittering down Daisy's back. In a flash, Northrup swung out, slashing at a dark-headed man. Crimson blood sprayed Northrup's face. That was all she saw before the moving mass of men converged on Northrup, and he disappeared beneath them.

She could not see what was happening but she could hear the sickening sounds of flesh being pounded and skin being torn. The floor swayed beneath her feet as the memory of that night in the alley came back. Flesh ripped open by long black claws, the metallic scent of blood soaking the air.

Daisy slumped against the doorway. She knew that smell, mixed with something wild and rangy. Wolf. Her muscles seized, her breath ratcheting as the urge to run consumed her. *Do not run from them.* He'd commanded it of her when they'd come. And she knew to the depths of her marrow that he'd been literal in the directive. She was not to run, or her life would be forfeit. Despite instinct, she trusted him more, even if the memory of death made her knees shake.

But Northrup was already up, his feet as light and quick as a pugilist's as he bobbed and weaved between three men. His coat was gone. Blood covered his exposed shoulder and flowed from a deep gash across his collarbone. The ginger man lay limp upon the floor, his head resting a few feet away from the body. Blood flowed from the stump of his neck and colored the white marble crimson. Daisy fought to keep from fainting.

Before her eyes, Northrup was changing. Fangs gleamed in a mouth that seemed wider, his jaw larger, while his eyes had shifted position in his face, tilting up at the corners and glowing. The men who attacked him had changed the same as he, with claw-tipped fingers and fang-filled mouths. Fear made her insides recoil, yet Northrup was beautiful in his savagery. Sinewy muscles, showing through the rents in his shirt, bunched as he lunged and took a man down with a punch to the jaw. Despite herself, Daisy felt a surge of something that felt unsettlingly like pride.

The feeling snapped abruptly as a large, rough hand curled around her neck and squeezed. Crying out, she struggled only to find herself wrenched against a hard body. Claws bit into her skin, deep enough to feel their sting.

"MacRanulf," shouted a coarse voice from behind her. "Shall I take her head then?"

Northrup drew up so quickly that the man he'd been

fighting fell flat on his face. Panting lightly from exertion, he glared at the man holding Daisy. Groans came from the floor as the men around him struggled to stand. One fiend grabbed his own jaw, which skewed oddly to the side, and wrenched it. A crack rang out as the joint snapped back into place.

The man holding her stepped slightly to the side, and Daisy caught a glimpse of him. Whipcord lean, he was only a few inches taller than she, but powerful. Blond hair curled about his head in angelic fashion. But his features were coarse and brutal. "I'm here ta fetch. So come like a good dog, eh?"

"Lyall." Northrup's lip curled, revealing bloodstained teeth. "Come over here and fetch me yourself."

Hot breath hit her cheek as Lyall laughed. "'Twas a good try, MacRanulf. But I think I'll be keeping hold of these sweet goods for now." He turned to regard Daisy. Amber eyes gleamed in interest. "Seems a shame to let loose such a luscious morsel before takin' a bite."

Northrup's hands curled into fists but he didn't move.

Lyall chuckled again. "As I thought. Come. Ranulf awaits."

Daisy did not expect to be taken to Mayfair. Nor to be taken there in a luxurious town coach with a strange coronet and the Ranulf coat of arms emblazoned upon its black lacquered doors.

She sat stiffly upon the crimson leather seat and tried to keep from catching Northrup's eye. It was clear he wanted no part in looking at her. He hadn't said a word since entering the coach and accepting the clean clothing Lyall had tossed to him with the order to "get dressed." Daisy had been rather proud that she hadn't gaped at the display, for Northrup's chest had been…stunning. There was no other word for the network of sinew and muscle that made up his arms and torso, the taut, smooth skin, or the way it all flowed in perfect harmony to his movements as he washed himself off with the wet rag they provided. He'd dressed quickly and proficiently. And never once looked her way.

They now sat at opposite sides of the coach, Northrup's gaze withdrawn and brooding. The man at his side sent leering glances at Daisy now and again. He had not been provided with a change of clothes but sat in a shredded shirt that was more red with blood than white. However, both he and Northrup had already started to heal, and what were once gashes now were little more than seeping cuts. As to the unfortunate fellow who had his head taken courtesy of Northrup, they'd left him where he lay upon the floor of Northrup's front hall.

The coach rounded onto Park Lane, and the grip on her arm tightened. Having enough, she shook her arm free and glared at the man called Lyall. "What do expect me to do?" she snapped. "Throw myself from a moving coach? I see no need to paw me to excess."

He uttered a short laugh. "We wolves like to paw. Lick and bite too. Or hasn't your lover shown you?"

She wouldn't look at Northrup to see his reaction. Instead, she shrugged and made a show of inspecting her nails, which unfortunately had gone quite ragged after last night. "If you know Northrup at all, you'll understand when I do not blush at your coarseness."

He grinned and let a finger run down her arm, making her skin crawl. "You like it coarse then?"

Perhaps she was the only one who saw Northrup's fist curl. She rather thought Lyall shouldn't see it so she leaned back against the squabs as though in complete comfort. "Baiting Northrup isn't working, and it is boring me."

He laughed again, but his nostrils flared, his amber irises growing slightly larger as he did. A shiver ran down her spine. She turned her gaze to the window. They'd come upon the grand residences that housed London's finest. Daisy worried her lower lip. Who was this Ranulf? And how was he tied to Northrup?

The coach stopped before the gates of a house so grand that she couldn't see it all at once.

"What is this place?" Daisy asked Northrup, to break the unbearable silence and, admittedly, to force him to look at her, damn him.

Azure eyes flicked to hers. His mouth was flat, the dark slashes of his brows drawn as if in annoyance over her presence. "Ranulf House."

"Ranulf? That is your name."

He didn't look at her but stared out of the window. "It was my father's house, long ago."

"Your father?" Daisy's fingers dug into her thighs as she leaned forward. "Tell me what is happening, Northrup."

He sighed, and she couldn't help but notice the lines of exhaustion that bracketed his mouth, or the gravel in his voice. "My father was The Ranulf, King of the Lycan Clan for Western Europe and Scandinavia."

A strangled sound escaped her. "But I thought he was the Earl of Rossberry."

"Those titles are our human ones. But here, among the lycans, I am simply Ian Ranulf or MacRanulf for formal occasions." A bitter smile pulled up his lips. "In truth, the title inheritances are a farce." He looked at her sidelong.

"One tends to question when a man doesn't age or expire. My father had been Northrup and I Rossberry since my birth in 1753."

She still could not wrap her thoughts around the fact that he was so old. Not when he exuded the physical beauty of a man in his prime.

"Viscount Mckinnon is a newer title," he said, not seeing her disquiet. "We would let the titles revolve between us, disappear for a number of years into Scotland, then return as a grandson, father, son, what have you."

"It's all quite the show, is it not?" said Lyall with a laugh.

Northrup ignored him. "My father's burns were going to be a problem, however. No getting around that sight. So eventually, I'd have played the part of Northrup anyway."

Daisy remembered the old Lord Rossberry. Scars had covered over seventy percent of his body, giving his skin the appearance of oak bark. She had never met him but heard that his temper had been mercurial, running from taciturn to violently rude. She couldn't say that she blamed him.

Heavy iron gates pulled back, and the coach drew inside.

"So then who is The Ranulf now?"

"Conall," he said. "My little brother."

Lyall snarled. "He is The Ranulf."

Northrup's straight brows tilted upward. "So we are often reminded."

Lyall bared his teeth, showing upper and lower fangs that had lengthened to long points. Daisy took a small, bracing breath, but Northrup merely reclined against the seat back as if he owned the coach and gave him a bland look.

"Any time you care to face me on sporting ground, Lyall," he said, "I'll be waiting."

The coach rocked forward and then came to a stop. Northrup did not wait for the footmen, but in a smooth motion he leaped from the coach to land lightly upon his feet outside. He allowed a mere moment to tug his cuffs down and then he strode toward the open doors. Never once looking back to see what became of her.

She was going to meet a king. Daisy refused to look down at her dress, lest she whimper. Men might call it a silly female whim but the proper outfit gave one strength and confidence. Her ruined, showy dress was not the ideal gown in which to greet royalty.

"There is something I don't understand," Daisy said to the man at her side.

Lyall sneered as if to say he wasn't surprised. She ignored the look. Her curiosity was too great to keep quiet, and Northrup was striding ten paces ahead. So she would have to ask Lyall, even if he was an ass.

"If Northrup is the elder brother, why is he not king?"

"Because he did not make a bid for the throne."

"Make a bid? I suppose Lycan society does not follow the same laws of succession?"

Lyall shrugged lightly. "More or less, but we live forever, aye? So a king might always hold the throne, which can be a problem if said king becomes lax or is no' a good ruler." Something dark flickered in his eyes. "At some point, every king must be challenged. Back in 1815, Ian's father, Alasdair, was king, but he suffered a great blow when the ice witch burned him alive. There are some wounds even a lycan does not come back from. He held the throne for a time, but it was clear he was no' in his right mind to keep leading.

"It was Ian's right as first born to take up the challenge and fight his father for the crown, but he was no' interested. So Conall stepped in and did what was right. He beat Alasdair soundly and took the throne."

Daisy's mouth fell open before she quickly shut it. "They were supposed to beat their father?"

He nodded. "Mayhap kill him, if it is a true fight for the crown. It is our way."

Daisy watched Northrup walk down a long corridor lined with exquisite white marble adorned with gold paint on the lintels. His shoulders were straight and proud, with not a sign of hesitation or fear showing. She felt a new appreciation for the man he was. "Perhaps Northrup was civilized and caring enough not to want to hurt his own father."

Lyall snorted at that. "It was no' a hostile coup. Alasdair was willing to step down. Damage sustained in such a fight is temporary, more a show of strength than a true beating. In truth, Alasdair was more hurt that the man to face him wasn't his firstborn and beloved son."

"You're very loyal to your king," she said. "Were you loyal to Alasdair as well?"

He made a sound of annoyance. "I am loyal to the Clan Ranulf, whoever may lead it."

"So then, were Northrup to become king?"

Lyall's mouth twisted. "I don't hold with cowards, lass. Were he a true alpha, he would have taken the throne."

Northrup's hand clenched, and Daisy knew he had heard. She turned her eyes back to Lyall. "Northrup may be many things, but he is not a coward. That much I know."

Chapter Twenty-one

An alpha, my boy, is not the beast with the greatest strength but with the greatest will. Know your mind, boy. Know it without hesitation or reservation and ye shall lead them.

Ian strode into the Great Hall of Clan Ranulf, and his father's long-ago words rang through his bones. Here, in this hallowed court, he felt the power and will of his ancestors. Designed to impress, the walls and floor were lined with onyx marble, creating a void of black in which only the golden throne at the end of the hall shone bright.

His father had sat there for clan business. His father had expected Ian to sit there one day too. Conall sat there now, his black eyes watchful as Ian drew near. Conall, the younger brother who used to dog his steps, pleading for a bit of Ian's attention. Ian had taught him to fight, tried to teach him the concept of justice. But he had failed at some point, for the reports Ian had heard from the refugee lycans that Lena sent to his home told a dark story of dominance, greed, and mismanagement.

Worse, if those tales were to be believed, Conall had also formed an alliance with the human gangs around inner-city London and now preyed on the weak and the poor.

Ian bit back a sneer of disgust as he stopped before the dais. Conall lounged upon the throne as if it were a bed, one long leg thrown over the armrest, his booted foot swinging an idle rhythm. Aye, his brother was strong, no doubt about it. Muscles dominated his frame, barely hidden beneath the modish clothes he wore. And he was without hesitation. But did he have the will? Ian would soon find out.

Do what is right. Take control of your clan.

His clan. The thought was smoke and seduction, whispering in his veins, creeping along his skin. He had lost everything because of his lycan heritage. And now his world had turned full circle.

Conall gave him a thin smile, his eyes calculating. "And so the prodigal son returns." His black gaze narrowed. "After running amok in Highgate, it seems."

Ian almost snorted. Is that what Conall would call it? And what of the *were* he'd captured? Ian wanted answers, but he had to be careful. Behind him came the scent of Daisy. He ignored it. It was too easy to lose control where she was concerned. Damn it all, he hated having his weakness so close at hand. Considering his options, he realized he'd have to taunt Conall just enough to show he did not care, but not enough to challenge him. Wonderful.

"Conall," he said by way of greeting.

His brother snarled. In an instant, he was before Ian, his hand wrapped about Ian's throat. "Pardon?"

Claws sank into Ian's neck. The faint sound of Daisy's muffled distress stayed his tongue. *Easy, lass.* Ian met his brother's eyes. "Ranulf," he corrected with false ease.

Sharp teeth flashed as Conall smiled. "Better." He let Ian go with a shake.

Ian stood steady.

Conall strolled about him, circling. "What are you doing mucking about in my territory, brother?"

Ian cut him a glance. Did Conall think he'd make excuses? "Looking for the mad werewolf, *brother*."

"Ah, yes, this mythical werewolf that none of my men have seen hide nor hair of."

Ian gave a humorless snort. "So then what was it you captured last night?"

Conall stopped. His dark brows lifted in an expression much like Ian's. "I captured nothing. Though I did hear that my brother has now been connected with two 'wild dog' attacks."

For a cold second, Ian couldn't answer. He hadn't expected Conall to deny having the *were*. It did not make sense. Worse, there was something in his brother's tone that gave him pause. They'd grown so far apart that Ian could no longer be sure if Conall was lying or not. And that concerned him greatly.

"Are you trying to tell me that I imagined fighting that *were* last night? Or the fact that your men took it down with Ranulf darts just moments before they tagged me?"

Conall laughed shortly. "I've no idea what you've imagined."

Ian reached into his trouser pocket. "Tell me then, did I imagine this?" He tossed the silver dart he'd kept onto the floor where it clattered against the black marble and then spun about in indolent fashion.

From the grumbling that erupted around the room, Ian knew the lycans all recognized the dart.

Conall stopped and turned on his heel. He glanced at it

before looking back at Ian. Not a shade of emotion on his brother's face. Ian had to commend him for that.

"What is it I am supposed to be seeing?" Conall said, still not bothering to look at the dart.

Ian smiled thinly. "Right. I'll play. That there, dear brother mine, is a Ranulf hunting dart. One of four that found its way into my chest last night," Ian snapped. "After the *were* that was attacking me received his fair share of darts."

"And yet, no clan members of mine were out hunting *weres* last night." Conall turned to Lyall. "Or am I mistaken?"

Amusement lit Lyall's expression. "No, Sire." His cold amber gaze settled on Ian for a moment. "Nor would a member of my guard take down MacRanulf without just cause."

Anger turned Ian's blood hot. Lyall, the bastard, would say anything Conall asked him too. Being a lycan, Lyall's age did not show, but he was older than all of them and had been beta to Ian's father. Back then, Lyall had been like an uncle to Ian, caring for him and his family in all ways. Until Ian had refused the throne. Then Lyall turned from him and swore loyalty only to Conall.

Conall strolled away from the dart. "D'ye care to call Lyall a liar then?"

Yes. "I've no wish to call him anything." *Other than a canny little lickspittle*.

If Conall and Lyall insisted on lying, there was nothing Ian could do about it. He yearned to shove the stickpin he'd found in Bethnal Green under Conall's nose and demand an explanation, but it would be tantamount to a challenge. So he glanced at the crowd of lycan assembled in court instead. Some were familiar; some were new.

All were richly dressed. Yet none of them had been seen among Ian's human familiars. What had gone on here? Had Conall isolated them so much from human society? It was a dangerous thing, for lycans needed human contact to stay sane. "Have ye all missed the stench of werewolf trailing all over our city?" Ian asked.

"My city," Conall said, a fair amount of warning coloring his words.

"Our city," Ian retorted. "Or is Ranulf no longer a clan?"

A shift went through the crowd, uneasiness tightening the air and tingeing it sour. These lycan were too used to subservience. Ian could see it in their stance, the way they looked to Conall not with respect but hesitation and fear.

"The question should be why ye care, brother." Conall came toe to toe with him, and Ian smelled blood on his breath. "You left the clan long ago. You're in no position to ask questions. That I gave you leave to even live in this city should have you bowing in gratitude."

"The werewolf's existence is a danger to every man, not just the clan," Ian said. "He needs to be put down before he exposes us and hurts others."

"There you go again with your speeches." Conall strolled around Ian. "A sorry way to get attention." Conall rubbed his jaw, and for a moment, he looked so like their father that Ian felt a stab of grief. "Which sets me wondering...given as you're the only lycan claiming to have seen this wolf, well, brother, perhaps you are the one doing these deeds."

Ian laughed. He could not contain it. "Do I look like a *were*?" Once a man shifted fully into a wolf, he was done for. It was the warning hammered into every lycan's brain from the time they were weaned.

"No," Conall admitted, holding the irritating, smug smile that had Ian itching to swipe it off. "But then one needn't be fully changed to inflict good damage, aye?" His dark eyes narrowed. "I hear ye took Alan's head with one swipe."

If Alan was the lycan lying dead in his front hall, then yes he had. And he'd do it again. The bastard had been poised to launch a killing blow on Ian.

Conall's claws tore free. One gleaming tip touched the corner of Ian's right eye, pushing in just enough to hurt. "After all, we have claws too, don't we?"

Ian stared at his brother. "Enough. Why do you persist in claiming there is no *were*? Bloody hell, man, the beast has attacked at least five humans. Will you disgrace your own throne—"

He saw Conall make the decision to move a second before he acted. The hit took Ian hard in the solar plexus. Ian doubled over, the urge to strike back setting his claws free. He'd been stupid to fall for Conall's baiting. Not with Daisy in the same room with him. So far, she'd stayed quiet. He'd kiss her for it later. But he would not make the mistake of thinking Conall wasn't aware of her.

"You do not question The Ranulf," Conall snarled. "You do as you are told."

Ian sucked in a hard breath. "I wasn't aware that you were telling me anything, Ranulf." *Christ, man, keep your mouth shut.*

Another blow caught him in the temple. He saw stars.

"Had enough?"

No, hit me again so I can rip your throat out. Ian bit his lip hard to keep his mouth shut and stayed bent over.

Conall's boots came to view. "Your talk comes close to sedition, Ian. Verra close." Conall leaned down to look

Ian in the eye, and his voice went soft with menace. "An' I'm fair aching to see you cross that line and have this business done with."

They stared at each other when a sweet feminine voice broke their stalemate. "I saw the beast."

Ian ground his teeth as he cursed six ways to Sunday.

All eyes turned to Daisy. "Ah, that is, I saw the beast, sir," she corrected.

Bloody woman. His claws punched free, at the ready, for no one was touching her. No one.

Daisy ought to have kept quiet, but seeing Conall lay his fists into Northrup had made her stomach turn and inflamed her sense of justice. The words tumbled out of her mouth before she could think better of doing so.

Dark eyes looked her over, and she found herself quailing.

"And who is this?" Conall asked.

"Mrs. Craigmore of Mayfair." Daisy inclined her head. She had no desire to offer her given name to this brute. "I was witness to the second killings." Damn. How did one address a lycan king? "Your Highness."

A lock of hair fell across the lycan leader's brow as he tilted his head and studied her. Northrup's brother did not wear his hair long. Did he not, then, officially mourn his father's death?

"Yet you survived?" He sounded dubious.

"By mere chance," she said. "But I saw the beast before I blacked out. His movements were odd, like a wolf's yet also like a man's."

A stir went through the crowd. Daisy hadn't known what to expect when she'd entered the court of the lycans. These people looked just like any other. But their scent was wild, calling to mind grasses and windswept meadows. They did not smell human. The notion made her shiver.

Northrup stood like a statue, not acknowledging her, but she saw the subtle flare of irritation in his eyes as he stared blindly forward. She felt another qualm of guilt. She hadn't meant to interfere.

Surprisingly, Conall's voice gentled. "And have you seen my brother and this werewolf at the same time?"

"Well..." Daisy paused. "No..."

The lycan king smiled pleasantly. "Then how do you know it is not he?"

"They do not have the same scent," she said without hesitation, but her heart was pounding. Did they all truly believe Northrup could do these deeds? She remembered the wild look in Ian's eyes just before he attacked her and she swallowed hard. It would be easy to place the blame upon his head. Perhaps that was what his brother had wanted all along. She didn't understand their ways and feared that she was in over her head.

Each step of Conall's booted feet sounded in the quiet of the hall. She clenched her hands as he came before her. His face was broader than Northrup's and not quite as refined. He had coal-black eyes, but they shared the same auburn hair color. He was a touch shorter than Northrup and a bit stockier. Certainly he did not possess the same air of natural grace that Northrup exuded. For all of that, it still unnerved Daisy to look into a face so like Northrup's, yet not.

Conall studied her with equal scrutiny. "What do you know of scents, little human?"

"Enough to know that Northrup doesn't smell like the beast that accosted me."

Conall waved an indolent hand. "I'm thinking you seek to protect your man."

"I am not!" She was. And from the gleam in his eyes, the lycan knew it.

"The sense of smell is a very powerful tool, I will give you that." His nostrils flared a bit as he drew in her scent. The very idea caused a ripple of disquiet along her skin, as if she were being considered for his evening meal. "She smells lovely," Conall said to Ian without taking his eyes from her. "Like spring flowers."

Northrup's expression was almost bored. "Aye."

Conall took a step closer to her, and Daisy caught the scent of him as well, of wet grass and turned earth. Not unpleasant, but nothing like the heady fragrance of Northrup. Conall's dark eyes roamed over Daisy. Frank appreciation flared in their depths.

"Delicious. Is she yours?" he asked Northrup as his gaze strayed to Daisy's bosom.

"No." The word was so flat and lifeless that she might have been a piece of misplaced furniture.

The heat of Conall's body warmed her arms, and Daisy swallowed down her urge to step back. His lilting voice, holding more of the Highlands than did his brother's, rumbled in her ear. "D'ye hear him, lass? For all your defense of him, he won't even claim you." He ran a callused thumb over her cheek, and she fought not to wrench her head away. "Does it no' shame you to discover that your man is a coward?"

Northrup stood tall and still in the middle of the court. She shouldn't speak. She knew it was stupid to do so, but seeing Northrup surrounded by jeering fools who used the strength of their numbers to intimidate made her blood boil. "Nothing about Northrup shames me."

If anything, her words irritated Northrup, for his jaw tensed.

A puff of air caressed her cheek as Conall laughed. “Fool girl. Too blind to know real power when she sees it.”

Her insides went liquid as his claw slowly dragged over her jaw, not hard enough to cut but to let her know how much it would hurt should he choose to. She held steady. “I know true power when I see it.”

He did not miss the scathing bite of her words. The claw stopped at her jugular and pressed just a bit harder. “Shall we test the theory?”

Daisy looked at Conall through lowered lashes and licked her lips in a show of nervousness, but it had the desired effect as his nostrils flared again. “I hardly believe you need to prove anything, Sire.”

He stared at her for a hard minute and then ran a finger slowly over the swell of her bodice as if considering what he might do with her.

Northrup’s voice broke the silence. “I spoke to Lena.”

Conall’s jaw clenched. “Did you now?” He turned away from Daisy, and her insides sagged with relief. “Turned errand boy for the frozen bitch, have you?”

Northrup’s mouth curled. “Perhaps I have.”

Conall’s hands went to his hips. “Out with it then.”

Northrup’s smile grew. “Oh, I think you can imagine what she might say, brother.”

The entire court seemed to buzz with nervous energy upon hearing of this mysterious Lena. Whoever she was, she held a position of power. Dozens of shining eyes turned to Conall, waiting, it appeared, to see what their king would do.

Suddenly, Conall snorted. “Keep your counsel, brother. It is inconsequential to me.”

Northrup's mouth kicked up at one corner. "I would expect not, brother."

Conall returned Northrup's look but his tone grew hard. "You will cease this talk of werewolves. And if I find you anywhere near another human death, I will take your head, Ian Ranulf."

Surprisingly, Ian bowed his head. "As you wish, Ranulf." He was too complacent, Daisy thought with trepidation.

Apparently his brother did not know, or consider, Northrup's more canny tendencies, for he made a sound of satisfaction. "Now that that is settled, there is one more bit of business before I'm done with ye." He turned back to Northrup. "Payment for Alan."

A ripple of excitement went through the hall, and Daisy's stomach clenched, for it held the taint of violence in it. Fangs lengthened, and the rangy scent of wolf grew deeper. All of it directed at Northrup.

Northrup didn't flinch. "Get on with it then."

"As you wish." Conall's black eyes found her, sending a chill of ice down her spine. "And let the lass watch."

Chapter Twenty-two

It was going to hurt. Hurt badly. Most men thought of torture in an abstract manner, never knowing precisely what they were in for. Ian knew. And although he'd like to think of himself as brave, a large part of him wanted to turn tail and run.

He took a breath and walked calmly out of Ranulf Hall and toward the open balcony doors. Flanked on both sides by members of the pack, he couldn't see Daisy, but he knew she was there. Her scent touched the air, an elusive tease that heightened his senses. He didn't want her to see and vowed that he would not beg, no matter how much he might want to.

Conall followed at a leisurely clip as the party moved down the terrace steps and onto the large expanse of parkland backing the house. "No trophies today, lads," he called out before slanting Ian a glance, and the crowd grumbled its disappointment. "Not this time."

Relief washed over Ian in a wave that dissipated too quickly. So he'd keep his appendages and eyes. They'd grow back eventually, but he was admittedly a vain man in regard to his appearance and didn't fancy the idea of walking around maimed, even for a short while. And hell, regrowing a limb hurt almost as much as the injury.

Shit. He started to shake as the pack stopped and surrounded him in a wide circle. Relax. Pain grew worse with tension.

Conall strolled to the center of the circle, keeping his back to Ian. "No trophies, aye, but pound for pound he'll feel the force of Ranulf. He took one of the pack"—Conall's black gaze scanned his subjects—"when he's no' willing to come into the fold as one of us." His eyes landed on Ian, cold and calculating. Conall knew nothing of true calculation, just brute force.

Two lieutenants drew near. One ripped off Ian's shirt and the other clamped irons around Ian's wrists and neck. The heavy silver-dipped chains, designed to weaken lycans, clanked as they fell to the ground before being pulled tight by the lycans in charge of keeping him tethered. But he wouldn't fight. This was as much his show as it was Conall's.

Wrists chained, he stood tall and looked around at the lycans who would mete out his punishment. Some he knew, old lieutenants of his father who wouldn't look him directly in the eye; others were younger and lusting for a bit of blood sport.

When Ian spoke, his voice rang strong and clear. "I accept the penalty for taking another lycan's life. For the law is clear." He turned his gaze to Conall and held it. "The leaders of Clan Ranulf have always upheld our laws. As is their right and privilege. For who else has the strength to protect the innocent? Or the bravery?" His voice rose on a wave of pride he didn't see coming, and his words came out a roar. "*Dei Dono Sum Quod Sum!*"

Around him, Ranulf's men raised their fists to the air and returned the cry, caught up as he was by their clan motto.

"Cease!" shouted Conall, his skin molting with rage.

Spittle flew from his lips as he stalked forward. "Will ye let this bastard play you the fool and distract you with his speeches? Hear your king and show what the true power of Clan Ranulf means!"

On a grumble, the lycan men settled down. They knew better than to ignore their alpha's command. Conall flashed a bit of fang at Ian as he spoke. "Teach him respect, lads. Claws and fangs!" With that chilling allowance, Ian's brother walked out of the circle and folded himself into the gilded chair a beta had set out for him.

Daisy stood next to the chair watching Ian, her skin ghostly white and her eyes wide with fear. *She shouldn't have to see this. It will scar her. I'm sorry, lass.*

It was the last thought he had before they came for him.

Northrup was letting them tear him apart. Daisy pressed a shaking hand to her mouth as lycan after lycan came forward to slash, bite, kick, or hit him. His body jerked with each attack, blood spraying and flesh ripping open. His face was now unrecognizable, his trousers hanging in crimson-soaked tatters.

Bile rose in her throat. It was too much. Too much like the night of her nightmares, too much pain for one man to endure. Her stomach contracted, and she swallowed hard, blinking back her tears, but she would not look away. If he had to endure, she would endure too. But why had he agreed to this? He might have run. Daisy ground her teeth as she realized that had he run, he would have had to leave her behind. The scene before her eyes blurred.

The warm morning air grew thick and fetid with the

stench of blood and sweat and the growing tang of aggression and excitement. There was a method to their torment. She could see that, but it was not going to last. The crowd swelled closer, the attacks becoming more brutish, one on top of the other. They'd soon break into a frenzy. She could feel it. The men had shifted at the start of the violence, their jaws elongating, mouths filling with fangs, their fingers lengthening, claws bursting from the tips. Despite herself, she pressed against the chair in which Northrup's treacherous brother lounged. She glanced at his strong profile and repressed the urge to do him violence.

"Don't like what you see?" Conall asked, not bothering to take his eyes from the carnage.

If she opened her mouth to speak, she would surely vomit. A particularly hulking lycan threw himself at Northrup, his blow opening a huge rent across Northrup's once magnificent torso. Northrup didn't make a noise as he doubled over and blood poured from his mouth. Daisy swayed. *Let it end. Let it end.*

"Perhaps I should have allowed them to take ears," Conall muttered.

"You sick, bloody bastard!"

The man lifted a slanting brow, an expression disturbingly similar to his brother's. "My parentage is secure," he said with a cold smile, "but I can appreciate the sentiment." He glanced at Northrup. "My brother thinks he knows me better than I him. He thinks he will not turn, that he'll take the beating, go free, and the clan will admire him for it." A disturbing chuckle rumbled from Conall's chest. "He knows nothing."

Conall stood and glanced at Lyall, who leaned against a nearby tree. "Lyall." Though Lyall was several feet away from them and Conall's voice did not lift beyond the level of normal conversation, Lyall stood straighter. "Finish him off when he strikes," Conall said to him. Lyall gave a short nod and pushed off from the tree.

"No!" Daisy hissed, turning on Conall. "No. You said a lesson, not death."

"Did I?" He shrugged. "I can't say as I recall those words."

She took a step toward him, fighting the need to hurt him. "Liar. You made him believe he would go free."

"Och, that's not so much a lie as a tactical maneuver, lass. I needed him weakened." His amused expression traveled over her before dimming. "Ah, but it is a shame that I'll have to be involving you. A fine bit of skirt, ye are at that." A look of true pity filled his dark eyes as he watched her. "Normally, I don't fancy hurting females. It isn't sporting." He frowned, but then it cleared. "Let us call this an unfortunate circumstance of necessity, eh?"

Daisy's heartbeat sped up as he stepped closer. Her answering step back had his nostrils flaring as though scenting a chase.

"I'll have him turned," Conall said with a jerk of his head toward Northrup, who was being kicked in the hip. Northrup's eyes were vacant, as if he'd moved his mind elsewhere. "And I well know his weakness."

A blow to her cheek sent her sprawling on the ground. Somewhere beyond the ringing in her ears, she heard a shout halfway between a roar and a snarl, but then a kick to her midriff took her breath. Crawling along the ground on wobbling limbs, her mouth worked in a wordless cry, her fingers digging into the cool earth.

Vaguely, she was aware of chaos breaking out around her. Lycans ran toward a commotion. *Ian.* She saw him in the corner of her eye. He'd risen to his feet and was straining against the chains, his eyes flashing fire. Blood streamed from his lips, thickening his words. "You will no' touch her."

Conall grabbed Daisy by the hair, and pain exploded along her scalp as he hauled her up. "Come and stop me then, brother!"

Northrup snarled, thrashing his arms to get free. One of the brutes holding him went flying forward from the force. The lycans struggled to get hold of Northrup as his body grew in size, ripped flesh and muscle swelling and shifting with the crackle of bones. Fur sprouted along his arms, and over his chest and face. He lunged, his elongated snout snapping at limbs. And then the pack fell upon Northrup, dragging him under in a flurry of fangs and claws. Blood sprayed. He would fully turn. And they would kill him.

Fury surged through Daisy's body so strong it felt like another kick to her gut. She lashed out, grabbing Conall by his soft cods and wrenching them. The man screamed high and sharp as he fell. Daisy stumbled free, the rage within her vibrating. Truly it felt as though the ground rumbled. And then it was. It took a moment for her to realize that the lycans around her were falling, grabbing onto whatever they could to stay upright.

Still hunched over, Conall tottered around like a drunken sailor as he glanced wildly about. Daisy turned for Northrup. *Save him. Get him free.* He lay in a heap as the earthquake made the others scatter. Two beasts still had a hold on him and were trying to drag him away.

Daisy took a step toward him and then fell when the ground heaved up in great chunks of pungent earth. Another surge went through her. It felt like need, as strong as lust but with a painful force behind it. The ground around Northrup exploded in a spray of earth and grass as thick tree roots flew upward. One of the lycan blinked in shock as a thick tree root shot through his chest, and his life ended in a gurgle of terror.

The pack froze for a horrified moment and then they flew into action, running for their lives as tree roots shot from the ground to spear or coil around their victims. Dark gratification burst through her at the sight. *Run. You cannot hide.* The words had barely formed in her head when a tree root sprang forth to claim Lyall, lifting him high and tossing him like rubbish.

Strengthened by it, Daisy pulled herself up. *Fear me.* Beside her, Conall looked at her as if seeing a ghost. She smiled with grim satisfaction, the feeling of fearlessness like a drug in her veins. *Run away, little wolf, or I shall kill you.*

Conall's eyes went round. Then he took off in a sprint toward the house, narrowly missing a tree root coming for his neck. She saw no more of him as she staggered toward Northrup's limp form. She was almost there when a hand grabbed her arm. She turned, her fist raised and ready to strike, caution be damned, when she saw the familiar face of Jack Talent.

"Let us collect him," he said in a rush, his green eyes flashing with terror, "and leave this cursed place!"

Chapter Twenty-three

Agony had its own special burn: sharp and breathtaking. Ian lay as still as he could. Every rock of the carriage slashed pain through him with lightning-hot intensity. His world was dark, yet loud, blood covering his eyes, blood roaring through his ears. *Blood, blood, blood.* He almost sang it aloud. Christ, he was becoming giddy with pain. The carriage hit a bump, and he groaned, tried to move his arm but found it bound against him.

"He's bleeding through the sheet!" Daisy's voice. Strained and rasping. He didn't like hearing it like that.

Talent's dry lilt replied. "Can't be helped. He's more slashed than whole."

Good to know.

"Oh, God. God!" Soft hands fluttered over his hair, the only place that did not scream for relief. "So much blood. Look at him! Just look...His face...God." She petted him again and he turned his head into the touch, which unfortunately made him whimper like a lad. The stroking stopped. "He's going to die, isn't he?" A sob.

He liked the sound of that sob, bastard that he was. It spoke of regret.

"You're being overly dramatic," said Talent. "It doesn't suit you. He's a lycan. A good thrashing won't kill him, just hurts like the devil."

Aye, and didn't he know it. Simply taking a breath sent fire coursing through him. Ian concentrated on Daisy's scent to avoid the pain. Her scent was strong now, enveloping him. The scent of Daisy and woman. Despite his pain, his mouth watered. His head was pillowed on her lap, he realized. What he wouldn't give to be there when he was fully healed. He tried to open his eyes. It didn't work.

"A thrashing? They tore him apart!" Gentle fingers ran through his hair, and *he* almost sobbed. It felt too good, that touch.

"That was the idea, wasn't it? At least they didn't take any parts," Talent observed with typical pragmatism. "Stop your worrying. We wrapped him tight enough in that sheet. Won't lose any bits of loose meat that way."

The hand in his hair tightened. He grunted, and the grip quickly eased. But not her voice. "You're sick!" Daisy snapped. "All of you, sick."

Talent let out a tired sigh. "It is what it is. My lord knew what he was in for and accepted it. Why can't you?"

"Accept torture without turning a hair?" Her laughter held a touch of hysteria. "How could he let them do this?"

"What a question," said Talent. "When you were like a grape ripe for the plucking from the moment Lyall put his hands on you? Do you honestly think his lordship would leave you to such a fate? I can only thank the devil that you had the sense to stay quiet."

"You were there?" Daisy voice grew shrill, the grip

in his hair going tight again before easing over him like the flutter of butterfly wings. “And you did nothing to save him?”

“Are you cracked? You think I would have usurped his lordship’s authority to *save* him? You think he would have accepted such an indignity? Crazy, fool woman…”

“No worse than an impudent, vain…valet! If that’s what you even are. No valet I know talks back in such a manner.”

“And no lady I know goes stumbling into such trouble, yet here you are!”

They’d be tossing him aside to get at each other’s throats in a moment. And Ian rather liked the plump pillow of Daisy’s thighs.

“Shut. Up.” His voice was as coarse as coal, but they heard.

“Oh!” Hands fluttered around his hair. “Northrup? Don’t move! We’ll be home soon and…” She touched his earlobe. Past the burn of his wounds, he concentrated on her soft, warm fingertip as if it were the only thing in the world. “We’ll get you well.” She didn’t sound so sure, but she went back to stroking his hair.

“Be fine,” he mumbled. Speech wasn’t advisable; his face moved too much. White spots exploded behind his lids and nausea pulled at his gut. When the fingers stilled, he made one last effort. “Just don’t stop.”

Her scent touched him as she leaned close. “Stop what?”

Suddenly every gash and gouge screamed, and raw agony had him weeping inside. His throat worked. God, he wanted to scream. Razor-sharp fingers of pain dug into him, scraping his bones. He need to go someplace it couldn’t get him. To darkness.

"Touching me," he whispered, and then gave up the fight.

Daisy stroked his hair until they reached his home. She held his fingers—the only bit of him that wasn't injured—after Tuttle and Talent unwrapped him from the bloody sheet shrouding his body. She kept a hold on his fingers, but averted her eyes when Talent lifted him into the deep copper tub in Northrup's bathing chamber. And clenched them tight when he lunged forward on a scream as the water hit him, his face a horror of gashes that went bone deep. The sight made her want to sob, but she bit it back.

Talent leaped forward, grabbing Northrup's bloody jaw and forced something down his throat. Whatever he gave Northrup made the man slip back into oblivion. Tuttle cooed under her breath as she handled him with the gentle deftness of a mother.

"A little bit of witches brew will make this easier." Tuttle held his shoulder as Northrup went limp once more, his broad chest sinking into the water, the wounds turning it crimson. He slid down until he was submerged to his chin. Daisy could only wonder if "witches brew" was just that, or simply an opiate. She couldn't be sure of anything anymore.

"Fresh, pure water is the best thing for a wounded lycan," Tuttle said to Daisy. " 'Clean them up, let them heal' is what they say. No one knows exactly why that is, but I'm not one to question a good thing." Still, the elder woman shook her head at the sight of Northrup. "If he's been worse, I've not seen it."

Worse didn't begin to cover the damage. His expressive lips were torn open, exposing his teeth in a gruesome grin. His eyes were swollen shut and blackened. Gore, blood, and dirt matted his hair, covered every inch of him. How? How could he heal from this?

Talent bustled around the chamber, pulling out a pot of the same concoction Tuttle had used on Daisy before and a stack of thick towels. "You shouldn't be here."

Her fingers laced with Northrup's. "He said to keep touching him and so I shall." She glared at the hostile young man before her. "And if you say one more word about it, I'll thrash *you*."

Talent scowled, and Tuttle chuckled as she poured water over Northrup's face and hair. "I suspect you would at that, lass."

Despite Daisy's doubts, the water was working. Before her eyes, the edges of his gaping flesh slowly began coming together. As the flesh grew, blood ran from the wounds. A gruesome sight, and yet he appeared to ease just a bit more. Daisy caressed the backs of his fingers with her thumb, soothing him in the only way she could. She hated the way his brow pinched in an expression of deep pain, and the way the corners of his mouth twitched as if repressing a scream. Part of her wanted to shake him for accepting such torture. The other wanted to crawl into the tub with him, curl around him, and cry.

She did not let him go when Talent took him from the tub, dried him off, and began rubbing the ointment into his skin. The fresh scent of chamomile and lavender, with an underlying bite of tea tree, filled the air. "Soothes his nerves," Talent muttered reluctantly to Daisy. "Eases the itching that comes with new skin." Skin that was covered now not with deep rents but with lumpy pink slashes that wept a clear liquid.

Daisy kept her eyes firmly on Northrup's face. She would not dishonor his sacrifice by looking upon him in his vulnerability. "Will he heal completely?" It would not matter; her regard for him wouldn't change if he remained in this scarred state. Only Northrup was a bit vain about his good looks, and it hurt her to think of him suffering for the loss of them.

"Of course he will," Talent said. "His age and his blood will see to that. He's a Ranulf. Purest blood a lycan can have." His hands worked rhythmically against Northrup's skin. "Makes him strong, where an ordinary lycan would have succumbed."

"But his father..."

"Was burned," Talent said emphatically. "Fire destroys flesh. Eats it, if you will. Cuts merely separate the flesh. Much easier to heal from that."

"This was why you did not worry?" she asked.

Talent set the pot of ointment aside and wiped his hands on a towel before looking at her. His green eyes were hard in the flickering lamplight. "I didn't worry because worrying doesn't change a damn thing." He pulled the sheet over his master. "Fate is fate."

Chapter Twenty-four

Hours passed and day gave way to night. Daisy watched in fascination as Northrup slowly healed. First, only pink lines marked where he'd been abused, and then the slashes across his face faded. Presently, he was whole and breathtaking once more.

Daisy's hand slid along the sweeping curve of Northrup's jaw where the skin was as smooth as a lad's now. Down, along his strong neck, she went, and then back up, across the high plane of his brow.

The room had grown ghostly quiet while Northrup slept, with only the occasional crack and hiss behind the grate to punctuate the silence.

Before leaving them, Talent had carried his master into the bedchamber and tucked him into the massive tester bed that dominated the room. Though young, and mouthy, and surly, the valet cared for his master with a loyalty that required respect. He'd left her standing by Northrup's prone form with the brusque instructions to "make herself useful and rub some ointment on his lordship's face now and then."

"Blighter," she muttered as she picked up the jar and dipped her fingers into the slightly greasy ointment again. The substance went on cool, but as she worked it into Northrup's skin, it began to warm. It was the same ointment that Tuttle had given her days ago, when Daisy had been bitten. Whatever the concoction was, its healing properties were beyond the pale. Tuttle had insisted that Daisy use it again on her stinging, swollen cheek. Within minutes, the pain had gone. She hadn't looked in a mirror, but suspected the swelling had subsided as well.

Northrup did not move as she worked on him, but the tightness around his mouth eased with each pass of Daisy's fingers until finally it was gone. The bedside lamp had been turned low, and its light played over the crests and hollows of his countenance. He would never appear soft, not even in sleep. His features were too sharp, the angle of his dark brows etched into a permanent slant of concentration. Knowing he slept soundly at last, she released the tight rein she'd kept on her gaze and let it wander downward.

Daisy's breath caught as she took an unabashed look at Northrup's uncovered chest. He was gorgeous. Perfectly balanced between sheer strength and elegant economy. Lean, flat muscles defined the dips and planes of his torso and rose and swelled along his wide shoulders and long arms. Golden ivory in the low lamplight, his skin was a smooth canvas that highlighted all his glorious definition. Were it not for the gentle rise and fall of his chest, she'd think him a sculpture. Endymion lying in wait for Selene.

Indeed, he might have been a sculpture save for the dusting of copper and bronze hair scattered along his upper chest. Hair that lovingly surrounded little flat nipples of light brown. On his left pectoral muscle was a fist-sized tattoo. Daisy had heard of such things but had never seen one up close before. Northrup's was of a black wolf's head with *Dei Dono Sum Quod Sum* inscribed around it in bold script. Rusty memories of her Latin primer came to the fore.

"By the grace of God I am what I am," she whispered. He'd shouted it earlier, and she had to smile at how very fitting the motto was. The tattoo appeared to move as he breathed with the even cadence of sleep.

Her mouth went dry, her fingers curling into a fist. She would not touch it.

Ye gods but the sheet was too low around his waist, stopping at a line of dark auburn hair that peeked out a little bit farther with each exhale of Northrup's breath. The muscles beneath his belly button lay flat like a plate of armor above the narrow plane of his hips, the skin stretched so tightly over them that the veins stood out, one of them leading a path down below the sheet.

Flush with heat, she bit her lip hard. She wanted to trace that path with her tongue and pull the sheet away to reveal the rather large bulge hiding beneath it. A delicious image, ripped in two as he tensed on a sharp breath, his eyes snapping open and his hand shooting out to grasp her wrist. She yelped as he wrenched her toward him.

Daisy fell upon his chest with an undignified "Oomph!"

Northrup blinked once, then immediately his eyes cleared, and he relaxed his hold. "Are you well?" His voice was a rasp of sandpaper, but strong.

Stiffly she nodded, the shock of his sudden movement still upon her. "You?"

He scowled as if taking stock, his eyes darting over her face. "I feel as though I've been used to fill a mincemeat pie."

"How vivid," she croaked and, unable to hold up the weight of the night any longer, she let her head fall to his shoulder with a thud. He felt as warm and solid as he looked.

Beneath her, his chest shook with a small laugh. "That bad?"

Her deep, shuddering breath was the only answer she felt capable to give. He smelled too good. Of ointment and Northrup. She burrowed her nose deeper, searching for the pure scent of him alone.

His fingers combed through her hair, parting the tangled curls that tumbled free now. A gentle stroke designed to comfort. "He hurt you. For that, he will pay."

Her cheek worked against his skin as she swallowed. "It is over now."

Northrup made a sound of disagreement but did not stop his explorations. "You did well, Daisy-girl. You stayed quiet and demure . . . mostly."

Daisy pinched at his side, and he yelped. "Of course I did," she said.

His body moved as he shook his head. "I should not have fought them when they came for us." Carefully, he touched her cheek. "It gave Conall the knowledge to use you."

"You chose the best course with what you were given, and I'll hear no more about it." Her breath stirred the hair upon his chest, and his nipple hardened. Her finger crept closer to the little nub. "Who is Lena?"

Beneath her palm, his heart pounded. "An ally at one time." His voice was careful, quiet. "Now it seems I have none."

You have me. She almost said it when she felt him move and could have sworn he was smiling. His voice drifted down, and there was a definite lilt of amusement in it. "Did I detect a note of jealousy in your voice just then, Daisy-Meg?"

Yes. "You detected curiosity, you arrogant sot."

He grunted. "Of course. A thousand pardons, madam." He did not sound conciliatory in the least.

She relaxed her hand, and her fingers moved a fraction, the very tip of her nail touching the flat edge of his areola. Northrup stilled, and her muscles tensed, her skin heating. She wanted to pet him, to feel the strength of his musculature and the silk of his skin. She forced herself to speak instead.

"What did Lena have to say to Conall?"

Northrup's free hand fell to her waist. He had a big hand, and it was warm as it smoothed slowly up her side, stopping short of her breast before easing back down to her hip. She closed her eyes and almost purred in pleasure.

"Nothing to Conall," he answered somewhat roughly. Again came that slow, easing caress that held nearly all her attention. His hand stopped. "She wants me to take him from the throne."

"To challenge him and become the king?"

Northrup's grip tightened at her waist. "She thinks I'll be a better leader. But I've no interest in the role."

"Why not? Is it not your birthright?" She touched one curling auburn hair upon his chest. A light touch that perhaps he wouldn't notice. But his breath caught, before he let it out slowly.

"I don't want to be a lycan." He said it so softly she almost didn't catch it. "I want to live as a normal man." His fingertips traced the seam at the side of her bodice. "Live a normal life."

Normal. After what she had seen and done this night, she could see the vast appeal of normalcy. And yet when she thought of Northrup living and acting as every other man, she found herself frowning.

"I should think I would find you rather dull, Northrup, were you a normal man."

The heartbeat beneath her ear grew to a rapid tattoo as he tensed. His fingers threaded through her hair to cup the back of her head. Gently, he held her against him. "Thank you."

The whisper stroked along her skin. He said no more as he continued to play with her hair. They sat as such for a long moment, until her side hurt from the pinch of her corset and she made to rise.

He stopped her with a touch to her cheek. Ensnared, she blinked down at him, aware that her mouth parted with her quickening breath, and that her skin suddenly felt too hot. The thumb at her cheek moved in a halting stroke that had her trembling.

"I didn't let you go," she blurted out inanely.

He stilled. "No," he said. "No, you didn't."

A smile wavered at the corners of his mouth as his gaze grew unguarded. The heat and yearning there took her breath. Suddenly, he wasn't smiling anymore. His voice cracked between them. "Daisy, let me..."

He pulled her down as he rose up.

They met in a melding of lips and tongues, slow and decadent, and it sent a sigh of sweet relief through her.

On a breath, he lifted her up and beside him to lay her down upon her back. His lips never left hers as he slid against her, holding her close before cupping her neck with a strong hand. Her legs were in a hopeless tangle with her skirts, her arm trapped against the wall of his chest, but her lips were in perfect accord with his. She licked inside his mouth, a warm wet glide that uncoiled something hot and thick within her. Ian made a sound of contentment within his throat as he kissed her and then pulled away to look at her beneath sleepy lids.

"This," he whispered thickly, "this is what I thought of when they had me. Touching you." He kissed her again, again. "Tasting you." He touched her cheek, his mouth brushing over hers. "You were my safe harbor."

She traced the silken path of his brow with a shaking finger, then pulled him close. He was so very strong, warm, *present.* Holding him close, she could acknowledge how afraid she had been for him. How much she wanted him.

They explored each other slowly, deeply, nipping and sucking, their hands bumping as they reached for each other and held each other steady. The languid sensation made her head spin, and her body grow heavy. His hand glided up her ribs to cup her breast. She arched into the touch, her belly pressing against the hard length of his cock bunting up between them. They both whimpered at the contact, their kiss shifting its intensity.

"I love this gown," he murmured, licking a path across the low line of the bodice. The touch was fire along her skin.

"A strumpet's gown," she answered breathlessly.

"Precisely." He kissed the swell of her left breast. "You should have one in every color."

Suckling the tender skin at the base of her throat, Ian rolled onto her, his hands at her waist, hips, rubbing, urging her on. The hard press of his body, the smooth shift of his muscles against her palm felt so good that she shook with the need for more, to rub skin to skin, to lick a path down his chest and take him in her mouth.

His shoulders were granite under silk. She could write a sonnet on the beauty of his shoulders, a symphony about the bulge of his biceps. She sank her teeth into one, testing its hardness, and he groaned.

"Ian." She took his lips in a greedy kiss that explored his taste.

He broke off with a smile. "Ian," he repeated, nipping her lower lip. "Finally, you call me Ian." Their eyes met, and a bolt of tenderness hit her with unexpected intensity. "Took you long enough," he whispered, his hand smoothing back a curl at her cheek.

He was alive, and whole, and looking down at her with heat and affection in his eyes. When had he become so necessary? She could not afford necessary. Suddenly she couldn't draw a proper breath. A spike of pain shot down the side of her skull with enough force to make her gasp.

Ian's brows knitted. "Daisy?" He touched the curve of her temple with a finger.

She blinked, trying to ease the feeling away, but a film settled over her eyes, all at once too bright yet wavering. She closed her eyes against it. "I..." A sharp breath left her as another bolt of pain attacked her head. "My eyes."

He eased off of her. "Your eyes?" Another gentle touch. "What, love? Where does it hurt?"

Daisy let out a frustrated breath and flung her legs over the side of the bed, an altogether undignified move as she was too far away and had to slide along the mattress. "I'm sorry. I can't...I cannot do this."

Ian held her shoulder as she made to leave the bed. "Daisy, calm yourself." His hand lay warm and heavy, a comfort. She tried to ease it off but he wouldn't be budged. "Tell me what is the matter."

Fighting tears, she pressed a shaking hand hard against her eyes. "I can't see properly. There is this blur and"—she waved a helpless hand—"lights..."

"A migraine?" he said softly. At times she forgot that he was a physician. He was very near, his arm steadying her shoulder, and she let herself rest her head on his bare shoulder. The action made her brain slosh within its bed of pain, and she hissed.

"Yes," she said on a breath. "They come when I'm..." She didn't want to talk. The pain behind her skull made her feel brittle, capable of shattering with one wrong move.

Ian's arms came around her, and he pulled her close, holding her as if she were a hollow eggshell. "When you are under great stress." He cupped the back of her head with his palm. "Christ, you should not have seen what occurred this night. It is my fault."

Tension rode over her shoulders, building with force until she found herself pushing at his chest with clenched fists. "It is!" she cried in a low voice. "Of course it is, you..." Her fists rubbed over his chest, half a caress, half grinding into his flesh as if to imprint herself there. "Don't you ever—" She broke off when he gathered her nearer, his lips grazing her temple.

She gave his shoulder a light punch. "No. Don't kiss me! Don't you ever do that again."

"Kiss you?" he teased softly, and doing just that.

She turned away, tears leaking out of her eyes like little traitors to her will. "Let them hurt you like that." She glared up at him but could see only a sparkling blur of his face as if viewing him through thick bottle glass. "You fight, damn you! Damn me too, if it comes to that." And then she was sobbing, burrowing her head in the shelter of his chest. "They tore you apart."

"Och now." His callused palm cupped her cheek. "Did ye fear I'd lose me pretty face?" he said, drawing out his brogue as though he knew she liked to hear it.

"Of course." She nudged his ribs with her fist. "What else is there to admire about you?" When he bent his head down to peer at her, she rested her forehead against his. "Certainly n-not your inane conversations." Her fingers curled about his shoulders as he peppered her face with soft kisses. "Or your r-ridiculous jests."

He gathered her tightly once more and soothed her with gentle strokes as she cried. His chest was a fortress, his arms battlements. Her cheek pressed against the warmth of his pectoral muscle and she heard the steady drum of his heart.

"Come." A tug on her bodice made her stiffen, and he uttered a short laugh. "If you think I intend to offer you anything more than comfort at this moment, I fear ye've greatly underestimated my sense of honor, lass."

The sound of his Scottish coming out unfettered had her crying all over again, and he *tsked* as he turned down the light and quietly undressed her in the dark as efficient as any maid.

The sheets were smooth and cool as she slid between them in nothing but her chemise and drawers. Ian followed her in and then spooned her against him. The feel of his hard body so warm and solid against her back steadied her.

"Be at ease now," he said on a breath as his strong fingers tunneled into her hair and dug into the tender spots along her scalp, scattering blessed relief in their wake. His dark voice drew her into dreams on a promise. "I will not let you go either."

In the thin hours of the night, Ian left a sleeping Daisy under Talent's guard and headed for The Clock Tower at Westminster. Big Ben, some called it. He remembered it being built. He sprinted toward the looming tower and nearly threw himself at its limestone walls. Up he climbed, hand over foot, scaling the intricately carved edifice with ease.

The wind howled in his ears as he neared the top, moving past the gilt letters along the base of the large clock face: *Domine Salvam Fac Reginam Nostram Victoriam Primam—O Lord, keep safe our Queen Victoria the First.* He was in no mood to think of the queen. The thought of gaining her attention caused a fine shudder to work through him. He had turned his back on her when he'd turned his back on the clan and he had no wish to return to that life.

Only when he'd passed the bellhouse and reached the iron-clad spire did he slow down. He vaulted over the gilt-and-cast-iron railing on the topmost steeple and sucked in a deep breath of London air, a witch's brew of scents and tastes. Nothing of the *werewolf.* It was if it had been plucked from this earth. But Ian damn well knew it hadn't been.

Below, the black surface of the Thames rippled like snakeskin in the moonlight. Tiny pinpricks of light marked the windows and lamps of London, a glittering web of stars in the dark. Though he was not afraid of heights, his stomach turned, for the temptation was there, to jump. From this great height, it must be nearly like flying. His fingers curled into his palms until he felt the bite of his nails. A breeze lifted his hair as he gazed down at the river, undulating and black. To fly free. He could do it. Only he'd land, his head smashed open but still alive, unable even then to die. A choked laugh escaped him as he pictured himself lying upon the pavers like a broken marionette, forced to wait while his body slowly healed.

Had it felt like flying to Maccon?

Maccon. Blackness danced at the edge of Ian's sight before he brutally shoved the name and the feelings that came with it back into the deep, dark hole in his heart. He would not think about that. Not ever again.

Ian had much practice ignoring that particular pain so the darkness quickly passed. Ironic because it was that adaptability that had dragged him down into a half-life of apathy. On a sigh, he moved to the edge of the tower and took a calming breath.

But calm was hard to keep tonight. Restlessness had pulled Ian from Daisy's bed and out here where he could think.

Inside his pocket, the moonstone stickpin lay like a ballast, weighing him down. He didn't want to look at it, or touch it, unnerved as he was by the very sight of it. The last time he'd seen his own pin, he'd been burying it with Maccon. Conall had one. But he wouldn't willingly part with the piece. Why then was it pinned to a woman's corpse? Had Conall meant for it to be found? Was it a taunt? And if so, why?

It didn't matter. Whatever Conall was playing at, he was involved in this madness. And it was a kick to Ian's solar plexus.

Resignation settled in his bones. He knew what must be done. And if it cost him his soul, so be it, for he could not live this half-life any longer. But he needed a plan. He needed allies, and not the bloody SOS, who would want to control him. Only one thing was certain: Daisy was his to protect until it was done. With a sharp inhale, Ian sat up straight. For the first time in years, someone needed him. The sense of purpose stirred him. He felt alive, not merely moving through each day but alive in a way that made his blood sing.

Tilting his head back, he gazed up at the moon and the lace-thin clouds that drifted in front of her glowing face. The sky behind it was so deep and close that he fancied he could sink his hand into it and pull back with inky fingertips. Alive. The wolf inside of him felt it too. Emotion, anticipation, and surprising joy welled up within with a sudden force that had him panting. He let the feeling crest and held it until his chest vibrated.

As a lone wolf, he was forbidden to do it. In so doing, he would be stating his intentions to the lycan world. But centuries of instinct could not be denied. A howl tore free, rising and falling in a long wave that spoke of his return and his promise to the woman.

Chapter Twenty-five

The sign on The Book Shop door said CLOSED. Daisy did not bother knocking. She was expected so the door was unlocked. The Book Shop. Ha! Leave it to practical Poppy to pick a name for her bookshop that was utterly lacking in any lyricism and so very...literal. As much as Daisy loved her older sister, she sometimes yearned to crack through her indomitable and proper facade.

Daisy's heels clicked as she strode along the narrow hall, past the shop entrance, and toward the private areas at the back of the building. She left Tuttle and Seamus waiting in the carriage, though not without a bit of fuss, for they both feared for her. They needn't. Not here.

The familiar scent of wood polish mingling with book mold and linen paper touched her nose. Light slanted in from the backdoor window, landing in a square block of gold upon the dark, wood floor. She moved through it and yanked the door wide open before slamming it behind her.

Before her spread a little green square of a garden

enclosed by the walls of surrounding buildings. A quiet oasis in the midst of the bustling city.

Blinking in the brightness of the sun, Daisy lifted a hand for shade and found two sets of eyes upon her: one set gleaming green and curious, the other shrewd and brown.

"You look as though the very devil were on your heels," said her eldest sister, Poppy.

Daisy opened her white parasol, lined with copper satin to keep the sunlight out, and walked toward her sisters, who sat at the little table nestled beneath the lacy shade of a budding willow.

"Perhaps he is." She took her seat as Miranda set out a glass of iced tea and a plate before her. "Or perhaps the devil is a woman, and I am she."

At that statement, she put away her parasol, helped herself to a ham sandwich, and took a hearty bite.

Miranda's brow arched delicately. "Care to explain?"

Thoughtfully, Daisy chewed and let her sisters wait, but her eyes went to Poppy, who looked somewhat... hesitant. Interesting. Her eyes narrowed, and Poppy's did in return. Daisy took a careful drink of deliciously cold tea, thankful for the way it soothed her sore throat, before addressing Miranda. "Well, dearest, it seems strangeness runs through our family after all."

"No!" Miranda went pale but a smile tugged at her lips. "You didn't!" She leaned forward in excitement. "You started a fire?"

"No." Daisy shot a look at Poppy, who'd remained surprisingly quiet. "Nothing quite so...exotic...Dirt!" she shouted, no longer able to contain her ire. "Of all the gifts I could have received, I am left with dirt."

She shoved back from the table and leaped up to pace in front of her shocked sisters. "Panda gets to play with fire, and

I get filth. How very disgusting. Have you any idea what lives in dirt? Bugs! Worms!" She flung her arms up in disgust.

"Daisy, dearest," Miranda pleaded, "calm yourself and explain."

"Yes," Daisy whirled about, "of course." She stopped and clasped her shaking hands. "It appears, love, that when *my* ire is stretched to the limit, I can make the earth move. And... tree roots appear." She flung her hands once more. "Honest to goodness tree roots shot from the earth and speared people!"

At this, both sisters went white.

"Tree roots?" Miranda intoned. She got up and caught hold of Daisy's arm. "Sit and tell us what happened."

Daisy let herself be led back to her seat. She took another sip of tea before recounting what had occurred the night before. Well, not all of it. She left out her kiss with Northrup. Miranda certainly wouldn't approve. Despite not wanting Northrup when he wanted her, Miranda fervently objected to the idea that Daisy might get involved with him. Which both irked Daisy and made her love her sister for her protectiveness.

"It was my doing," Daisy said to them. "I felt it in my bones. I caused the earth to heave and crumble. I caused those roots to burst free. It felt like want and power."

She frowned, trying to explain, but Miranda nodded and clasped her hand. "Like a need trying to break free. And then a shiver of pleasure when it does."

Daisy squeezed her fingers. "Yes, exactly."

They shared a look in which they both grew distressingly misty-eyed before blinking their tears away and taking a bracing breath.

"I thought it only me," Miranda said, after taking a moment to collect herself.

"Indeed." Daisy turned her gaze on a silent Poppy. "I thought so as well. And yet one of us appears to be not the least bit surprised…Poppy Ann Ellis Lane!" She lurched forward in her seat, her fists rattling the plates upon the table as she glared at her sister. "You knew this might happen. Do not try to pretend you didn't. You are the smartest of all of us. And the oldest. You knew, didn't you?"

Silence filled the garden as the younger Ellis sisters stared at their eldest sister. Poppy had gone as still as the statuary gracing the four corners of the garden. She blinked back at them for one tense moment and then inhaled sharply as if bracing herself.

"I knew."

Two simple words and the garden erupted into a volley of shouts, Miranda's being the loudest. She stood to glare down at Poppy like an avenging angel, stray wisps of her red-gold hair stirring in the breeze.

"You knew?" Miranda hissed. "You knew how alone I felt with this burden. I felt a freak, an aberration of nature, and you *knew* it was not solely I who possessed strange powers?"

Poppy's expression remained frozen, and her eyes were hollow. "It hurt me to keep quiet, Miranda. But it was not my place to warn Daisy or speak of your power unless absolutely necessary."

"How could it not be necessary when I was turning things to ash?" Miranda shouted.

"If you had been seriously out of control, I would have helped you," Poppy said calmly. "As it was, however, you handled the situation quite nicely."

Another round of cursing broke forth but this time Poppy's clear voice cut through it all. "Sit down, the both of you. Now."

Something in her tone was so like their mother's that Daisy found herself obeying, and Miranda shortly followed.

"Explain," Miranda said.

"Of course," Poppy said. "You are elementals."

"Elementals?" Daisy parroted. The sun seemed too bright, the air too hot in the face of such discoveries but she was not inclined to break up the conversation to move indoors.

Poppy's expression was serene. "Beings who can control the elements. In the past, elementals were touted as witches, many of them burned at the stake."

Daisy shuddered and leaned back in her seat. "Witches. Lovely. Though with your temper, Panda"—she sent a small smile toward her irate little sister—"I can fully imagine the moniker."

Miranda had clearly learned quite the number of colorful hand gestures during her time with Billy Finger and used one then. Daisy stuck her tongue out before turning back to Poppy. "How did we get this way?"

"You inherited it from Mother. Elementals are usually women, and the trait passed on to the daughters. It was she who forbade me to speak of it unless asked."

"And you simply obeyed?" Miranda asked. "Even when you knew what it was doing to me?"

Poppy blinked. "I took a vow. As First Daughter, it was my duty to keep the secret. Only if you sought to do harm should I interfere. Only if you sought personal gain. You did neither but merely sought to suppress your talent, Miranda. What good would it truly have done to tell you when you didn't even want to use it?"

Miranda's teeth clicked together. "That statement is so utterly wrong that I don't even know where to begin."

Poppy looked away first, her fierce, straight brows furrowed with emotion. She was wrong, Daisy knew, but either would not admit to it or didn't fully see the fault in her logic.

Daisy's mind fairly reeled. Not just Miranda, but all of them were different. And their mother had known. She thought of her beautiful and ethereal mother who had died giving birth to their little brother; the poor little mite hadn't lived past the first day. From the looks on her sisters' faces, Daisy knew they too thought of that devastating loss. "What could Mother do?"

A long sigh lifted Poppy's breast. "Her powers were a lot like yours, actually. She could influence nature. Remember the way she had with animals?"

Miranda's lip wobbled. "God, I'd forgotten. She used to say that she 'told' the rats to stay out of our pantry." Her voice broke on a laugh. "I always thought she was having me on."

Poppy nodded stiffly. "Nature gave her strength. She yearned for the countryside. She hated London."

They'd lost her too early. Some days, Daisy missed her so much it was an ache in her chest.

"And Father?" Daisy asked, breaking the silence. "I suppose it is the practice of elementals to keep their husbands in the dark?" She glanced at Miranda. "You are in trouble now, pet."

Poppy's mouth thinned in clear defiance. "Father did not know of Mother's talents. Only of Miranda's, for obvious reasons."

"But not of yours, I gather," Daisy supplied. When Miranda sat up straight, she gave her a repressive look. "Come now, she called herself the first daughter. You can't have imagined she doesn't possess one either."

Poppy actually grimaced. "Or mine."

"What is it?" Miranda snapped.

Poppy sighed again and then slowly moved her hand forward. Her long, blunt-tipped finger touched the tea pitcher, pebbled with condensation as it warmed in the sun. A shiver of air drifted over the small space, ice cold and clear. Before their eyes, frost moved over the glass. Laces of ice soon covered it, and the tea within froze solid.

"Well, at least that explains iced tea on a bookseller's salary," Daisy said. "Might we have iced cream next time, Pop?"

Poppy's look was frigid.

"Does Winston know?" Daisy asked.

"No. And he never will."

The threat was clear and chilling.

"Bloody hell," Miranda muttered, still gaping at the frozen tea pitcher.

"Bloody hell is right," Daisy snapped, crossing her arms in front of her. "You have fire, she has ice, and I have dirt." When they both stared at her, she made a noise of disgust. "Fire and ice are elegant, brutal powers. I hate dirt! And, really, what can one do with it?"

"Oh, I don't know," murmured Poppy. "It sounds to me as though you used it quite effectively to fell your enemies."

Daisy batted back one of the curls tickling her cheek and looked away, refusing to be persuaded.

"And it wasn't the mere moving of dirt, was it?" Poppy said. "You mentioned tree roots. Which makes me believe that nature is attuned to you, as it was with Mother." She glanced at the patches of spring crocuses growing along the borders of the newly budding flowerbeds. "I suspect you have more power than you think. Why not try speaking to the flowers?"

"Speaking to the flowers?"

How very ridiculous. She glanced about her. True, each blade of grass, every flower had its own scent, which she could detect as clearly as the tea before her or the lemon cakes on the stand. If she were very still, she could hear the little flowers stirring in the breeze and the tight buds straining to break free from the willow overhead. Cautiously, she took a little breath and let go of the strange swirling that somehow lived within her belly, a power that seemed to have always been there, had she thought to look for it.

The air about the table seemed to crack and writhe with a strange hissing sound that Daisy realized with a start was the growing of things. Something brushed against her ankles. Grass. Grass shooting from the ground, growing high. The timid little cluster of crocuses bloomed a full, deep purple. Miranda gasped as the rose vines attached to a trellis at the back wall exploded in a riot of lush, vermilion color and sweet, tender fragrances.

The garden darkened a touch, shade from the willow now in full bloom. Golden petals rained down like snow as its branches swayed in the breeze. The heady perfume of flowers and fruit thickened the air. Daisy sucked in a breath and cut the energy off.

"Well, now," Poppy plucked a brilliant green apple from the tree at her side, "I wouldn't call that display inelegant."

"No, it was wonderful," Daisy retorted airily, though her insides were shaking. "I shall be the belle of the garden club."

Miranda chortled into her glass of tea.

Daisy tapped her nails upon the tabletop, drumming out a hollow rhythm. "What I don't understand is why now? Why hadn't I seen some hint of this talent before? I am older than Miranda. Ought I not to have come into my power before her? Bloody hell, she burned Father's warehouse to the ground when she was ten years old."

A thoughtful expression came over Poppy's features. "It usually manifests during a time of great stress." She looked at Miranda. "Panda was a special case, for she had it as a tot. For me, and others, the power made itself known when I felt great danger and the need to defend myself."

"Believe me, sister," Daisy said darkly, "I've had need to defend myself before now." Oh, what she would have given to have used this power when Craigmore had lived.

"That is true," Poppy said. "But you've a sunny, caring nature, dear, despite your efforts to shock."

Daisy resisted the urge to squirm, but Poppy continued in her maddeningly pragmatic tone. "Surely there were some signs?"

Daisy thought on it. "Craigmore loved orchids," she said slowly. "Somehow, they always died, immediately. Shriveled up in their pots. And then there was the ivy." She bit back an evil smile. "Remember how thickly it grew over our house? It covered Craigmore's study windows no matter how many times the gardener tried to rein it in." Daisy laughed lightly. "I remember thinking, 'Good, grow so thick that he never sees sunlight.' And it did."

She sighed. "But nothing like what happened last night."

"Many elementals do not manifest their powers unless someone they love or care for deeply is in danger," Poppy said.

Again, two sets of eyes pinned her to the spot with their piercing stares. Her cheeks heated.

"You were defending Northrup," Miranda said in a hollow voice. "Do you . . . you couldn't possibly . . ."

"Care for him?" Daisy supplied, with a tinge of bitterness. "Would it be so very surprising? He is kind and charming. Never mind that he was being torn apart, his flesh cut to shreds because he was keeping me safe." Her chin lifted a touch. "Is it so very wrong of me to want to protect him? To feel gratitude?"

Miranda's eyes remained watchful. "Is it gratitude? Or are you falling in love with the man?"

Daisy crossed her arms over her chest. "I do not see why it would concern you if I was, which I am *not*."

"Because he will break your heart. Likely, he is toying with you to—" Her mouth snapped shut, a look of horrified embarrassment widening her lovely eyes.

"To make you jealous," Daisy finished for her. She hated saying the words aloud, but they were hovering in the air between them regardless. "After all, why would he want me when he's seen you?"

Miranda paled. "I never said that, or thought it. I only meant that he has a history of dallying with women."

"No, sister, it was precisely what you meant." Daisy drew away from the table and stood on weak limbs. Her throat was beginning to hurt most dreadfully. "I cannot fault you for thinking so. You are quite the most beautiful woman I've ever seen. Why should Northrup want another?"

Daisy held no illusions as to her own appeal. She was pretty, very pretty. But her attractiveness was, as her husband had constantly reminded her, common, lusty. She'd never told a soul how she'd overheard Craigmore offering for Miranda and being forced to make do with her when her father refused to part with his favored daughter. *I wanted the beauty, and I got the barmaid, good for nothing more than being passed around.* Why should Northrup think any different?

"Daisy," Miranda said softly, "don't say that. I simply do not trust his motives. I never have. He did everything he could to drive a wedge between me and Archer."

"I cannot speak to Northrup's actions in regards to you and Archer." Daisy gathered her parasol and gloves. She needed to leave. The garden was too small, too overladen with damned flora thanks to her. "But I do know this. The man you do not trust saved my life, repeatedly. And suffered for it. Might we give him that small credit?"

Miranda's lips pursed but she gave Daisy a stiff nod.

Daisy took a breath and stood. "He has been a friend to me." The word "friend" felt wrong on her tongue but she forged on. "I'm not falling in love. I may act foolish now and again, but I'm not a fool." A lie, because she knew she was the worst sort of fool.

"All right," Ian said when he could no longer keep himself from asking the question, "where is she?"

It irked him that he had to ask Talent. It irked him that he'd woken up in his bed alone. He'd had plans. Plans that included sinking into a soft, warm woman blessed with a particularly tart tongue. After returning late in the night to slip back into bed with her, it had been the only thought on his mind, and he'd fancied she would finally be compliant. Ah, well, the best laid schemes and all of that.

Talent slanted him a glance as he helped Ian into his morning coat. Despite the growing craze for the sack suit, neither man found the cut appealing. The shapeless style had no elegance about it. In that, at least, they were of an accord. On other things, however…

"She has ensnared Tuttle in her little web," said Talent shortly. "They set out at daybreak. To where I cannot say." *Or care.* The rest of the sentiment was clearly written over his expressive face.

Ian craned his head around. "With Tuttle?" Two women out alone with that beast on the loose. He tensed, ready to stalk out of the house and hunt the blasted woman down. Perhaps take Daisy over his knee. The thought held appeal in more ways than one. The woman had the most lusciously round arse…

"Hold your water." Talent adjusted the line of the suit shoulders. "They took Seamus with them."

Ian grunted. Seamus was a strong lad. All right, a brute. Easily six and a half feet of pure muscle and speed, the lycan stable master was as good protection, if not better, than Talent. Tension eased a bit in Ian's gut. They'd be safe with Seamus.

But the scowl remained as Talent fussed about with his cravat. Ian's skin itched and felt too tight for his frame. He couldn't credit it entirely to the healing. She was out of his sight and he…

He didn't like it.

"Did they say when they would return?"

At this, Talent's open features pulled into a sneer of disgust. "Henpecked already, are we?"

Ian could only grin. What did a boy know of it? Only a boy would view anticipation as a trap. Despite various aches and pains that lingered, Ian felt a certain lightness in his chest. So she hadn't been there in the morning. There was always later. Always that taut pang that hit him the moment they set their eyes on each other. Always that catch of his breath right before he took her in his arms.

Ought a man ignore such pleasures simply because the rest of the world was falling down around him? After nearly a century of being numb, he rather thought not. He deserved a bit of pleasure, damn it all.

Talent gave Ian's sleeve a tug that was a tad too efficient, and Ian turned his attention back to him.

"You don't like her."

Talent's shoulders hunched as he kept about his business.

Ian laughed and inspected the sets of cufflinks lined up in their case like good little soldiers. "Admit it. You'll be no use to me until you do." A set of garnet studs winked in the sunlight. Perfect. "I won't have you brooding when there's work to be done."

Talent swatted Ian's hand away from the studs and plucked up a pair of gold-and-black-enamel links, stylized into small skulls. "Gems for night. Gold for day." Deftly he took hold of Ian's cuff and pinned a skull in place. "She's a distraction."

"Of course she is," Ian said. "The best sort."

"Look what trouble that's given you so far," his valet muttered. Ian knew that Talent liked his life set up in well-ordered categories, and one should never bleed into the other.

Ian's hand dropped, and the other was grabbed. "You don't like anyone who takes attention away from you," Ian countered. "Had you your way, the whole household would revolve around your dramas. I've never seen a vainer man pretend to be so humble."

Talent snorted. "You possess a mirror, eh?" Ian had to concede the point as Talent brusquely began brushing his coat.

"Be one thing if you'd tup her and have done with it." The brush whacked his shoulder. "Instead, you're having conversations." Talent drew the word out as if tasting something foul. "An' walking around like a barmy nabob with your head in the clouds and a grin on your face."

Another whack found him between the shoulder blades. "What's it done but bring trouble to our door. You could have taken all four of those wolves without breaking a sweat, were it not for worrying over her. Let's be done with her, I say. Get her out of the house and—"

Ian caught Talent's wrist midstrike. "I believe we can both concede that my propensity for picking up strays has yet to be regrettable." He let his gaze bore into the lad's. "Pray, do not give me cause to think different."

The young man's eyes narrowed into green slits, and Ian leaned in a touch. "Whatever your feelings for Daisy may be, put them away. You will watch over her as instructed." He did not bother to add a consequence for failure. There was no need. The thing was either done or it was not.

Talent held his gaze for a second more and then broke it. "Talking like a proper gent again, are we?" When Ian let him go, Talent straightened his own cuffs with care.

Ian grabbed his walking stick and headed for the door.

"Least you're thinking clearly now," Talent said. At that he trailed off with more mutterings under his breath.

Pausing to inspect his form in the mirror, Ian remarked more from idleness than true curiosity, "Hmm?"

"I said she's right about one thing," Talent answered in an overloud voice. "You get your cock up and your Scots goes hanging out in the wind. Pretty soon, all one'll have to do is look for The Saltire flapping over your daft head, and your brother will know when to strike!"

Ian gave the boy a warning glare before striding out of the room. But Talent's irritating voice chased him down.

"She makes you weak, Ian!"

Chapter Twenty-six

Death lived in this dark alley. Winston could smell it long before he approached. A London Particular had drummed up early in the morning, and now the fog was thick as pudding and just as murky, despite the noonday sun that must be burning overhead. Their lamps did little more than reflect the light back into their eyes, turning the fog around them into a living, writhing thing. So they turned them down low and stumbled along.

They ought to have turned back, or perhaps have waited until the fog lifted, but the chase was upon them, and Winston sensed its end. He needed to see this done.

Even so, he pulled out his revolver and had it at the ready as they drew closer.

Sheridan's voice was a thin echo in the murk. "We ought to have brought backup."

"Mmm."

The dark outline of a building emerged, its windows and door shut tight against visitors. From there came the foul, overwhelming stench of rot, of death.

"I know that smell, sir."

Unfortunately, Winston did too.

"A body's in there." The younger man moved closer to Winston's side.

"Mmm."

Was it Ned Montgomery's, a man otherwise known as the perfumer? Word on the street had it that the perfumer hadn't been seen in at least a week. Was it he inside? Or one of his victims?

Backtracking, prodding, and pondering had finally brought to light that the man had a personal connection with both the victim Mary Fenn and the missing Lucy Montgomery.

The scuffle of Winston's shoes sounded overloud in the quiet. Somewhere beyond came the steady drip of water and the discordant strains of a violin perhaps. Sheridan's breath chuffed at his ear.

"Doesn't feel right, sir. Feels like a trap, it does."

Cold danced up Winston's spine at the words, and the feeling of being watched oiled over him. His fingers tensed around the gun.

"Mmm."

"'Mmm'?" Sheridan glowered at him, no more than a bit of eyes and a flattened mouth in the swirling stew of fog that danced over them. "Is that all you're going to say?"

Winston held up a hand for silence, his eyes searching the alleyway from whence they'd come. Mud-brown fog seemed to part and close as though breathing them in. His ears filled with the sound of his pounding heart and each labored breath he took.

Slowly, he cocked his gun, the click like a thunder-clap in the quiet. Beside him, Sheridan moved to do the same when a figure burst through the fog, a snarl of rage igniting sheer terror in Winston's gut even as the thing slammed into them.

Sheridan's shout was cut short, his copper-bright head snapping back as he flew into the side of the old shack. The wall cracked on impact. Winston went tumbling, a shot going off wild and wide.

Scrambling back on his ass, he lifted his gun to aim. A blur came at him, dark and hulking, and then white-hot pain sliced through his cheek with one blow. The gun clattered to the ground. Blood poured into his mouth, filling his nose. He retched, his arm coming up in defense as another blow fell, cutting him to the bone.

Screams. He heard his own. His world slowed to jerks and thumps upon his body as the thing came at him. Through the blood, he saw it: the long jaws, flashing fangs, hands half human, half beast. A wolf. And a man.

Werewolf.

The word popped into Winston's head like a nightmare as he slammed down against the wet, packed mud of the alley. The beast lunged. A killing blow, its mouth open wide with fangs and fetid breath, ready to tear his throat out.

And then there was only air.

The form of a man was before him, grasping hold of the beast with inhuman strength. In a haze of red blood, Winston saw the man lift the beast high and toss it. A yelp rang out and another as the man moved off, the sound of him beating back the beast clear, despite the ringing in Winston's ears.

Blood bubbled in his throat and poured hot down his chest and between his legs. His life's blood slipping away. It numbed him and made his eyes want to close.

"Wouldn't want to lose Mother over this." A deep voice

touched with ice. Then something felt his neck. He hadn't the strength to look. He was too heavy. Too cold.

Arms lifted him. As if he were a child. He forced his eyes open and came face to face with an angel. It must be so. The man's skin glowed with silver light as if he were made of ice and glass. Inhuman. And...Christ, were those wings?

His vision dimmed, the feeling of being borne up, of bobbing in the wind made his head light and his wounds scream. A great whooshing sound filled his ears. He chanced a glance and saw only fog speeding past and the sculpted, icy profile of a man who look oddly familiar. As did his charm.

Despite his pain, everything in Winston focused on the silver charm pinned to the man's lapel. He knew that charm.

With the last of his strength, Winston grabbed hold of it and tore it free, the metal cutting into his palm. Then he let the darkness have him. It pulled him down into an eternal rest, and he found he welcomed the embrace.

Daisy was already coming in as Ian strode down the stairs toward the main hall. He paused midstep, overwhelmed by the sight of her looking so sunny and fresh, a true flower with her bright hair curling in profusion around her face. She noticed him in the next instant and stopped short, her cheeks flushing as their gazes locked, and then her lids lowered to hide whatever it was she felt.

She makes you weak. His hand curled round the balustrade. Part of him feared he might careen down the stair and fall flat on his face before her. Christ, he didn't like the sensation. But Daisy, her locks ablaze in a nimbus of gold from the light pouring in through the window, was a sight from which he could not turn away.

He had hated seeing her fear last night. He hated that this thing wanted her.

Mine. A ridiculous sentiment, given that his heart could not afford to claim her, but one that wouldn't go away.

"You're going out," she said first, her voice music in the quiet of his house.

"Seems you've already been." Damn but he sounded unhinged, affected. Aye, she made him weak, to be sure. But alive. So very alive.

"I went to visit my sisters." Her eyes clouded for a moment. "We meet on Tuesdays for breakfast."

He took the last few stairs at an easy pace and came to stand in front of her. The sweet scent of her, untainted by perfume, enveloped him, and he forced himself to speak lightly. "Are you well?"

"Yes." She gave him a slight, practiced smile. "My headache is gone, and Tuttle's potion patched me up quite well."

Gently, he touched her temple, not missing the way she stiffened. The reaction slashed into his heart but he forged on. "I'm glad." He let his hand drop. "However, I was referring to what you saw."

Her jaw tensed but she met his eyes with an even gaze. "That was horrid. But you are healed so I shall not dwell on it."

The fingers of a memory pulled at the edges of his mind. Of the earth quaking and men screaming. He'd been too lost in pain to remember it clearly. Perhaps he'd been hallucinating at that point. As neither Daisy nor Talent remarked upon it, he figured it must be so. But he'd been close, too close, to fully turning, and that scared the hell out of him. *She makes you weak.*

"It pains me that you had to witness it," he said softly.

"It pains me that you had to endure it," she said just as softly.

Quite suddenly, all he wanted to do was kiss her, to taste her flavor, lose himself in the decadence of her succulent mouth once more. His flesh tightened with need. Need enough to make him lean toward her. But her expression cried out *Stay away*, so he stepped back and put a distance between them.

"Need you rest now?" he asked. "Or would you like to come out with me?"

Her eyes widened as she blinked up at him in clear surprise. "Where are you going?"

He smiled at her, a devious grin he knew she wouldn't be able to resist. "Somewhere proper ladies would not dare venture." He offered his arm. "Somewhere foul and most likely dangerous."

A smile crept over her features, turning her from lovely to breathtaking. "Oh, la. If it were truly dangerous, you'd endeavor to keep me away from it, Northrup." But she put her slim hand on his arm anyway. The contact felt a balm to the irritation that had been plaguing his insides since he'd woken to find himself alone. How did she manage it? To always say and do the exact thing to keep him going.

"True, but that wouldn't stop you from trying to follow, now would it?"

Her smile was the sun itself. "How very clever of you to realize you've been bested and admit defeat now."

Although he laughed, his heart clenched with sudden, brutal force, for he feared truer words had not been spoken.

Chapter Twenty-seven

Tell me about her."

Daisy's soft voice cut into Ian with the stealth of a switchblade as they waited for a skiff to take them to their destination. Standing beside her on the wooden docks, Ian tensed. Talking about *her* was the last thing he wanted to do. The very idea made him sweat.

"Her who?" Lovely response. Made him sound like a bloody night owl.

The corner of Daisy's succulent mouth lifted but the smile didn't reach her eyes. "The woman whom you seek in redheaded whores."

Jesus. Where was this coming from? What did she want of him?

"I no longer seek whores, luv." Not when what he wanted stood less than a foot away.

Again that look, pitying, accusing, and sad. It made his insides itch and his collar go tight.

"Ian," she said softly, "do not play games now."

Ian. The sound of his name on her lips surely did make him weak.

Blue eyes pinned him. "Was it truly another? Or is it... Is it my sister whom you think of when you bed them?"

Right. She'd been visiting with Miranda just now. Lovely.

He must have scowled for Daisy made a furtive move, as if to place a hand on him in placation. "I will not judge you for falling in love with her," she said quickly, insanely. "Who wouldn't love her? I love her to distraction myself. But after last night..."

White teeth dug into her bottom lip, denting it, but she faced him without flinching. "I need to know. I won't be a substitute for what you cannot have. Especially not if it is my sister's shadow you mean to place me in. I will not be that woman, Ian."

Brave, proud lass. Something inside his chest shifted.

"And if I should tell you that you are more than what I craved before?" he asked. "That you are not a substitute, or distraction, but a balm, would you believe me? Or accuse me of saying what I would in order to get you into my bed?"

Her expression grew pinched. "You cannot deny that is the tactic most men would employ."

"So I am buggered no matter how I answer?"

She flinched.

When he spoke, his voice came out rough and angrier than he'd like, for he could see her skittishness. "There is only one thing you truly need to know about me, Daisy-Meg. And that is that I will not lie to you. Ever." His fingers curled over the silver wolf's head of his walking stick. "I told you before that it was not your sister who made me want to seek ginger-haired lasses. That was truth."

She nodded with a jerk of her head, but her eyes did not clear. "But you did fancy her."

"Oh, for God's sake!" He threw a hand up out of sheer irritation and a passing dockworker flinched. The man gave Ian a wide berth as he walked around them, and Ian lowered his voice. "Yes, I fancied her, but it wasn't what you think."

Surrounded by swirls of fog, her heart-shaped face glowed like a fine pearl. "What do I think?"

"That I was so beguiled by her beauty that I lost my mind to it." He made a sound of disgust.

"Well..." She frowned.

"I'll tell you, and then we'll have no more talk of your sister. I'll not have her standing between us, aye?"

Again she nodded stiffly, but she'd flinched at his use of "us." Out of surprise? Or distaste? His hand shook as he raked his fingers through his hair. He wouldn't lose her to this. Not this. Damn Miranda. And damn himself too for letting the world believe she meant more to him than she did.

"Part of it was her looks. Her ginger hair and green eyes mostly, mind. I've had plenty of beautiful women in my life. Enough to not be turned into a panting pup by appearance alone." By God, it wasn't redheads that plagued his dreams now. Not even a little. He took his eyes from Daisy's golden locks.

Her voice was hesitant, unbelieving. "If it wasn't her appearance, then what?"

Thick, cold fog seemed to creep down his throat and smother his nostrils. He struggled not to pull at his collar. "She was a supernatural. Like me."

Around them, commerce teemed with activity: dock-workers and sailors, streetwalkers and pickpockets went about their daily lives. Here, standing beside a wooden piling, it was just him, just her.

"Most humans would likely think I was mad if I revealed my true self. I thought she would understand. I found the notion of not having to hide what I was attractive. And she was loyal. So very loyal to Archer."

Daisy was silent for a moment, her head tilted slightly as though she were contemplating. Which he gathered she was. How could she not ponder on his humiliating confession of neediness? Again came the feeling of suffocation, the air too heavy, the smell of brine and fish overwhelming. His hand convulsively clutched his thigh.

Daisy saw the action. "If not Miranda, then who is the redheaded woman you seek?"

He hated the softness in her voice most of all. Perspiration bloomed along his upper lip as he stared at the mucky brown water of the Thames. When her pointed silence grew unbearable, he made himself say it. "My wife." He swallowed. "Una."

Saying her name was akin to calling forth her ghost, and his hackles rose in defense. Under the cold eye of scrutiny, Ian didn't really know what he was after when he bedded women who resembled her. Forgiveness? Another chance? Revenge? His thoughts were muddled, and part of him resented Daisy for making him examine his motivations.

Daisy's eyes were wide when he looked back at her. Hadn't expected a wife, had she? Perhaps she thought him incapable of love. If only that were true. It would have saved him much. He almost laughed, save his chest hurt too much. "Not to worry, she's been dead some seventy years."

Daisy's bottom lip pushed out. "I did not think you had her tucked away somewhere while you dallied about, if that is what you are implying."

"Didn't you?"

"No. You are too honorable to treat any woman so poorly."

"You are the only one who seems to view me as honorable," he said with an unfortunate rasp in his throat.

Her expression did not alter but stayed hard, piercing. "What happened to her, Ian?"

I thought I could stand it, Ian. I was wrong to hope for the best. They'd both been wrong to hope.

His nails turned to claws, catching on the fine weave of his trousers. "She died."

"How?"

You destroy everything! You and your... beast. Just by being.

His jaw clenched. For a moment, he wanted Una in front of him so badly he could taste it. "Of a broken heart."

"Oh."

Yes, oh, he thought with a silent shout. He saw Daisy's frown of disappointment and wanted to punch something. He took a ragged breath, and then another.

"Did you... did you no longer fancy her then?"

His laugh was light, sardonic, yet it burned like acid in his throat. "Who said I was the one to break her heart?" God, if only Una were here. He would put his hands around her slender neck, and wring it.

Possession of an excellent sense of smell was not always a boon. Beautiful in its own way, the River Thames was nevertheless a foul place to be. Overcrowded on the dock with the sweating bodies of men laboring to lift and transport huge crates as well as the riffraff of hawkers, vendors, pickpockets, and cutthroats—and the whores who serviced them all.

But on the river, well, one could not get away from the thick, burning stink that came from the millions of gallons of raw sewage that emptied into it twice daily, nor the briny dampness that clung to one's hair and clothes.

A fact that had Daisy breathing through her mouth and resisting the urge to burrow her nose in the folds of Northrup's coat. It couldn't be any better for Northrup, whose senses were no doubt stronger than hers. But he sat erect and alert as their hired skiff bobbled across dark, glossy waters toward a ramshackle-looking barge moored near the Waterloo Bridge. Only a certain tightness around his eyes and nostrils betrayed that he too was suffering from the smell.

At some point, Northrup had quietly taken her hand in his, pulling it close. He had yet to give it up. Now and then, he would idly play with the tips of her fingers in a gesture that she realized was subconscious. She had yet to take her hand back, for the touch left her feeling warm and cosseted. Were she to concentrate too greatly upon the sensation, she'd crawl into the circle of his very capable arms and nuzzle his well-formed mouth. Kiss and suck those lips until she forgot everything. A shiver lit through her. God, he'd been delicious last night. And she wanted more. Always more.

Which was insanity. A wife. He'd had a wife. One that he had obviously loved. She had seen that much in his eyes. A wife whose ghost he sought in so many others. And yet the woman had her heart broken by another. Daisy had wanted to ask by whom and why, but instinctively, she knew he would have cracked if she'd asked more just then. She wouldn't do that to him. Because she cared. She needed to end this...thing between them. Now, before she sank in too deep.

Weary and confused, she turned her head to find the haggard-looking man who rowed them staring at their clasped hands. The muscles along the back of her neck tightened. Words such as "strumpet" and "jezebel" came to her mind unbidden, filling her with thwarted rage. Why was it that her affection for men, her *need* was so very vile, while a man's was simply touted as natural?

Northrup felt her tension, for he looked down at their linked hands as if suddenly aware of them. His brows drew together in a puzzled frown, and then his nostrils flared and he brought her hand against his flat stomach. His blue gaze settled on the man before them.

"I don't recall paying extra for the scenic route, Clive." His expression, for all its outward pleasantness, held a hard glint of warning.

Clive flinched and put his legs into the next row. The oars slapped through the brown water and the skiff cut into the light wisps of fog with a smooth whoosh. "Scenic route's free for favored customers, guvnor."

Northrup flashed a set of even, sharp teeth. "Just get us there before I lose my breakfast."

Clive cackled with good nature. "Never was a good waterman, was you, milord?"

It was then Daisy truly noticed the gray cast to Northrup's skin, but it was of little matter, for the dark, hulking shape of the barge now loomed before them, the craft rocking gently against the slow-moving waters. Clive maneuvered them to the side of it, where its hull spread out over the water in a wall of dull, black-painted wood.

Barnacles and slick algae clung to the old wooden vessel, various creaks and groans an ominous sound among the clangs and whistles that rang out over the river proper. A ladder made of graying rope and dubious-looking slots of weathered wood dangled over the side, and Daisy mentally cursed the fashion for narrow skirts.

She was grateful that Northrup went up first, for the idea of stepping onto the ghostly craft alone did not appeal. His step was light and sure, and he soon disappeared over the side. After a moment, his head popped over the edge, and he gave her an encouraging smile.

"Up with you, old girl, or risk missing out on the fun."

Hands on hips, she glared. "Call me 'old girl' again, and I'll leave you here."

Northrup merely winked. "I am certain Clive would be most willing to give you another scenic tour of the Thames. Wouldn't you, Clive?"

" 'Twould be my great pleasure, milord," Clive called back, his bleary eyes alight with the prospect as he ogled Daisy.

Northrup held out a hand. Glaring promised murder, Daisy grabbed the ladder.

With Clive holding the bottom and Northrup calling down various cheeky suggestions, she managed it to the top, and despite wanting to kick him rather badly, she happily accepted Northrup's warm hand and stumbled onto the abandoned deck.

"There's no one here," she said, allowing him to draw an arm about her waist and hold her close. The dank air was cooler on deck, a chill that seemed to run over her and coil about her ankles.

A growl sounded deep in Northrup's throat, and he raised his voice, his gaze not on hers but on the empty deck. "Oh, there is someone here, and if they've a mind to keep their throats intact, they'll leave off."

On that rather odd request, the air about them stirred and suddenly it was warmer.

Making a sound of annoyance, Northrup led her forward, their steps hollow against the damp wood as they went to the captain's cabin.

The door opened easily, and Daisy found herself stepping into a riot of color and light. Saffron silk damask lined the walls that glowed like fire in the light of a dozen Moroccan lamps. Her footsteps were muted as they moved over jewel-toned carpets made in the East. Before her, lay a great table of golden ormolu, on which a lavish buffet had been spread. The foul scent of the river receded in favor of roast beef and hot rolls. She could not help but blink in stupefaction.

"Lord Northrup," came a deep voice from the far end of the room. "Precisely on time, as always. And you've brought a guest."

It was only then that she noticed the man lounging in a throne-like black chair inlaid with mother-of-pearl. The man himself was as stunning as the room, his caramel-colored skin light compared to the shining raven hair that rose from his high brow to flow like ink around an exquisitely carved face. He turned his eyes to her, and a little breath left her. They were eyes of the palest green jade that seemed to glow with an inner light.

Northrup heard the sound and his grip on her waist tightened a fraction. She might have laughed at the possessive gesture. Certainly the man before her was handsome, but there was a coldness in him, an oddness that left her feeling on edge. The man seemed well aware of the effect his appearance had on the uninitiated, but the look in his eyes was weary and resigned, as if he took no joy from it. Daisy was left with the oddest feeling that he resented his own beauty.

He wore not the attire of a proper modern gentleman

but something out of the previous century: blue satin breeches, a lacy jabot at his throat, and a frock coat of aquamarine satin embroidered with tiny chartreuse dragonflies. His voice was smooth and welcoming as he stood.

"Welcome to the *Marietta*, madam." He bowed with grace before gesturing to the seat beside him. "Please, do me a great honor and join me for a bit of refreshment." His words ran together in a thick syrup of sound, the lilt in them foreign yet pleasing. An American southerner, if Daisy had to guess.

Famished, she moved to accept the seat to which he gestured, but Northrup put a staying hand on her arm. "I think not, Lucien." Northrup's mouth twisted wryly as he glanced down at Daisy. "Many an unfortunate innocent have sat down to sup with a gim, never to get up again."

Northrup drew out a chair for Daisy, decidedly away from Lucien, before sitting in the one Lucien had offered to her. "Poison or sleeping draughts are their most-loved weapons. Never share a meal with a desperate gim, *mo gradh*. Or risk it being your last."

Lucien laughed at that, a deep rumbling sound that unnerved her, despite its warmth. "I am greatly aggrieved at the charge, Ian." His smile was the uncoiling of a snake as he took his seat. "Even if it is true."

"A gim?" Daisy asked, finding her voice at last.

Lucien's strange green eyes settled on her, and in the candlelight, they seemed to glow. "GIM—short for Ghost in the Machine, *ma chère*."

She turned to Northrup, who, for all his talk of poisoning, settled back into his seat with casual grace. "Yes, a GIM. It is what we came to see."

"Whom." Lucien's drawl, though still mellow, had a bit of steel beneath it when he addressed Northrup. "If you intend to come for a visit, Ian, I expect a measure of politeness."

Northrup inclined his head, all sense of play having fled from his expression. "Quite right. A thousand pardons. I forget myself." He placed a hand upon Daisy's forearm. "Daisy, may I present Mr. Lucien Stone, formerly of New Orleans, Louisiana, now leader for the London faction of the *GIMs*."

Lucien gave a stately nod as Northrup continued. "Lucien, may I present—"

"The lovely widow Craigmore," Lucien finished for him. "Your paramour of late, if gossip is to be believed." When Daisy sat up in ire, he smiled. "Though according to my sources, we are not quite there as of yet. Are we, my dear?"

"I expect you to play nice as well, Lucien," Northrup warned.

"Mmm." With a languid hand, Lucien picked up a glass of red wine and took a long swallow, somehow managing to make it look delicious to Daisy's parched mouth. "Certainly, *mon ami*."

She rested her hands in her lap for fear of reaching out for the wine. "If the two of you are finished baiting each other, would one of you tell me what or who is a 'ghost in the machine'?"

Lucien set his wine down. "It is quite a tale, as tales go." He plucked an icy-looking grape in his mouth and sucked it dry with relish. Daisy's mouth watered. "There are," he continued, "certain individuals who possess a great desire for life. Unfortunately, circumstance is never kind, and their life ultimately ends."

"Doesn't it for everyone?" Lord but the grapes looked refreshing.

He took another one. "One would think. However, these individuals refuse to go gently into that cold night, as it were. And so they wait, without a body to warm them, a soul drifting in search of a home. When lo and behold, this poor, lost spirit finds an opportunity."

"A dying body," Northrup put in, his eyes narrowing on Lucien as the man licked up another succulent grape.

"Yes," said Lucien. "A perfect home, for the body is soon to be vacated."

"And so," Northrup continued, "this spirit pushes out the rightful spirit of the dying body and takes possession."

"Crassly put but accurate." Lucien toyed with the stem of his wine glass. "But there is a problem."

"The body is still dying," Daisy said. The story had set her heart to a slow, hesitant rhythm and lifted the little hairs along the back of her neck.

He beamed. "Exactly! Fortunately, with every problem comes a solution. For upon possession, if the gods are smiling down"—Northrup's snort was ignored—"a being appears."

Lucien took another drink, and Daisy swallowed, mimicking the action and wishing the wine were sliding down her throat. Northrup's hand fell upon hers. The stern look in his blue eyes had her sitting back.

"He calls himself Adam," Lucien said, "as he ate from the tree of knowledge, and in so doing learned how to create his own beings. Adam will give the spirit the home it craves, restoring the dying body and turning it into a perfect, ageless shell."

"You mean"—Daisy swallowed—"you are a spirit using the body of another?"

His smile was all teeth. "In the flesh." He chuckled. "And a rather lovely body at that, wouldn't you agree?"

Daisy pursed her mouth, but he kept grinning. "You should have seen my birth form, sweetness. It was plain, odd, and gangly. The crowning glory of breeding cousin with cousin for generations." He gave a little bow with his head. "I was the very rich, very spoiled son of very white, very ugly planters." Another grape disappeared through his full, beautiful lips. "Oh, how they would roll over in their graves to learn that I now inhabit the body of a quadroon whore."

"Perhaps they would think you fortunate for a second chance at life," Daisy murmured.

"Doubtful, *chère*. One must not overlook the very real price to pay for this second chance, as you put it." His green eyes iced over. "The spirit must procure other bodies for Adam."

"And if the spirit does not?"

"Oh, but he must. For Adam builds in a rather clever fail proof." At that, Lucien undid the middle two buttons of his shirt and parted the linen.

"Good God," Daisy breathed, holding her own chest, for the sight pained her.

Embedded within the center of his chest lay a little glass window framed in gold, through which, beneath the cage of bone, blue veins, and flesh, pumped a golden heart, a miracle of clockwork gears and moving pistons.

Having seen a man merged with a wolf, Daisy knew the impossible possible. It still did not prevent her from leaning forward, her hand rising as if to touch the little window. She curled her fingers into a fist at the last moment, realizing the rudeness of the gesture.

" 'How many goodly creatures are there here,' " she quoted softly.

He gave her a knowing smile as he buttoned his shirt.

"'O brave new world! That has such people in it!'" he said, finishing the quote for her. "Knowledge is a wonderful thing, is it not? You see, my dear, if the ghost who now drives the machine should fail to comply with his maker's wishes, his heart will stop and the machine works no more."

"Is it worth it?" she asked. "To murder innocents in return for a life of servitude?"

The corners of his eyes crinkled. "Oh now, we've misled you, Northrup and I. One need not resort to murder. The dying are plentiful, especially in a city such as London. However, one occasionally grows weary of the search and may, if tempted, take an easier route in procurement."

With a lazy sigh, he poured himself more wine, sending forth a bouquet heavy with notes of currant and black cherry. "And we mustn't forget the certain, shall we say, benefits one acquires." He turned his gleaming eyes upon Northrup. "Which, presumably, is the reason you are here."

Releasing his proprietary grip on Daisy's arm, Northrup reached into his breast pocket to pull out the unicorn stickpin he had found in the perfumer's shack and passed it over to Lucien. "I found this pinned to the bodice of a dead woman in Bethnal Green."

"A lovely piece." Lucien swirled the pin between his fingers, making the unicorn dance. "But I needn't tell you what it is."

Northrup scowled at the pin. "No."

Daisy leaned closer to peer at the little pin. "Perhaps you could tell me?"

"The lion and the unicorn are the monarch's symbol," Northrup said.

Daisy nodded. "The lion for England, the unicorn for Scotland."

"Aye, but what you do not know is that upon ascension to the Ranulf throne, the British monarch presents a pin such as this to the Ranulf King as a symbol of good faith."

She blinked. "Does the Queen know? About lycans?"

"The Ranulfs are closely tied with the royal family. We share a direct blood tie with Queen Mary of Scots." His expression turned wry. "Queen Victoria knows of us. The royals always have. And though the British monarchs rule Scotland in the human world, The Ranulfs rule the subjects of the lycan world."

Northrup, rather than looking smug, seemed to flush at this. His lids lowered and he studied the place setting before him. "Recognizing our ties is essential to maintaining civil human-lycan politics. My father passed his pin on to me before he abdicated his throne."

Lucien smiled widely, much like the cat that ate the cream. "I take it this one is not yours?"

"No." Northrup's tone was final. "I can only assume it is the one Conall received from Queen Victoria."

Making a steeple with his fingers, Lucien's expression turned inward. "I've heard tell that Conall is on the outs with Victoria." He gave Northrup a stiff smile. "She always liked you better. It's no secret that Victoria was put out when you did not become The Ranulf. That has stuck in Conall's craw."

"True," Northrup said. "Since I refused the throne and he took it, Conall has hated me. Now a pin that would implicate both the House of Ranulf and the Queen is found at a murder scene."

"So," said Lucien, "you believe Conall might be stirring up trouble and letting the werewolf live to bedevil the Queen?"

Northrup's jaw tightened. "Last night, I was hit by

Ranulf darts, as was the *were*. Daisy and I were taken to Ranulf House. Conall feigns ignorance of the *were*, but I have little reason to believe him. Either he is taunting the Queen or me, or both. I do not know." He picked up the delicate pin and made the unicorn spin round. "Which is why I want you to find out what my brother is doing and why."

Lucien's mouth twitched with what looked like resigned humor. "Just so I have this straight. You want me to spy on the lycan king?"

They stared at each other as the ormolu clock on the wall ticked away the seconds.

"Well," said Lucien as he rang a bell by his side, "it appears we shall need Mary Chase."

Chapter Twenty-eight

"Who is Mary Chase?" Daisy asked while they waited. "And why do we need her?"

Lucien's strange eyes flashed on a smile. "Reconnaissance. We are the spies of the supernatural world, *ma petite*. For the right price, we can get into anywhere at any time. Observe."

Lucien became utterly still, and his gleaming eyes immediately dimmed. A caress of ice-cold air touched Daisy's cheek and then surrounded her breasts. Icy prickles rippled over her sensitive flesh, beading her nipples. She sucked in a gasp as a cold draft blew between her legs. "Oh!"

A vicious snarl burst from Northrup, and he was out of his seat, his hands fisting Lucien's collar. The man's head flopped to the side as if he were stunned. Northrup gave him a violent shake. Fangs sprang long in Northrup's mouth, his eyes going round and filling with blue. "I'll tear yer fuckin' head from yer neck, if ye don't leave off!"

The air about her whooshed past her. Lucien's prone

body jerked and he blinked, his eyes returning to normal. Still caught in Northrup's grip, he offered an innocent little smile to the snarling lycan bearing down on him.

"Temper, Ian. It was only a bit of fun."

Northrup was past hearing. His jaw cracked as it lengthened, the fangs in his upper and lower jaw growing longer. "Not with her." A snarl tore out as his claws sank into Lucien's neck.

The man gurgled as Daisy leaped up. "Northrup! Stop." He bared his teeth at Lucien, and the muscles along his forearms bulged. Crimson blood ran in rivulets down Lucien's neck and into his snow-white cravat.

"Ian." With a shaking hand, she touched his arm. He jerked as though shocked, his eyes, gleaming ice blue, turned to her, unseeing and wild. "Let him go, Ian. You don't want to kill him. Not truly."

Northrup cocked his head, his nostrils pinching as though he were inclined to disagree. His tense frame vibrated as a series of low growls rumbled in his throat. Daisy blanched but did not let him go. She had to trust in his promise not to hurt her. "Ian. Stand down."

On a shudder, his body began to ease back to normal and the confusion and rage in his eyes cleared, to be replaced by a possessive heat that made her blush. A grunt of acknowledgment left him before he turned away from her.

Northrup hauled his prey close, his nose butting up against Lucien's. "Play with yer own lass, aye?"

With a final snarl, he shoved Lucien back into his seat. The chair slid a foot before Lucien's boot heels stopped it. "A thousand pardons," Lucien said, panting. "I forgot myself."

Daisy, on the other hand, having just realized that the cold touch was Lucien, suddenly felt far from appeased. "That was you?" she said through her teeth.

The man held up his hands in apology, and she turned to Northrup. "I was wrong. Tear his hands off."

Northrup's eyes glinted with wicked humor as he winked at her, his smile feral and still showing a bit of fang. He turned back to Lucien and let his claws free. Lucien backed into his chair, his handsome mouth opening in alarm. "Here now!"

Daisy gave him an evil smile. Now that Northrup had calmed, he wouldn't follow through, but he put on a very convincing show. "I wouldn't be too alarmed, Mr. Stone," she said. "After all, it appears you do not need your hands to get into mischief."

Northrup took another step, making a great deal of growling, and Daisy almost laughed.

"Oh now, sweet, I do apologize." Northrup grabbed his flailing arm, and Lucien yelped. "I was disrespectful, and I was wrong. Now call off your dog!"

"I suppose we ought to let him alone," Daisy said with a sigh. "After all, I abhor violence."

Northrup chuckled and let him go.

"Quite good of you," Lucien muttered to Daisy. "I am in your debt."

The door opened and in walked a woman Daisy presumed was Mary Chase.

Sugar and spice and everything nice. It was all Daisy could think as the young woman glided toward them. Golden-brown hair, glinting like spun sugar, framed a heart-shaped face from which eyes of pale butterscotch glittered with bright, watchful intelligence.

Those eyes glanced over her, taking note and then moving on as if she found Daisy a rather boring addition to her day. Lucien, however, saw the way Daisy gaped.

"It is the eyes that snare you." Smoothing out his

rumpled coat with a shaking hand, he forced a wide smile. "As is their purpose. Crystalline eyes to draw you in. Entice you to tell us your secrets."

Daisy closed her mouth. "You pick your bodies well."

Mary Chase's petal pink lips quirked but she said nothing as she perched on the arm of Lucien's chair.

"Mary's"—Lucien ran a knuckle down the woman's arm—"delightful body is her own. As she had the choice offered to her moments before her first death."

Mary Chase accepted the man's touch with neither encouragement nor rejection. Her odd eyes rested a moment longer than proper on Northrup before sliding back to Lucien. "What is it that you want, sir?" Her voice was warm toffee, and some base part of Daisy bristled with pure feminine jealousy.

"Northrup here wants us to play shadow to The Ranulf." Lucien handed her the stickpin. "Are you up to the task, *ma petite*?"

Her butterscotch eyes settled on Northrup. "A dangerous thing to follow a lycan."

A slow, wry smile curled Northrup's lips as he took his seat once more. "Very dangerous. You might not survive."

Lucien laughed again. "Helping along our bargaining, are we, Ian?"

"Hurrying it along, more like," Northrup said. "We all know what it is I am asking."

Daisy leaned in. "Do *we*?" She rather hated being the ignorant party.

"Lycans can see spirits," Northrup said patiently. "For a GIM to spy on one is a tricky business." Well, at the very least, Daisy understood how Northrup had known what Lucien had been up to with his tricks.

"An understatement," Lucien cut in. "I don't lightly risk

the welfare of my brightest." Lucien's hand drifted from Mary's arm to the narrow curve of her waist, cinched in golden silk. Daisy could not help but admire the gown, or the woman for choosing it. Here was a woman who knew proper dress.

"One wonders why you don't volunteer for the deed yourself then," Daisy said.

At that, Mary Chase's gold gaze flicked to Daisy's. A small smile sparked in those strange orbs. "Because he needs the best," she said. "That would be me."

Humble girl, she was.

"What is that you want to know?" Mary asked Northrup.

Daisy tried to take her eyes from Lucien's roaming hand, but she could not as it slid slowly up to cup the young woman's small breast.

Northrup's seat creaked beneath his muscled frame. "The werewolf terrorizing London, does Conall have it? And if so, where?"

Long, dark fingers idly circled a budding nipple, a whisper of a caress. The woman leaned into the touch, slightly, subtly. Heat bloomed between Daisy's legs and spread over her flesh. She shifted in her chair, pressing her thighs together.

"That shall take some time, and finesse."

"Are you willing?"

The questing fingers stilled but did not give up their prize. The blunt tip of one finger rested gently over a hardened nub. Daisy swallowed, the tightness inside of her clenching. Her cheeks were surely aflame. Yet she could not move her eyes from the sight.

Mary Chase's small breast lifted and fell with the rhythm of her breathing, causing dark fingers to slide over the curve of flesh. A pale, feminine hand fell upon a muscled thigh encased in blue satin. Slowly, the hand stroked up to the bulge growing between his thighs. Daisy squirmed and gripped the side of her chair.

"I am always willing." The questing hand stopped, having found its prize, and squeezed. A blast of heat hit Daisy's cheeks.

Lucien's voice was surprisingly benign for a man who had a woman's hand on his cock. "There is the matter of payment, old friend."

Northrup's arm moved. A pile of pound notes scattered among the plates and goblets.

"Money is lovely, Ian, but I think I'll need something more this time." He made a show of straightening his cravat.

So they would have to pay for Northrup's temper.

Northrup's jaw tightened. "What do you want?"

Lucien let go of his moll and leaned back in his chair. "Do you know your brother will not work with the GIMs?" A cold look frosted over his features. "Rather, he'd prefer not to pay but to force our hand into providing services."

Northrup did not move. "What, Lucien?"

"You." His expression grew deadly serious. "You get that brother of yours off the throne and take it."

A bitter laugh escaped Northrup. "Why does everyone seem to think I'll be a better leader? Did ye no' think I might be inclined to hold it against you once I got there?"

"Ah, but that is why I shall also ask for your assurance that you shall treat us fairly." Lucien waved an idle hand. "Fairly, that is all. No favoritism. You could not ask for a better deal."

"I can ask for a hell of a lot," Northrup snapped.

He turned away and lowered his head. But Daisy could see the capitulation taking over his expression, and it made her want to shout in protest. He wanted a normal life. He would not do this. He could not.

"I'll need assurances as well," Northrup said. "I do this, and not only will you tell me what I want to know, but you will work for me exclusively until the *were* is dead. Daisy's safety will be as important to you as it is to me." He leveled a glare at Lucien. "I trust you understand the full extent of that importance."

Lucien's smile was the devil's. "Of course. She shall be as dear to me as... well, let us say a daughter, shall we? I wouldn't want you getting your fur up once more."

Northrup began to nod his assent but Lucien held up a hand. "To be clear, protection is null and void should you fail to become The Ranulf. As much as I'd love to help the lovely Daisy"—he glanced at her with humor—"I cannot risk all for nothing in return."

Dead calm colored Northrup's voice when he spoke. "When I challenge Conall, I will not fail." His eyes held with Lucien's. "But I will not do so until the werewolf is destroyed."

With a chill, Daisy understood. The werewolf was a threat to her. He could not risk his own life until he knew that she was safe.

"Northrup," Daisy said, coming forward, "do not do this. Not for me. There are other ways."

"There are always other ways," he agreed, not looking at her. "But this is the best." He gave a sharp nod to Lucien. "Done."

"Why did you do it?" Daisy asked him. "You told me you wanted out of that life."

Ian sat back against the squabs, as comfortable as he could get given that he'd been fighting off an erection for the better part of the hour and had only just got it under control. Damn Lucien and his antics. Ian had seen the display before, and he didn't give a fig if the sly GIM fondled his protégée. Daisy's reaction, however, was another matter altogether. Seeing her grow agitated with desire had set him aflame.

"You know why."

Her white teeth caught her lower lip and worried it. "I'm not worth this trouble."

"You *are*." Ian cleared his throat. "My course was set the moment those Ranulf darts hit me, lass. At least this way I'll know the GIMs will be watching over you. It isn't the best of arrangements, I grant you. They are a sly lot, but we needed the help. I can assure you, however, that once a deal is struck, they will hold up their end."

Daisy frowned. "I thought you were friends with Lucien."

"No one is truly friends with a GIM. Their very immortality is based on theft, which does not endear them to many." But Ian did not want to discuss Lucien or their deal. No matter the necessity, or the facts, Conall was his baby brother. The thought of killing him crushed Ian's heart. No, all he wanted to discuss this very moment was Daisy. And him.

"He beguiled you, you realize."

Daisy stiffened against her seat. "Into wanting the food?" With undue intensity, she studied the view outside of the moving coach. "I figured as much. I've never been so moved by a common grape."

He wanted to laugh at the way she so neatly sidestepped him. "That evasion was prettily done, my dear."

She sniffed. "I don't know what you mean."

Feeling fiendish, he nudged her skirts with the tip of his booted toe. Her red-and-cream-striped visiting dress, with all its flounces and bows, put to mind wrapping paper, an irresistible present that his fingers itched to unwrap. "Did it not affect you, the way he touched the ethereal Mary Chase?"

She edged away, her plump lips flat with annoyance. "Of course it did. How can one not be affected by such a disgraceful display?"

"Mmm." He rested the offending foot over his knee. "So those blushes were out of disgust, were they?"

She glared at the passing traffic.

A certain sense of glee lightened his chest. "See, I rather thought you found it arousing."

She did not bite but kept a bland face turned toward the window. "You would."

"Huh. Perhaps there was another reason you squirmed within your seat. I would blame it on luncheon, but as we've had none..."

She shot him a repressive look. "Now it is you who is being disgusting."

He laughed for the sheer joy of doing so. This was what he wanted from life, not death or clan machinations. Just her. Just them. "Daisy-girl, you are a terrible liar, did you know?"

"Ass," she muttered under her breath.

Planting his feet on the coach floor, Ian rested his elbows upon his knees, bringing himself into tempting proximity of her lush figure. He allowed himself one breath of her natural fragrance and felt it swim through his veins. "Are you saying you have no interest in that sort of activity?" Oh, but he was a bastard.

The bored look remained. "Voyeurism seems a rather unbalanced exchange."

"Were it not solely voyeuristic in nature?" He ran his tongue along the outside of his teeth and was gratified to see her twitch. Unbidden, images of the night before flashed through his mind, of her mouth opening for him and the feel of her abundant curves filling his hands as he pressed against her. By God, she'd bitten him. And he'd loved it. His fingers clenched. "Were it perhaps one man with one woman? *You*, I mean, with one man."

"Northrup." It was a strangled sound, a plea for silence.

But the devil in him had taken rein of his common sense. "Did you take a peek?"

She startled, but he could tell by the look on her face that she knew precisely what he was about. "What? No." Her eyes cut to his and then darted away, high color painting her cheeks red. "You were unconscious. It would have been rude in the extreme to take advantage."

"How disappointing." His smile grew. Ah, to tease her. He got more enjoyment from doing so than entertaining a bed full of women. Suddenly, it was not enough to face her. Ian moved to the space beside her, taking note of the way she tensed.

"And if I hadn't been?" His heart beat too quickly, the blood pumping through his veins too hot. "Had I been awake," he whispered in her ear, "what then?"

Her cheeks plumped on a repressed grin. "In minute detail."

Heat washed under his clothes, and he pressed his shoulder more intimately against hers, knowing it would agitate her just as it agitated him. "And then what?" His voice had gone rough and thick, not his own.

Daisy kept her eyes on the window. "From what I saw

of your torso, I think..." Little pearl teeth caught on her pouting bottom lip. "I think I should like to dip you in melted butter and lick it off."

A shocked laugh burst from his lips. His cock pushed tight against his trousers. He adjusted himself and took a deep breath to keep from hauling her onto his lap then and there. "I'm asking cook for butter when we arrive home."

A chuckle escaped before she pressed her mouth tight, but her eyes twinkled as she maintained her vigil of the road. "No, you are not. Even if you did, it wouldn't matter. I won't succumb."

He turned toward her, suddenly irritated. "You are evading this. Why? We are both unattached and healthy. And we want each other," he said. "Quite desperately."

Daisy drew in a sharp breath through her pert nose, but she faced him, her blue eyes steady and filled with the same desire that burned inside of him. "Yes, we do."

Gods, but her admission heated his blood.

"Then let us enjoy each other."

"Is that what we are doing?" She said it so earnestly that he almost smiled, save she also appeared distressed at the very idea. "Enjoying each other? Is that what this is?"

No. It wasn't what this was. Suddenly his chest felt too tight, and his jaw clamped shut.

Blonde curls trembled as she shook her head. "You can't even answer."

"Of course I can." He rubbed his chest irritably before glaring at her. "I want you. Now. Here. Is that clear enough?"

Heart thundering in his ears, he watched her in the ensuing silence. Her lovely face fell as if she'd expected withdrawal instead of a confession. "Yes." She averted her eyes, their brilliant blue depths going murky. "It isn't a good idea, Northrup."

The coach slammed over a rut and his teeth rattled. He ground them together. It was that easy for her, was it? And what of him? If he thought too closely on all that he risked, he surely would turn tail and run. And yet he was here, willing to try.

"This is bullshite," he got out at last.

Her head snapped up in surprise, her eyes going wide. "Pardon me?"

Such outrage. Oh, but he saw the hurt there too. The fear. His fist clenched on his thigh. "It isn't in your nature to turn from pleasure, yet you are."

"What do you know of my nature?"

"I know it is exactly like mine, made to enjoy sensation. You weren't afraid before. And now you are. Why? Tell me what has changed."

She gave a little laugh. "I don't have to tell you a thing."

"No," he admitted, calming. "No, you don't." Gently, like he would approach a frightened wolf, his hand settled over her smaller one to show her he could lead her from any danger. "But you can."

She stared down at it for a moment.

"This isn't about Miranda, is it?" His fingers tightened over hers. "For I told you—"

"No, that isn't it."

Ian ran a hand over his face in an effort not to shout. "Then tell me what it is."

"You wouldn't be a nameless tup in some alley!"

She inhaled sharply and looked away, hot color rising over her cheeks. A golden curl bounced over her ear, and he caught it with his fingertip. The tendril coiled around his finger as if a living thing. When she spoke, it was barely a whisper. "It would mean something with you." The bronze fan of her lashes swept down. "You would become a complication I wouldn't know how to manage, Ian."

Everything inside him tensed. His finger, still embraced by her curl, clenched and the strand slipped free. Part of him didn't want to speak. Part of him wanted to leap from the coach and run away. Were he honest with himself, it was the greater part of him. And yet he could not stop his mouth from slowly forming the words that the stronger, deeper part of him wanted to say. "I'm willing to risk complications to be with you."

A pained sound tore from her lips. "I don't know how to do this." Her mouth pinched as though tasting something bitter. For a moment, he feared she wouldn't speak, but then she took a deep, choppy breath. "Not when my heart is engaged."

"Daisy..."

She didn't appear to hear him.

"Bloody Craigmore," she ground out, viciousness twisting her features. "I know his words were lies, cruelty designed to torment." Her hands opened and clenched as she spoke. "And yet I still find myself believing them."

He threaded his fingers with hers, keeping his hold light no matter how much he wanted to turn and punch a hole through the coach window. "I'd rip his throat out were he still alive."

Daisy blinked back a tear. "It wouldn't have changed a thing. His words have infected me, made me believe that my lust is a sin and my pleasure a man's downfall."

"Is this why you never took a lover?"

Her eyes snapped to his.

"All signs point to a woman unaccustomed to proper male attention, love." His thumb found the pulse point at her wrist and caressed the silken spot. "Which is a true shame, as you are ripe for pleasure."

She sighed. "I wanted to. God knows I did. Only"—she swallowed visibly—"I thought it would make it worse. For me to have a taste of pleasure and still be trapped." A bitter laugh filled the coach. "Stupid. So utterly stupid that I let him win."

She said it more to herself, but he drew her near. "Entirely," he agreed softly before bending down to nuzzle her neck and inhale the sweet scent of her, like sunshine and life and happiness. It felt so good to hold her again, as though one day had been a lifetime. "I say we conduct a thorough investigation in the matter of your pleasure." His lips trailed over the fragrant skin under her jaw, and she shivered. "Consider me your willing victim."

This time, when she laughed, it was light, relenting. "Pest."

"Mmm." Not leaving the delicious spot on her neck, he reached out and pulled the shade closed. "The worst of the lot."

Her head lolled back on a sigh. "I wasn't supposed to like you, Northrup."

"Ian," he reminded her. His tongue touched her earlobe, drawing out another thready sigh. "And you were supposed to be a bloody pain in my arse."

Slowly he kissed his way down her slender neck. The plump swells of her bosom trembled with each light kiss. He unhooked the first clasp of her bodice, and she went still.

"Ian?"

"Hmm?"

"You aren't honestly trying to seduce me in a carriage, are you?" She sounded mildly amused and highly incredulous.

"Why not?" His voice was muffled against her breast,

the deep valley there a delight of curves and dips. Delicately, he ran the tip of his tongue along the line of her cleavage, and she made a little noise of surprise that had him as hard as iron in an instant. He eased down to kneel in front of her on the carriage floor, and then pressed in closer, kissing her butter-soft lips, her firm little chin, the side of her warm neck.

Daisy squirmed against him. Trying to get away, or trying to get closer, he couldn't be sure. He decided to find out. He nuzzled her neck and slipped the second hook free. "It's quiet." He kissed her left breast. "Private." Her right breast next. "Then there are the convenient bumps and sways."

"It seems so obvious." Despite the protest, her hand drifted down to slide into his hair.

He laughed, his breath hot against her skin. "I shall keep that in mind for next time, lest my creativity be permanently called into question. Keep that up."

Obligingly, her fingers stroked his hair, sending shivers of pleasure down his back. The next hook came free, and his knuckles grazed the underswell of her corseted breasts.

"All the times my mother warned me about being alone with men in carriages, I would think"—she lifted her shoulders a touch, nudging herself into the kiss he placed on her collarbone—"how prosaic. What true rake would dare?"

Ian lifted his head and caught her gaze with his. "Daisy-girl?"

The arc of her brow lifted.

"Hush."

Her bodice slid apart in a hiss of satin, and he almost groaned. Her corset matched the color of her eyes. A demicup design that lifted her breasts high. The shadow of her nipples taunted him beneath the thin linen of her combinations. His thumb found the first ingenious little latch release on the corset front, and he almost wept. God bless French lingerie designers.

Ian held her gaze, watching the way she panted lightly, her lips parted and her color high. He knew that she craved going down darker roads. His voice was not his own. It belonged to a beast with a raging cockstand. "I'm going to lick and suck your sweet tits, Daisy-Meg, until we're both dying from the pleasure of it."

Her lips rounded to a shocked O, a flush spreading from her cheeks down to the impressive swells of her breasts. He didn't miss the way her pupils dilated with desire and excitement. It fueled his.

"Because you deserve pleasure, lass." He flipped open a snap, the inhuman strength in his fingers making it easy. "You deserve to be well and thoroughly loved."

With each distinct click of her corset snaps releasing, her breath ratcheted and he fought not to fall on her like a man starved. Slowly, the corset parted, revealing its hidden prize. The tightness in his gut turned to near pain.

Her panting had grown hard and agitated as she waited, her blue eyes watchful. With a flick of his wrist, he set her corset free. She exhaled in a shuddering breath as though she too had been freed. Liquid heat flowed down his spine. Keeping his eyes on hers, he let one claw out and hooked his finger over the edge of her combinations.

Whip-fast her hand lashed out and grasped his wrist with surprising strength.

Ian froze. Daisy's eyes had gone wide and panicked, fear warring with desperate longing. Tension vibrated down her arm and into his wrist, and his heart kicked in his chest.

"I don't know what will happen either," he whispered, his breath growing as agitated as hers. In truth he could go limp, fail again, or perhaps fall so far and deep for her that he would not recover. And yet. "Let us discover it together, love."

Her throat worked on a swallow, but her eyes...they filled with trust. Pride swelled in his chest. The grip on his wrist eased, and slowly, surely her hand fell to her lap.

Ian held her gaze and then he pulled. The delicate fabric tore to her waist with a rending sound that shot through the tense silence.

"Sweet Jesus." It was more a prayer than anything. She was gorgeous. Full, creamy, teardrop-shaped breasts that thrust upward. Perfect tawny nipples the size of sovereigns that invited a man to linger. His hands covered the curve of her waist where her tender flesh had been abused by the binding corset. He smoothed his palms over the red marks, and she hissed as though his touch burned.

Perhaps it did, for he felt himself burning up from inside out.

"Poor lass," he whispered, brushing his lips over a red groove on her sweet belly. "Ye should be free and unbound like this always."

Her helpless laugh was cut short as he kissed his way up, his mouth following the path made by his hands. A groan escaped him as he cupped her lush breasts. His thumbs slid over the silken tips of her nipples, slowly, back and forth until they grew stiff and wanting. He gave them a little pinch, and her eyes squeezed shut, her lips parting on a gasp. The sight almost killed him.

His mouth fastened over one flushed tip, and she moaned, arching up into him. Ian's breath was unsteady as he drew the stiff nub in deep, learning her taste, the feel of her. She was delicious, maddening. He gave her a little nip. She squirmed against him, and he knew he drove her as mad as he felt.

Blood running hot and viscous as honey in his veins, he licked his way over to the other neglected breast and nibbled and sucked it until she was tugging at his hair.

She was so primed that he could probably make her come by doing this alone. Hell, *he* was dangerously near spilling his seed as it was. And wasn't that enough to make him shout in triumph? But it was too fast. Giving her one last, suckling kiss, he took a breath and sat back on his heels.

Beneath lids lowered in dazed arousal, she watched him, confusion clouding her eyes even as she waited to see what he would do. The coach rattled over a rough patch in the road, and her breasts bounced lightly, her nipples dark and wet from his ministrations. Ian almost fell upon her again, wanting to suck and tweak those swollen tips until she came apart in his arms. He fisted his hands at his side because he wanted more. Much more. *She* deserved more.

"Lift your skirts." His voice was guttural, brutal in its command.

Her soft mouth fell open, her eyes going wide. But he saw the flash of heat in those blue depths. They stared at each other, their breathing heavy and fast.

"Lift them high and show me your sweet cunny, Daisy-Meg."

A little gasp escaped her lips, her gaze turning fever bright at the demand. He held her gaze unflinchingly, the silence so thick it pressed upon his chest like a hand. For one lurching moment, he thought she might refuse, and then slowly, oh so slowly, her hands moved. Trembling fingers fisted her skirts, and lust surged like victory through his gut.

His muscles clenched as she gathered up her gown, the rustling of satin overloud in the silence. Trim ankles came into view, then the elegant line of her shins covered in red silk stockings. Ian wanted to laugh in delight upon seeing her naughty choice in hosiery, but he couldn't catch his breath. He licked his dry lips.

"Higher." It was a growl.

She struggled with the fabric, bunches of it slipping and sliding in her hands. Poor girl. Her breasts bobbled as she arched up, making room for the mass of her skirts on the bench seat. The lacy ruffle of knickers peeked out. The frilled edge of the gown eased over her dimpled knees. Ian swallowed hard, his shoulders shaking despite his wish to be still.

"Spread your legs," he ordered on a pant.

Shyly, she bit her bottom lip as she spread her thighs. The scent of her desire made his head light. Her hips came forward on the seat, the white length of plump, linen-covered thighs opening like flower petals to the sun.

"Wider," he said when the shadowed apex of her thighs remained hidden to him. His cock throbbed with impatience, wanting to push and thrust. He took a deep breath, willing it to calm. No longer was it a question of could he finish, but could he refrain from finishing too soon.

She made a little sound that had his fingers digging into his thighs for control, and then she moved, parting, revealing herself to him.

"Ah God." His hands shook as he put them on her thighs. Framed by the slit in her combinations and a nest of honey-gold curls, pink lips, as pouty and plump as her mouth, glistened in the dim light. "I could eat ye alive, *mo gradh*."

And then he did. Spreading her legs wider still, he kissed those lips, his tongue laving through her slickness.

"Ian!" Her back lifted off the squabs, mewling sounds breaking from her as she undulated against his questing mouth. She was honey and salt and so succulent the animal in him wanted to sink his teeth into her.

He gripped the soft abundance of her arse and hauled her closer. The way her hips gently rocked in time with his kisses drove him on, and he devoured her. His mind went dark, his flesh turning to liquid fire, and his heart threatened to pound right out of his chest. She was going to kill him.

Chapter Twenty-nine

He was going to kill her. Surely one could die from pleasure.

Daisy bit her lip to keep from screaming out. Slick and hot, his tongue lapped at her, each long lick sending heat coursing down her thighs.

Sagging against the seats she blinked up at the carriage roof, her breath coming in shallow bursts. Her damp palms clutched at the mass of her skirts for fear that they would slip and hinder his efforts. Dear God, nothing ever felt so good, so sinfully good as this. Sensation overwhelmed her, drawing her focus to the wet sounds of him kissing, sucking, to the air caressing her nipples still wet and throbbing from his earlier assault, and his tongue—his clever, devious tongue.

Her hand fluttered down to weakly cup the silky back of his head and keep him close. A whimper left her as he did something particularly decadent with his mouth, and she pushed herself into the kiss. He rewarded her by doing it again, a slow swirling glide that had her writhing.

A growl rumbled low in his throat. His big hands clutched her bottom, holding her still.

She was utterly open to him, her thighs trembling and her sex pulsing. "Ian." It was a plea.

He made a noise as if he were as helpless as she, but he did not stop, his mouth moving over her in a maddeningly steady rhythm, surely designed to torment.

In a haze, she saw his hand go to the fall of his trousers, his arm jerking as he worked to open the buttons and free his cock. *Cock.* She remembered when she'd learned that word. It was the same day she'd learned what it could do, how it made her feel, the heat and fullness of it inside of her. Before her marriage, she'd loved men, loved their bodies, their taste. A lump rose in her throat. She'd nearly forgotten.

Her gaze drifted down to the dark head between her legs, the sight of it making her insides clench. This man, this man above all others, drove her to distraction. She wanted Ian's cock now, driving into her, taking claim. Heat rippled up her torso, and her pleasure spiraled toward a precipice.

"Ian…"

He tilted his head, the strands of his thick hair spreading over her thigh in an auburn fan. He blinked up at her, slow and languid, as if he hadn't a care. But the devil lurked behind his innocent expression, sly and ready to tease. "Yes, sweet?"

Perspiration trickled between her breasts and down the small of her back. She licked her lips, forcing the words past her labored breaths. "I want…" She couldn't say it. Her cheeks burned as she looked at him in supplication.

His breath stirred her wet curls, making her twitch. "What do you want?"

Oh, the horrid bastard. She tried to nudge closer, but he held her back.

"You." She gasped as he planted another soft, searching kiss on her sex. "You. Now... God!"

Beneath the shadow of his lashes, his eyes were a blue flame, wicked and wild as they pinned her. "What is it that you want me to do?"

A shiver wracked her. He wanted the words. The look in his eyes told her he knew that deep down she yearned to say them, that the very idea of saying them made her burn hotter. Anticipation gathered in her limbs and made her heart pound as she thought of the words, the most sinful way to ask.

An evil smile curled Ian's mouth. "Well?" His tongue snaked out to flick over her swollen flesh, and she arched off the seat.

"Please..."

Slowly, he kissed his way up her torso. His lips closed over her nipple, giving it a light suck, and she moaned. "Please, what?" he whispered around the trembling tip.

His hips moved between hers, and she felt him there, the crown of his cock pressing against her entrance. He did not move, but fisted the sides of her skirts as his forehead rested on hers.

His lips hovered over hers, his breath an unsteady pant. "Tell me."

The carriage lurched, rocking as it turned up an incline, and Ian's cock nudged against her opening. He grunted, his throat working on a swallow, but he held steady. Waiting. She closed her eyes for a brief moment. She could feel his power, the restraint that had the muscles of his shoulders shaking. When she opened her eyes, their gazes collided.

With a flush of white-hot heat, she said the words that gave her power and set her free. "Fuck me."

His groan filled her mouth, mingled with her gasp as he plunged home, a smooth, gliding thrust that seated him to the hilt just as the carriage lurched to a halt. The penetration, the intimacy of it, nearly undid her right there, but the unmistakable sound of the coachman jumping from his seat made her freeze. A muffled curse left Ian as he too went utterly still.

Barely able to breathe or to think past the sensation of being filled with *him*, Daisy blinked up at Ian in horror. Ian stared back, his expression a virulent mix of pained impatience and growing wrath. Footsteps sounded just outside the coach door.

"My lord?"

"Leave off, George," Ian shouted in a strangled voice. A bead of sweat trickled from his temple down to his twitching jawline.

He glanced at her and moved his hips a fraction, a slight pull that sent a delicious ripple through her core. Murmuring a sound of impatience, he grazed his lips over hers, intent on exploring, but the coachman's strained voice ruptured the thick silence.

"But my lord..."

"I said leave off!" Ian's plea broke on a groan, his head falling against her neck as he struggled not to move. "Christ, I'm going to kill him."

"It's Lady Archer," said a frantic George. Daisy's heart seized. "My lord, she is out of her carriage and headed this way."

"Oh God!" Daisy shot upward, her nose colliding with Ian's chin as she shoved at his chest hard. "Get off. Oh do!"

Dislodged, Ian fell back with a curse as Daisy scrambled to get her skirts down. Her bodice lay gaping, her breast swaying in humiliating fashion. Miranda was here! Her sharp voice was just outside the door as she argued with George to let her pass.

"Damned meddling woman," Ian muttered as he tucked himself into his trousers. He moved to help Daisy but she smacked at his hands. He batted hers back. "I'm faster."

Wasting precious seconds, they slapped at each other's hands in a battle to re-dress her bodice until Daisy threw her hands up in the air. "Forget it. There's no time to re-lace the corset, and the bodice won't close without it. What are you doing?" she hissed as he began to pull off his coat. "Put that back on." A knock rapped on the door, and she jumped within her skin. "Bloody hell!"

"Daisy? Are you in there?"

Ian's smile was quick and tight as he kissed the tip of Daisy's nose and then swung his coat around her shoulders. "Chin up," he said as she struggled to put her arms through the long sleeves. He tucked a curl behind her ear. "And look the devil in the eye when she has a go at you."

Miranda's eyes widened as Daisy stumbled out of the coach, now parked in Ian's drive. Daisy took Ian's advice and met Miranda's reproachful look with a lift of her chin, though she could not quite pull off the pose with the dignity she wanted as her hair was tumbling down around her shoulders and her frame swayed on unsteady legs.

She clutched the edges of Ian's coat tighter together. "Not a word," she said when Miranda made to speak. "Not a single admonishment, Panda. Or I'll march right by and finish what I started in the privacy of Northrup's home."

The strangled sound of a masculine laugh came from behind her as Miranda's brow lifted. Ian, finishing the act of buttoning up, leaped down from the conveyance and gave her sister a courtly bow. "Lady Archer, a pleasure as always."

Miranda's mouth pursed. "I doubt it very much in this instance, Lord Northrup." Her green eyes cut to Daisy, wonder and wariness warring within their depths, but she took a deep breath and her expression fell to grief. "Oh, Daisy."

In an instant, Daisy pulled her into a hard embrace, heedless of her disheveled state. "What is it, pet?"

Miranda's arms held her just as tightly. "Winston," Miranda said against Daisy's hair. "He's been attacked by the werewolf."

Beside them, Ian snapped to attention. "Where? When?"

Miranda straightened. "I don't know. He's alive but just barely. Archer is with him." She turned back to Daisy, and her eyes glistened. For a moment, she looked like the little girl who used to follow Daisy and Poppy round the house, wanting to play. Their little sister, who was as annoying as she was dear. "Daisy, I'm so afraid for Poppy. If she loses Winston..."

Daisy's insides clenched. Winston Lane meant everything to Poppy.

Chapter Thirty

Truth, it seemed, hurt. And Winston hurt. All over he hurt. A screaming, fiery pain that ate at the left side of his face and ripped into his arm and chest.

Winston tried to breathe and gurgled on his own blood instead, a salty, metallic sludge that made him gag.

"Easy, darling. Easy." A cool hand touched his.

He fought a sob. Poppy. Her voice. Her touch. So familiar to him, it was like coming home. Home. Perhaps he was. The air was warm here, no longer cold and dank, the surface beneath him soft, not the uneven hardness of that dark lane where…

His hand lashed out, remembering the thing that attacked, the razor-sharp claws that tore into him.

A hand grabbed him, strong and steady. "Do not move. This is hard enough work as it is."

Who was it? His mind raced for the answer. Dark voice. Deep. A liar. Something tugged at his face, pulling at his cheek. He stiffened.

"Win," Poppy again. "Be still and let Archer sew you up."

Archer. That bastard. Fire burned over his skin and down his throat. They were all lying bastards.

"Sher—Sheridan?" He had to know.

"Knocked out cold," came Archer's detached voice. "Beyond having a bump on his head, he'll live."

Winston shifted, wanting to get away from the voice that seemed to haunt him with some unwelcome memory.

"Christ, there he goes again. Poppy, if you would."

Poppy's hands came down on his shoulders. "Win. Easy. Please."

He calmed because she asked him to and lay quiet as the pinch-pull at his face continued.

Water tinkled in a basin. And then came the cool feel of it along his neck and chest.

"Oh, Win." Poppy's voice, so soft. "Win, we'll see you well. We will."

He tried to focus. Slowly, the hazy outline of a head formed, a fiery nimbus of scarlet hair. Her severe brows were drawn tight. Poppy. His Hellenistic beauty, so strong and clean. His Boadicea, for he had thought of the goddess the moment he'd first laid eyes on her, fearing he'd never have a chance to win the fierce beauty who kept the world at bay with a glare.

Poppy. His wife, his one true partner. She'd never lied to him. Not her.

She leaned in close, her expression tender, though nothing could fully gentle the strength of her features. "Rest easy, Win," she said. "It is almost over."

Save it was just the beginning. The anchor of that knowledge fell upon his chest, dragging him down. His gaze came to rest on the glint of the gold chain she wore about her neck, the pendant well-hidden, as always, beneath her collar. But he knew its contours so well he could draw it in minute detail from memory.

That pendant, the tiny bit of gold fashioned into a goddess whose winged arms lifted up to form an arc like those of a phoenix rising. How many times had he seen it? Hell, he'd taken it between his teeth when Poppy rode him, her lithe body rising and falling above him, pert breasts bouncing in maddening rhythm. God, it made him crazed with lust when they made love in that manner.

He stared at the chain now, his hand curling tighter over the object he'd kept clutching since he'd torn it off his savior's cloak. Metal bit into his skin, a taunt. His eyes lifted to his wife's, and he saw her confusion and hesitation. Slowly he let his grip relax, and the little charm clattered to the floor at his side.

Poppy's eyes went to it and then flew to his. For it was the same charm. How well he remembered the first time she'd let him see it, during the first time they'd made love. How she quoted the poet Apuleius: *I am nature, the universal Mother, mistress of all the elements, primordial child of time, sovereign of all things spiritual, queen of the dead, queen of the ocean, queen also of the immortals...*

Winston had never questioned why Poppy wore the charm. He figured it a fancy born from her love of books and myth. Now, as he held her gaze and saw her tremble, he could only look away. He closed his eyes to her, for he'd seen in her what he inevitably saw in everyone: a liar.

Ian was not surprised when Archer joined him on the steps leading to the garden terrace where he'd gone to wait, not wanting to interfere with Daisy and her sisters' shared grief. Ian wanted to leave Archer House altogether.

Hell, he wanted to haul Daisy back in his coach and finish what they'd started.

If he weren't a randy bastard, he'd have admitted to being worried about the inspector. In truth, he rather liked Lane. Or at the least, respected him.

Ian stood and snubbed out the cheroot he'd been idly smoking in an effort to distract himself.

"I've a theory that smoking bodes ill for one's health," Archer said.

Ian gave a short laugh. "Seeing as I'll live forever, I will forgo that worry."

The man beside him chuckled in turn. "An excellent point."

"And anyway, you are the one who looks like hell."

Worry flickered in Archer's eyes, and Ian's hackles rose, but the look disappeared. Archer's mouth twisted in a parody of a smile. "It's been a long night."

"Tell me about Lane." Ian might have assisted, but Archer had the matter well in hand by the time he and Daisy had arrived. Quite frankly, Ian doubted his wolf could cope with the overwhelming scent of blood and mad werewolf mixed together without turning Ian into a snarling beast.

Archer let out a tired sigh and rubbed the back of his neck. "Extensive damage to the left side of the face, left arm, and anterior torso. Four particularly nasty incisions across the face, one that nearly bisected the masseter."

The masseter muscle being necessary if a man wanted to chew. "Christ."

"I got it all sewn." Tired lines bracketed Archer's mouth. "Thank Christ he was out then, or it would have been a mess." Archer took the cheroot Ian offered him with little more than a quirk of his lips.

When it was lit and blue smoke perfumed the night, he continued. "Must have put over a hundred stitches in the poor bastard. If he survives the shock and possible infection, he'll be significantly scarred."

They hung their heads for a moment, and Ian felt the tips of his claws threatening to break free. He wanted to tear into the beast that did this. Unbidden, he thought of Daisy and went cold.

"How did you find him?" Ian asked.

Archer finally turned his eyes to Ian. His expression grew tight and weary. "That's the strangest bit of all. He found us. Gilroy answered a knock at the door, and there he was, unconscious and a bloody mess."

Ian frowned, looking off into the garden. Who would have brought the inspector here? More importantly, how did he survive? Ian knew enough about his kind to understand that a full-on attack would only end when the victim's throat was torn out.

Tense silence filled the space between them. Was it ever going to fade? Did he want it to? Ian had been so angry with his old friend for so long that there were times he couldn't remember how or why it had started. And then all Archer had to do was come near him, and Ian wanted to rip him apart, rage and the feeling of betrayal threatening to consume him.

Standing beside the man now, Ian experienced an odd discomfort. Though it filled his mouth with bitterness, he knew the feeling to be remorse. Point of fact, he missed his friend. Disgusted in himself, he kicked at a loose pebble on the edge of the stairs.

Archer's voice broke through the quiet. "As to Daisy"—he dropped his cheroot and stamped it out—"she may want to stay—"

"She stays with me."

Archer's gray eyes widened as he looked back at Ian. "You're falling for her."

Ian's back teeth met. "You think it impossible?"

"Not impossible, nor surprising. Simply inadvisable."

Ian's temper flared, tightening his gut and making his wolf rise. "I believe I said the same to you a while back." And damn if his meddling wasn't coming back to bite him in the arse. "It did not appear to change your course of action."

The man refused to be cowed. "She's mortal."

Two simple words. And more than enough to lash him. Ian cursed and turned away. His fist curled with the urge to strike. Ice filled his veins. Christ. Unwelcome memories filled his mind like sticky pitch. Each beat of his heart hurt as he closed his eyes, trying to block the flood of images, but they came regardless. Una's once smooth face lined with winkles, her once bright eyes dull when she looked upon him. *Do not touch me, Ian. I cannot look at you without thinking of what I once was. Please leave me. I cannot stand the sight of you.*

His feelings, his hurt had no longer mattered. Ian dragged a breath through his clenched teeth. And another. The wolf inside him whined, circling and cowing. A plea. Aye, he knew better than anyone how stupid it was to want Daisy. Yet everything in him screamed in protest at the thought of giving her up.

Una's words continued to taunt him, pricking at his conscience. *It was a mistake, Ian.*

Dizzy, he placed a hand on the balustrade and felt his claws sink in deep. A black hole of despair opened up before him, threatening to suck him down. He knew with crystal clarity what his life would be like without Daisy in it, because he had lived it for the past eighty years. He might as well fall into that hole now and end it if that was the way of things.

Archer's voice cut through his nightmare. "While I was fool enough to act without fully understanding the consequences. You do understand. You've lived it, man. Don't go back there. Don't be a fool."

Ian whirled around. "I'll not have judgment from you!"

"Why? When you've judged me for years." He took a step into Ian's space and pointed a finger at him. Ian's wolf growled, itching to release its claws and fangs, but Archer did not back down. "It was never about you, Ian. I never wanted to hurt you."

"You knew how I felt about immortality. You knew the damage it had done to me and still you sought it." Ian slashed at the granite balustrade beside him, his claws slicing through the stone with a satisfying scrape. He'd let Archer in, revealing the pain he hadn't the courage to show another soul. "You threw my suffering in my face."

Even in the dark, Ian could see the dull red wash over Archer's cheekbones. "I never meant it to be like that. And you know it."

"Did you not? And what of introducing my father to that mad fiend?"

Archer had brought Ian's father into West Moon Club, a secret society of fellow noblemen obsessed with immortality. They soon got their wish when Victoria, a female demon claiming to be an angel of light, found them. She had promised them immortality if they drank an elixir, not realizing that in so doing, they would become like her, destined to crave the light of human souls. A mindless monster.

Ian's claws punctured his own palms. The bite of pain

spurred him on. "You knew my father was unhinged when it came to his quest for power and still you lured him with promises of untold strength."

Not being satisfied with the immortality granted to all lycan, Ian's father, Alasdair, had wanted more. More power, the impenetrable strength of a god. When he realized what Victoria truly was, he had wanted to leave. Victoria tried to burn Alasdair alive and succeeded in scarring him for life. And while Ian couldn't truly blame Archer for Alasdair's faults, he could blame the man for preying on them. "The worst of it is, that when I tried to warn you off, you told me to take a piss."

"And what of you?" Archer snapped. "When I turned to you for help after I'd changed, who told *me* to take a piss then? Christ, you tried to steal my wife out from under me!"

Ian's outrage deflated under that inescapable truth. He suddenly felt all of his one hundred and thirty years. His mouth quirked as he looked at his oldest friend. "Fine. We're both jackasses. You want to have a go and beat the shite out of each other, or call pax?"

Archer's hard expression eased. "You're only saying that because you can finally beat me."

" 'Finally.' " Ian snorted. "I could have beaten you before if you hadn't ambushed me when I was piss drunk."

Archer grinned. "That's your excuse, is it?"

"Prat."

They were silent for a moment before Archer glanced at him. "Does she make the risk worth it?"

Despite the years they'd been at odds, they still understood each other perfectly. Ian didn't hesitate to answer.

"It isn't a matter of choice, Benjamin."

The other man sighed. "It never is."

Chapter Thirty-one

He won't look at me." Poppy's words held the strength of smoke. Her lips trembled, and she pressed them together so tightly they went white.

Daisy cast a glance at Miranda, whose eyes creased with the same concern that Daisy felt. They had never seen their sister weak. She was their mountain: solid, unmovable. Now she sat listless in a chair by the hearth in Miranda's sitting room.

Winston slept in a room down the hall, watched over, for the moment, by Tuttle, who'd come from Northrup's house to serve as nurse. The woman fussed about, checking for fever and administering various concoctions, along with a liberal application of her ointment in an attempt to stave off infection.

Poppy picked at the loose folds of the dressing gown Miranda had lent her. "He turns away when I draw near."

Daisy's head throbbed. She wanted to lie down and sleep for a week, or find Ian and...She bit her lip. Between her legs, her flesh was still slick and sensitive with longing. Her cheeks burned with the memory of what Ian had done to her, and the base part of her craved more. But her sister needed her. Daisy's skirts rustled as she stood and went to Poppy's side. Resting a hand on Poppy's bright hair, she smoothed the glossy crown of her head. "Why, Pop?"

Both sisters knew Poppy well enough to know Poppy already had the answer.

Poppy turned her head to face the fire. Orange light danced over Poppy's high cheekbones, turning the red tips of her lashes bronze. "He knows."

Daisy's hand stilled. "About us? How?"

Slowly, Poppy's clenched fist opened and a little silver charm shone in the firelight. Daisy heard Miranda rise, but she kept her eyes upon the charm and leaned down to see.

Miranda's voice, soft with worry, drifted over the silence. "What does it mean, Poppy?"

Poppy's slender throat worked as she swallowed. "The SOS."

Daisy sighed and touched her sister's cheek, surprised to find it cold despite the heat of the fire. "Dearest, you aren't making sense." Which was unthinkable.

Pain and resignation clouded the depths of Poppy's eyes. "The Society for the Suppression of Supernaturals, the S.O.S. They exist so that the world never learns of beings like us.

"This," Poppy lifted the charm, "is their emblem. Winston had it in his hand when they brought him in."

Miranda's eyes narrowed. "They did this to him?"

Heaven help these people if they did. Need and strength shifted within Daisy's belly, writhing as if to break free. She saw the answering promise in the glint of Miranda's eyes. For the first time in memory, Daisy felt useful, capable of serving justice to those who wronged the innocent. And it felt like freedom.

Poppy's tone was resolute as she answered. "No. They saved him."

"How can you be sure?" Daisy asked.

"Because I am one of them."

"Oh, Poppy." Daisy's overskirts billowed around her knees as she sank to the footstool at Poppy's side.

Poppy's fist tightened around the charm. "I lied to him. Like all the others. I pretended to be something I am not. And now I am paying the price." A single tear trickled down her white cheek. "I made a lie of love."

Out of respect, Daisy turned from her sister's pain, yet her words made a fist around Daisy's heart and clanged like warning bells within her ears. She too was a liar. And it made her inexpressibly tired. She was tired of pretending that she didn't want everything with Ian, tired of resisting her baser nature. Suddenly, waiting felt like a cloak smothering her breath. Gathering her skirts, she rose.

"I'm sorry, dearest. I must go."

"What?" Miranda sat up straighter in her seat. "Why? Where?"

Suspicion darkened Miranda's eyes, and she obviously thought of the scene she'd come upon, of Daisy's dishevelment and Ian unrepentantly buttoning his trousers. Daisy refused to blush now or turn away. Her sister had no right to judge. But she saw no such judgment from Poppy, who looked at Daisy with understanding and yet such sorrow that Daisy's chest ached.

"She is going to live in truth," Poppy answered for her.

Old doubts made her insides roll, but when Daisy spoke her voice was clear. "Yes."

* * *

Ian prowled his room, walking the length of it in an endless loop, just as he had done since returning home alone. His pulse jumped, his fingers twitching with the temptation to reach out and grab her. Only she wasn't here. He yanked at his cravat, desperate to get the blasted thing off before it choked him. He ought to go out and run, get the need out of his system. But he didn't want to run. He wanted her. He wanted to finish what they had started.

The cravat ripped free, and he sucked in a breath. Damn, but he couldn't do those things. Not tonight. Her sister needed her. It was as it should be. She wouldn't come to him tonight. Perhaps she wouldn't come to him at all. Fine, he liked the chase. Always had. Only, for some damned reason, he wanted to be chased in return, just once.

His gait turned stiff and disjointed as he stalked to the sideboard in search of a drink. He needed something to ease this burning.

His cock was an iron staff in his trousers, his balls drawn up so tight they ached. He'd been inside of her. For one perfect, heart-stopping moment, he'd been clasped by her slick, warm…The crystal decanter in his hand clattered against his glass with too much force, cracking its side.

A hollow laugh burst from his mouth. "Bloody hell," he muttered before rubbing a tired hand over his face. Utterly undone by a woman, he was.

Ian blinked down at his unshod feet, not able to do anything else. A small hole was growing in his stocking, and his big toe worked to break through. He stared at the undignified sight. The sound of his own heart beating filled his ears, and then something else, the clatter of hooves and the creaking of a coach pulling to a stop. His heart clenched painfully. The dainty patter of feet alighted the front stair, followed by a rap of the knocker.

He closed his eyes and inhaled sharply and deeply. Vanilla, jasmine, sunshine, and *her.* His breath released in a burst of shock and hope. Bloody anxious hope that had his insides quivering and his fists clenching.

In the front hall, a feminine voice murmured before a light tread sounded on the center staircase, heading toward his room. Ian couldn't move. His muscles locked, his breath coming hard like a steamer. Each step she took sent a quiver along his hot, tight skin.

By the time the handle turned, he was shaking. The door creaked open.

She stood, framed by the light in the hall, golden wisps of her hair curling about her head like a halo and her summer eyes alive with equal parts hesitation and want. They stared at each other in the charged silence, and a flush spread over the tops of her plump breasts. His mouth was as dry as toast, his heart slamming to get past his ribs. She was so bloody beautiful.

On a breath, he was striding forward, each step hard and strong. She met him halfway, her slim arms going up and around his neck even as his hands tunneled into her hair to hold her still as he captured her mouth on a low groan. He devoured her, reveling in the feel of her pillowed bottom lip and the taste of her, like sweet strawberries and dark chocolate.

Ian groaned again and opened her mouth farther, desperate to have all of her. They stumbled back, her nimble hands pulling at his shirt as he ripped at her lacings. A small laugh escaped her and she caught his gaze with hers.

He found himself smiling back, inanely, like a green lad getting his first taste of sin. The soft promise in her eyes settled him a bit, eased him in a way he didn't understand. Gently, he touched her cheek, the skin there as smooth as fine satin. When he kissed her again, he took his time and savored her. He touched her with deliberation now, drawing out her pleasure, and his.

"You came," he whispered as his hands roamed over her. "I didn't think... your sister."

"I couldn't stay there," she said just as softly. "I needed..." Her blue eyes looked up at him helplessly.

He understood. She needed a release, to not think about the horrors around her. And yet it pinched a small part of him that it was all she needed. Selfish or not, he wanted her to need *him*. The way he needed her.

He said none of that, only gave her a soft kiss and nibbled his way down her warm, fragrant neck. "I'll give you what you need, my Daisy," he said against her skin. "I'll take care of you."

Daisy sighed and molded against him, her hands coming up to tug him back to her mouth. One small gesture and his heart nearly burst within his chest. Lust ratcheted within him. It fed hers, and their hands grew unsteady once more. Silken hair tumbled over his fingers and spilled around her shoulders.

He broke their kiss to allow her to wrench his shirt off. The shirt sailed overhead. Her bodice hit the floor with a slap as he walked her backward toward the bed, still kissing her. He couldn't leave her mouth. It was too delicious, quenching his thirst yet driving his hunger. She was quicker than he, helping him out of his clothes and getting herself free of that hideous contraption of a bustle when his shaking hands proved useless.

It was she who pulled him onto the bed with a sound of impatience. Her skin was satin against his, her body trembling and her breathing as rough and unsteady as his own, as if they'd just finished instead of having just begun. He breathed her in and let his hand slide down all that soft, smooth skin to cup between her legs. Gods, but she was wet. He felt the fine tension humming beneath all that softness.

"Are you afraid?" he asked between kisses he could not stop from taking.

He stroked through her wetness with a light touch, easing her legs open. Her eyelids fluttered before she focused on him. "Not with you." She looked almost surprised by this, but her gaze did not waver. "I'm not afraid of you."

Pride and lust and relief surged through him, setting his body aflame. She had seen him at his worst and still wasn't afraid of him. He kissed with little technique and all heat, his finger sliding in deep to lay claim, and she moaned. Ian pulled back, and she wrapped her arms about him as if she feared he would go. Not a bloody chance of that. But he had to look at her and drink his fill before he took her. When he did, pain returned to his chest and his gut. Mother of God. She was made for sin, made to be adored. She was an hourglass, sweet curves that turned a man weak-kneed and panting. Full breasts, tiny waist, and a gorgeously rounded ass that made him whimper.

"Daisy-Meg," he managed. "You light the moon looking as you do."

A smile spread across her face. She traced a path around his nipple, and a bolt of heat went straight to his cock. "And you put the sun to bed, wild man."

Wild man. He was, at that moment, kissing her like he was starved. Her legs threaded with his, her full breasts crushed against his chest as he moved over her. All that warmth and softness finally his. He nibbled on her bottom lip as he filled his hands with the plump miracle of her arse. She made a little noise that had him grinning like a fiend. He squeezed again and ground his thigh against the wet heat that called to him.

Sweet Christ, she was intoxicating. Finesse was impossible with her. Not this time. Not when he was so hot and wanting that he shook with it. Sweat trickled down his back as he slid his cock over her wetness to tease them both. Once. Twice. His arms trembled as they bracketed her, and his tongue plunged into her mouth the way his cock wanted to plunder her warm quim.

"Ian," she pled against his lips. "Now."

He gritted his teeth when she nipped his lower lip impatiently. "Wait. Let me give you more." He'd do right by her if it killed him.

Her legs spread wider, a call home. "Now." Sly devil that she was, she arched her hips a fraction, and suddenly he was in, tunneling into tight, wet heat. And he lost his mind.

A vicious oath tore from him as he pumped her, hard, harder than he ought to. He couldn't stop. She was warmth, all soft and malleable flesh. Her hot, clenching sex fisted his cock. So very good. His knees dug into the mattress as he struggled to gain leverage, to get in deeper. Grunting, he hooked one smooth leg over his elbow, and she moaned.

"Oh, God, Ian." Her breath came in pants, her creamy skin dewy and flushed. "Like that. Like that."

He kissed her fiercely as he pistoned hard and deep inside her. His free hand kneaded her round bottom and held her prone. Some dark part of him urged his fingers lower, down along the seam of her pert arse, to find the tight little rosette just below her wet sex. Her eyes went wide as he stroked it with his thumb. He stroked it again, adding just a bit of pressure as he did. Delicately, she bit her lip, and then the shock was his as she nudged herself against his thumb.

The beast within him roared. He slammed into her as his thumb pressed harder. And when it breached that tight barrier, she came apart in his arms.

"Ian!" A keening wail broke from her mouth, as her nails dug into his shoulders. She held herself taut against him, burrowing her face against his neck, sucking his skin there, as her sex milked his, drawing him deeper still. Lightning heat flashed down his spine and into his cock. He bucked on a shout, the orgasm hitting him so hard he lost his sight for one blissful, red moment.

Weak as a pup, he fell limp against her, his breath ruffling her curls. "Daisy," he said hoarsely. Every inch of him felt battered. It hit him with a jolt that not once had he thought of failing her. It hadn't even occurred to him that he would. Satisfaction and peace made his heart light as he closed his eyes and gathered her in his arms and turned onto his side. "Daisy," he said again. It was all he could say. And in that moment, it was everything.

Chapter Thirty-two

They lay in a languid tangle of limbs, so intertwined that she wasn't sure where she ended and he began. One of his strong arms snaked under her neck and around her shoulders to hold her close, as if she might try to get away. Their breath moved in a gentle panting cadence that spoke of physical exhaustion, their lips brushing together with each inhale.

Idly his big hand cupped her breast, his clever fingers toying with her nipple, lightly playing over the stiff tip and setting her insides to clench once again, despite the liquid-warm contentment that made her want to melt into the bed. She arched into his touch, her thighs tightening against his in reflex, and he growled low in his throat. Their lips melded, gently, lightly, a flicker of wet, warm tongues that sent another impossible flood of heat through her.

"I think I may have come close to dying just then." Even as he spoke, he tweaked her nipple as if he couldn't stop himself from touching her.

Nor could she. Her hand smoothed up over the strong slab of muscle that flanked his spine and was gratified to feel him shiver, too. "I think I did die," she said.

Their lips touched as if drawn together like magnets. A sip, a taste before he pulled back slightly, his devilish eyes studying her face, and his expression careful. "You'll be wanting to go back now? To your sister?"

Her heart stilled. Somehow she found her voice. "Panda is with Poppy." She licked her tender lips. "Do you want me to go?"

They were so close that her ribs compressed with each sharp rise of his chest. Her hand flattened against his shoulder blade, holding him still, holding him, for she suddenly saw the vulnerability hiding beneath his pride. He did not know the power he had over her.

The hand at her breast stilled, but held her, warm and possessive. "Do you want to go?"

"You cannot answer a question with a question," she hedged.

His brows drew together in a fierce scowl, but it was need that burned bright in his eyes. His hand slid down her ribs and settled on her hip. The long length of his cock rose up between them, heated steel that pulsed against her belly in an insistent tattoo. "I..." His fingers bit into her flesh. "Stay. Stay with me."

"I don't want to go," she admitted in a rush as his hand moved to her bottom, hauling her so close that she lost her breath, and his mouth found hers. His kiss was fierce, tender, and filled with yearning as he rolled onto his back and pulled her on top of him. Every inch of her felt sore, heavy, and aching from their play, her breasts, limbs, sex, even her ass, God help her, and yet when her wet folds slid over his cock her insides tightened in anticipation.

"Then ride me, Daisy-girl." His voice was rough with sex and utterly seductive. "Do what you will, and I'll follow."

Emotion caught hard and fast in her throat. Beneath her palm, his heart pounded. Just as hers did. He'd given the power back to her. He'd given her control, and all she wanted to do now was cherish him, adore him with her touch. His eyes closed just before she placed a soft kiss on one eyelid and then the other. Trembling, she traced a path of kisses along his jaw and down the strong column of his neck. He was better than caramels, richer and saltier. She reveled in his taste as she licked and sucked the tender skin at the base of his throat and nibbled the hard line of his collarbone.

He turned his head toward her, seeking her mouth. Their tongues twined, their kiss open-mouthed and so hot she thought she might faint. Strong hands gripped her hips, guiding her. Moving as through water, she lifted up and found the wide tip of his cock. Their eyes met, and she paused, her nipples skimming over his hard chest with every labored breath she took.

"It was you I needed. No one else but you," she whispered and then pushed down, impaling herself onto that wonderful, thick, long cock.

Ian groaned, his strong body bowing as if he'd been shocked. His brilliant blue eyes blazed up at her. She flowed over him, letting herself go free. The long, rangy muscles along his torso and arms bunched and trembled as she worked him, his eyes never leaving hers. "You'll stay." It was a husky rasp, as much a plea as a demand, and Daisy's heart turned over in her chest. "Every. Night."

Her hand tunneled into the cool silk of his hair and grabbed hold. Ian's nostrils flared as she clenched her inner walls, squeezing his thick length that pulsed inside of her.

"Every night, Ian," she countered, unwilling to let him look away.

The desperate fight left his eyes to be replaced with something that looked like joy. Grinning like a boy, he tumbled her over, pouncing with playful fervor. "Glad we have that settled," he said as she laughed breathlessly. His grin widened and, without warning, he flipped her onto her stomach, intent on a different play. Her hair fell around her face, and she heard the sound of his sudden, ragged intake of breath. Everything in her froze. Her back was to him.

His growl cut into her. "What the fuck?"

Humiliation washed over her in a wave of sour sickness, and she scrambled to get up, get away. But he was too fast for her. His hand lashed out, snatching up her wrist, his powerful thighs pinning her hips, holding her facedown on the bed.

"What the hell is this?"

That position, that exposure. She could not bear it. Rage surged like hot fire, and she bucked.

"No," she screamed. "Do not!" Her legs thrashed against the bed, tangling in the sheets. With one arm she swung out, sending a glancing blow off his jaw. "You will not touch me."

"Daisy!" Hands clasped her arms. She reared, her head smashing against his nose. "Oof! Christ. Daisy, stop."

She would not be held down again. She would not. A body fell upon her. *No!*

"Daisy-girl," his voice crooned. "Calm yourself, lass."

Not *his* voice. But Ian's. Ian's voice. Something in her stilled. Ian's body on top of her. Not pressing but holding, his strong arms a cocoon.

"That's it, luv." Lips brushed against her hot cheek. "It's me. Only me." He kissed the corner of her eye, and she realized that tears leaked from them. "It's all right. You're safe."

The fight left her on a sob.

Ian's strong body trembled, and she knew it was from rage held in tight check. Rage at seeing the network of red slashes along her lower back. One moment of relaxing her guard and he had seen. He rested his head next to hers on the bed, close enough for her to see his expression. Daisy closed her eyes against it.

"Ah, my sweet, lass," he said brokenly. "What did that bastard do to you?"

Shame was a hot tar coating her insides, clogging her throat. "I can't."

His hand smoothed down her forearm. "You can. Haven't you realized yet? I am yours, whether you will it or no."

She sobbed again but took a quelling breath, squeezing her eyes shut to stop the tears running down. "He found out I wasn't a virgin," she said at last.

Dark memories filled her mind. The disgust she'd felt in having to bed Craigmore on their wedding night. The sick feeling of him on top of her. Craigmore's ugly face twisted into something hideous and profane as he raised his hand high and smacked her.

She licked her lips. "There was a riding crop."

Ah, the pain. She could remember it still. The way he'd ripped her gown from her, somehow pinning her down as he unleashed his fury upon her back. It had taken a week to heal. And the scars stayed. A red crisscross to forever mar her lower back. She supposed she ought to be thankful they weren't raised.

"Did he..." His breath caught. "Did he—"

"No." She opened her eyes to find him looking at her with compassion. It hurt almost as much as the telling. "He'd already had me, hadn't he?" A bitter laugh left her. "He never touched me again. He called me the worst sort of filth. 'A whore whose foul cunt was poison to a man's sword.'"

"Filthy, fucking bastard," Ian hissed, his teeth clenching.

Her lips twisted. "That he was. But, in truth, he only said what society believes."

"No—"

"Yes," she said. "A true lady remains a virgin for her husband. She doesn't go off bedding the stable lad. Or the tailor's son." She lowered her lids. "He might have been the vessel, but I was the source of my shame."

Ian's forehead fell lightly against hers. "Christ, that bastard twisted your mind." When she opened her mouth to protest, he kissed it gently. "That rotten piece of filth hurt you because he was a coward and a bloody hypocrite."

Daisy swallowed hard. "I thought I was over it. But then you saw my back, and..." She closed her eyes. "I feel such shame. For letting him do that to me. For giving him cause to do it in the first place."

"Daisy-girl."

"And nothing can change it," she hurried on. "I'll always carry these marks. The ugliness of it. *I* will always be ugly because of it."

He moved then, his hand brushing away the mass of her hair cascading down her back.

"No," she said, twisting to move her back from view. "Don't..."

"Yes." His lips found a mark and pressed there. "You

are the most beautiful woman..." He kissed his way along a red path. "...I have ever laid eyes upon."

"Ridiculous—"

He raised his head to spear her with a glance. "Ever."

A warm hand cupped her bottom and gave it a squeeze. "Ah, Daisy-girl, when you look at me with those eyes, even if they're scowling at me from over your shoulder as they are now..." He smiled. "You light me up."

She clung to the soft bedding. She could not take his kindness, didn't know how. She wanted to run away, but he wouldn't let her. Firm but gentle hands held her as soft kisses assaulted her senses. He slid over her, his body a weight that anchored. So often she felt as if she might float away in the darkest part of the night and not a soul would be there to see her go.

"Ian." Tears clogged her throat. She wanted to say so much more, but didn't know how to say the words—she'd never said them to anyone.

He traced the groove of her spine with his lips as if he could erase old hurts. "I wouldn't take away a single scar for all the world, if it meant changing the woman you are today. I—"

She spun round and silenced him with a kiss. He kissed her back, soft yet fierce kisses that punctuated his former words. Her throat ached as she wrapped her arms around his neck. "It might never fully go away, Ian." She searched his face for any sign of wariness. "These old fears. As much as I try to change, I might fall back into darkness now and then."

Gently, he threaded his hand through her curls, spreading them about her. "We are all imperfect creatures, love. I don't want perfect. I just want you."

Pressed against his lean body and wrapped within the

security of his arms, Daisy felt that lost part of her self finally return and slip into place. She might have wept in gratitude. "Foolish man... Lovely, foolish..." But he was her fool, and so she kissed him and then smoothed a lock of his hair back from his brow and studied his face, the sharp angles and sweeping planes that held both strength and vulnerability. "I could love you, you know."

A look of bemusement clouded his eyes, as if he wanted to believe her but couldn't, and Daisy's heart squeezed in response. She saw him reach for the careless expression he often wore, but he failed, and his voice came out rough when he spoke. "I could love you, too."

Chapter Thirty-three

Sometime in the night, Ian awoke with a suddenness that had him lurching upward. Panting as though he'd run miles, he stared unseeing in the darkness. His heart pounded painfully within his chest, and for a moment, he couldn't place where he was. Beside him, a feminine form stirred and a soft hand smoothed his bare thigh. Something in him eased. Daisy.

Sweat rolled down his temple as he gazed down at her. Sweet, luscious Daisy. At the sight of her, need, longing, and tenderness rolled within his heart with such force that he wanted nothing more than to gather her up and squeeze her tight.

The wolf inside him didn't brood—he lived in the now. And the wolf was clamoring for Ian to make Daisy his in all ways. But the man in him was lost in the past.

I will never be like you, forced to roam this world alone. A thing not of nature but of fearsome myth. Pain sliced through him at the remembered words. Christ. His stomach pitched.

Ian swung his legs over the edge of the bed. He was going to be ill. Grabbing his dressing robe where it lay slung over a chair, he wrenched it on as he fled. His breath came in harder pants, his heart going like a metronome.

Running blindly now, he found himself in the garden, the grass wet and cool beneath his feet. Moonlight warmed his skin. His kind felt the moon's rays as humans felt the sun's. Even with the warmth and the power of the moonlight, his insides were ice cold. He fell to his knees but still he felt as though he were falling. Falling without a thing to cling to. Bloody hell. He was done in.

His breath came out in a wheeze as his fingers dug into the moist, fragrant earth. He wanted to be happy. He wanted it with every fiber of his being. *You know as I do that my very existence is wrong. Every breath I take is an exercise in selfishness. I will not wait out my fate.*

Ian's arms buckled. Why? Why must he think of Maccon now? But Ian knew. And he ground his teeth so he wouldn't shout. It didn't help. Black spots dotted before his eyes as he struggled for air.

Footsteps sounded behind him, and he whirled around, landing on his ass. Christ, he hadn't even noticed her approaching.

Daisy stopped short at his movement. Her unbound hair undulated and coiled down to her waist. Moonlight caught the golden strands and turned them silver. Her eyes, indigo in the night, were wide and troubled. Ian's fists curled tighter. He couldn't say a word, find a jest to hide behind.

"You are hurting," she said.

His chest heaved, the feeling of falling making him dizzy.

Her bare feet sank into the grass as she drew near. Closer, and he shook with the need to run. But she was upon him, her body emanating heat. He rose upon his knees as she stopped before him. Without a word, she wrapped her arms about him and drew him close. He shuddered and clutched the skirts of her dressing gown.

"Ian," she murmured, "hold onto me."

The acceptance in her voice choked him. His claws snagged on the satin as he clung tighter.

"I had a son." The confession broke from him without thought. Acid burned in his throat. "Maccon."

Her fingers sifted through his hair.

"He was perfect. A good lad." The weight on his chest crushed into him, and the words came out hard. "Brooding at times, but a smart lad." Ian's throat worked. "I was so proud."

"Tell me, love," she whispered.

"Una. She was human. We met before I had reached maturity. She told me that our differences wouldn't matter."

Daisy continued to hold him and keep him steady while his heart raced and his chest ached.

"Then I became lycan. I did not age, and she did." He closed his eyes and pressed his face into the safety of Daisy's bosom. Her heartbeat strong and true. "It did not matter to me. I loved her still. But Una could not stand it. Nor could she stand the wolf within me.

"And Maccon. She made him her confidant, told him that his life would be an endless misery, that he would become an animal. Stupid, bloody Una." A growl of rage rumbled in his chest. He hated Una in the end. "Maccon was thirty, so close to the change. There are signs when the time approaches. He tried to enjoy life, women, but he began to withdraw. And then he... Shit..."

Ian could not breath. "He fucking killed himself... Christ..." His voice was too high, too thin.

Daisy's arms held him tight, so tight he could not fall through the black hole that opened up beneath him when he thought of Maccon. Maccon who had flung himself off the high tower of their ancestral keep in Scotland. Maccon's head crushed on the pavers, blood pooling around him. Maccon's body twisted and broken.

"Ian. Oh, Ian." She rocked him gently.

"He left a note. Said he would not turn into me. Wouldn't become a thing destined to be alone. Trapped in a body that would not die."

And everything in Ian's world had stopped. He would no longer be a lycan. He would ignore that side of himself. Until now.

"Una faded away after that." And cursed him with each dying breath she took. He hadn't found it in himself to grieve her loss until years afterward.

"A broken heart," Daisy whispered, and then kissed the top of his head. "Ian, love."

"God, I am a hypocrite," he said. "I tell you to let go of the past when I cannot release mine."

Her hand was in his hair, stroking, petting. "Perhaps there are some things we can't let go of, but simply accept as over."

He would. If she was his future, he would accept the past for her.

She held him until he could breathe properly, and the black thing that threatened to take him slipped back into the shadows. Ian's grip upon her skirts eased, and his hands slid to her hips. "He did not want to become like me. He didn't want to be a monster." When he looked up at her, she touched his cheek tenderly.

"You are not a monster, but a man." Her fingers spread, bracketing his jaw. "The best man I've ever known."

Ah, but she killed him. She had cut out his heart and taken it for her own.

"I want to marry you." He winced, cursing himself for letting the words spill out.

Daisy's hand fell away. "What?"

He wouldn't let her go. "It's happening again, and I can't seem to fight it. I want to be with you. Take you to the theater, to parties and balls. I don't want the world to assume you are my mistress because you deserve to be a wife. A wife who can hold her head up high when out in public. My wife. And it tears into my soul because I should not want it. I should let you go."

He leaned into her. She smelled of cool silk and warm roses. She smelled of home. "I am afraid, aye? Bloody terrified of history repeating itself." He wrapped his arms about her waist and held on tightly. "But I want you more. Do you understand? I feel free when I am with you. Happy. You are the gift I never saw coming."

She was quiet, and he knew it would end now. But a man could ignore his fate for only so long. Soft hands touched his cheeks, saving him from further humiliation. She tilted his head back, and he made himself look at her.

"Then have me," she said, throwing him off kilter.

He blinked up at her, not understanding. "Have you not heard a word I said, lass?"

Her cheeks trembled as she smiled, a weak smile but there, shining in the moonlight. A rustling sounded around them, fingers of grass brushed his bare legs as they began to lengthen. "We've both lived in fear for so long, denying what we are to the world, to ourselves. And what good has come of it? I don't want to live that way anymore, Ian."

Her finger traced his ear. "I am afraid, too," she said. "Afraid that when the time comes, I will not be any different than Una."

"You are already different than Una. You are... you." Brave, proud. His other half.

Fragrance bloomed as the grass grew lush and wild flowers burst free beneath the moon's bright glow. It was magic perhaps, or all in his mind. He did not care. Not in this moment when his hope had finally returned. His only care was for her.

Daisy's thumb traced his bottom lip, and he caught it up as she let go of a sigh. "But I'll have you," she whispered. Joy surged through his chest like wildfire. "Because I too want you more than I am afraid."

He pulled her down into his lap, and she laughed a bit as he peppered her face with kisses.

"Daisy." He tumbled them down onto the dewy grass, now thick with flowers, and rolled on his back to protect her even as his hands slipped into her gown. She made an appreciative noise. Greedy thing that she was, she ripped his robe open and ran her hands over his chest. His beast preened right along with him. A sigh escaped her when he pulled her close, laying them skin to skin.

She raked her fingers through his hair. "This is madness, Ian. You know that, don't you?" But her gaze was without fear.

He brought her closer, until there was no space between them. "And yet it is the only thing that has ever felt completely right." His mouth found hers, and he drank her in. His Daisy-Meg. She would be his wife.

In the comfort of Ian's bed, Daisy smiled. *I want to marry you.*

She'd awoken in his arms, her fingers threaded through the strands of his hair that shone with glints of copper and bronze in the morning sun. Barbaric and untamed, his hair might be, but Daisy rather liked it long. She'd stroked the glossy mane, enjoying the feel of it running through her fingers, until he opened his eyes with a smile and a sigh. He'd canted his head into her touch and closed his eyes with a grunt of satisfaction.

"So it's true," she'd said. "Wolves do like to be petted."

"Men too." With a contented grumble, he'd moved his warm, hard body over her, and then into her, making them both sigh as he sank deep.

He made lazy love to her in the morning sun, whispering wicked things in her ear, kissing her mouth until she fell into a haze of lust and need. He made her laugh and dive under the covers when he rang for a bowl of melted butter. And she'd made him cry out and beg when she followed through on her promise.

She ought to be afraid at the depth of her happiness, yet she was not. When she thought of marrying Ian, and of sharing mornings just like this with him, she felt not shame or worry but a fluttery warmth that made her lay a hand upon her belly to calm herself. And yet she was calm. Surprisingly so. He would not hurt her. He'd seen her worst and not turned away. In the comfort of their bed, Daisy smiled, too.

Now she could relax, and perhaps the throbbing headaches that plagued her of late, the sore throats, and the constant tightness in her muscles would fade. In fact, she would celebrate now by soaking in a hot bath.

Sun dappled the room with brilliant strips of gold as she padded naked over to the bathing room. Waiting for the tub to fill, Daisy brushed out her hair. A glimpse in

Ian's full-length mirror stopped her short. Just below her hairline was a red bump. It might have been the odd pimple or a bug bite, but the sight of the sore sent a violent chill through her, for it lay in the exact spot where the werewolf had bitten her. With trembling hands, she inspected it.

Hard and red, just touching it made her heart flip. Dread clamored like warning bells. Daisy swallowed with difficulty and prepared to dress instead.

Chapter Thirty-four

Ian had woken up surrounded by the soft warmth of Daisy. If there was a better way to greet the day, he could not think of it. They had continued their play, and his happiness had swelled. But when he'd finally left her to dress for the day, dark thoughts began to creep in.

She would marry him. Despite everything he'd confessed, she had agreed. The baser part of his soul wanted to haul her down here, find a priest, and bind her to him now, before she came to her senses. But he knew full well that marriage vows were not a guarantee, nor a promise, of everlasting happiness.

A feeling much like guilt writhed in his guts. He should have left things as they were and not pressed her into this rash action. Guilt and fear. Fear was gaining. Every time he stopped moving, it crept along his spine with insidious hands. What if she came to regret him? What if he couldn't stand seeing her age and die?

Dressing without the aid of a missing, and most likely surly, Talent, Ian spent the time waiting for Daisy to finish her much longer dressing ritual by going for a walk in his garden. Prowling his garden would be more accurate. He longed to run, but had no intention of leaving Daisy alone.

When he thought of what she'd endured, his blood boiled. If the bastard Craigmore weren't already dead, Ian would surely tear his cods off and feed them to him.

No closer to feeling content, he ended up in the corner of his terrace, taking solace under the shade of a potted peach tree as the sun started to rise higher in the sky and the heat of the day took hold.

Through the twitter of birdsong, he heard the light swish of skirts as a woman approached the terrace doors and then her scent as she opened them to step out into the sun. Unfortunately, it was the wrong scent. A wash of ambergris and figs touched his nose. Her golden brown hair gleamed in the light and then darkened as she walked beneath the shade of the peach tree.

"Ranulf," Mary Chase said with a nod of her head.

He'd ignore her cheek for addressing him by his brother's title for now. "Miss Chase. You have news for me?"

"Yes, Sire." Spending much of her time in her spectral form lent her physical body an effortless grace as she glided closer. "I believe I've found your werewolf."

Ian tensed. "You've been following Conall." He knew this; thus he knew what was coming. In his heart he was almost glad. Glad to have a reason to overthrow his brother that did not involve the machinations of others. Despite what sort of leader Conall was, or what he had done, he was still Ian's brother. Regret and soul-deep sorrow was the constant mix of emotion when Ian thought of Conall.

Mary Chase's luminous eyes took in his struggle, and she lowered her lids as if in sympathy. "I believe so."

Her rosebud mouth opened to continue but she suddenly stiffened.

Ian turned to watch Talent walk onto the terrace. He'd been aware of Talent drawing near but hadn't thought that Mary Chase would realize it so quickly as well. GIMs did not possess the lycan's superior sense of smell. His curiosity grew as Talent skidded to a stop upon seeing her.

His valet's face twisted in an ill-disguised sneer of disgust. "You."

Mary Chase's expression remained serene. "Yes, me. How observant you are, Mr. Talent."

Dark clouds gathered over Talent's countenance. Any moment now the lad would go off. Ian didn't understand the animosity between them. As far as he knew, they'd met only twice before, and on both occasions hadn't exchanged more than two words, but Ian needed to hear information, not play nanny to bickering children. "Your news, if you please, Miss Chase."

Mary inclined her head in that floating manner of hers. "Last night, Lyall and Conall talked about the werewolf and Ian Ranulf. I could not get too close, but I heard them say they were going to address the problem tonight."

"How?" Talent asked.

She flicked him an irritated glance but looked to Ian when she answered. "I don't know what they plan to do, but they are going to Buckingham Palace."

Ian straightened. "That little bugger."

The palace was abandoned and so large and isolated by its massive grounds that the howls of a werewolf might go unnoticed.

"They are set to go at midnight," Mary said.

"Then we will go there before they can move him."

"You can't be thinking about trusting her." Talent's scowl twisted. "She's an unholy body thief."

Mary Chase bristled. "And you? Whose identity do you steal when you think no one is looking?"

Talent went as white as paper and then five shades of red, but he got ahold of himself and turned his back on her. "Sir," he said to Ian, "let me take you in. If it is a trap, at least I'll be there to help you."

"I need you to watch over Daisy." Talent frowned, and Ian placed a hand upon the lad's shoulder, for he knew the tenderness of a man's pride. "I'm leaving you to watch my heart, Jack."

The lad appeared a bit mollified but Mary Chase's expression made it clear what she thought of Talent's assignment, and the color was soon rising once more up Talent's neck. Ian stepped between them before any more squabbles broke out.

"The *were* dies tonight." A surge of adrenaline lit over him at the idea. "When we are done there, I am going for Conall."

"As you wish, Ranulf." Mary Chase left the terrace in a delicate swirl of skirts and flowing hair.

"I don't trust her," Talent muttered as he watched her go.

But Ian's mind was on other things. Such as how the hell he was going to take down the *were*. And what he was going to do with Daisy.

Back in his cage. The wolf cowered in the corner of it, as far away as he could get from the stink of his waste that spilled across the floor. They didn't clean the cage anymore. Didn't give him drugs to numb the pain. Pain. Pain. Pain. A chant that went through his head as he slammed his aching skull against the walls.

"Stop."

The wolf lunged at the bars, his teeth snapping, claws raking against the thick iron in an effort to get to the lycan. But the man danced back with a laugh. Taunting fuck.

"Temper, lad."

Lad. The lycan called him that when the wolf had been a man. The man inside the wolf surged to the skin for a moment, screaming his hate and rage as well. He hated the lycan, too.

The lycan's grin widened. "Ah, your rage is a glorious thing. Yet you aim it at the wrong man. Have you not been kept safe all these years? Safe from execution? Hell, you've even had a woman, as deformed as you are."

His woman. The man inside the wolf cried out in sorrow.

"Your clan cared for you." The lycan stepped near, his eyes flashing. "When he was the one that put you in the grave!"

The wolf whined, his legs wobbling beneath him. Buried in the dark. Hardwood coffin above his head. His fingers worn to the bone as he clawed his way out, through the wood and earth. Agony knifed into his skull, and he howled.

"Ah, yes, you're remembering a bit of it, aren't you?" The lycan's voice turned soothing. "Remembering how he left you behind. How he went on with his life, let your mother rot, as if she was nothing, until she too faded away."

Dizziness threatened. He remembered the lycan with the blue eyes. A calm voice. Safety. Comfort. Home. The man inside wanted to remember. But the wolf did not. The wolf ground his head into the stone wall, letting the pain lance him and take away the memories, as the man raged and rattled about within the wolf's brain.

"And now he has your woman. Likely he's fucking her right now."

Man and wolf went wild, slamming as one into the bars. The wolf's bones cracked. Blood flowed, his fangs scraping iron and tasting it on his tongue. And the lycan just laughed.

"Soon, Maccon. Soon ye can have yer revenge."

Daisy made her visit when she knew Miranda was out consoling Poppy, who was distraught over Winston's withdrawal. Otherwise, Daisy would not be able to face this.

Although she wasn't expected, her brother-in-law received her immediately.

"Daisy." Archer's silvery eyes traveled over her face in concerned assessment. "Are you well?"

Nerves swarmed like angry bees within Daisy's belly as she clutched the ends of her cloak. "That is the problem, Archer. I'm not sure."

His handsome face darkened. "Is it Northrup? Has he done something to upset you?"

She rather thought Ian would be in for another thrashing should she answer yes. A wobbling smile touched her lips, for despite his taciturn demeanor, Archer cared for her like a brother. "No, nothing like that. Ian is... He is good to me, Archer."

Some of the tension left Archer as he nodded, sending a thick, black curl falling over his brow. "I never thought I'd say this, but I am glad." The edges of his mouth pinched as though he fought to keep from speaking. "He was my closest friend, you know. Once upon a time."

Archer scowled down at his hand, and she wondered if he was remembering when he'd been altered, half man, half demon. Miranda had loved him regardless, and

Daisy could see why. He was loyal and honest. A good man.

"Ian has changed," he said. "I see in him the man he was before."

"If he ever lets himself swallow his pride," she said, suppressing her sad smile, "I think he would ask to be your friend once more." God, she hoped it was true.

Archer made a masculine noise of ambivalence, designed, she supposed, to make her think he didn't care. Unfortunately, she needed him to care, for Ian's sake. For a moment, she couldn't breathe past the pain and terror that clutched her heart.

"He'll need you, Archer," she said when she could speak. "Even if he won't admit it, he will."

His head shot up, his eyes alert and worried. "Tell me why you are here, sister."

With a shaking breath, she unclasped her cloak. Daisy swallowed hard. "I need you to look at something. In a professional capacity," she added when Archer's eyes widened.

His expression turned to stone, and she knew he was hardening his heart, much as she prepared to do. When he spoke, his voice was calm, authoritative. "Let us go to my library."

Chapter Thirty-five

What are you reading?" Daisy asked a silent, dour Northrup, who thumbed through a small leather notebook as they sat in a small corner table at the Plough and Harrow, where they had stopped to take supper.

She could not think of him as Ian when he was like this. Not when he brooded like a stranger. Soon after she'd returned from Archer's house, Ian's manner had changed. Just as thoroughly as his donning of new clothes. So thoroughly, in fact, she had not been able to summon the courage to tell him what she must.

Although polite and attentive when need be, Ian was distant now, avoiding her gaze and fidgeting as though his skin were too tight for his frame. It was he who had suggested they dine out. "Out" being among people and away from the threat of privacy, and the bedroom, she supposed bitterly.

She swallowed down the ball of hurt that seemed lodged in her throat. Had he regretted proposing to her? Perhaps it was for the best. She needed to tell him…

Terror rushed over her so quick and cold that her breath hitched. Her fists bore down on the scarred wood of the table.

"Well?" she pressed, if only to speak and not cry. Later. She would think about the future later. "Are you going to respond? What do you have there?"

Northrup's wide shoulders hunched as far as his perfectly cut coat would let them. "Winston Lane's notebook."

"Ian! You can't steal Winston's notebook."

His brows furrowed as he read. "It appears that I can and did, luv." His fingers tapped an idle beat as the scowl on his face grew.

"It's amoral to steal from an invalid."

He made a noise but did not look up. "It's amoral to let a man's attacker go free, too. I should think the ends justify the means here."

"Bosh." Daisy sat back, her chair scraping a bit on the wood floor from the force. Around her was the happy laughter of men drinking at the bar and the warm scent of good food. Usually, the familiar pub was a balm when her nerves were frayed. Tonight, it served only to exacerbate her upset. She pointed to the battered notebook.

"What is in there that has caught your undivided attention? May we start with that?"

Daisy did not believe for one moment whatever it was had him in this mood. It was her. A war of emotions played over his face as they stared at each other from across the divide of the table. Fear, yearning, and frustration flickered in his gaze. His knuckles stood out bone white against the worn wood, and as much as she longed to cover his hand with hers, she did not. Not when she knew in her belly that she was the cause of his current torment.

Finally, he blinked and let go of a breath with a long sigh. "Lane was attacked at the perfumer's shack. They found Lane's assistant, John Sheridan, at the scene. According to these notes, Lane discovered that the perfumer was a Mr. Ned Montgomery, who, incidentally, was secretly engaged to Miss Mary Fenn, the first known victim of the werewolf."

"Ah, so the perfumer is our killer."

"No. The perfumer is most likely the chap we found in the shack."

Daisy repressed a huff of annoyance. "You're not making very much sense, you know."

"If you'd let me explain, I might." Northrup ignored her glare, but she saw the wry humor in his expression as he thumbed the edge of the notebook. "The perfumer had a sister, Miss Lucy Montgomery." Northrup's eyes gleamed with a dangerous light. "Aside from being Ned's sister, Miss Lucy was also employed as a nursemaid at Ranulf House. It isn't a far stretch to assume that she had been nursing a lycan plagued with syphilis." The gleam grew deadly. "My bastard brother has been lying to me."

"It might be a coincidence. Perhaps Conall isn't involved at all." Daisy knew that no matter what Ian said, the notion of killing his brother ate at his heart.

"And what of the stickpin?" Northrup countered.

"Perhaps someone nicked that stickpin from him."

"Nicked?" Northrup repeated with a repressed smile. For a breath-stealing moment, his blue eyes warmed and her insides fluttered, but he shook his head as if to clear it, and the connection was broken. "A nice thought," he said with his silk-and-gravel voice.

"Well, could it be yours? Maybe someone *nicked* it from you."

He didn't laugh at her tease. "No, lass. My stickpin is long gone." A shadow of grief fell across his face. "I buried it with my son."

She touched him then, because she couldn't bear not to any longer. His hand was warm beneath her palm. "Maybe it isn't that stickpin at all, but one that resembles it. Victoria was crowned forty-six years ago," she added when he shook his head. "It was so long ago, you can't expect your memory to hold so well."

His smile was wide and wolfish. "So you blame my faulty, old-man memory, do you?"

"You are not old."

An amused snort filled the air between them. "I am going on one hundred and thirty-one."

"That is different," she said tartly.

"Oh?" His brows slanted upward, his smile shrewd. "How so?"

"You have the vigor and appearance of a man in his prime, as you well know, you arrogant bastard." She tried to sound annoyed, but for the first time in the day, he was acting himself. She hadn't realized how much she need his teasing, his joy, *him*.

Northrup's white teeth flashed. "Yes, vigor is quite important, is it not?"

"Do be serious, Northrup."

"Ian."

"Ian," she corrected, something inside of her squeezing tight.

His expression softened at the name, and she leaned closer, noting the way his nostrils flared and how the look in his eyes grew heated. She swallowed, her mouth dry. But the moment died when he spoke again. "Stickpin or not, have you an explanation for Miss Montgomery's both working at Ranulf House and being intimately associated with not only a victim but the perfumer?"

Daisy did not. "We must warn her then. Is this what you plan to do tonight?"

Slowly, his thumb stroked her knuckles. "No, sweet, I believe Miss Montgomery is long past help. Lane describes her as being fair of hair, blue eyed, and pretty." Ian's lids lowered. "The woman we found in Ned's shack might have been so once. And Miss Montgomery was let go from Ranulf House about a month ago due to illness. Cancer, she claimed. But I'd bet my hat that it was syphilis, given to her by this mystery lycan who is now a *were*. Lane apparently thought as much, too."

"Well." Daisy sat back. "It appears that Winston is a better detective than you gave him credit for."

"He is a good man," Ian said. "And I will not let his attack go unanswered."

"Then tell me what you plan to do," she said, not without a little exasperation.

He hesitated for a fraction of a second. "Well, that's the thing, love. It appears that Conall has been hiding something in Buckingham Palace."

"Buckingham Palace." She did not want to hear this. She did not.

"The one and only."

It stunned her how well she could read him now. And she did not like what she saw. "Do not tell me you plan to break into Buckingham Palace."

He did not so much as blink. "Fine, I won't."

Wily bastard. "You are mad."

Ian grinned in acknowledgment, but he remained undeterred. "It's not as cracked as you assume. Only a few guards remain to watch the palace. Which is most likely why Conall has been using it. The little shite probably loves to thumb his nose at Victoria by hiding the werewolf there."

"Only a few guards." The table creaked as she leaned over it. "And if you get caught, you can be charged with high treason."

"I will not be caught."

Daisy had to take a breath to keep from shouting. "Just how do intend to get in?"

Ian blinked then. "I'm taking Mary Chase with me."

"Oh-ho no." Daisy's hand curled into a fist upon the table. "Not that, that... moll."

His lips quirked. "She is not a moll. All right, perhaps she is, but she is also a very good spy. I need her to guide me in."

"Of course you do. Perhaps she'll let you feel her bosom as well." And Daisy would hunt her down and claw her gleaming, golden eyes out.

Being a fool, Ian wagged his brows. "D'ye think she might?" Squinting, he stroked his chin. "Perhaps she would at that, gratitude for me bringing her into danger, I suppose."

"Oh, stop!" She tossed the table linen at him, which he ducked with a laugh. "I am going with you," she said when he straightened.

He laughed again, and not without a little humor. "You see, lass, there is where you are wrong. You"—he pointed a long finger at her scowling face—"are going to be nice and safe at home with Talent keeping guard."

She grabbed the finger and hauled his hand, and thus him, close. "I do believe you must be suffering some malady of the mind if you think that will come to pass."

"Daisy..."

"I am not without resources, Ian."

Her curt response gave him pause. "What are you saying?"

Daisy took a breath. "I have a power as well."

Oddly, he didn't look as shocked as she expected, but rather relieved. "Were you planning to tell me anytime soon?"

"I'm telling you now. I found out the night you let your despicable brother tear you to shreds. And"—she braced herself—"it involves dirt."

"Dirt," he repeated.

She wrinkled her nose. "Bother. I hate dirt."

When he lifted his brows in exaggerated query, she sighed. "You see, I can move the earth, make it quake, part, surge, and so forth. I can control the plants, trees."

He closed his eyes. "I did not dream those lycans being speared by tree roots, did I? Or the flowers in the garden."

"I fear not."

Azure blue eyes opened. "Daisy-girl, I cannot tell you how much it pleases me to hear that you can defend yourself when threatened." His fingers, still caught in her grip, threaded through hers and Daisy felt the warmth of his affection. Something in her relaxed.

The grip on her fingers tightened, and he jerked her against him. "But if ye think that such revelations will cause me to take leave of my senses and put you in the direct path of danger, then ye've gone as daft as a wee loon."

It appeared that Daisy had not gone "as daft as a wee loon."

Ian's colorful phrasing aside, she could not fully justify coming along with him. One fool breaking into Buckingham Palace was enough. She wouldn't distract him by waiting outside, a sitting target for whoever happened along. So here she was, cosseted away like a bloody child with Talent to nanny her while Ian ran off with Mary Chase.

Smothering another curse, she glared into the crackling fire burning merrily away in the small upstairs library hearth. Beside her, Talent brooded for reasons of his own. When she could no longer take his burning stare, she turned to glare back at him. "It was his idea for you to watch me, not mine, so kindly stop looking at me in that manner."

"Of course it was his idea." He crossed his arms over his chest. "Before you came along, he relied on me for important tasks. Now I'm stuck watching over one of his women."

One of his women.

The little rat. Talent thought he knew how to get to her, did he?

"Is that why you do not like me?" She gave Talent a thin smile. "I know you don't. You have made that quite clear."

Talent smirked. "I wasn't going to deny it." He leaned forward suddenly, and his broad cheekbones flushed. "I don't like you because you make him weak. You distract him."

"Well, I'm here, aren't I?" Daisy's words came out in a hiss. "While he's off with that GIM."

She expected Talent to jump on her weakness but he looked equally disgruntled. "She's an unnatural piece, that one." Quickly he crossed himself.

"Does everyone revile the poor GIMs?" Daisy asked, a little shocked by his vehemence.

His lip curled. "Poor GIMs? They're body thieves. Unholy. The dogs of our world. And untrustworthy."

"Northrup trusts her. It should be good enough for you." *And for me,* she thought with a qualm.

"He's a fool around women," Talent said with a sneer. "Loves them too much."

Daisy's nails tapped along the arm of her chair as she studied the young man. He wasn't particularly handsome, not in the traditional sense of the word. Though hard, his features were even and well-formed. She suspected that when he smiled, he would be devastating in his own way. And he was not a boy, no matter how often Ian treated him as such. Talent continued to frown into the fire.

"Are you in love with Northrup?" she asked.

He jumped within his seat, his mouth hanging open. "You *are* barmy."

She offered a smile. "Stranger things have happened. And you do go on rather like a jealous lover."

"Good God," he snarled before leaping up to pace. "In love with him?" Talent spun on his heel and glared down at her. "He is like a father to me. Do you understand? I've been with him for years. Years, I've witnessed his loneliness. And now you come along, and he's out of his head."

Daisy's fists clenched. "Yet you begrudge his happiness with me?"

"Because he will not survive it when you leave," Talent shouted. "He was better off closed up. Better off not feeling."

She did not know what happened to the man to make him have such a dim view of life, but she understood his fear. Feeling too much was a dangerous endeavor. It was on the tip of her tongue to shout at him that she would never leave Ian. Doing so would be like ripping out her own heart. But that would make her a liar. Try as she might to forget what she knew, the truth could not be ignored. It burrowed into her heart and made her feel ill, and so very frightened that she wanted to curl up and hide. Daisy sighed and sank back deeper into her seat. "You're right."

Whatever cutting retort Talent had been about to utter died a quick death in the face of her confession. "What are you going on about now?"

Daisy's bottom lip trembled, and she ducked her head, cursing herself for crying now, and in front of him of all people. "I shouldn't have let it go so far," she whispered. "I am not for him."

She might have laughed at the way Talent's head cocked to the side, his expression utterly confounded. But she couldn't. Not when her heart was breaking. Damn it, but Ian had been right; distraction worked for only so long.

"You..." Talent ground his teeth before continuing, "You make him happy."

It was an admission dragged out with the greatest reluctance. Of that Daisy was sure. She did laugh then, but without any humor. "Yes. And he makes me so very happy, too." She sniffled as she went as leaky as a blasted kitchen tap. With a sound of disgust, Talent handed her his kerchief.

"Thank you," she said. "You know, I never used to cry. It seems all I'm capable of now."

"If you make him happy, and he makes you happy," Talent said, "then why should you care a whit what I say?"

She looked up at him through her watery gaze. "Admitting that you aren't all-knowing now, are you?" When he glared, she smiled. "I am human, Jack." Tears welled up again and she blinked hard. "I'm going to die." She swallowed hard. "Eventually, I will die, and he will remain."

He opened his mouth to protest when a sharp noise

from below brought him up short. He stilled and held up his hand as if to bid her quiet while he listened. The sound came again, of breaking glass. His green eyes gleamed with determination as he looked at her. "Stay here."

Daisy lurched to her feet, her heart pounding a wild rhythm. Before he could move away, she caught his arm. "Don't go down there."

Talent looked at her hand upon his arm and then up at her with pointed annoyance. "Are you joking? Of course I'm going. It's my duty."

Daisy didn't let go. Talent might be abrasive and pompous half of the time, but she couldn't see him hurt. "It might be the werewolf."

"I bloody hope so. I've been itching to get my hands on that bastard." He tugged at her grip. "Let it go, will you?"

"No." She clutched him harder. "Ian said you weren't a lycan. How do you even expect to fight it?"

Talent snorted. "Now you ask me?"

"I trust Northrup's judgment," she said. "But you have no idea how strong that thing is."

He laughed with equal parts mirth and outrage. "Hell, woman, I am a shifter."

She had no idea what a shifter was, but it did not sound very impressive. "A shifter is what exactly?"

"Bloody... A shifter is its own beast. I can shift into any living thing." An evil smile spread over his face, and then the air about him shimmered and his body distorted. It was a quick thing, a blur of movement.

Daisy gave a cry of shock and nearly fell on the floor.

Talent laughed. "What? Don't like what you see?"

She gaped back at herself. He'd turned into her! Her face, her figure dressed in Talent's clothes looking back at her.

"Good God," she sputtered. A thought occurred to her, and she yelped. "You were that blasted crow who followed me!"

The air around him stirred as he shifted back. "Quick one, aren't you?" He leaned in, and all the humor leached out of his expression. "I can turn into anything," he said with emphasis. "Even another werewolf."

When Daisy blinked back at him, too dumbfounded to speak, Talent laughed, heartily. She'd been correct. He was devastating when he truly smiled. "Haven't you learned, woman? You've fallen off the map. Here there be monsters."

Another crash stopped him cold. With a firm hand, he guided her to the chair and sat her down as if she were a child. "Now let me go handle this one."

Chapter Thirty-six

In the course of a life as long as Ian's, a man learned to be grateful for small mercies. Therefore, he was extremely grateful that the Queen eschewed living in Buckingham Palace. Breaking into the monarch's property was damning enough without having to worry about running into her person. Since she was not currently in residence, nor had been for some time, minimal security was in place. Two guards patrolled the insides, bored men who played of brag while passing a flask of gin between them. They were currently sleeping off the effect of the laudanum Mary Chase had snuck into their gin. Even so, Ian's footsteps made not a sound as he walked down the dank, dark corridors in the upper hall. Must thickened the air, cobwebs and dust gathering in corners. A rather sad state for the magnificent structure.

He hadn't come empty-handed. Armed with two silver hunting knives and a loaded dart gun, Ian intended to put the *were* down in a humane fashion and walk out with his own head intact. It was one thing to attack the *were* while defending another, but he would not dishonor them both by doing so if the thing were caged.

A ways in front of him, Mary Chase's specter floated along, her form pearly white and translucent. She retained her shape and was able to give the appearance of walking when she was so inclined, but more often it was easier and faster for a GIM in spirit form to drift.

But the longer they roamed the massive palace, the more agitated he grew. Not a soul stirred, nor was there any sign of a werewolf having inhabited the place. The hairs lifted along the back of his neck. Ian's pace quickened, his jaw growing so tight that it throbbed. When they'd come full circle yet again, he stalked toward Mary Chase's ghostly form.

"There is nothing here!" he hissed. "Not a bloody thing."

She frowned, the skirts of her diaphanous dress wavering in a phantom breeze. "We are too late."

Ian punched the wall, not giving a damn that he'd torn through the damask. "There was never a *were* in this place." He punched the wall again, and the picture frames rattled.

"Sire..."

"Do not call me that!" Ian raked his hand through his hair and felt the sting of his claws. Why lure him out here? To get him away from Daisy? Ian went cold for one tense moment. But his heart eased. Talent would protect Daisy.

Even so, Ian itched to return home. "They've laid a trap and we've fallen right into it."

Hovering beside him, Mary's spectral form frowned just before her eyes went wide with fright. Her thin, ghostly voice whispered "No," and then she disappeared.

Ian's hand reached out in a reflexive attempt to pull her

back when Conall's voice rang out from beyond the palace walls. "Ho-there, brother. I've got your little puppet by the neck. Come out and play nice, will you? Or shall I pull on her strings?"

Ian's blood went hot as he ground his teeth.

"Come along then," called Conall. "There's a good bitch."

Conall, Lyall, and six of their guard stood in a semicircle on the Queen's back lawn. Pale moonbeams highlighted his brother's face and made it appear narrower. Otherwise, it was like looking in a bloody mirror. Ian knew then that part of him would die along with Conall this night.

Mary Chase stood placid and unmoving, as though Conall's large hand was not curled around her neck and squeezing tightly.

"Let her go." Ian set down his weapons. "She's got nothing to do with what's between us."

"Your little spy?" Conall shook Mary hard. Her hair tumbled over her face but she did not move. "Making bargains with the devil's minions now, are we?" Sneering, he tossed her away from him, and she fell to the ground with a thud. "Go," he said to Mary, "before I change my mind and rip your clockwork heart out."

She sprinted away without a word.

"So then, brother," Conall said, "will you be challenging me now? Or were you planning to slink about all night?" He came out of the shadows, and Ian noticed that he was kitted out in formal attire, the Clan Ranulf kilt wrapped about him in a bright swath of crimson and blue, a lacy jabot frothing at his throat. He'd been expecting Ian's challenge then, as it was the custom for the king of Ranulf to wear court dress when confronting a bid for his throne. It made it a bugger to fight, but then an alpha didn't fear such trivial things.

"Now will be fine with me." Ian pulled off his coat and tossed it. The bones in his neck cracked as he rolled his shoulders.

The lycans around them circled close, watching now to see who would be alpha.

Lyall stepped forward. "Is it to be a formal challenge then, Ian Ranulf? I'll need to hear the words."

Ian hesitated for a mere second, for there was a light in Lyall's eyes that made Ian think the lycan was pleased. He hadn't expected that. Regardless, Ian stood straight and faced his kind. "I, Ian Alasdair Ranulf, hereby challenge Conall George Ranulf for the throne of Ranulf, as is my right, by blood, birth, and will."

He gave Conall an assessing look. "Or will you concede defeat and step down?" It had to be said. The rules demanded it. And Ian wanted there to be no contention when he took his throne. The very thought made his body hum with impatience, his wolf alert and clamoring for blood.

Conall laughed as he undid the jabot and took off his coat. "I'll give you this," he said. "You've kept your humor."

Lyall spoke up. "Challenge has been issued." He bowed his head toward Conall. "Will you accept, Ranulf?"

"Aye," Conall's tone was almost bored, but Ian saw the gleam of anticipation in his brother's eyes.

"Well, then," Ian unsheathed his claws and his fangs extended, "let's be at it."

They came together in a fury of fist and claws. Snapping fangs missed Ian's neck by a hair. Ian swept a leg under Conall's feet and took him down with a thud. His claws sank into Conall's wrists, pinning him.

"Is that the best ye got, brother?" Conall spit at him.

Ian didn't flinch. "You are the one on the ground. Yield, Conall, and end this madness."

Conall bared his teeth. "Death first."

Death. Ian knew it would come to this, and yet seeing his brother beneath him, his heart recoiled and his soul screamed in protest. "Da wouldn't have wanted us to come to this."

"Da was a mad dog who deserved to be put down. And you were nothing more than his bitch." Conall lurched forward, his teeth snapping. "You want my throne, then try to take it like a true alpha."

Ian squeezed Conall's wrists until he felt the bones bend. "True alpha," he spit out. "You rule by fear, no' respect." A red haze blinded his world for a second. He snarled, his teeth aching to rip into Conall's neck.

His brother merely laughed, not bothering to get free. "Respect? You've let the GIMs and the SOS goad you into trying to take my throne, you bloody fucking puppet."

"Little shite." Ian smashed his forehead into Conall's nose and felt the satisfying crush of bone. "You know nothing of my motives."

Blood seeped over Conall's lips, coloring his fangs red. "Nor you mine. You're barely a lycan now. Told what to do and how to do it by a society that would destroy our kind if they knew."

"Which is why we keep the knowledge from them," Ian ground out. "Or have you forgotten?"

"I forget nothing." Conall bared his teeth. "And if you thought I'd just roll over and let you take what's rightfully mine, then you're a bloody fool, too."

With a burst of strength, Conall lunged and threw Ian off balance. Claws sliced at Ian's chest. A blow to his head had him reeling.

"When I finish with you," Conall said, panting, "I'm going to take your woman and give her a taste of true alpha cock."

Ian roared. Ignoring the pain, he slammed into his brother, punching and slicing, until hot slick blood covered his hand and hit his face. Pinning his brother, Conall jerked and swung out at Ian. But Ian wouldn't let go. His hand curled around Conall's neck, and his claws dug in until they hit his brother's spine. A fraction more and Conall would be dead.

Conall froze. Blood ran in rivulets down his face and over Ian's fingers as he stared back at him.

"You are done," Ian said through his teeth. "Your life is in my hands, to end or to spare. You know it." Ian squeezed just a bit harder and Conall gagged, blood bubbling from his lips, "But more important, they know it."

Conall's gaze darted to the group of lycans who stood tall and silent, watching and waiting. Even without looking, Ian could feel the change in them, the shifting of their loyalty to him. They knew Conall had been vanquished; it was just a matter of what sentence Ian would mete out.

"I am Ranulf, by right and by will." The rightness of it rushed like the tide through Ian, and his wolf howled within him.

Beneath Ian's hand, Conall's throat moved on a swallow, but his eyes flashed defiant. "Finish it then."

The sight cut into Ian. Christ, this was his brother. He knew Conall's scent as well as his own. He'd held him when their mother had passed on. His wolf did not need more blood, nor did Ian. With a sneer, he lifted his brother high and then tossed him. Conall landed on the grass with a thud.

"No," Ian said, looming over him. "I'll not make it so easy for you." He leaned over and hauled Conall up. "You get to live, knowing that I bested you, that I gave you mercy." Ian stood tall and looked at his clan. "Conall Ranulf is hereby banished from Clan Ranulf."

"Bastard." Conall's arm hung at an odd angle as he staggered to his feet.

"Aye, that an' more, brother." Ian advanced on him. "Now tell me where the werewolf is before I chain you and have your balls cut off." Ian didn't want to kill him. But he could make him hurt.

"For the last time," Conall shouted in a ravaged voice, "there is no *were*!"

Ian took another step, but the fight was draining out of him. Instead, he felt a sharp tug of dread. Facing his brother, he ripped the stickpin from his pocket and tossed it at Conall. "Explain this then."

With his good hand, Conall caught it. He glanced down at the pin and his brows furrowed. "Where did you get it?"

Ian held his gaze. "Pinned to the bodice of a dead woman in Bethnal Green. A woman who wore the same perfume as every damn woman who has been killed by the *were*."

Conall studied him for a long moment in which not a soul stirred. Then, with rough movements, he limped over to the bundle of clothes lying on the ground and ripped something free from his jabot.

The bit of gold sailed through the night before Ian plucked it from the air. Even as his hand closed around the metal, Ian could feel the blood rushing from his face and his heart stuttering within his chest.

"That's my pin," Conall said.

A buzzing sound filled Ian's ears as he looked back at his brother. "You truly thought I'd made up the werewolf as an excuse to take your throne?"

"Aye." Conall took a hobbled step closer. "It's not my pin, Ian," he said watching him with wary intent, because Conall knew, just as Ian did, where the other pin had ended up. "It's Maccon's."

A block of ice formed in Ian's stomach, and his blood congealed. "No." He couldn't say anything more. Sweat trickled down his back. *No!*

Pity filled Conall's eyes. "Lyall told me there wasn't a *were"*—

Ian heard the hiss of the sword a second before it sliced through Conall's neck. Conall's mouth hung open in surprise, even as his head hit the ground with a heavy clunk. It wobbled there, as his body fell beside it. Lyall stood on the other side, sword in hand and his own mouth open in shock.

Chapter Thirty-seven

Ian could not move or speak as he stared at the beta who had just killed his brother. For a thick moment, they said nothing, and then Lyall looked at the sword in his hand as if he couldn't understand how it got there. "I told Conall that ye crafted the tale of the *were* to make him look incompetent."

"You..." Ian's voice failed him, for his body was still numb and his brain still trying to make him believe that his brother was dead.

"Aye." Lyall let the sword fall. "And the fool believed me. Just as you believed that Conall was controlling the *were*." His gaze went to Conall's body for a second before shooting up to Ian. "The clan needed a true leader. The clan needed you."

Acid rose in Ian's throat, and he swallowed. "This was all to get me to be ruler?"

"Got you out of that bloody pathetic state of self-pity, did it not?" Lyall's face went red. "You should have taken the throne when it was offered. Instead, you let your brother nearly run us into ruin!"

Low in Ian's gut, a tremble started, working its way up his back. "Where did you get this pin, Lyall?"

"Maccon gave the pin to that girl. The *were* is Maccon."

"Lies." It was all Ian could say. Not Maccon. His son was dead. He had buried him. Grieved over his grave for a full night and day. Grieved in his heart every day thereafter.

"He'd already made the change. You buried him, damaged but alive. Poor lad clawed his way out and ran straight to Ranulf Hall. Only you were gone, and I was there."

It wasn't true. Every cell in Ian's body screamed in denial. "His head was split open, his neck broken. He was dead."

Slowly, Lyall shook his head, and Ian saw the truth in his eyes. "He just needed time to heal."

"Why would he—" Ian's breath hitched. The *were* was sick with syphilis.

Lyall nodded as if seeing the understanding come over Ian's face. "He had the pox. Said he didn't want you or Una to see him that way. Hell, it's why he tried to kill himself."

Blood thundered in Ian's ears as he finally looked at the man who had turned his life upside down. "Have you no sense? No notion of what was in store for him?"

Lyall's chin lifted. "Gave him a nurse, didn't I? Made him as comfortable as I could. Didn't expect him to turn when the nurse died. But when he did, I saw the opportunity for what it was."

It was all Ian could do not to be ill. Bile surged up strong and burning. *Sweet Jesus.* Ian wanted to sob, beat Lyall's face to a pulp, only he was frozen. Rage pulsed through his temples and set his teeth grinding. "Why?"

He bit back a growl, his limbs quivering with rage held in tight rein. "Why did you keep him from me?" Ian's body came to vivid life. "Why, you twisted, mad fuck—"

"He asked." Lyall took a shuddering breath. "Jesus, he *begged.* I could not deny him. I loved him like a son."

"He was my son! No' yours!"

The belligerent look in Lyall's eyes flashed to fury. "He should have been mine!"

Ian's heart lurched. "You never even looked at Una."

"I could give a shite about Una!" Lyall flung his arms wide. "I never found a woman who could give me offspring. You did! You, the favored son, who didn't even want the throne, who let an incompetent rule. You, who would have killed Maccon had you known."

"I would have tried to help him! I would not have let him suffer."

"You would have bloody put him down."

"Where is he?" Ian roared.

Lyall palmed the sword as though it could keep him safe. "You were supposed to think Conall was to blame for everything. After you killed him, that's what you would think, aye?" He shook his head. "After all, I couldn't have you distracted by another human. So I let Maccon out to play."

Daisy. In one leap, Ian tackled Lyall. They rolled, grass and sky a dark blur. Lyall might have spent his life as a beta, but he was strong and a born fighter. Lyall's body shifted and grew, his wolf rising so close to the fore that he barely appeared human. Sharp teeth sank into Ian's arm, hitting the bone. On a shout, Ian punched Lyall hard in the temple, once, then twice. The side of Lyall's head dented in as his skull cracked and his hold on Ian failed.

"No," shouted Lyall. "I'll not die because of another fucking Ranulf!"

Before Ian's eyes, Lyall turned to full-out werewolf. Fur tickled his nose, the wild scent of beast clogging his throat. And then Ian was tossed back, flying into the air by the superior strength of the wolf. Bloody hell, the man had turned with the ease of breathing. He'd set his wolf free. Ian's mind reeled at the possibility, while his wolf howled to be free as well.

Let me. Just let me.

Claws gouged the flesh on Ian's shoulder as Ian rolled at the last moment. Another swipe of Lyall's claws nearly eviscerated Ian.

On a growl, he kicked Lyall's snout. The *were* barely staggered. He was too strong in this form. Putting his back into it, Ian lunged, tackling the wolf and crushing its ribs. Lyall twisted, his hind legs finding Ian's exposed belly and sinking in. Pain burst in brilliant color behind Ian's lids. Blood pooled in his mouth. He caught sight of the glowing moon and he thought of death, and Daisy. Everything slowed, his breath, the beat of his heart.

You failed her too, MacRanulf. She'll know it when she dies. Lyall's thoughts were in his head, ringing as clear as a death knell.

Daisy.

Lyall was stronger. But an alpha's will was greater than strength. This conniving bastard would not take another thing from Ian. Conviction rushed like wildfire through his flesh. Without another thought, he burst forward, urgency and need burning his blood. Strength and power as he'd never experienced surged through him with such force that he barely felt the pain lancing his body. On the next breath, he was on four legs, and Lyall was scrambling back.

Free. Free.

His wolf was a shout in his mind. Not his mind anymore, but the wolf's. And he lay trapped, unable to control his limbs. Panic rose like acid.

Calm.

Oddly, the wolf soothed him. The wolf knew what to do. Daisy. Save her. Kill Lyall. These things were simple in its mind. The wolf would take care of him. He would protect his mate. On a snarl, he flew up and clamped down on Lyall's neck. His teeth sank past thick fur, into the other *were*'s tender throat and slicing through the jugular. He shook the dying wolf like a rag, severing his spine, ending his life.

Blood coated his tongue as he let the *were* drop. The wolf felt a keen surge of victory, but deep in the corners of his mind, the man cried for all that he'd lost. The lycan men around him kneeled, but the wolf didn't acknowledge them.

He was already running across the lawn, his paws sinking into the grass, his heart threatening to burst. For he knew he would be too late.

It was too quiet. Daisy sat in the chair with her knees drawn up and her arms locked around them. It was a childish pose, but she did not particularly care at the moment. Talent had been gone for too long. There had been no sounds of fighting, no call for her to come out. It was as if he'd up and disappeared. Cursing, she got to her feet and paced the floor. All was silent. Still. Too still. She could not stay here, waiting for whatever it was to come up and claim her.

Going to the French windows that opened up onto a small balcony, she looked out into the dark night. The only light came from the gibbous moon overhead. The marble terrace gleamed icy blue, punctuated here and there by the dark shadows of potted trees. Just beyond lay a wide lawn that stretched down to the glittering river, winking through a row of stately trees.

Ordinarily, she would think it madness to leave a house for the outdoors. Only right now, she felt the moonlight on her face and saw the sway of the tree limbs and felt the call of nature. Out there was her strength. She felt it now just like a rush of warm light through her veins. Out there was where she would be safe. Gathering her skirts with resolve, she went out to the balcony and then hefted herself over the edge. Her footing was sure as she climbed down the trellis. She'd climbed up and down her father's trellis many times before. The naughty daughter who snuck out at night to carouse in taverns because she craved laughter and life so very much she'd rather take the risk and live it. How she missed being that girl. Emotion clogged her throat as she jumped lightly from the last rung and landed with sure feet.

Creeping along, she made it as far as the middle of the terrace when she realized something was amiss. The coppery tang of blood touched her nose. Walking on heavy feet, she followed the smell to the stairs that led to the garden. Her heel slid a ways as she came sharply to a halt before a black pool of blood on the white marble.

Breath caught in her throat as she slowly turned toward the spill. A scream rose and died on her lips. Talent lay in a heap at the foot of the stairwell. His right arm was a stump, his body ravaged. She thought him dead but he moved as if hearing her. One green eye, bloodied and raw, opened. His lips worked for a moment.

"Run."

She couldn't move. Couldn't leave him to this.

He snarled. "Run!"

As if giving her wings, his command made her fly down the stairs and toward the garden. Her sweaty fingers slipped on her skirts as she lifted them high. A rose garden flanked the sides of the terrace where, in June, the thick, sweet scent of their blooms would surely perfume the air. Now, however, they were merely hard, twisted roots, cut short for the winter. A low, distinct growl stopped her cold on the path. Everything in her went still. Past the thundering of her heart and the panting of her breath came the click of claws upon the marble and the wild, noxious sweet scent of wolf and sickness.

He was behind her. Convulsively, she swallowed. On trembling legs she turned.

Up close, she finally got a good look at him. His head was deformed, massive tumors pulling his eyes far apart, sending his jaw askew. Amber eyes held such pain that Daisy felt not solely terror but pity as well. Pity that died when the *were* snarled and headed for her. A surge lit through Daisy in answer, the strange feeling of power and pressure that throbbed in her belly and down to her fingertips. The ground rumbled for a moment, and then the sharp crackle of rose bushes growing rent the air.

Daisy's insides quaked. *Faster. More.* The hard, thorny branches grew up and out, creating a wall around her. The *were* attacked, running so fast that Daisy's breath caught. The impact cracked the branches. Knife-sharp claws slashed at the wood, splintering it.

Fear surged through her limbs and her power slipped. The roots faltered. *More. Stronger. Focus.*

Thorns and branches wrapped tight around werewolf limbs, holding the beast off but not stopping him. One foreleg broke free, and then another. The wolf's eyes were on her, a promise gleaming in them. Daisy edged back, her heart pounding, her breath caught in a ball of terror in her throat. Desperately, she drew on the feeling within her, and the rose branches snaked out, tangling around the *were* again and again. But it was not enough. With a bone-shaking howl, the beast writhed and the branches shattered like glass.

Daisy stumbled back, her strength sputtering like an empty lamp. The werewolf stopped and cocked his head as though confused. Daisy's jaw clenched tight enough to ache before she forced herself to ease, trying to ignore the blood that caked the *were's* coat. Talent's blood. She froze upon the ground, too terrified to do any more but wait.

He limped forward, one foreleg shorter than the other due to his humped back. Light from the house windows hit his molted coat, highlighting the open sores that plagued him and the wounds from the thorns. Quite suddenly, she wanted to cry. This was her future, too. This suffering and deformity.

"You hurt, don't you?"

Halting, the *were* whined and shifted his weight from one leg to another. A world of agony lay in its eyes.

"I'm sorry," she whispered, her voice too thin.

His head lowered, yet a growl rumbled in his chest. In a flash, he snapped his teeth at her, snarling and growling.

Her fingers clenched on air. Ian. She wanted Ian. *Please let him be on his way.* "Let me help you. I want to help you."

He whined again, his massive head swaying as he cowered. *Pain. I feel pain.*

Daisy's heart skipped a beat, for she distinctly heard the words within her head. Licking her dry lips, she tried again. "Let me talk to the man."

He shuddered violently, keening.

"The man," she said. "Let him come, and I can help you both."

The wolf sighed, and his head sank down. The snap and pop of his bones filled the night as he shifted, and Daisy was left staring at a man.

No better off in his human form, his naked, twisted body fell to a heap upon the marble. There he trembled, the sores that covered him weeping and swollen. Disease had destroyed this man, ruining his body and his reason. She feared she might be ill.

A gnarled hand lifted to the massive tumor on his head that had deformed his face into something barely human. A pitiful cry broke from him. "Kill me," he rasped. Bleary eyes lifted to hers. "I cannot live as this…"

Daisy's heart threatened to pound out of her chest. "I cannot…"

He snarled, smashing his fist into his skull. "Kill me. Kill me." He howled, his body rocking. "Pain. Too much."

Would someone take pity on her were it she who suffered? Did he not deserve compassion? A sob tore from her. "Let me get someone to help you."

His voice grew thready, his displaced eyes desperate as he looked at her. "You. I want it to be you. Please…" He curled in on himself with a groan. "Please, Lucy. I tried to find you."

Lucy. He thought she was his love. All this time, he'd been looking for his love. She blinked back her tears.

"These other women…smell of you but were not…" A growl rumbled in his chest and fangs grew. "They were not…"

"But I am here now," Daisy said quickly, soothing him with her voice and praying he would not notice his mistake. She thought of Alex's ravaged body and swallowed hard. "What can I do for you?"

"Take my head."

She blanched. Anything but that.

His breath rattled. "Shred my heart with silver. A knife. I cannot live like this. And it will come back, the madness. The wolf wants to die, too. You promised to help him."

For a long moment, she could only stare. To kill in cold blood was something beyond her. Yet to live as he did, it was no life. Her eyes burned with unshed tears. Again came the hard rolling of her stomach and the urge to cast up her accounts. She took a deep breath. "All right."

He didn't stop her as she stumbled away, past Talent, who had either passed out or died. She was too afraid to look. Moving stiffly, she found the butler's pantry and the silver carving knife within. Her heart beat a fierce tattoo, her mind numb to all thought but one. She might have run away, yet she could not. She would help this man, this harbinger of her fate.

His skin was clammy, his breath a wheezing rattle as she knelt beside him. His eyes, however, were lucid as he gazed up at her. "I am sorry," he whispered. "For all of it."

Tears blurred her view of him. "I know." Extreme pain, tumors, and madness, they were the tools of destruction for those suffering from syphilis. A fate worse than any death. Yet she could not make herself move.

"Not your fault." His voice was gentle, and when she looked down at him, he touched her arm. "Never was."

God, he appeared a man no older than thirty. How long had he been like this? Her arm shook so badly that she could barely raise it. Her nerves jumped when his hand closed over hers. His gaze grew dazed. "I only wanted to see you once more, Lucy Love."

"Of course," she whispered. "I wanted to see you, too. Rest now. Everything will be all right."

In the end, it was his strength and her hand that plunged the knife down between his ribs, past muscle, and into the heart. With a hard jerk of his body, he wrenched the knife back and forth, all the while Daisy's hand caught below his, the hilt of the knife slippery against her skin.

The man took his last breath in a gurgled sigh of blood.

On a cry, she scrambled far away from him and curled up by a ravaged rose bush. Weary to the bone, she rested her head upon her arms and sighed. It was done. For him. Her fear, however, went so deep that she could not think to move.

Her small peace was shattered when the terrace doors slammed open with enough force to send one hanging on its hinge. A scream leaped up in her throat as an enormous brown wolf charged onto the terrace. It skidded to a stop when he spied her. Daisy's mouth went dry. Dear God, but it was magnificent. This was not the poor, deformed creature she'd help pass on but a full-out wolf, enormous in form, but graceful and proud.

The beast's thick, auburn coat gleamed with blood, his wild blue eyes intent upon her. And then the bottom fell out of her world. Those eyes. Ian's eyes. Oh, Ian. She wanted to scream in rage and sorrow. Ian had turned.

Daisy put a hand to her breast to ease the pain there. The wolf growled. She did not move, but her mind raced. She'd spoken to the sick *were*. The wolf had set the man free. Could she reach Ian? She would. She had to.

"Hello," she said calmly—a lie for her heart threatened to burst, it pounded so hard. "I know you," she said slowly, softly. "I've been waiting to meet you."

The wolf whined, cocking his head a touch. He took a tentative step forward.

"Yes," she said, pretending that her breath wasn't ragged, that her fingers did not shake. "Come to me. Let me touch you."

With a grunt, it moved, a quick lope that had it knocking against her, his big head nudging her shoulder hard. A gasp burst from her, but she did what instinct prompted and threaded her fingers through the dense, coarse hair at the wolf's neck. The wolf's eyes narrowed, not in aggression but pleasure.

With a sigh, she stroked his fur. "If you're here... you must have had to protect Ian." It was the only reason Daisy could think of. Ian simply wouldn't lose control of his wolf unless it had been his last choice.

Yes. Save you.

She heard the words inside her heard, and the voice was Ian's and not. It was rougher, more primal. The wolf's.

Daisy's breath caught and her eyes burned. "You've done well. So well."

Save you from the were. Its blue gaze moved past her to rest on the dead man. A keening noise sounded low in the wolf's throat, and it turned away from the sight as if it pained him.

"I am so proud," she murmured as the wolf bunted his snout under her chin. The hit rattled her teeth. Before she could move, gentle fangs took hold of her lower jaw. But the wolf did nothing more than hold her still. A claim.

With a smile, she pushed him back. "No more of that." She was insane, but could only hope the wolf understood. It seemed to, for it simply panted and nudged her once more.

Daisy wrapped her arms around his neck. "Let him come back," she whispered. "I cannot lose him."

The wolf whined, and she stroked his fur. "He knows

how to set you free again. He will. But I need him now." The wolf stilled, and her heart thundered. "Ian," she pled, "come back to me. Come back."

Dread pulled at her insides for a cold moment and then the wolf stirred. Bones cracked and popped, the body around her arm shrinking. In the next breath, she felt smooth, hot skin, and Ian was in her arms, as weak as a pup as he fell to his knees. His chest heaved as he glanced up at her with reddened eyes. "I think," he said, "I am going to be ill."

He clung to her, his body damp with sweat and shaking. Daisy held him close. But she felt him stiffen as he caught sight of the twisted body on the ground. All color leached from his face, and he wilted.

"Maccon." Such pain in that utterance.

Daisy's blood stilled. Maccon? She glanced at the poor body of the man and back to Ian, who tore himself from her grasp and stumbled forward. Devastation marked every line of his countenance. *I had a son. Maccon. He was perfect. A good lad.* Her head went light. Oh God, Ian's child. A sharp pain lanced her chest. *Ian. What did I do?*

Ian's breath rattled as he sank to the ground next to the body.

"But he died," she said, in a panic. "You said he died."

Ian did not look at her. "He'd already turned." His throat worked. "I-I did not know." Lightly, as if he feared the body would break, Ian gathered his son against himself. Maccon's head lolled back, his eyes sightless and staring.

Daisy gripped herself so tightly her knuckles cracked. *No, no, no. Not this.* "I killed him." Such a stupid thing to say. What had she done?

"Yes." Ian did not take his eyes from his son.

"Ian..." Her voice cracked. "I'm...I did not know."

He didn't seem to hear her. "Lyall had him. All this time. Watching my son go mad. A grand joke."

"Lyall?" She thought of the crafty lycan who'd been Conall's right hand. He'd been the one to capture them at the cemetery. He'd been everywhere.

"Lyall kept him when he turned. All this time he was playing Conall and me against each other. He used Maccon so I would challenge Conall. And it worked." Ian's shoulders lifted on a breath. "My brother is dead. And my son..."

"Oh, Ian." Were Lyall here, Daisy would kill him. Yet she knew in her bones that he was already dead. Ian would not have let him live after such a betrayal.

"Are you hurt?" Still Ian would not look her way.

Suddenly she was glad for it. She could not bear to see his eyes, and the accusation there. She deserved it, but she could not bear it. "No. I... he..." Daisy couldn't bring herself to say that Maccon had begged for death. It sounded like an excuse. She wouldn't excuse herself for it.

Ian's head fell forward, his hair swinging down to hide his face. Shame choked Daisy as she watched him. She wanted to say she was sorry but knew it wouldn't matter. When he finally spoke, his voice was a broken thing that made her heart ache. "I need to bury him."

She licked her dry lips. "I'll help you."

"No!" He took another breath. "Just... just go into the house."

She went, because it was the only thing she could do for him.

Chapter Thirty-eight

It was not Ian who sought her out hours later but Talent. Daisy stirred from her cold spot on the settee as he limped into her bedroom, his battered body bandaged up like a mummy.

"You should be in bed," she said. Her throat ached and her eyes burned, but the man before her looked like hell.

He slumped onto the seat beside her and closed his eyes. "Doesn't matter where I am," he said. "I'll hurt like a bitch regardless."

"Your arm..." It was missing below his elbow. Guilt flooded her at the sight. He had been defending her.

"Will grow back. Eventually." He did not sound very concerned, merely annoyed. "Jesus, it's cold in here. Haven't you any notion of how to start a fire?" He cracked one eye open. "Or are we feeling sorry for ourselves?"

She didn't rise to his bait but stood and lit the coals that had been laid out, and then found her thick shawl to drape over him. Talent grunted in acknowledgment and kept his eyes closed. He didn't try to speak anymore, for which Daisy was truly grateful, but simply sat with her for a long while as they stared into the fire. Every bone in her body hurt. She ought to go home, only that place didn't feel like her home. Ian was her home. And she'd destroyed it. Eventually, she knew he'd seek her out and tell her to go. Until then, she would remain hiding away in cowardly fashion and aching to hold him.

"You had no choice."

She sucked in a breath at the sound of Talent's voice. It took her a moment to find her own voice. "It doesn't matter."

"It should. Maccon was insane, and hurting." He turned his head to look at her. "I heard him beg you."

Daisy winced, but he kept on. "You did him a kindness. Ian will understand. Hell, you called him back after the wolf claimed him. He ought to be thanking you."

Her laugh was weak and pained. "It was his will and the wolf's trust that brought him back. Not I. And as for his son, I fear logic and emotion never go hand in hand."

"No," Ian said from the door. "They don't."

Daisy and Talent stood up as one.

Ian stepped into the room, his expression implacable. He'd cleaned himself up and dressed. Yet he looked so defeated that she wanted to run to him and beg him to let her hold him. But she did not move. They stared at each other from across the room, the tension between them pulled as tight as a bowstring. Daisy could not think of a word to say to make things right.

Talent frowned and then stirred.

"Utter one word, Jack," came Ian's fierce growl, "and I'll rip yer sharp tongue from yer mouth."

Well.

Talent's mouth snapped shut. With a terse nod, he left

them. Ian slammed the door shut behind him and stalked across the room.

All protest died on her lips as he hauled her against his chest in a bone-squeezing embrace and he buried his face in her hair. He stood shaking, holding her as if she might be snatched away.

Nothing had ever felt better than his embrace. She clung to him and wished that it would never end.

"Don't," he pled when she started to speak. His grip tightened. "Just... don't. Not yet."

Whatever she felt at that moment receded in the face of his disquiet. He eased only a little when she slid her hands up and cupped his cheeks. Firelight turned his features into a patchwork of gold and amber angles and reflected in the haunted sheen of his eyes.

"Ian," she whispered, because she knew he liked his name upon her lips. Then she kissed him. He made a sound close to a whimper and then fell into the kiss, a man gripped by need.

She pulled back and touched his face. "Ian, you don't need to..."

"I do need." A cracked, raw sound left him as he rested his forehead against hers. "I need more than you know."

He unsheathed one claw and reduced her gown into tatters with stunning adeptness. Cold air shivered over her skin as he tumbled her onto the bed. Soft bedding enveloped her, and then he was there, the long length of his body pressing her deeper into the covers, the wool of his suit warm and rough against her nakedness.

His knuckles grazed her damp sex as he unbuttoned the fall of his trousers. The hot length of his cock fell against her thigh, and Daisy undulated against him. Unsteady hands slid along her arms to capture her wrists. Their fingers twined, and he lifted her arms above her head.

His kiss was a desperate thing, without finesse. "I don't know any other way," he said against her mouth. "I don't know how else to show you."

His eyes were wild and frightened as he gazed down at her, pausing as if to see if she understood. She was pinned to the bed, his thighs holding hers so wide apart that she felt the exposure acutely, and with it, the need to be filled. Her heart knocked against her rib cage. For suddenly, she did understand. She blinked back the mist blurring her vision and tightened her grip upon his fingers.

"Then show me your way," she whispered.

A deep shudder racked his frame. She expected him to act, to take her with quick brutality, but he did not. He simply looked at her, his eyes wide open, hiding nothing, letting her in. What she saw took her breath. He was utterly beautiful to her just then. And she knew her heart and soul was no longer her own.

Holding her gaze, he tilted his head and kissed her, a soft, open-mouthed kiss of melting heat. The tip of his cock nudged her opening, drawing her attention until it was the only thing she could think on. She wiggled against him, impatient and hurried. But he would not let her rush. Murmuring soothing words against her mouth, he gentled the kiss once more, his silken tongue dipping, tasting with smooth strokes.

Only when she panted with need and small cries left her mouth did he ease into her. Slow enough for her to feel every inch tunneling through her flesh, filling her up. She shuddered, her thighs aching to move. But she was pinned. And he was withdrawing with the same steady deliberation. Invasion, retreat, he worked an undulating rhythm that tormented. All the while, he kissed her, working her mouth as he worked her.

Her body shook, perspiration blooming along her heated skin. God, but this could become essential. A woman could want this every day. All the time. The feeling within her was almost angry, a blinding, dark thing that had her biting his lower lip before licking to soothe it.

He squeezed their twined fingers, his thrusts growing harder, his breath coming in shallow pants. She was burning up beneath him, the feel of his clothes heightening the sensation. She wanted to feel him without barrier.

His deliberation fractured into desperation. Groaning deeply, he dropped his forehead to her neck, burrowing there as he pushed deep.

A shiver lit over her skin, through her flesh, and into him. He shook with a violent tremor, but stopped. "Ah, God, I need—let me..." Shuddering, he withdrew, and before she could think, he turned her around to take her from behind. He stilled, remembering, perhaps, what had happened the last time he had tried. His big hand trembled as it pressed against her belly. "Please, Daisy, will you let me?"

The very idea set her aflame, released something wild within her, but his hesitation and concern for her was a kick to her heart. Her voice was barely a whisper when she responded. "Yes."

He expelled the breath he'd been holding. Stepping away, he ripped free of his clothes and then came back to her, his breathing as ragged as her own. She groaned as he nudged her legs apart. Daisy's eyes fluttered closed as she slumped forward and lifted her hips to him.

"Christ," he hissed as he sank in deep, and then his hands grasped her hips and he took her. It was brutal, savage, and Daisy shivered from the shocking pleasure of it, her mind crying out *yes*. And *more*.

Ian's body surrounded her, holding her, keeping her. His strong teeth, so unlike the wolf's, clamped down on the soft junction of her shoulder, and Daisy shattered. He followed her with a sharp cry as he strained against her.

In the resounding silence, he fell onto the bed next to her and threw an arm over his eyes. His glistening chest heaved as he lay there, struggling for breath. She moved to touch him, and he lowered his arm. Daisy's vision blurred as she saw the raw pain in his eyes.

"Ian."

"You brought me back." His voice was a ghost of itself.

"You came back. I wanted to be afraid, but I knew in my heart that you would."

"I came back to you." Without another word, he curled against her, burrowing his face into the crook of her neck. She held him tight as he silently wept for the loss of his son, and even his brother. Eventually he calmed, his long body becoming loose and warm against hers. As they drifted off to sleep, her last bit of peace shattered when he whispered, "They all die."

They would have to talk. Eventually. Daisy knew this. Pull the thorn out quickly, was what her mother used to say. But she didn't want to. She didn't want to see Ian hurt any further. And she knew he would be. So she let him sleep. And sleep Ian did, his big, lean body taking up their bed in a sprawl of golden limbs and tousled auburn hair. He slept like the dead. Grief could do that to a person, make them seek the oblivion of sleep rather than face the day. Daisy knew from experience.

Acting the coward, she dressed and then watched over

him until the sunlight crept up his long legs and played with the flat muscles along his back.

When he finally stirred, she went to him. Sleep mussed and grumbling, Ian tugged her near, wrapping his arms about her waist and resting his head in her lap. He seemed to breathe her in, his chest lifting with it. His fingers plucked at her dressing gown. "You're dressed," he said from the comfort of her lap. It sounded like a complaint.

Though it made her want to smile, she couldn't. Softly she stroked his silken hair. A lump rose in her throat. "It's midday."

"Is it?"

"Mmm." She smoothed a strand of hair between her fingers. Ian sighed and nuzzled against her. So very wolfish, she thought, a smile rising at last. But the smile faded. "Ian." She laid her hand upon the crown of his head. "Ian, I am so sorry."

Tension tightened along his body. She felt him swallow. His voice was low but controlled when he spoke. "Talent was in the right. You did Maccon a mercy." Lightly, he traced along the swirling pattern in her skirt. "I was coming to do the same thing, love. I... He did not deserve to suffer.

"Last night," he said after a moment, "when I..." A rough exhale sent warmth against her belly. "I thought I was too late," he rasped. "I thought—" He sucked in a deep breath. "Fuck."

She hugged him close. "Had I known, I would have waited for you. I wish I had done so with all my heart."

He didn't seem to hear her. "I couldn't bear it, Daisy, if you'd died. I don't want to live in a world without your light. Letting my wolf free did not matter if it saved you."

He looked at her as if seeing her for the first time and

he lifted his hand to slowly trace the contours of her face as if imprinting them in his mind.

"I love you." He said it so simply, without reservation or shame. As though he'd said the words to her a thousand times.

It took her breath and shattered her heart.

The corner of his lips quirked in a repentant smile. "I should have told you before but I haven't... I haven't said the words in a long time."

Quickly, she pressed a hand to his jaw, running her thumb across his bottom lip. "Hush." Her insides were tearing apart. And it hurt. It hurt so badly, she thought she might wail. But she forced herself to say what she must. "Hush, Ian."

She bent over and gave him a soft, quick kiss and almost sobbed. "You needn't..." Her mouth wobbled, threatening to betray her, and she took another breath. "You needn't feel obliged to say those things."

He went utterly stiff against her, his expression recoiling as though he'd been struck. Daisy forged on, making herself speak quickly. See the deed done. "I know you care, Ian."

"Care." His voice was flat, his eyes narrowing. "Care? Obliged?"

He sat up full, and she drew away, sensing the inevitable explosion. But he wouldn't let her go far. Strong hands whipped out to clasp her upper arms in an unbreakable grip. Her heart cracked at the pain swimming in his blue gaze.

"I tell you I love you. Words I vowed never to say to another again." His fingers bit into her soft flesh. "And you think them spoken out of obligation?" His voice turned sharp, cutting. "Out of some warped need to... coddle you?"

"Ian," she whispered, for her voice wouldn't obey her any more than her heart would. "You're hurting me."

His eyes widened, and he let her go as if burned. With a curse, he jumped up, oblivious to his nakedness. "Aye, and you are hurting me," he snapped. "Or are my feelings so unworthy as to not merit discussion?"

Daisy got to her feet. "Don't be ridiculous. Of course they matter."

"Oh?" His brows slashed upward. "I tell you I love you. And in turn, you spout utter rot. Do I mean nothing to you?"

"Yes!" Oh, but the walls were closing in on her, his questions making her too hot, too agitated. "I care for you as you care for me."

"Care," he snarled, tossing up a hand. His eyes flashed blue fire. "I'm beginning to hate that word 'care.' Fuck 'care'!"

He paced toward her, gathering her in his arms again, his eyes wild but his touch careful now. "No more deflections, Daisy-Meg. It's just you and me here. Tell me. Tell me why you cannot accept that I love you." Doubt flickered in his troubled gaze. "Why you cannot say that you love me."

She wrenched herself out of his embrace and stumbled back when he moved toward her. "Because you cannot love me. You should not," Daisy shouted. "I am not for you, Ian Ranulf. I am mortal, if you remember. I will die."

He flinched then. "Aye. Some days that's all I think of, and it cuts me to the soul."

She gasped, pressing a hand to her throbbing head. "And you ask me why I resist?"

"I know why you resist," he retorted. "Why I resisted for as long as I did." He took another step closer. "And

I told you before, I'm willing to risk the pain to be with you, Daisy mine." Ian's expression darkened as he bore down on her. "Yesterday you were willing to try. Yesterday you agreed to become my wife."

Yesterday her life was filled with hope. She wrenched herself out of his embrace and stumbled back. "Yesterday, I didn't fully appreciate the reality of what we would be to each other." She paced away from him and the look of betrayal and pain she'd put in his eyes. "I don't want do this while you're hurting. I don't want to say these things now."

"Then don't say them!"

"Someone has to. I know how much it devastated you to lose Maccon." Her stomach pitched as he winced. "And if we continue on this way, it will happen to you again." She tried to touch him but he flinched away. Her hand curled into a fist as she let it drop. "I can be unselfish for once. I can do that much for you."

The whites of his eyes were red and glassy as he glared at her. "You're running away. Again."

"Yes," she said, backing away. "I will not be another regret, Ian. I cannot be the one to cause you pain when I die and leave you behind." Pain lanced through the center of her skull, and she ground her teeth. "Love should not be the destruction of another. Talent was in the right. I make you weak, Ian. I cannot bear the thought of making you weak. Not you, the strongest man I've ever known."

He stared at her for a long moment, his head cocked as if he were confused. But the clouds cleared, and he appeared almost angry.

"Christ." He strode forward. His mouth took hers in an open, heady kiss that spoke of frustration and desperation. She gave as good as she got, sinking into him because this was the last time she could. On a groan, his kiss gentled, exploring, coaxing. And when they finally parted, he gazed down at her.

"You never made me weak," he said, giving her a little shake. "You make me strong." His big hands smoothed up her arms. "Just knowing you're in this world makes me want to live in it, makes me want to fight."

A small sob broke from her lips, and his gaze grew tender as he brushed a kiss along her temple. "No, my Daisy-Meg," he said against her hair. "Never weak, but infinitely strong."

Sunlight gilded the swells of his shoulders and turned the ends of his hair into bronze. When he spoke, his voice was clear and firm. "I would be a god with the power of your love. If I knew that I had it."

He touched her cheek. "But I cannot do it alone. I cannot bow and scrape for each scrap, hoping you'll see what I see in us. I won't have you by default." A small smile lifted his mouth. "Ah, but if you gave it to me freely, I swear on my soul I wouldn't let it go to waste. With everything I am, I'd give it back to you in return. I'd keep ye, love ye till my last breath, lass."

Softly, he kissed her. A promise. It was all she ever wanted. He was home, peace, and happiness. And it split her in two. A hole lay in her chest where her heart had been, and she felt as though it bled straight through her skin and onto her clothes. Everything in her turned cold, then hot. Why did he have to make it so hard? Why did he have to fight her? She wanted to kick and bite him for her pain, for his. So she turned from him.

Ian simply followed her with his head. "Tell me that you don't love me, Daisy." His chest heaved. "If that be the case, tell me and I'll let you go."

Tears leaked from her eyes, scalding her skin as they ran free. "I cannot."

He exhaled with a deep shudder, his grip easing. "Then why—"

"I'm dying, Ian."

The statement snapped like a whip, making his head rear back and his body tense. She closed her eyes on a sigh, defeat suddenly making her utterly weary.

"What—" He swallowed audibly.

"Maccon," she croaked. "He bit me on the night he first attacked." Quickly, she licked her dry lips. "I've had headaches, sore throats, dizzy spells...I found the sore yesterday morning. Archer confirmed it. I have syphilis."

His frozen stance shattered with a burst of agitated movements.

"Where?" His hands were already fumbling with her gown.

"What does it matter—"

"Where!" He'd gone as white as chalk, his eyes awash with pain and denial. And it wrenched her heart anew.

Too tired to resist, she lifted up the thick fall of her hair to reveal the small, round sore. His fingers hovered just above it, shaking. He bit his bottom lip hard and gave one sharp shake of his head. "No."

She forced herself to look him in the eyes. "I'm done for."

"No." He took a shallow breath. "There are treatments."

At this, she allowed a small smile. "You know better than anyone how effective those treatments are, Ian. They're almost worse than the disease."

"I'll care for you. You won't be alone. We will find a cure. I swear it."

"Ian... You know what lies in store. Pain, fevers, sores,

deformity, madness. You said yourself that you would have helped Maccon go."

"Because he was already more than half gone!" Ian gave her a little shake. "I will not do that to you, so don't you fucking ask that of me, Daisy. Do not dare!"

She let him see the resolve in her eyes. "That existence is not life. I won't do it, Ian. Do not ask me to become that."

"No..." His expression crumpled. "No, Daisy, no." A sob tore from him, and he buried his head in her hair. "I won't let you. I can't—"

She cradled him, cooing under her breath as he cried. His arms wrapped around her, a vise that wouldn't let go as his lean frame shook. "Do not do this. Please. I can't lose you, too."

"No, love," she managed. "Not now. There's time yet."

She let him undress her and helped him with his clothes, their kisses soft, silent, his hands shaking as he touched her everywhere, mapping the topography of her body and she his. His gloriously strong body that would never age, never grow ill. He was the miracle that she could never be as a human.

Slowly, they relearned each other. There, in the sanctuary of their bed, with him, his touch, his taste, she was timeless, eternal. She was whole. She held onto the feeling until he finally slept, his limbs entwined with hers.

Rest, however, eluded Daisy. Carefully, so as not to wake Ian, she slipped from the bed and went out onto the balcony. Moonlight turned her skin marble white. Staring down at her bare arms, she thought of her life. She had not lived it as she ought. A cold rage swept over her, and her hands shook. She had not taken control of her wants and needs. And now her chance for happiness would go to waste. Daisy bowed her head and struggled not to scream. But as her breathing slowed and calm descended, a thought swirled within her, tantalizing with possibility. She straightened. Could it work? Could she do it?

Ian did not stir when she came back inside and padded on silent feet into the dressing room. Anticipation and fear sent her blood to racing as she prepared to head out. Of the two emotions, fear was the greater. The unknown had always frightened Daisy, but she would face it now. She only prayed that Ian would understand when he learned what she had done.

Chapter Thirty-nine

Ian's fist nearly broke through the front door of Archer House. He pummeled it with all the terror and pain that gripped his soul.

"Open up!" His shout ripped his throat raw. "Open, damn you!"

Before he could howl and shred the door to bits with his claws, it whipped open.

Miranda stood in shocked fury, her green eyes glinting. "Northrup, have you gone mad? You scared my butler into his closet—"

"Where is she?" He shook with the need to hold Daisy. Waiting only made his wolf whine and his muscles twitch.

The sight of Miranda blinking in confusion nearly brought him to his knees. He knew in his gut that she hadn't a clue where Daisy had gone. He'd known the instant he'd woken up alone that Daisy had left for good.

Bile surged in his throat. His knees cracked hard against the flagstone. She was gone. He felt it, felt her soul slipping away from him and leaving him ice cold. Leaving him alone.

A hand touched his shoulder. "Ian," Miranda whispered fiercely. "Where is my sister?"

Fury and despair had his fangs sinking into his lip and tasting blood. She'd given up. Quit on him. A keening cry tore through the air. He realized it was his.

Words felt like broken glass in his mouth. "She's taken her own way out."

Her footsteps echoed in the silence as Daisy walked slowly across the Waterloo Bridge. She was afraid. So very afraid and cold. It made her want to turn tail and run, back to Ian and his warmth. Wrapping her arms about her middle, she kept going. A thick fog had come up, shrouding the bridge in murky gray bunting, punctuated only by the ghostly glow of the gas lamps.

She would not think about him. About her family. Her life. Her step stuttered. Think about Maccon. What he'd become. Deformed. Grotesque. In agony. She shivered, her steps slowing.

The mad beating of her heart overshadowed the mournful wail of a foghorn and the clang of a buoy. Her lips trembled, her breath coming short.

I am afraid. I want to go home.

Her fingers curled around the cold, slick wood of a piling as she stepped onto the pier. Just beyond, the barge floated at anchor as if waiting for her to pay a call. What if he said no? What if she had to inhabit another body? Bile rose in her throat, threatening to let loose. Her muscles tensed as she moved to pull herself up. The water below her raced onward, making her dizzy.

Ian. What would he think? Would he understand that

she had no other choice? Would he find her repugnant? Shame burned in her belly. On a cry, she tore away from the piling. "I cannot."

"You can. Because you are no coward."

Daisy jumped at the sound, a scream clogged in her throat as a figure emerged from the fog.

The man stepped closer, his familiar features illuminated by the weak lamplight behind her.

His voice was a low melody in the dusk. "I've been waiting for you."

"You've been watching me."

"Yes."

She ought to be furious, but he had promised Ian. "Then you knew I would come to ask—"

"Of course." He gave her a wry smile. "We are, after all, the ears of London."

Her insides trembled. He would make dying easy. She knew that now, and she didn't know if she appreciated the gesture. *I am afraid.* She blinked down at the hand he held out.

"Salvation is yours," he said. "The question is, how much are you willing to sacrifice for love?"

There, glinting in the black bed of his gloved palm, it lay. A silver charm in the form of a goddess, with the wings of an angel.

Chapter Forty

It wasn't easy to find Ian. Aside from his home and Ranulf House, both of which were unnervingly empty, she hadn't a clue where to look. As a last resort, she went to Miranda's home.

Her sister ran out into the hall to meet her.

"Daisy! Where have you been?"

Daisy tried to smile, but she was too weak. Her body felt odd, heavy yet light as if she might float away from it at any moment. The heart within her chest was like a ballast stone, an uncomfortable bulk that stretched against her breastbone—a sensation, she was assured, that would lessen with time. "Later, pet. I need to find Ian. Do you know where he is?"

Miranda's eyes pinched. "He was beside himself. He thought..." She clenched Daisy's arm. "He was under the impression that you went off to kill yourself."

Guilt speared her, and with it, a cold fear that he would find what she'd done even worse.

"Well, obviously I did not," she said briskly, and then winced at her own callousness. "Panda, where is he?"

"Oh, how glib you are acting. You scared the devil out of me, Daisy! I... Oh, Daisy, Archer told me about what's happened." She teared up. "You must know that we will help you."

Daisy stroked Miranda's cheek. "I'm sorry to have worried you all. It was a misunderstanding. Everything will be all right now, dearest."

"That is supposed to be what I say to you—" Miranda stopped short and studied her with a keen eye. "You look odd. Lovely, but... odd."

Well, she felt odd. Daisy could no longer bite back her impatience. "Panda! I need Ian. Now." Indeed, if she didn't see him soon, she might scream.

"He's at the Plough and Harrow," said a male voice behind them.

Talent limped forward on limbs still healing. "He's gone out of his head. I came to see if Lady or Lord Archer could talk him down"—cold accusation burned into her—"because I thought you were gone."

"How did you get in?" Miranda asked.

"Flew through an open window."

Miranda blinked in surprise, but Daisy was already gathering her skirts.

"Daisy, wait!" Miranda searched her face. "I'm sorry I stood in your way. He loves you so."

"I know." And the knowledge gave Daisy the strength to run to him.

Clemens was in a state when she arrived. The whey-faced barkeep paced in front of his tavern, wringing his hands and muttering about crazed noblemen.

"He threw everybody out," Clemens told her. "Had his man give me a sack of coins and said he'd buy the use of the place for the night."

Daisy moved to go in when he blocked her path. "He ain't in his right mind, lassie. I'm fearing for your safety."

She meant her touch to be light, but she ended up all but shoving Clemens to the side in her haste. "I've nothing to fear from him."

He was sitting at their table, a forlorn figure hunched in the near darkness of the deserted tavern. From Clemens's warning, she feared he'd been drinking or had possibly destroyed the room, but he simply sat, alone in the quiet. Elbows on the table, his head in his hands, he didn't see her approach. For a moment, she wondered if he knew she was there.

"Get the fuck out."

She stopped at his harsh command, and her stomach dipped.

Ian didn't lift his head to acknowledge her as he spoke in a dead, flat voice. "I don't care who you are or what you want. I've paid for this space. Now go."

Her lips trembled in a smile. Ridiculous that she should be smiling now, but it was that or cry. "Ian," she whispered.

His lithe body tensed so hard that every muscle along his shoulders and arms stood out in fine relief against his shirt. His chest lifted on a deep breath, and she knew without doubt that he was scenting her. In a rush, he exhaled. Slowly, as though he were afraid to look, he let his hands fall and he raised his head.

Red rimmed the azure color of his eyes. Thick auburn stubble shadowed his jaw and throat. A stain, whiskey perhaps, spread over the expanse of his rumpled linen shirt. He looked ghastly. He looked wonderful.

She expected him to come to her, but he didn't move. He stared at her for a long moment, his lower lip twitching, his eyes wide and agonized. Daisy fought the urge to fidget. Her blood moved like sludge through her veins, a painful feeling, compounded by the ache in her chest. Part of her wanted to run away; the other part wanted to run into his arms.

His voice cracked through the silence. "You left." A grimace of pain twisted his features. "I thought you had—" He bit down on his lip and swallowed audibly.

She ground her fists into her skirts to keep still. "I know. I'm sorry, Ian. So sorry."

Ian blinked as if her words were a physical blow. "Where did you go?" His teeth clicked together. "Why didn't you wake me?"

Daisy's hand floated up to her chest to rest there. How was it that her heart still hurt? "I..." She couldn't find the courage.

"Why are you hovering there?" he said quietly, not moving, barely breathing. "Are you afraid of me then?"

She took a step closer to him. "Never."

His jaw clenched as his gaze slid away. "Perhaps you should be. I'm in a rare temper just now."

"You don't appear to be."

He snorted softly, without humor. "For future reference, lass, a wolf's always dangerous when he's gone still." His mouth curled in a parody of a smile as his hands clenched into fists. "And I'm of a mind to 'stroop yer backside,' as ye so kindly put it once."

The hurt surrounding him made her eyes water. She would make it up to him. With everything she had, she would make him feel loved and cherished.

"You still don't scare me, Ian Ranulf."

His eyes fluttered closed for one pained moment. When they opened, they shone brilliant blue. "Then come here." He exhaled with a ragged growl. "Come here. Let me touch you, if you're real." His throat worked. "I want to touch you. I need to touch you."

"Ian." She took a shuddering breath. "I did something."

He heard the regret in her voice, and his eyes grew watchful. "What?" His voice was flat, afraid. "What have you done?"

She hugged herself tightly. "What I had to do." He wouldn't understand. "Ian...I...I am frightened that you—"

He moved before she could blink, catching her up, hauling her against him. His mouth was on hers in an instant, tender, demanding, thirsting. She kissed him back, holding him tightly because he was her home, her other half, and she hadn't felt whole or safe until he touched her.

He broke the kiss first, but he didn't let her go. "Hasn't it seeped into your thick head yet, Daisy-Meg," he whispered, his hands roaming her back, neck, shoulders, "there isn't anything you can do that will make me stop loving you. You might break my heart, but it is yours anyway."

Daisy sobbed, the tension in her breaking until she couldn't hold herself up. She could no longer give him her heart, but he had her soul. Always. "Ian...I should have told you, I know."

Cooing under his breath, he sank down into a chair and pulled her closer. It was then she felt how much he shook, deep tremors that racked his frame. But his voice was steady and his touch tender.

"There now, lass." His fingers threaded through her hair. "I understand."

"I'm sorry I scared you. I couldn't think of another way. I..." She stopped and picked at a loose thread along his collar.

"I understand, Daisy. I do. I'm not happy you left me to think the worst, mind you, but I understand your fear." He kissed her temple. "We will work it out, I promise."

She held him tighter and burrowed her face into the warm crook of his neck. Those hours she'd been gone. Hours of hell and fear. For both of them. "I love you, Ian. So much."

He stiffened, and she could feel the pounding of his heart against her ribs. A sigh left him, soft and gentle.

"Well, thank Christ for that," he said on a breath.

Odd that she could feel him smile, but she knew he did. Ian always smiled with his whole body.

"I went to Lucien."

The muscles surrounding her turned to rock. Before she could explain, he grabbed hold of her upper arms. His nostrils flared. "What did you do?" It was a whisper of fear.

With shaking hands, she pulled open her cloak and undid the loose blouse she wore. Her tender ribs couldn't bear a corset just now. Ian made a strangled sound as she pulled the blouse open to reveal the line of golden stitching between her breasts, below which ticked her golden heart. Lucien had explained that "due to the delectable attributes of the female anatomy, a window won't do." Hence she was stitched back together.

"Ah, Christ." Ian's fingertips hovered over her breastbone. "Tell me you didn't." He clasped the back of her neck hard and pressed his forehead against her. His ragged breath fanned her face. "Ah, hell, my sweet Daisy-girl, why?"

She closed her eyes and wrapped an arm around his neck. She needed to hold him. Uncertainty made her bones shake. "You know why."

"Aye, that I do. And it tears at my heart." He swore again and then hugged her tight. It felt so much like home that her throat constricted. "My brave love."

"I know it is not the most attractive alternative—"

"It's beautiful," he cut in fiercely. "If it's you, it is beautiful."

She pressed her lips to the strong, warm column of his neck, where his pulse beat true. "It is you who are beautiful. Heart and soul."

He held her as if she were a fragile thing, not the indestructible shell she had become. But she knew he was not content. Not by half.

"How many?" he asked as he stroked her back.

The question was clear. She shuddered again. For a cold moment, she was back in Lucien's barge, feeling her life end, the icy, sick dread of it, and the blinding pain of rebirth. She'd been violently ill for an hour afterward and wished for true death more than once as Lucien held her hair and patted her back in sympathy.

She swallowed several times before she could speak. "One."

Ian eased back to look down at her in surprise. "One soul?"

"One soul, and one hundred years of service to the GIMs."

One soul in place of hers, for she'd already given hers to Ian. One hundred years because the GIMs valued her connection to Ian and the lycans more than they needed souls. So she would work with the GIMs, collecting information, being their champion with the Ranulf court. A strange thrill shot through her at the thought of being useful. Hers was a brave new world. If she had Ian in it, she could face anything.

His jaw worked in quiet fury. "It should have been me. I should have offered in your stead."

On a sigh, she cupped his cheek. "It was my choice, my sacrifice. I've no regrets, Ian."

His frown was slow to dissolve, and she gave him a little nudge upon his hard shoulder.

"You talk of thick skulls," she said. "Haven't *you* realized? You are life. You are the reason I want to wake each morning. The inspiration for my every breath. I took salvation, Ian. For I too would be a god with the power of your love. If I knew I had it."

He touched her cheek softly, so softly. "That you do, Daisy-girl. Always."

"Then"—she pulled him close—"I swear on my soul I won't let your love go to waste. With everything I am, I give it back to you in return. I shall keep you and love you till my last breath."

She saw the realization break over him, that she was like him now—immortal. No longer would he have to see her age as he stayed the same. For as long as they had each other, they would never be alone again.

His smile was the brilliance of the moon as he leaned down to kiss her. "Till my last breath."

Epilogue

Ian and Daisy's wedding was a rousing affair, filled with drinking, dancing, and the occasional Scot bursting into song—never mind the antics of the lycans. Indeed, the bride and groom were quite shameless in their open displays of affection. So much so that come time to depart, the groom simply tossed his bride over his shoulder and carried his woman off. The bride laughed the whole way out.

"Show-off," muttered his best man, Archer. Though no one was fooled. Least of all his own wife, who gave him a secretive smile and tugged him home shortly thereafter.

As for Poppy, she returned to an empty house. For three months she had endured this painful, solo homecoming. Three months and it did not get any easier. She went through the motions of removing her hat, lighting the lamps. Things must be done, life must go on. Life would go on, even if every breath she took hurt, even if her joints ached when she moved. Sorrow and loneliness were an insidious evil, for they lived in the mind. One could not take a tonic and see them dissipate.

Minutes passed as she stood in the center of her abandoned home. She would not hear his footstep on the landing or smell the fragrance of his pipe when the sun set and the teakettle whistled. And she would not feel the warmth of his arms holding her when the rest of the world assumed she was too strong to need comfort. She *was* strong. Only, she was no longer whole.

Once the flames are ignited, they will burn for eternity.

Please turn this page for an excerpt from

Chapter Thirteen

Miranda put the unpleasantness of murder out of her mind. She would enjoy herself with Archer, if not for her sake, then for his. And surprisingly, they did enjoy the day. The museum was enormous, its collection of wonders vast.

When the hour grew late and most patrons made for home, Archer slipped an obscene amount of money to the guard to allow them to stroll the upper floors uninterrupted. Miranda was glad for it. A day spent in public with her husband made her painfully aware of how life was for him. Her heart filled with tenderness when she realized what this day out cost him.

They stopped to study Greek sculptures in one of the upper galleries, and she turned to him, intent upon offering her gratitude.

"Why haven't you left me?" Archer interrupted, scattering her thoughts.

"What do you mean?" But she knew. Her throat went dry and sore. How could she tell him, when she hadn't truly admitted it to herself?

They stood alone in a small alcove facing an ancient frieze. He gestured toward the stairs where the sound of patrons leaving the museum drifted up. "All of them think I am a killer."

He ran a finger along the balustrade at his side, watching the movement. "Morbid fascination compels society to tolerate me. But you..." Archer lifted his head, yet would not turn to face her. "Why haven't you left? Why do you defend me? I... I cannot account for it."

"You cannot account for a person coming to your defense when it is needed?"

"No. Never."

His quiet conviction made her ache.

"I told you, Archer, I will not condemn you based on your appearance alone."

His stillness seemed to affect the air around him, turning their world quiet. "Come now, Miranda. You heard all that Inspector Lane had to say."

Caught, Miranda's breath left in a sharp puff, but he went on.

"Sir Percival called my name moments before he was murdered. Another servant saw someone dressed like me leaving the grounds. All very damning. Why did you not leave then?"

Miranda's heart pounded loudly in her ears. "How did you know I was there?"

He made a soft sound, perhaps a laugh, and fell silent. So then, he would not answer unless she answered first. So be it. She would say it. "It was you. That night. You are the man who saved me in the alleyway."

Stillness consumed him, as if he'd frozen over. "Yes."

She released a soft breath. "Why were you there?"

Archer studied her quietly, a man of stealth waiting to

see which direction she would bolt. "It was as you guessed those years ago. To kill your father."

She knew it, but still the admission shocked her. "But why? What did he do to you?"

"Damage enough."

She bit the inside of her lip to keep from cursing his reticence.

The silence between them stretched tight until Archer spoke, low and controlled and just a bit bemused. "I admit the desire to kill one man, *your* father. Yet you do not question that I might kill another?"

She met his gaze without falter. "Capable, yes. But you did not. Just as you did not kill my father when you had the chance."

He blinked. Surprise? Or guilt? For an endless moment, she waited.

"You have given me your word, Archer, and I will believe it." It was a true answer. But not the whole truth. "I will not run from you."

The wool of his frock coat whispered against marble as he turned to fully face her. She stared back, unguarded for a pained moment. Warmth filled his eyes. He understood. He took a quick breath, and his voice dropped. "You've no notion of the effect you have on me."

The words gave a hard tug to her belly. She closed her eyes and swallowed. "If by effect, you mean finding yourself in uncharted waters, wondering whether you are coming or going…" She stared at his shirt, watching his breath hitch. "Then I fear you have the same effect on me, my lord."

Cool quiet surrounded them, highlighting the soft rush of their mingled breathing. Slow as Sunday, his hand lifted, and a wash of heat flowed over her. But his hand moved to the hard mask at his face. The mask came off with a small creak and a burst of Archer's freed breath. Light hit his features, and Miranda froze.

"Has my face gone blue?" he asked softly when she stood with her mouth hanging open like a haddock.

His lips curled as he enjoyed his joke.

Lips. She stared at them in shock. She could see his lips. Behind the carnival mask, he wore a black half-mask of smooth silk. It molded to his face like a second skin, revealing the lines of a high forehead, a strong nose, and a sharply squared-off jaw. The mask covered almost all of his right side, down along his jaw to wrap fully around his neck. But the left side... The tip of his nose, his left cheek, jaw, chin, and lips were fully exposed.

The shock of seeing all-too-human skin upon his face rendered her nearly senseless. His complexion was olive toned, showing some Mediterranean origin in his background. How on earth the man could have sun-bronzed skin was a mystery to her. He must have shaved before they left, for his cheek was smooth. Grooming his face for a world that would never see it. A pity.

A small cleft divided his square chin. But his lips called her attention once more. They were firmly sculpted; a sturdy bottom lip that almost begged to be bitten. The upper lip was wider than the bottom and flared gently in perpetual humor. Roman lips. She hadn't thought...

"You keep gaping like that, and the flies will come in."

She watched in fascination as the lips moved, amazed to hear his familiar rich voice coming from them. One corner lifted. "Are you going to stare all day? Should I have a self-portrait done for your contemplation?"

She looked up into his eyes, heavily lidded and deeply set, though covered with some sort of black cosmetic, kohl perhaps. Not an inch of his true skin color showed around his eyes. Even so, there was kindness in those endless gray depths. His eyes drew a person in and kept one wondering.

"Yes," she said.

Archer's jaw twitched. " 'Yes,' you are going to stare? Or 'yes,' you would like a portrait?"

Despite his teasing, he was uncommonly still, poised as though she might bite.

"Yes, I am going to stare," she said crisply.

"Why are you cross? You said you didn't like my other masks. I offer you a different view."

"You walked around wearing those terrible masks, filling my head with all sorts of horrible visions and... and..." Her hand flailed in front of his face. "And all along, you could have worn this."

His lips compressed, but they couldn't thin entirely. "What makes you think that there isn't a horror lurking still behind this mask?"

"It isn't the horror," she retorted. "It is the subterfuge." The line of his brows rose beneath the mask. "Those carnival masks must not be comfortable in the least. Blast it, you can't even eat or drink wearing them!"

He crossed his arms over his chest and looked away.

"Why, Archer? Why shut the world out?"

For a moment, she thought he might not answer.

"I don't want pity." He glared at the stern visage of the Greek centaur before them. "I'd rather have fear."

His voice was a phantom, haunted and alone. Miranda's fingers curled into fists to keep from reaching for him. But she understood him. Deep down, she knew she would rather the world see her beauty and overlook the pain. It had stung when he had called her a false front, because he was right.

"And me, Archer?" she whispered. "Would you have me fear you as well?"

"No!" He stopped and stiffened. "I'd rather have you imagine all sorts of horrors than study my face and believe that there is a chance a normal man might be hiding underneath."

She flushed hotly. It was the very thing she'd started to imagine.

Light from a flickering gas lamp caressed the sharp angles of his jaw, the high planes of his cheek as he lifted his chin. "Because there is not. I am not so twisted as to wear this thing if I were whole and untouched."

He glanced at the stairwell as though he'd like nothing more than to flee. "Perhaps we should go. It is getting late."

He moved to put on the mask once more, and her hand flew to clutch his arm.

"Don't," she said gently. The muscles beneath her hand hardened like granite yet he did not pull away. He loomed over her, his newly revealed features inscrutable, all the more because she did not yet know the subtleties of them. Without the warm rumble of his voice, he seemed almost a stranger to her for a moment, but for the scent of him and the familiar lines of his form.

"You startled me, Archer. That is all. I had no right to rail at you." Absently, her thumb caressed the fabric of his coat. She forced it still. "Thank you. It is a gift you gave me, and I am the richer for it."

Flushing and unable to meet his eyes another moment, she let him go. His silence was almost unbearable, but she could not turn from him. She had promised to stay. She gripped the cool balustrade and hoped it might keep her in place.

On a sigh, his stiffness released, and his hand came down to rest next to hers. "I felt you," he whispered. "That is how I knew."

She raised her head, and the world seemed to fade down to a narrow focus of just him, just her.

"I feel you," he said, "whether stalking me through the streets of London, or hiding behind a screen in my library." His words were soft as bunting, buffeting her skin, shivering inside of her.

Her hand opened on the balustrade, fingers stretching toward his. The very tips of their fingers met, the touch sparking between them like a current.

Archer's finger grazed hers. "I feel you. As if you were connected to me by an invisible string." He touched his chest. "I feel you here. In my heart."

She couldn't think past the mad pounding of her blood. She swallowed painfully. "I feel you too."

He sucked in a sharp breath.

Miranda stepped closer, closer to the heat of his body, to the place where her senses came alive—toward him. Her hand trembled as she touched her breast. "I feel you here," she said, both an admission and the true reason she could not leave him.

The corner of his lush mouth quirked. His legs moved into the folds of her skirts, and they were standing but a handbreadth apart. She felt his legs tense, a gather of his resolve. His hand lifted.

She watched it come, his broad shoulders blocking out the light from the windows at his back. The swells of her breasts rose and fell over her bodice with a rapid rhythm. Gently he touched her, his fingertips brushing the upper curve of her left breast, and she gasped.

"Here?" he asked thickly.

A tremulous smile touched her lips as a sudden weightless anticipation filled her, making her head spin. "There."

Smooth leather burned a path to her neck. Archer watched his fingers, the line of his mouth stern, the look in his eyes almost angry. Then, as if in answer to a challenge, he lowered his head. Miranda's breath ratcheted in her chest, became trapped by her corset. Unable to bear it, she closed her eyes.

Soft lips pressed against her breast, barely a touch that sent a bolt of feeling through her heart.

"Archer."

"Miri." His breath steamed against her fragile skin. "*Sono consumato.*"

Slowly, oh so slowly, his lips took the path his fingers made. Up, up, over the curve of her breast to the indent just above her collarbone. Not quite touching her, but skimming the surface. Hot breath ebbed and flowed in waves over her skin as he explored with unhurried languor.

"I am consumed," he whispered against her ear, and she shivered. "By you." Soft lips grazed her jaw in an agonizingly slow trail toward her waiting mouth. Her eyes squeezed tight. She could not bear it. The heat in her was fever bright. No part of him touched her, except that mouth. But oh, that mouth. It destroyed her composure as it moved with steady deliberation toward her lips.

The tip of his nose brushed against her hair as his lips touched the corner of her mouth. A universe of nerves occupied that small corner of her mouth. One touch was enough to leave her dizzy.

Archer held still, trembling as she did. The tips of her breasts brushed against his chest as she struggled to gain equilibrium. Liquid lust surged through her veins like wildfire. She wanted to move, do something rash, crush her lips to his and simply take, press herself against him and ease the heated ache between her legs. She did none of those things, only clutched her skirt like a lifeline as he moved his open lips just above hers.

His breath left in a pained rush that flowed into her. In, out, in. Still he did not kiss her, but let his lips brush against hers as if he knew, just as she, what would happen should their mouths truly merge. She wanted more. She wanted a taste. Her limbs quivered as she let her tongue inch forward, slip out between her parted lips. Of a like mind, Archer did the same. Their tongues touched.

A choked cry broke from her, the silken wet tip of his tongue sending a bolt of heat to her core. Archer made a sound close to pain. For a moment, their tongues retreated. And then.

She flicked her tongue, a small lick. And found his again. The sound of their breathing filled her ears as their tongues caressed, retreated, and met again, learning each other. Every flick, each wet slide of his tongue felt like a direct touch to the center of her sex, until she throbbed there, grew so hot she feared she might combust.

Their lips never melded, only danced with the possibility of it. It was not a kiss. It was something infinitely worse. It was torture. And God help her if she didn't want more.

Their breathing became pants. Her fingers fisted her skirts with near violence. His tongue slipped deeper, lighting across her lips, invading her mouth for one hot moment. Miranda moaned, her knees buckling. Archer's big hand clasped her nape, hard and impatient. Now he would kiss her, take her. *Now.* Her body screamed for that sweet release.

He wrenched his mouth away even as his arm crushed

her against his hard chest. Her heart leapt to her throat, her senses jumbled and confused until she heard the strange thump of something hitting the wall behind her. She froze, panting softly, her nose buried in the black folds of his suit coat for what felt like an eternity but was at most a moment in time.

Archer swore sharply and then moved, leaving her teetering on her feet. She righted quickly and found him glaring around, his frame held tight as a spring. But the long hall behind them was empty. Slowly he turned his attention to the wall before them. The silver hilt of a dagger embedded deep in the plaster still quivered from the impact.

Archer's breath hitched visibly, his eyes narrowing to slits. The force of the throw was unmistakable. Had he not acted quickly, the wicked dagger would have now rested deep within Miranda's back.

"What the devil?" she hissed, disbelief and sheer terror making her voice unsteady and her heart pound.

A mad cackle echoed in the empty corridor behind them, and Miranda started. The voice was neither feminine nor masculine—only evil. Footsteps sounded in the far end of the gallery, near the end of the corridor where shadows dwelled.

Archer squeezed her shoulder. "Stay here."

He took off running. Grabbing her parasol with one hand, and her skirts with the other, she followed. The long corridor veered right, opening to a larger hall and the stairs to the lower exhibits and great court. There the devil stood, paused at the top of the marble stair. He lifted his head, and her heart skittered. Were it not for the man's smaller size, one might have thought him Archer's twin. The villain wore a suit of black and a matching carnival mask that covered his entire face.

"Hell," Archer said.

The man gave a mocking salute and then turned to fly down the stairs. A dash to the high marble balustrade found the stairwell empty; the villain vanished as if by illusion.

"Hell and damn." Archer's hand came down upon her wrist. "Stay here. I will come back for you." His tone brooked no argument, but his touch was gentle. "Stay here."

She hadn't the time to protest before he took hold of the railing and leapt over it, straight down the stairwell.

The spark of true love
can never grow
cold…
Please turn this page
for a preview of
Winterblaze.

Winterblaze

London, 1873, Victoria Station.

Winston Lane could never recall the impetus that prompted him to leave the confines of his first class railway compartment and step back onto the platform. The whistle had sounded, long and high, indicating that they would soon be off. And yet, he'd felt compelled. Was it for a quick draw upon his pipe? The need for a bit of air? His memory was muddled at best. Perhaps it was because the whys did not matter. From the moment he'd stepped off that train, his life had changed completely. And it had been because of a woman.

Now *that* he remembered with the vividness of a fine oil painting. Great billows of hot, white steam clouded the cold air upon the platform, obscuring the shapes of the few railway workers attending to last minute duties, giving their movements a ghostlike subtly. Idly he watched them, interested as always in the activities of the common man, when through the mists she emerged. It might have been lyrical had she been gliding along in peaceful repose, but no, this woman *strode*. A mannish, commanding walk as if she owned the very air about her. And though Winston had been raised to appreciate ladies who exuded utter femininity and eschew those who did not, he'd snapped to instant attention.

She was tall, nearly as tall as he, this assertive miss, and dressed in some dull frock that blended into the fading light. The only spot of color was her mass of vivid, carnelian red hair coiled at the back of her head like a crown. So very red, and glinting like a beacon. One look and he knew he had to have her. Which was rather extraordinary, for he wasn't the sort prone to impulse or rash feeling. And certainly not about women. They were interesting in an abstract way, but one was much like any other. At one and twenty, he was already set in his ways, orderly, bookish, and logical. Save there was nothing logical about the hot, hard pang that caught him in the gut as she walked by, her dark eyes flashing beneath the red slashes of her brows.

The pipe fell from Winston's hand, clattering upon the ground as he stood frozen, surely gaping like some slack-jawed idiot. She did not appear to notice him, but kept walking, her long legs eating up the ground, taking her away from him. This, he could not have. In an instant, he was after her.

He nearly broke into a run to catch her. It was worth it. The scent of lemons and book leather enveloped him, and his head went light. Books and clean woman. Had God ever divined a more perfect perfume? She was young. Perhaps younger than he was. Her pale skin was smooth, unlined, and unmarred, save for the little freckle just above her earlobe. He had the great urge to bite that little lobe.

She did not break her pace, but glanced at him sidelong as if to throw out a warning. He did not blame her; he was being unspeakably rude approaching this young lady without a proper introduction. Then again, they were the only ones on the platform, and he was not fool enough to let her out of his sight.

"Forgive me," he said, a bit breathless, for really this woman was fast on her feet, "I realize this is rather forward, and usually I would never—"

"Never what?" she cut in, her voice crisp and smooth as fresh linen sheets, "never proposition young ladies who have the temerity to walk unescorted in public areas?"

Well, now that he thought of it, she really ought to have a guardian with her. She did not appear to be from great wealth, so he wouldn't expect an abigail, but a sister or an aunt perhaps? Or a husband. A shudder went through him at the thought of her being married. He mentally shook himself, aware that he'd been staring at her, memorizing the sharp slope of her nose, and the graceful curve of her jaw.

"I would never presume to proposition you, miss. Indeed, should any such scoundrel approach you, it would be my pleasure to set them to rights." And now he sounded like a prig, and a hypocrite.

She smirked. "Then let me guess, you are a member of the Society for the Protection of Young Ladies and Innocents and want to make certain I realize the perils of walking alone." Dark brown eyes flashed as she glanced at him, and Winston's already tight gut started to ache. "Or perhaps you merely seek a contribution?"

He could not help it, he grinned. "And if I were, would you listen to my testimony?"

Her soft, pink lips pursed. Whether in irritation or in

amusement, he could not tell. Nor did he care. He wanted to run his tongue along them and ease them back to softness. The image made him twitch. He'd never had such importunate thoughts. Yet speaking to her felt natural, as if he'd done so a thousand times before.

"I don't know, is your testimony any good?"

Like that, he was hard as iron. His voice came out rough. "While I am certainly capable of extolling the virtues of my testimony, there is only one way for you to truly find out."

When she blushed, it was a deep pink that clashed beautifully with her hair. "Well, you certainly talk a good talk," she murmured, and his smile grew.

They neared the end of the platform. Behind them the train gave one last, loud whistle.

His cheeky miss quirked one of her straight brows. "You'll miss your train, sir."

"Some things are worth missing, and some are not."

Coming to the iron stairway, she stopped and regarded him. When she spoke again, her voice was hard and uncompromising. "What do you want?"

You. "To know your name so that I might come to call upon you properly." He made a leg, the extravagant sort he'd done at court recently. "Winston Lane at your service, madam."

For the life of him, he did not know why he'd held back giving her his full name. The lie shamed him, and he moved to correct the blunder, but those pink lips twitched again and good intentions flew from his mind. What would it take to get her to truly smile? What would she look like flushed with passion? His skin went hot.

Her dark eyes looked over his shoulder. "Your train is leaving."

The platform beneath his feet trembled as the train groaned out of the station. He didn't even look. "I find," he said keeping his eyes upon her gloriously stern visage, "that I no longer wish to leave London."

Unsurprisingly, she held his gaze without a blush or one of the coy looks the ladies in his sphere would have employed. "Do you always act the fool?"

Never. But he didn't have to say it. She read him well, and her eyes suddenly gleamed with acceptance. Slowly, she held her hand out so that he might take it. "Miss Poppy Ann Ellis."

Poppy. For her hair, he supposed. But to him, she was Boadicea, Athena, a goddess.

It was all he could do to keep himself from bridging the short distance between them and putting his mouth to hers. Instead, he took her hand with due formality. His gloved fingers curled around hers, and something within him settled. He shook only a little as he raised her hand to his lips. "Miss Ellis, I am your servant." *Always.*

Yet even as he spoke, fate was conspiring to make a liar of him.

THE DISH

Where authors give you the inside scoop!

♥ ♥ ♥ ♥ ♥ ♥ ♥ ♥ ♥ ♥ ♥ ♥ ♥ ♥ ♥

From the desk of Kendra Leigh Castle

Dear Reader,

I admit it: I love a bad boy.

From the Sheriff of Nottingham to Severus Snape, Spike to Jack Sparrow, it's always the men who seem beyond saving that throw my imagination into overdrive. So it's no wonder that this sort of character arrived in my very first Dark Dynasties book and has stuck around since, despite the fact that most of the other characters either (a)wonder why he hasn't been killed or (b)would like to kill him themselves. Or both, depending on the day. His name is Damien Tremaine. He's a vampire, thief, assassin, and as deadly as they come. In fact, he spent much of *Dark Awakening* trying to kill the hero and heroine. He positively revels in the fact that he has few redeeming qualities. And I just. Couldn't. Resist.

Writing SHADOW RISING, the third installment in the Dark Dynasties series, proved an interesting challenge. The true bad boy takes a special kind of woman to turn him around, and I knew it would take a lot to pierce the substantial (and very stylish) armor that Damien had built up over the centuries. Enter Ariane, a vampire who is formidable in her own right but really remarkable because of her innocence, despite being hundreds of years old. As a member of the reclusive and mysterious Grigori dynasty, Ariane remembers nothing of her life before being turned. All she knows is the hidden desert compound of her kind, a place she has never been allowed to leave. She's long been restless... but when her closest friend goes missing and she's forbidden to search for him, Ariane takes matters into her own untried but very capable hands. Little does she know that her dynasty's leader has hired an outside vampire who specializes in finding those who don't want to be found—and that once she crosses paths with him, he'll make very sure that their paths keep crossing, whether she likes it or not.

All of the couples I write about have their differences, but Damien and Ariane are polar opposites. She's sheltered, he's jaded. She longs to feel everything, while Damien's spent years burying every emotion. And she is, of course, exactly what he needs, which is the first thing to have actually frightened Damien in... well, ever. Damien's slow and terrifying realization that he's finally in over his head was both a lot of fun to write, and exactly what he deserved. After all, redemption is satisfying, but it's not supposed to be *easy*.

Between Damien's sharp tongue and sharper killer instincts, Ariane has her hands full from the get-go. Fortunately, she finds him just as irresistible as I do. Like so many dark and delicious bad boys, there's more to Damien than meets the eye. If you're interested in finding out whether this particular assassin has the heart of a hero, I hope you'll check out SHADOW RISING. I'll be honest: Damien never really turns into a traditional knight in shining armor. But if you're anything like me... you won't want him to anyway.

Enjoy!

Kendra Leigh Castle

Kendra Leigh Castle

♥ ♥ ♥ ♥ ♥ ♥ ♥ ♥ ♥ ♥ ♥ ♥ ♥ ♥ ♥

From the desk of Jennifer Haymore

Dear Reader,

When Meg Donovan, the heroine of PLEASURES OF A TEMPTED LADY (on sale now), entered my office for the first time, I mistook her for her twin sister, Serena.

"Serena!" I exclaimed. "How are you? Please, take a seat."

She slowly shook her head. "Not Serena," she said quietly. "Meg."

I stared at her. I couldn't do anything else, because my throat had closed up tight. For, dear reader, Meg was dead! Lost at sea and long gone, and I'd written two complete novels and a novella under that assumption.

Finally, I found my scrambled wits and gathered them tight around me.

"Um," I said hopefully, "Serena...that's not a funny joke. My income relies on my journalistic credibility. You know that, right?"

She just looked at me. Then she shrugged. "Sorry. I am Meg Donovan. And though the world might like to pretend that I am Serena, I know who I am."

"But...but...you're dead." Now I sounded like a petulant child. A rather warped and quite possibly disturbed petulant child.

She finally took the seat I'd offered Serena, and, settling in, she leaned forward. "No, Mrs. Haymore. I'm not dead. I'm very much alive, and I'd like you to write my story."

Oh, Lord.

I looked down to rub the bridge of my nose between my thumb and forefinger, fighting off a sudden headache. If this really was Meg, I was in big, big trouble.

Finally I looked up at her. "All right," I said slowly. "So you're Meg. Back from the dead."

"That's correct," she said.

I studied her closely. Her twin Serena and I have become good friends since I wrote her story for her, and now that I really looked at this woman, the subtle differences between her and her twin grew clearer. This woman was about ten pounds thinner than Serena. And though her eyes were the same shade of blue, something about them seemed harder and wary, as though she'd gone through a difficult time and come out of it barely intact.

"So who was it that rescued you, then?" I asked. "Pirates? Slavers?"

Her expression grew tight. Shuttered. "I'd like to skip that part, if you don't mind."

I raised a brow. This wasn't going to work out between us if she demanded I skip all the good stuff. But I'd play along. For now. "All right, then. Where would you like to start?"

"With my escape."

"Ah, so it *was* pirates, then."

She gave a firm shake of her head. "No. I meant my escape from England."

"That doesn't make sense," I said. "You'll be wanting to stay in England. Your family is there." I didn't say it, but I was pretty sure the man who loved her was there, too.

"I can't stay in England. You must help me."

I clasped my hands on top of my desk. "Look, Meg. I really like your family, so I'm sitting here listening to what you have to say. But I'm a writer who writes happy, satisfying stories about finding true love and living happily ever after. Is that what you're looking for?"

"No!"

I sighed. I'd thought not.

She leaned forward again, her palms flat on the desk. "I need you to write me out of England, because I need to protect my family, and..."

"And...?" I prompted when she looked away, seemingly unwilling to continue.

"And...Captain Langley. You see, as long as I stay in England, they're all in danger."

I fought the twitch that my lips wanted to make to form a smile. So she did know about Captain William Langley...and she obviously cared for him. Whatever danger she was worried about facing meant nothing in the face of the depth of love that might someday belong to William Langley and Meg Donovan.

"I see." I looked into her eyes. "I might be able to make an exception this time. I will do whatever I can to help you protect your family."

Note that I didn't tell her I'd help her to escape. Or to get out of England.

A frantic, wonderful plan was forming rapidly in my mind. Yeah, I'd write her story. I'd "help" her keep Langley and her family safe. But once I did that, once I gained her trust, I'd find a way to make them happy, to boot. Because I'm a romance writer, and that's what I do.

"Thank you," she murmured, glassy tears forming in her eyes. "Thank you so much."

I raised a warning finger. "Realize that in order for this to work, you need to tell me everything."

She hesitated, her lips pressed hard together. Then she finally nodded.

I flipped up my laptop and opened a new document. "Tell me your story, Miss Donovan. From the moment of your rescue."

And that was how I began to write the love story of Meg Donovan, the long-lost Donovan sister.

I truly hope you enjoy reading Meg's story! Please come visit me at my website, www.jenniferhaymore.com, where you can share your thoughts about my books, sign up for some fun freebies and contests, and read more about the characters from PLEASURES OF A TEMPTED LADY.

Sincerely,

Jennifer Haymore

♥ ♥ ♥ ♥ ♥ ♥ ♥ ♥ ♥ ♥ ♥ ♥ ♥ ♥ ♥

From the desk of Jill Shalvis

Dear Reader,

Ever feel like you're drowning? In FOREVER AND A DAY, my hero, Dr. Josh Scott, is most definitely drowning. He's overloaded, overworked, and on the edge of burnout. He's got his practice, his young son, his wheelchair-bound sister, and a crazy puppy. Not to mention the weight of the world on his shoulders from taking care of everyone in his life. He's in so deep, saving everyone around him all the time, that he doesn't even realize that *he's* the one in need of saving. It would never occur to him.

Enter Grace Brooks. She's a smart smartass and, thanks to some bad luck, pretty much starting her life over from scratch. Losing everything has landed her in Lucky Harbor working as Josh's dog walker. And then as his nanny. And then before he even realizes it, as his everything. In truth, she's saved him, in more ways than one.

Oh, how I loved watching the sure, steady rock that is Josh crumble, only to be slowly but surely helped back together again by the sexy yet sweet Grace.

And don't forget to pick up the other "Chocaholic" books, *Lucky in Love* and *At Last*, both available wherever books and ebooks are sold.

Happy Reading!

Jill Shalvis

Jill Shalvis

♥ ♥ ♥ ♥ ♥ ♥ ♥ ♥ ♥ ♥ ♥ ♥ ♥ ♥ ♥

From the desk of Kristen Callihan

Dear Reader,

I'm half Norwegian—on my mother's side. If there is one thing you need to know about Norwegians, it's that they are very egalitarian. This sense of equality defines them in a number of ways, but one of the more interesting aspects is that Norwegian men treat women as equal partners.

Take my grandfather. He was a man's man in the truest sense of the term. A rugged fisherman and farmer who hung out with the fellas, rebuilt old cars, smoked a pipe, and made furniture on the side. Yet he always picked up his own plate after dinner. He never hesitated to go to the market if my grandmother needed something, nor did he complain if he had to cook his own meals when she was busy. My grandfather was one of the most admirable men I've known. Thus when I began to write about heroes, I gravitated toward men who share some of the same qualities as my Norwegian ancestors.

Ian Ranulf, the hero of MOONGLOW, started out as a bit of an unsavory character in *Firelight*. All right, he was a total ass, doing everything he could to keep Miranda and Archer apart. So much so that, early on, my editor once asked me if I was sure Ian wasn't the real villain. While Ian did not act on his best behavior, I always knew that he was not a bad man. In fact, I rather liked him. Why? Because Ian loves and respects women in a way that not many of his peers do. While he feels inclined to protect a woman from physical harm, he'd never patronize her. For that, I could forgive a lot of him.

In MOONGLOW, Ian is a man living a half-life. He has sunk into apathy because life has not been particularly kind to him. And so he's done what most people do: He's retreated into a protective shell. Yet when he meets Daisy, a woman who will not be ignored, he finds himself wanting to live for her. But what I found interesting about Ian is that when he begins to fall for Daisy, he does not think, "No, I've been burned before; I'm not going to try again." Ian does the opposite: He reaches for what he wants, even if it terrifies him, even with a high possibility of failure.

While Ian certainly faces his share of physical battles in MOONGLOW, it is his dogged pursuit of happiness and his willingness to love Daisy as an equal that made him one of my favorite characters to write.

Happy Reading,

Kristen Callihan

Find out more about Forever Romance!

Visit us at
www.hachettebookgroup.com/publishing_forever.aspx

Find us on Facebook
http://www.facebook.com/ForeverRomance

Follow us on Twitter
http://twitter.com/ForeverRomance

NEW AND UPCOMING TITLES

Each month we feature our new titles
and reader favorites.

CONTESTS AND GIVEAWAYS

We give away galleys, autographed copies,
and all kinds of exclusive items.

AUTHOR INFO

You'll find bios, articles, and links to personal websites
for all your favorite authors—and so much more.

GET SOCIAL

Connect with your favorite authors, editors, and
other Forever fans, and share what's important to you.

THE BUZZ

Sign up for our monthly romance newsletter,
and be the first to read all about it.